THE PLEA

Joan Lee is a former British socialite who writes about a milieu she knows well – the privileged circles of the rich and famous, their exclusive clubs and parties.

JOAN LEE

The
Pleasure Palace

PAN BOOKS
London, Sydney and Auckland

First published in the United States 1987 by Dell Publishing Co., Inc
This edition published 1989 by Pan Books Ltd.,
Cavaye Place, London SW10 9PG
© Joan Lee, 1987
9 8 7 6 5 4 3 2 1
ISBN 0 330 30633 2
Printed and bound in Great Britain by
Richard Clay Ltd, Bungay, Suffolk

Dedication

To my daughter, Joan, for giving me the first push, and to my husband, Stan, for supporting me all the way.

Also, to Jonathan Dolger, Jackie Farber, and Charlie Spicer. They know why.

Prologue

The gala charity party was at last under way.

Held aboard the largest luxury liner in California's sprawling San Pedro harbor, it was being hailed as the social event of the decade.

Earlier that evening a bottle of champagne had been cracked over her hull by Jaafar al Hassad, the Arabian billionaire who was the chief investor in Nick Tyson's floating luxury liner. Christened *Pleasure Palace,* she had cost one hundred seventy-five million dollars.

Tonight *Pleasure Palace* had been donated by her members for this star-studded occasion. Proceeds from the evening's affair would benefit millions of starving children throughout the world. All three television networks were on hand to film the event.

The ship's dock had been turned into a sparkling fairyland over which thousands of balloons floated on multicolored ribbons. As rock music thundered from the disco below, the guests were ceremoniously piped aboard and escorted through arches made of fresh flowers. Atop the gangplank, they were greeted by the smiling stars of some of television's most popular series.

A gleaming Rolls slid into its allotted space on the pier. Sitting in the backseat, Nick Tyson turned to look at his bride-to-be as the car came to a halt. His deep blue eyes appraised her possessively. Aware that she was shivering, he placed his arm around her, and she snuggled close.

"Nervous, darling?" he asked in his soft southern accent.

"No, not really. I guess the devil just walked over my grave." She smiled. "Isn't that a silly expression, Nick? I wonder what it really means."

The chauffeur opened the car door and reached down to help her out. Then Nick took her hand and guided her up the gangplank.

"Let's take the private elevator, Jan. I don't feel like sharing you with the TV cameras."

As the mirrored elevator slowly lifted them up to Nick's private stateroom, Jan Julliard stared at her reflection. Her honey-colored hair was cut shoulder length, framing her beautiful face. Her pale green eyes seemed to hold exotic secrets. Her black Halston sheath caressed her magnificent body, touching it in all the right spots. At twenty-seven she was lovelier than she had been even at nineteen.

Turning from the mirror, she glanced at the flawless eight-carat diamond on her engagement finger. Nick had given it to her earlier that evening. Jan looked up at the man she was about to marry, thinking as always how incredibly handsome he was. Their eyes locked for a moment as Nick gave her one of his slow, easy smiles. But scurrying around in her mind was a niggling little thought: *Was he totally over his infatuation with Cat Bracken?*

She pushed the thought away as quickly as it had come.

"You don't think getting married wearing black will be unlucky, do you?" Jan asked, her voice filled with laughter.

Nick brushed a strand of hair from her face, then impulsively moved his hands over her body. She reached out for him, put her arms around his neck, and planted a gentle kiss on his mouth. Nick held her closer, wrapping his arms tightly around her.

"It won't be long now," he whispered. "There's been so much wasted time. You, my love, are all I'll ever need from this moment on."

Taking her arm, Nick walked her out of the elevator and into his private suite. Jan had never seen him so happy, so excited about what lay ahead. He took a deep breath as he looked at the radiance of his bride-to-be and thought, *Nothing can go wrong now. Nothing.*

They clung to each other for another long minute; then he bent down and whispered in her ear, "You look so beautiful, Jan. Did I remember to tell you that I love you?"

Patting her bottom and blowing her a kiss, he headed for the door.

"You just hold on to that thought while I go upstairs and give everything a final once-over. Then when I come back, we'll get the hell on with this wedding of ours."

He gave her one final smile and then, without another word, he was gone.

The chief security guard was sweating. Thaddeus Johnson prayed that everything would go without a hitch. He was understandably uptight; a lot of heavy bread and heavy jewelry would be on board. Everything had to go smoothly; no fuck-ups.

As he went from deck to deck, his eyes were sharp and wary, missing nothing. He watched sleek limousines pull silently into their parking spaces and studied the beautifully gowned women alighting with their wealthy escorts.

Johnson couldn't help thinking it must be goddamned terrific to be rich. *Jesus! My wife and I could live for a year on what the fuckin' flowers alone must have cost!*

Suddenly his thoughts were interrupted by one of the guards calling him on his walkie-talkie.

Cynthia Tyson stepped out of her limo. She paused, then gazed vaguely about. Her face tightened. Would Nick, her son, be angry with her? She had told him that she wouldn't attend the evening's festivities, but that was before she had known. Everything was different now.

A deluxe coach arrived with a party of young actors and actresses from various Hollywood studios. They would soon be mingling with the guests, providing their own brand of glamor.

Cynthia followed them on board ship.

Nick Tyson watched the captain greet the passengers as they came aboard. Everything seemed to be going perfectly. Almost every new arrival was instantly recognizable. Virtually all of them had been profiled in *People* or been a TV guest of Carson's or Merv's. There was hardly a nobody in sight.

Nick was glad he'd listened to his public relations advisers, glad he had let them convince the board members to provide their ship for this affair. It was the best publicity send-off that *Pleasure Palace* could possibly get.

He idly took a glass of champagne from a passing waiter. Sipping it, he silently studied the beautiful people milling about. Most of the guests were trying not to seem too obvious as they glanced around to see who was there and, even more important, who wasn't.

The huge frame of Nick's partner, Jaafar al Hassad, blocked the light in front of the doorway where he was standing. Catching Nick's eye, Jaafar blew a spear of smoke from the thin black cheroot he was smoking. His

beautiful wife, Leancia, stood next to him; they were insep-
arable.

Leancia's beauty was flawless. She was tall and slender,
quietly self-possessed and imbued with a quality of rare
elegance. Her jet black hair was pulled back from her
brow, which showed off the perfect symmetry of her face.
The dark green emeralds she was wearing were said to be
worth a king's ransom.

Nick wondered how many people on board knew Leancia's secret.

He stood staring for a moment, then lit a cigarette.
What a jewel of a ship she was.

With easy assurance, he moved his six-foot frame
through the crowd, listening to the laughter and overhear-
ing the whispers of conversation. All the time he was fully
aware that he had accomplished exactly what he had set
out to do.

Nick was proud and happy with his success, yet he
found that he felt a rare sense of dissatisfaction. A dark
cloud crossed his handsome face as he thought of his
mother.

Cynthia had become such a recluse, so out of things
lately; she was living as if a veil had been tightly drawn
around her life. Certainly her husband's terrible sickness
and subsequent death were to blame. Nick's full lips softened into a melancholy smile as he remembered the seemingly perfect love that his parents had shared.

He had to admit that he felt a sense of relief when
Cynthia had decided not to attend the evening's festivities.
And yet the relief was mingled with his ever-present feeling of guilt, his sense that he had in some way neglected
her. He wondered if he should call her.

But then his attention was distracted by a long-limbed model who had a generous mouth and taffy-colored shoulder-length hair. He watched as she turned her laughing face to the bearded young man next to her. A soft breeze from the ocean caught her dress, causing it to cling. Nick noticed the line of her full breasts. There was a mixture of elements about her that reminded him of Jan, his own beautiful bride-to-be, who was waiting for him in his suite.

Walking to the railing, he flipped his cigarette over the side and watched as it hit the water. Then, glancing at his watch, he saw that it was time for him to go belowdecks to the disco. After Cat Bracken finished entertaining the guests, he would place a call to Cynthia.

As he elbowed his way through the crowd, Nick shielded his eyes from the flashbulbs that were popping like firecrackers.

"Wonderful ship, Tyson! Impressive gathering. You've done yourself proud."

The board chairman of Brandon Oil drifted away before Nick could reply. Crowds of additional well-wishers began to gather around him.

He spent a moment mingling, watched them laughing, flattering, and seducing each other. The buccaneer business tycoon from Denver kissed the glamorous countess from Milan as she fondled the diamond necklace encircling her neck; the much-lionized fashion designer was with his current schizo boyfriend; the Italian director whom every woman under eighty had the hots for was there; the sixty-nine-year-old playboy, one of Nick's happy investors, was wearing a facelift to match the youthful look of his eighteen-year-old Nashville nymphet; the gossip columnist with venemous tongue and stiletto pen was saying nothing and observing everything; and the silver-haired talk-show host was smiling his famous smile as he smoothly glided among the crowd of notables, secure in his fame, basking in his power.

They were the rich and the powerful, the crème de la crème of society, a microcosm of the so-called elite; they were all strutting and preening and were all so pleased to be part of this, the snobbiest party of the year.

Extra bodyguards moved continuously through the crowd. They were dressed as guests so no one would be made uncomfortable by their presence. Every time they caught Nick Tyson's eye, they gave him a nod as if to let him know they were on the job.

Nick turned and headed in the direction of the small elevator that would take him down to the disco. He stopped for a moment; his blue eyes narrowed as he watched a man and woman smiling together as if over some private joke as they waited for the elevator.

The man was Mark Squire. His handsome, intelligent face was full of laughter. He spoke animatedly in perfect French to an exotic-looking woman who was flirting shamelessly with him.

Nick was in no mood to talk to him; he remembered how jealous he once had been of Mark Squire's relationship with Jan. Yet for a moment he felt a flash of sympathy for the man—Mark was losing her today.

Nick waited in the shadows until the couple were inside the elevator and the door closed behind them.

Moving toward the exit sign, he took the back stairs to the disco. As he entered, the sound level was a few decibels above deafening. The enormous room looked like a surrealistic circus, an orgiastic playpen where adults could let it all hang out. The deejay was playing a hot, sexy number with a pounding, primitive beat as couples on the crowded floor erotically swayed and shook, pelvises grinding; the music throbbed and blasted a wild, frenzied tempo.

Nick walked over to Cat Bracken, who was laughing and holding up her hands as if trying to ward off the popping flashbulbs.

As she turned she saw him. With a smile and a spontaneous hug, she gave him an exaggerated kiss.

"Nick, how lovely to see you!"

Her voice was low and throaty. Cat looked beautiful, and she knew it. She did a fast, sexy twirl as if showing herself off for him.

"Well, what do you think?"

Her large, round eyes were sparkling.

Nick took in every detail of her appearance.

"I think," he said slowly, "you'll knock 'em dead. You're a hit, a smash, a superstar. You'll move far and fast. You'll have it all—everything Cat Bracken ever wanted."

"All my dreams will come true, is that it, Nick?"

Cat flicked her long, silver hair from her eyes. As she continued, there was a tone of reservation in her voice that had not been there before.

"Maybe not *all* my dreams, Nick."

She smiled a lazy, sexy smile and moved toward him. Gently but firmly, Nick took her wrists and eased her slowly back, keeping her at arm's length. Cat drew in a deep breath as she looked at him with a special, tender expression on her face.

"You know I love a million things about you, Nick."

Then a flicker of sadness touched her glistening eyes.

"It's really over between us, isn't it? I understand. But you do know that I wish you and Jan everything good in your marriage. Truly, from deep down inside me."

"I know you do, Cat."

For one split-second, their eyes locked. Then Nick turned and left; he took the steps leading to the glass-walled deejay's booth two at a time.

The lights dimmed, and the dancers moved off the floor. There was an expectant silence as Cat walked toward center stage.

The TV cameras at the back of the room followed her, zeroing in on the raunchy, sensual swing of her hips. The strapless, silver lamé jumpsuit she wore complemented perfectly the magnificent turquoise and diamond necklace around her neck. Her silver hair cascaded in tangled curls, and her blue eyes looked out at the audience like cool chips of ice.

Onstage, she stood tense and silent as she waited for her drum roll. Hearing it, she picked up the wireless mike; a kittenish smile played around her lips. Then with a slow movement of her torso her body language showed that she loved them. The flashbulbs popped; with a wild shake of her head, Cat started to sing in a low, husky voice like a silken thrush; her honeyed notes filled the room with a deep, rich earthiness.

As the cameras rolled, Nick watched the scene from the booth above. He moved close to the window and looked idly out over the crowd.

Suddenly his eyes narrowed and focused on one face.

He stood motionless, momentarily transfixed. The woman's face was so white, so deathly pale, so totally consumed by hatred, that he felt himself jolted as if by an electric shock.

He gestured desperately, futilely, trying to catch Cat's eye, trying to send her a silent warning.

Dear God, he thought, *something awful is going to happen.*

He couldn't stop staring; he stared in horrified fascination at the gun that was pointed directly at Cat.

And nobody seemed to notice.

Nick forced himself to move, stirring as if from a stupor. He fumbled with the doorknob; his legs felt like lead as they propelled him down the stairs, pushing through the crowd to reach the stage. He seemed to be outside his body, watching himself in slow motion. He had to reach Cat.

Another round of applause. Another drum roll. Then a sea of glittering confetti dropped from the ceiling onto the stage. Copper and gold flying saucers skimmed across the glass-topped ceiling. A smoke machine filled the room with ghostly silver fog in a dazzling display of state-of-the-art pyrotechnics.

Cat was standing at the edge of the stage with her arms outstretched. The crowd drank her in; the music broke and the lights began to dim. There was a deafening clash of cymbals. Flashing colored strobes bounced off the dark blue lacquered walls.

The music grew louder, rising higher, beating faster, throbbing harder. The disco seemed to move and shake, as if with a life force of its own. A fierce frenzy of sound filled the atmosphere like a solid mass, building on its own wild energy, pulling the watching crowd deep into its vortex.

The cheering onlookers were ecstatic as Cat continued to tantalize them. Her movements were incredibly sensual. She strutted like an enchanted rooster, taunting, teasing, and flaunting her sexuality. The audience was all smiles, smiles prompted by music, by alcohol, by 'ludes, by cocaine, and especially by love for Cat Bracken. All seemed to sway as one, hypnotized, intoxicated by the mood of the moment, watching her move, listening to her sing.

No one heard the shots being fired. No one knew that a tragedy had taken place.

Only Nick Tyson knew.

Chapter One

The runaway boy huddled in a doorway was cold, hungry, and very frightened.

Mark Squire was an orphan. His parents had died in a flash fire when he was three years old. Aunt Emily, his father's older sister, had taken him to live with her. There was a warm, natural bond of affection between the two of them.

One day without warning, Emily Squire died of a massive heart attack. Mark was fifteen when it happened.

After her death, he was made a ward of the state and placed in a halfway house. The institution gave shelter to orphans, abandoned children, and delinquents.

Mark hated every day that he spent there. The attendants in charge of the boys were tough. They made sure that discipline was maintained any way they could.

Mark was a tall, good-looking boy with straight blond hair, a warm complexion, and serious brown eyes. He was bright and outgoing, but he longed for the day when he could leave the home and be on his own.

The first few weeks in his new environment, he was hassled by the bullying older boys. After a couple of fights, they soon learned that he wasn't afraid of them. Bored with their games, they began to leave him alone.

All except Big Willie.

Big Willie was the toughest of the jocks—a balding eighteen-year-old homosexual with a heavily muscled body and arms covered with lewd tatoos.

Big Willie took an instant shine to Mark; he bluntly

announced that he had selected him to take care of his own sexual needs.

From that moment on, Mark's life was hell. Every time he was within earshot, Willie would laugh and call out to him in his whining, nasal voice, "Nothin's wrong with a male lay, pretty boy. You oughta be flattered 'cause Big Willie wants you to be his pussy."

Willie would then make lewd gestures and call out, "Here, pussy, pussy, pussy. Here, pussy, pussy." Meanwhile, anger raged in Mark.

Standing a head shorter than the massive Willie, all Mark could do was lash out with invective. "Fuck off, asshole. I'll break your cruddy head if you come near me."

Saturday was Mark's turn to clean out the week's accumulation of dog manure. The three nondescript mutts who lived inside the fenced run had very active bowels.

Mark was just shoveling the last pile of turds into a wheelbarrow when he was seized in a viselike grip. He couldn't move. Terror ran through his body; he felt himself tremble.

Then he heard Willie's voice. He felt a hand reach down and squeeze his genitals.

"Very nice, pussy. You got yourself a big one."

Mark was horrified to feel an erection start to build.

"Relax," Willie whined, trying to pull Mark's trousers down. "Ain't nobody can see us here. My boys are watchin' out for me."

Mark felt fear race through him as he smelled Willie's fetid breath. The more he struggled, the more Willie squeezed. In desperation he forced himself to relax.

"That's better, pretty boy," Willie whispered. "You're startin' to enjoy it. I didn't wanna handcuff ya an' call the boys. No need for a gang bang when Willie wants sweet boy for himself. Hey, I'm gonna show you heaven."

A wave of adrenaline surged through Mark's body. His rage turned into a thousand atoms of energy. Maniacally, he flung Wet Willie off him. Grabbing the spade, he heard himself yell, "You lousy faggot! You ugly, cruddy, dirty son of a bitch!"

Swinging the spade with all his might, Mark hit Willie, smashing him into the wheelbarrow.

Big Willie lay there moaning in pain, facedown in the stinking dog excrement.

Mark knew he was going to be sick. He leaned heavily on the wheelbarrow and vomited his guts out.

Then he ran. He ran and ran across the fields until he thought his heart would stop. He kept running until he reached the highway. Sitting down on the soft shoulder, the boy began to cry. Great, heartrending, racking sobs came from his shaking body. Then through his tears, Mark saw a big rig barreling down the highway.

He ran toward the speeding transport, waving and shouting, hoping to flag it down. The huge truck slid to a screeching stop, and he jumped aboard.

Riding north, Mark stared out the cab window. The country music on the radio was loud. Jake Birmingham tooled the big truck down the highway as if it were a toy.

"Driving cross-country sure bores the piss outa me, boy," he said in a strong southern accent. "We got us about six more hours afore we hit Brooklyn. Can't wait to unload this crap an' find me some action."

He started to laugh.

"I tell ya, boy, you gotta be real cool when you hit that town. Yessir, you gotta look sharp an' act sharp. The broads are wise, the cops are wise—even the jerks are wise. Everybody's a wiseass in the Big Apple.

"Where ya headin', boy? How far before you want I should let ya off?"

Mark kept staring out the window, thinking he could get off anywhere and it wouldn't matter. Any goddamned place he wanted to. He was leaving Baltimore forever. Brooklyn sounded as good a place as any to him.

"I'm heading the same place as you," he finally answered, his voice tense.

"Listen, boy, I ain't tryin' to zap ya. It don't mean no shit to me who you're runnin' from or why you're takin' off. So just relax, huh? You been sittin' there like ya gotta pole up your ass."

Mark grinned. Then he found himself rocking with laughter. He couldn't stop. *A pole up my ass!* If the guy only knew.

He started to relax, telling himself everything was going to be all right. He began to nod. Minutes later, he drifted off to sleep.

Mark was awakened by the trucker shaking him. The cab door was open. They had reached Brooklyn. As he jumped to the pavement, Jake smiled at him, gunning the big rig.

"Take care of yourself, boy. Be sure ya stay away from the creeps out there."

The truck roared out of sight. Mark stood waving; his lips silently formed the word *thanks.*

Standing alone in the street, he stared into the darkness. Which direction should he take? His body tingled with an eerie sensation as the quiet of the night enveloped him. He could hear the rapid beating of his own heart. An involuntary shiver ran through him.

The trucker had dropped him off in a slum neighborhood, bordered by broken-down buildings. They stood menacingly against the night sky, looking like crumbling dinosaurs from an ancient past.

As he started to walk, Mark peered nervously into the dark corners and alleyways. He was trying hard not to let his fear turn into panic. Yet he sensed someone out there. He could almost feel the scrutiny of unseen eyes. The stench of rotting garbage filled his nostrils. It seemed to be strewn everywhere.

Passing what appeared to be an empty lot, Mark heard a sudden rustle. A whining voice called out to him.

"Lookin' for games, pretty boy? How's about a trade?"

A rusted streetlight threw its beam onto the face of a black man holding out a nearly empty wine bottle to Mark. His eyes were flecked with yellow like a snake's. His cadaverous face stretched into a wide grin, revealing teeth that were stained and rotting. Mark stood for a moment, transfixed. The man was breathing hard; his heavy, sour breath enveloped the boy's face.

Shit, Mark thought. *Not another creep.*

He turned and ran panting into the night, running to get away. He covered block after block until the stitch in his side made him stop. He leaned against a doorway gasping for breath, his heart beating rapidly.

It was then that he noticed his surroundings had changed. He was in a different neighborhood.

The street he was on had rows of neat little stores. He found himself standing beside the red and white pole of a shuttered barbershop that was in the center of the block. From there Mark could see if anyone was approaching him from either end of the street.

He claimed the empty doorway for his own, planning to leave at dawn. Wearily, he huddled in a corner listening to the sounds of the night.

* * *

Every morning at daybreak, Antonio Bono walked the six blocks to his barbershop. As he turned west on the last block, he could see into the doorway of his shop.

This morning he noticed a figure huddled in the shadows. *A junkie*—that was the first thought that flashed through his mind.

Antonio Bono was not a fearful man, but he hesitated for a moment. Then he approached cautiously. The boy's blond head turned to face him. He looked like a nice, clean-cut kid, but his eyes were flecked with fear. He didn't look like the sort that spelled trouble. Maybe he was a runaway.

Bono kept his voice low and soothing as he spoke.

"So you saw my sign in the window, huh? And you got here early for the job—now, that's smart. I like that. It means you really wanna be a barber's helper, right? The pay's not much, but you'll learn a lot."

Mark's face acknowledged nothing. He looked wary, mistrustful.

Taking the key out of his pocket, Bono continued talking. "Well, it's time to open shop. Every morning I come early. Gives me time to get the water boiling for the first shavers. I always have hot soup every morning. You and me—we'll have a cup, okay?"

The pale morning sun was starting to rise. Mark studied the face of the man talking to him. It was a nice, craggy, kindly face. Some of the fear that had etched itself into his own features during the blackness of the night was beginning to fade.

"Come on in, kid. We got work to do. Don't lollygag about. You got floors to sweep and brass to polish. And you might as well take the 'Boy Wanted' sign out of the window. An early bird like you deserves the job."

* * *

Within the week the old man and the boy were friends. Mark told him everything about himself and learned in return that Antonio Bono was a widower with no family.

The boy grew to love Bono and his Tonsorial Parlor. Over the three sinks in the old-fashioned shop hung well-worn black razor strops. They dangled above porcelain mugs containing the finest ivory-handled badger shaving brushes. Mark never tired of polishing the brass taps and dusting the spotless green bottles of shampoo. The shop reeked of vanilla from the many bottles of hair tonic; the shelves were laden with salves and sprays and perfumed pomades.

Antonio Bono enjoyed teaching Mark everything he knew about barbering. The boy became part of the old man's life, sharing his apartment, sleeping on a cot in the spare room.

A year passed; Mark had never been happier. He gained confidence in himself. He also became aware that he was ambitious. He soon convinced Bono that they should do ladies' hairdressing, too. He suggested spiffing up the back room and making it into a salon. A big new apartment building was being built across the street, and there wasn't a ladies' hairdressing salon anywhere in the neighborhood. Mark was certain that the women living in the building would become their customers.

Antonio Bono listened to him. He closed his gnarled hand on the boy's shoulder.

"I'm too old to learn new tricks. But, young fella, if it's a hairdresser you want to be, then Bono will lend you the tuition. You can pay me back later on."

Mark enrolled in a beauty school to obtain his operator's license. By the time he passed the state boards, the building across the street was completed, and he was a licensed hairdresser. He set out to learn every phase of the beauty business; he was a fast learner.

The years sped by. At age nineteen Mark Squire was a happy, handsome young man. His body was thin yet muscular; his blond hair was shoulder length. He had great natural style, a pleasing personality, and big brown eyes that turned the ladies on.

Mark loved women, everything about them. Women sensed it, and they returned his affection.

He lost his virginity in a pizza parlor owned by Rosa Magnelli, located just two blocks from the barbershop. Her husband was serving a three-month jail sentence. Rosa was constantly horny and hungry for sex at the time when she met Mark.

She took him into the back room of the pizza parlor and asked him to help her move some crates. Once alone with him, she locked the door and reached for his crotch. She traced the outline of his penis with her fingertips. Then she tugged down his pants and pulled up her skirt.

Mark felt himself breathe deeply. Rosa was wearing no panties. He stared silently at the black curls of her pubic hair; they were wet and glistening. Excitement flushed through him. He had never seen the private parts of a woman before.

Rosa slid down onto his penis.

"First time for you, isn't it, kid? Just relax—Rosa will lead you through it."

She started to undulate back and forth until, with a shudder and a great cry, she came. Mark could feel himself about to come, too.

So this was it. This was fucking. He plunged deep inside of her; his strokes were strong and powerful.

The intensity was so great as he spurted into her that he felt like shouting. The sensation was better than anything he had ever known before. He wanted to prolong it, but it happened too fast. It was over too soon.

Rosa told him it would be even better the next time.

She was right. It was.

In the ensuing months, she taught him cunnilingus, fellatio, and every trick she knew, no matter how kinky or erotic. Mark was young and inexhaustible and eager to learn. He became an adept lover with incredible control. Rosa was earthy, passionate, and insatiable. Her lust seemed boundless. She could give him an erection by just looking at him. With raw animal passion, Rosa Magnelli made screaming noises whenever she came. Her young lover made certain that the whole street heard her.

Mark moped for three days after her husband came home from jail. It took an orgiastic weekend with a twenty-year-old manicurist to help him get over it.

Over the next two years, Mark made love to many women. He would listen to their stories, flatter them, soothe them, and make wonderful love to them. He was always totally honest in his relationships. He told each and every one that he wasn't interested in long-range commitments. They, on the other hand, hardly ever believed him, no matter how clearly he spelled it out.

"Mark, I think I'm falling in love with you."

"You and I could really have a fantastic relationship."

"I'm not the kind of girl who'll fence you in or make demands, I promise."

"I'm looking for a free relationship, just like you are."

Mark's antennae would rise. He knew these words marked the beginning of entrapment. It would be the last time he bedded whoever it was that said it. Besides, he simply didn't have time for emotional involvements. His only responsibility was to himself. Mark Squire intended to reach the top of his chosen profession.

Six years after Mark arrived on the scene, Antonio Bono's Tonsorial Parlor was thriving. At first glance, everything seemed the same: there were the same three chairs, the same old-fashioned bottles, the same leather strops and brushes, and the same sweet aroma of vanilla filling the barber shop.

But beyond the new side entrance was the recently added salon. Its decor was in a vivid scarlet red—very, very macho—lovingly painted by Mark. There were two black leather chairs, two sinks, a dryer, and a perm machine.

This was Mark Squire's private kingdom.

One morning as Mark was opening for business, Bono told him he intended to sell the barbershop.

The whole street was scheduled for an urban face-lift. A syndicate in the fast-food business wanted his shop. They were prepared to meet his price.

Antonio Bono planned to leave for Arizona after selling his property. His doctor had convinced him it was the best place for his arthritis. Over the previous few months it had been becoming increasingly difficult for him to hold a pair of scissors.

The older man studied Mark all the time he was telling him this. Finally, he paused for a moment; there was a look of open affection in his eyes as he scanned the young man's face.

"You've been one of the good things that happened in my life, young fella, ever since the first day you took that broom over there and swept the floor. I've considered you my partner for the last two years. I thought maybe I'd try to convince you to move out to Arizona with me, but I figure you'd be bored to death out there. Now I want to give you something."

Mark nodded mutely, waiting for what would follow.

With a slow smile, Antonio Bono handed him one of the old porcelain shaving mugs with the faded gold lettering that read ANTONIO BONO TONSORIAL PARLOR.

Mark stared at the old man, a puzzled look on his face, as Antonio pointed at the mug.

Mark reached for it. Inside was a neatly folded check.

Unfolding it, his eyes widened as he read, *"Payable to the order of Mark Squire . . . fifteen thousand dollars."*

"Good God!" he exclaimed incredulously. "I never expected—I never thought . . ."

He stared at the check. After a few seconds Mark took a deep breath. "I can't accept this. I can't take your money, Antonio. It wouldn't be right. You've done so much for me already. I just can't take it."

He started to press the check back into the old man's hand. He couldn't trust himself to speak.

"Oh, yes you can, young fella. You're gonna take this. I ain't a poor man. It's no gift, either. You've earned it. Now go and make me proud of you. Get out there and become the biggest man in the beauty business. Go do all those things you're always talking about—go to Paris and study with those fancy hairdressers. What the hell, why not? You got your start from one of the best—Antonio Bono of Bono's Tonsorial."

The old man laughed, showing his gold-filled teeth.

"You got the know-how, boy. You got it all going for you."

Mark grabbed Bono by his arms and hugged him; his heart was too full for words.

Chapter Two

Jan Julliard was beautiful.

Five feet seven. Waist-length, honey-colored hair. Pale green eyes, as changeable as the many colors of jade, heavily fringed with feathered lashes.

Jan was an only child whose parents were killed in a plane crash over the Swiss Alps when she was fifteen. Jan had been at boarding school at the time. In fact, she had spent most of her teenage years at The Merriam School for Girls, since her parents traveled constantly.

After graduation, Jan was too impatient to opt for college. She felt she'd had enough of school. Having been left a comfortable inheritence, she was eager to be on her own and get on with her life. So she rented an apartment in Manhattan; she had been living there now for the past six months.

This morning she lay supine on her exercise mat, breathing deeply and listening to the music blasting from the speaker. Her body was filled with nervous energy. She stretched one long leg toward the ceiling and bit on her lower lip as she concentrated on the perfect arch of her foot.

Stretching to the beat of the music, her expression became reflective. Her soft lower lip curved into a smile as she thought of the man she had met in the elevator the day before. Well, perhaps it wasn't really a meeting. He had said nothing to her, although he had most definitely complimented her with his eyes.

Jan's reverie was interrupted by the ringing of the phone on the floor next to her.

"Hi, Sarah. What's up? What am I doing? My stretching exercises—can't you hear the music? Hang on a minute till I turn it down. I want to tell you about the delicious-looking man who was in my elevator yesterday. I found out he lives in this building."

Putting down the phone, Jan turned Crosby, Stills, and Nash down to a lower volume. Then, settling onto the mat once more, she pushed her heavy golden hair away from her face.

"Okay, ready?" she asked, placing the phone comfortably on her shoulder.

"For God's sake, Jan, get on with it, will you? I'm dying of curiosity."

Jan laughed and tucked herself into a yoga position.

"Well, let's see. I'd guess he was about thirty-two." She paused.

"It was the oddest thing, the way he stared at me, scrutinized me. He was very sexy-looking. You never saw anyone with such a definite air of self-confidence about him."

"Okay, Jan, I get the picture. Now, tell me the important stuff. Did he come on to you? Did he make a move? The question is, what the hell happened?"

"Nothing, you idiot. I just met him in the elevator. But I know who he is. His name is Russell, Daley Russell, and—"

Sarah interrupted her.

"Daley Russell? Shit, I'm impressed! I mean, really impressed. Daley Russell happens to be the hottest photographer around. And rumor has it he's the greatest cocksman of the year. I've seen pictures of him. God, I do think he's good-looking; dark, passionate, and with a wonderful ani-

mal lust about him. Oh, how divine to make it with someone like that! I'd just love to get him into my pants."

"Stop, stop! I can't bear any more," panted Jan, pretending to be caught up in Sarah's passionate description
of the man in the elevator.

The two girls had shared a friendship throughout boarding school. Sarah came from divorced parents, both of
whom had spoiled her horribly. She couldn't stand either
of them. At school she developed a quick wit and a force-
ful personality, as well as a very sharp tongue. Her fre-
quent disobedience had given her a reputation as a rebel.
As a teenager, she had been heavy, bordering on fat, and
she was endowed with an overly generous nose. All
through her school years she had endured the nickname
Jumbo. But after graduation, all that had changed.

Sarah Hartley had just turned twenty. She was no longer
fat, and her nose was almost perfect, thanks to her mother's current lover, who happened to be a plastic surgeon.
Her teeth had been wired and straightened, and her brown
hair frosted and tipped.

Ever since she had been living in New York, Sarah
rarely awoke without a warm male body next to her. But
none of her affairs ever lasted long. Her usual scenario was
seduction followed by dismissal.

She didn't like many people and would often bitterly
recall the unhappy memories of her childhood, viewing her
world through dark, smoldering, angry eyes.

At The Merriam School, Jan had held out her hand in
friendship to Sarah, taking her into her special coterie—
Jan Julliard, the prettiest, best-liked girl in the entire
school.

"Jan," she said, an edge of sarcasm in her voice, "why
do I have a distinct feeling that you're not telling me everything?"

"Because, Sarah Hartley," Jan replied with a giggle, "you just happen to have a damned suspicious nature. And on that note, I shall disconnect, hang up, and see you later."

Placing the receiver onto the phone, Jan remained in her yoga position for a few minutes longer. Then she showered, wrapped herself in a terry robe, and rummaged in her closet for something dynamite to wear. Tonight she and Sarah were planning to visit a couple of clubs. New York's night life was constantly exciting; the city vibrated with its own special energy.

Later that evening, as they alighted from the taxi outside Club Fantasia, it was pouring. Ignoring the impatient overflow crowd waiting to be admitted, a doorman dressed in black leather stood behind the roped entrance and swung his pony tail. Seeing Jan at the edge of the crowd, he winked at her; she winked back. He had a thing for beautiful blondes, and this one was a nonstop knockout. He watched appreciatively as, followed by Sarah, she edged her way toward him through the pressing bodies.

Jan smiled when they reached him, sensing that what was needed was a positive attitude. He unhooked the rope and let the two girls enter, giving them the feeling that they were being admitted to a very special private party.

Angry cries of "What about us?" erupted from the crowd outside, who were still waiting in the pouring rain. The doorman stared past them with disdain, ignoring their pleas. Tonight, as always, he found most of those seeking admittance to be a bunch of desperate nobodies, mostly wash and wear, with absolutely no style.

After all, he was the undisputed master, the one who decided who entered and who did not. He picked his people as carefully as a casting director. It was important to get just the right mix at all times. Sugar and spice—that's what was wanted inside.

He next admitted a caped crusader, followed by a bald-headed black man wearing a full lion's skin and not much else. A purple-haired lady on roller skates glided past him. She was a regular.

"Now, which one of these men will I bed down with tonight?"

There was a half-smile on Sarah's lips as she mused aloud, surveying the gyrating male bodies crowding the dance floor. She knew what men wanted, and she knew she would always use that to get what she herself wanted.

Wrinkling her nose, she sniffed the air delicately and ventured another observation.

"Someone here is smoking some heavy-duty grass."

Then she spotted a bizarre-looking male sitting alone, staring into space, moodily chewing on his fingernails.

Sarah whispered to Jan.

"Wow, now there's a sexual prize. That's Joey Detroit. He's a rock 'n' roller—a real comer. Maybe he's the one I'll stalk tonight."

With a predatory look on her face, she turned her back on Jan and sauntered over to the lone man's table.

Jan shook her head, a bemused expression in her eyes. Like a spider spots a fly, Sarah had spotted her prey and was now off and running.

A brash young man with layered blond hair walked over to Jan.

"This is a bloody fuckin' terrific club, ain't it, luv?"

His accent was unmistakably cockney, with a raucous twang to it. He was wearing a silver shirt with a heavy lace jabot. His pants were velvet and skintight. The bulge in front was awesome. To top it all off, he wore glove-leather hip boots. He looked like a cavalier from a bygone era.

He aimed a finger at Jan while eyeing her up and down.

"Hey, pretty bird, 'ow about you movin' that body of yours onto the dance floor? Then after a session or two, maybe we could shift our relationship into another gear?"

He stood with his pelvis thrust out.

"Just a little action on the floor, that's what Alfie digs."

Jan thought, *Why the hell not?* He was trashy, but his accent was cute.

She headed for the dance floor with him. The music was hitting with force. Alfie dived into the crowd. He moved as if he had grease under his feet. His dancing was wild and splashy, with dramatic twists and turns. He repeatedly threw his head back, his eyes closed in reverie. Jan watched him as she danced, intrigued by someone who was narcotized by his own performance. She wondered if his whirlpool of energy ever ran down.

Suddenly, at the edge of the dance floor a voice shrieked out:

"Alfie, Alfie, there you are! I've been looking all over for you."

Alfie stopped dancing immediately.

A thin, elegant black man sporting a gold-rimmed monocle walked onto the crowded floor. He slapped Alfie playfully on the cheek, then kissed him gently on the mouth.

"I thought you might be here. What on earth are you doing, you silly little bugger? I can't let you out of my sight for a minute, can I?"

Alfie stood looking coy, like a small boy who had been caught with his hand in a cookie jar. The other man removed his monocle. His black eyes stared at Jan, eyes that were glazed and held no humor. She could tell he was high on something. He spoke quietly; his lips were curled into a half-smile, almost as if to charm her.

"This boy is mine," he whispered. "I like boys, but I

also go both ways. If you care to join us, you're welcome. It might be fun."

Jan stared at the black man, her green eyes icy cold. Then she turned and walked off the dance floor. She stood for a moment watching Alfie. There he was again, twisting about with wild gyrations and swiveling moves, thrusting his pelvis seductively.

Jan could see tiny beads of sweat standing out on the black man's face as he watched him. She was sure he was anticipating the sexual pleasure that Alfie's lascivious moves were promising.

Shrugging her shoulders, she turned and walked away.

The ladies' room was empty. She opened her purse and took out a joint. Lighting it, she inhaled deeply, feeling a lovely buzz. Then she brushed her hair and lip-glossed her mouth.

"Hey, we all make mistakes," she said, speaking to the empty room. Then, breaking into peals of laughter, she thought about Alfie. There would be no shifting gears for him tonight. Black cock, that's what he'd be taking care of.

The more she thought about the incident, the more salacious her fantasies became and the more she laughed. She put out the joint and started to regain her composure. She couldn't wait to find Sarah and tell her what had happened. That scene was right up her alley.

Chapter Three

Daley Russell resumed pacing. He glanced at his desk calendar: Friday the thirteenth. Somehow he just knew this was going to be a very shitty day.

Where the hell was Erin? The bitch was late as usual.

He reached for the phone and dialed, fighting for composure as he counted the rings.

His voice was soft, with a sarcastic edge to it, as he spoke into the mouthpiece.

"Did I wake you, Erin? I mean, am I disturbing you?"

Then he started to yell.

"Whaddaya mean, you overslept? I don't wanna hear any more excuses! As a model, you're an unprofessional dumb-ass bitch!"

Daley Russell could be either a charmer or a tyrant. Today he wasn't a charmer.

"This," he yelled to a visibly shaken assistant, "is the last time that bimbo ever pulls anything like that on me!"

He stalked back and forth with angry energy, a catlike grace in his stride. With a wild, sweeping motion he knocked photographic prints and layout sheets to the floor.

Daley Russell was slight of build, with dark unruly hair. His face, though deeply tanned, was beginning to show the passage of time. His black eyes could fleck with myriad colors, depending on his mood. Today they looked like the eyes of a predatory jungle animal.

His faded jeans seemed comfortable. The cashmere sweater he wore was old but expensive. His feet resembled a small boy's in beat-up sneakers. They were Daley's trade-mark. Scorning shoes, he wore them with everything.

"Temperamental bitch," he muttered to himself. "Now what am I gonna do?"

Daley Russell photographed the most beautiful models in the world, then bedded down most of them. He was New York's top fashion photographer and a celebrity in his own right. He and his lens seemed to be one. His was a gaudy talent, always capturing outrageous shots.

He glanced down at the gold Rolex on his wrist. It was four-thirty—too bloody late for the agency to send him another model.

The buzzer rang. It was the doorman, Eddie.

"Mr. Russell, there's a messenger here with a package for you. You have to sign for it. Shall I send him up with it?"

"No, keep him there. I'm coming down." Daley's voice was tired and cranky.

After signing for the package, he decided to take a walk. He considered wandering over to his main studio. He was still in a black mood. They were shooting a commercial there. He could always lose himself in the darkroom.

His trained eye could not have missed the young woman in the lobby who was idly checking her mailbox. He realized that she was the same one he had seen in the elevator a couple of days ago—really quite beautiful.

Daley changed direction and slowly walked over. He deliberately paced around her, eyed her up and down, and stared for a long time. He continued studying her as if she were on display.

"Hello, whoever you are. I am compelled to tell you, in all modesty, that you have just been scrutinized by the greatest photographer of our time. This may sound flip, but it just so happens that you are in a position to do me an enormous favor. I can see that all your component parts are terrific, but it's actually your hair I need."

Never once taking his eyes off her, he played with her hair as he continued.

"Great. Just great. Your hair is even more glorious than the bimbo's. Now then, I need you to come upstairs and help me out. You'll be perfectly safe. I promise not to hassle you."

A few seconds passed before Jan smiled. Daley's intense eyes remained fixed on her.

Finally, she replied. "Are you putting me on?"

He favored her with his first smile of the day. "Daley Russell kids thee not."

Jan laughed in reply, standing as if uncertain what to do.

Daley took her hand. "Come on, I promise not to bite."

A few minutes later, his assistant opened the door to Daley's apartment. It was large and airy and contained very little furniture. The walls were white, and the floor was black. Old and new Nikons were carelessly piled in a corner. Daley's gofer had removed all traces of his earlier temper tantrum. The large wooden table was neatly stacked with photographic prints and layout sheets.

He positioned Jan on a chalk-marked spot on the floor. When he spoke, his voice was businesslike.

"Okay, stand there and face the wall. Mike, flip up the music, then set the wind blowers on her hair."

Daley held out his hand. His assistant handed him a camera.

Jan stood frozen to the spot as her hair was whipped around her. The music kept blasting from the stereo. Catching the beat, she started to move with it.

"That's it!" Daley cried. "Go with the music. Come on, that's the way. You're terrific. It's just what I want. Sensational! Don't stop. Now, toss your hair about. Move your fingers into it. Deeper. Faster. Wilder. Let yourself go, lady. That's it! Hey, did anyone ever tell you you've got a real classy ass?"

Daley laughed and spoke again.

"A few more shots, and it's time for my analyst. I'm planning to fire the son of a bitch today."

Daley moved around the room like a panther, clicking his camera. Then, flipping off the music, he moved next to her and kissed her soundly on the back of her neck.

"Thanks, pet. You're quite a thoroughbred. I owe you one. You saved me a lot of grief."

A mildly wicked grin gave Daley the demeanor of an impish little boy. With a wink, he walked over to Jan and slowly lifted her chin toward his face. When he spoke, his voice had a caress in it.

"Someone knew just what they were doing when they put you together. You've got great legs, sensational bones, and a super skeleton. All the ingredients you need."

Daley kept scrutinizing her features. He paused for a moment, as if making a decision. Then he continued.

"I'd really like to do some test shots of you. Why don't you drop by the studio next Saturday? Make it around two, and be prompt. I hate people who waste my time."

Jan's mind was racing as he walked her to the door. A career as a model was something she had never seriously considered. She realized she was getting excited just thinking about it.

Closing the door behind her, Daley reached for an already-rolled joint and lit it. He still couldn't believe that Erin had held up a shooting. For all her faults, she had always been a pro. He tried to think of an explanation for her behavior but could come up with nothing that satisfied him.

The telephone's sharp ring cut into his musing. He yanked the receiver off the hook and grumbled a hello.

It was his wife.

They had married eighteen years before and had been separated for fifteen of them. She had been a gorgeous, dark-haired virgin whom he had gotten pregnant. He'd had no choice but to marry her.

Three months later she had had a miscarriage.

Her widowed father, an Italian, had been the owner of the photography studio Daley worked for. The old man was a master photographer, a true artist who taught Daley almost everything he knew about the art. Later Daley added his own special flair, and it wasn't long before he attracted the attention of top fashion editors. *Vogue, Glamour,* and *Mademoiselle* all bid for his work. He became the toast of the high-fashion industry. Life was one big party—just the way he wanted it.

Always irresistibly drawn to women, Daley had gone from one affair to another. When his wife found out, they agreed their marriage had become just a whimper, so they split. However, they maintained a reasonably friendly relationship; neither of them had ever bothered to file for divorce.

"Daley?" she asked.

He shifted the phone to a more comfortable position. "What's up?"

"Wish me luck. I'm getting married. My husband-to-be is planning to run for Congress. But he needs the respectability of a wife, not a live-in lady friend. So I need a divorce."

"A divorce? Well, whaddaya know? So the guy you're marrying is running for Congress? Boy, that's terrific. I'm really impressed. I hope he makes it."

He took another long drag on the roach he was smoking.

"You can handle the divorce any way you want to. I wish you the best."

Hanging up the phone, Daley leaned back in his chair, smiling to himself and feeling a sense of satisfaction. Life sure was a pisser. His wife was finally getting married. His smile grew broader. That meant Daley Russell would soon be a free man. Not that being married had ever made a difference. He'd always done just as he wanted.

But freedom. The word had nice ring to it.

Minutes later he picked up the phone and dialed a number. It rang for a while. Why the hell didn't she answer?

Two more rings, and still nothing.

He was just about to hang up when he heard the disinterested voice of an answering-service girl.

"Is there any message?"

He felt like saying, *Where the hell is she? She's been with me for the past few nights. If she isn't here now, I wanna know who else she's putting out for.*

But he slammed down the phone without speaking.

Erin hadn't shown up at the modeling session either. He shook his head. She wasn't with him, and she wasn't home. Obviously something better had come along for her.

His mouth turned down in a slight grimace at the thought that occurred to him. Perhaps it was time for Daley Russell to switch ass.

Chapter Four

The March sun cast a warm glow over Manhattan, as if to herald spring. Its rays seemed to soften the contours of the city's tall, hard-edged buildings.

Jan was feeling keyed up, nervous, excited, and scared all at the same time. With a positive stride, she walked quickly to the East Side, heading toward Daley Russell's studio. Today was the day he had said he planned to take test shots of her.

Occupied with her own thoughts, Jan was oblivious to the admiring glances of the males who passed her by.

On arriving at Daley's studio, she hesitated near the doorway for a minute. Then, before entering, she glanced at her watch. Two o'clock—she was right on time.

As she walked through the black-walled rooms, Jan peered into the open alcoves filled with camera equipment. She saw no one. She began to feel foolish and embarrassed, certain that Daley had forgotten all about her.

She was about to leave when suddenly the pounding of music split the air. It seemed to come from somewhere above her. Noticing stairs to the left, she walked up and opened the studio door on the next landing. Inside, the frenetic beat of an old Bill Haley record was blasting from twin stereo speakers.

Daley was dancing by himself in the middle of the floor. Seeing her, he grinned and beckoned her in.

"Jesus, I'm friggin' terrific!" he shouted exuberantly.

Jan watched, fascinated, as he continued to dance. He was whirling around the room like a spinning top.

"Great exercise!" he called out to her. "It sure gets the old ticker moving."

As he undulated his body to the wild rock rhythm, he reminded Jan of a jungle savage flailing in the frenzy of a tribal ritual. He seemed to be intoxicated by the music, propelled by self-feeding manic energy. His feet, in red sneakers, moved like a teeny-bopper's across the floor as his gyrating body bobbed up and down.

When he finally stopped, he studied his watch intently, checking his pulse. Then he smiled as he turned to her.

"Perfect, just bloody perfect. I do this twice a day. It keeps my juices flowing. Some guys do push-ups, some play volleyball, but Daley Russell rocks with the Rockets."

Moving with catlike grace, he flopped down onto a pile of pillows. He lit a joint and handed it to Jan; his dark eyes regarded her expressionlessly as she refused it. Jan wanted to be sure that her senses were very sharp while she was alone in the studio with Daley Russell.

Smiling again, he motioned for her to sit down.

"Wow." Jan grinned, sliding down among the pillows. "You really are one terrific dancer."

"Lay back, relax," Daley said, pulling on the joint. Jan was aware of his scent of lemon cologne. He started to nuzzle the back of her neck.

"You know," he said, a soft rasp in his voice, "sometimes the very best sex happens in the most unexpected places. What if you and I were to have a nice friendly fuck here and now?"

Daley's hand started to slide ever so slowly up her thigh. *The horny bastard,* thought Jan. Boy, did she have his number. *Test shots, my ass! A fast Saturday roll in the hay, that's what's on his mind.*

For a moment she thought of decking him but decided against such theatrics. Awkwardly, but with as much dignity as she could muster, she rose to her feet from the mound of pillows. Her face was flushed and angry.

"Hey," Daley crooned, "you look like you're about ready to shoot me down. So it's no fuckin', eh? Too bad."

He fixed her with his dark eyes for a few seconds, then stared down at his crotch and talked to it. "Guess you're not as bloody irresistible as you thought, little fella. Sorry —it looks like no action for you today."

Jan allowed herself a smile at his remark.

Daley jumped up in one fast motion and pointed a forefinger at her.

"Now that we've decided the lady's not for screwing, let's bloody well get to work. I want you to undress and drape this sheet around you. Think of something fantastically sexy, and look radiant, vulgar, and virginal at the same time."

Jan glared at him. "Forget it. I have no intention of doing nude shots."

Daley glared at her. "Are you kidding? Don't be an idiot! It's time you got to know me. My field is fashion, not porn. I want your clothes off so the sheet can cling naturally. Its purpose is to lend softness and texture to the shot, and to cover the rest of you. It's the fantastic bone structure of your face and neck that I plan to emphasize, not your mammaries. Now move your ass, and wrap that thing around you."

Seconds later, Jan was alone in the dressing room preparing for the session. A jumble of thoughts whirled around in her head.

What would it have been like to make love with Daley? Her mind was filled with delicious speculations. She had probably missed a fantastic experience. A smile crossed her lips. A moment ago she had rejected the man, and now she was fantasizing about him.

She'd had only two brief affairs before, neither of them very satisfying. But she never wanted to be easy. Maybe it was old-fashioned, but she knew she was a total romantic. Jan liked the courting ritual, the trappings of romance. And she wanted desperately to be in love.

Her musings were interrupted by a call from Daley.

"Let's go. I'm not getting any younger."

Daley was fast. He clicked away endlessly, seeming to take a dozen shots of every pose. Jan loved every minute of it; she moved her head, tossed her hair, and curled her mouth in a variety of soft, sensuous smiles. She found herself feeling strong and sure about what she was doing—not a bit insecure. As the stereo music kept blasting, she teased and flirted with the camera, high in energy, feeling herself totally turned on. She sensed that Daley, too, was charged with a feeling of excitement.

"Hold that pose," he growled. "I want to set the strobes. These shots are gonna be great. Okay, now the light is perfect. Sometimes when the light is just right, it's almost like God is on my side. You're beautiful. You're sheer fantasy. It's just you, me, and the camera having a love affair."

His words practically tumbled over themselves, as if trying to keep up with his clicking camera.

"You know, I'm betting you could really make it in this game. Hell, you should be playing in the big leagues; London, Rome, Beverly Hills—all the fancy watering holes of the world. Everyone loves new and beautiful faces."

Jan became almost hypnotized by the feverish clicking of Daley's shutter. Then suddenly it stopped.

She watched him put his Hasselblad down. Slowly stretching and wiping the sweat from his face, he walked over to the pile of cushions.

In one fluid motion he fell on top of them. In a matter of seconds he was asleep.

Jan dressed and pinned her mass of honey-blond hair with a couple of hairpins as she wandered back into the studio.

Daley was awake.

"Hello," he greeted her.

"Hello, yourself," she replied.

She was thinking that it had been an unforgettable day, but that now it was coming to an end. There was no more hot pulse from the music, no props. Daley looked so vulnerable sitting there that he almost melted her defenses. Suddenly a very strong feeling of affection for him surged over her. She knew she liked the man and hoped he would be her friend.

Daley looked at her for a long moment.

"You know, kiddo, you were fuckin' great today. You'll make a wonderful model." Then he added slowly, "That is, of course, if you want to be."

He paused as a new thought struck him.

"Monday I'll be shooting a spread for *Mademoiselle.* They want me to use a hot new hairdresser by the name of Mark Squire. Why don't you get here at ten in the morning? Let him play around with your hair and see what he comes up with, okay?"

A slow smile spread across Daley's face.

"And now that I know that getting laid is out with you, I herewith turn you loose because I have to get on the horn and call up the bimbos."

Jan smiled back at him. "Thanks for a wonderful day. It was possibly the most exciting one of my life."

* * *

Returning to the studio Monday morning, Jan felt a little bit edgy. Daley was totally involved with his lighting equipment and all but ignored her.

Four very beautiful models walked out of the dressing room. Within minutes, a makeup artist was applying shading and pancake to their already heavily made-up faces.

During this, the girls stared at Jan with hostile eyes, as if they were wondering how much of a threat she might be. Who was she? Was she sexier than they? Was she prettier? More photogenic? Did she have that special appeal that went beyond being just plain beautiful? Was she being groomed to be this season's next star-quality model, next year's new face? She wasn't from their agency—of that they were certain.

Jan felt like an impaled insect under their cold-eyed scrutiny.

"Are you a model," the perfect brunette asked, "or a stylist?"

Before Jan could answer, the door to the dressing room opened again and a spectacular blonde walked out. Her features were virtually perfect—and her expression implied that she knew it. She walked over to the chalked outline on the floor with studied indifference; she ignored the other models and looked around as if she were waiting to be admired. Her expression seemed to say, *I'm here. Now you may start.*

Getting no reaction, she combed her hair delicately with long, tapering fingers. When she finally caught Daley's eye, she gave him a bright, provocative smile.

He lifted his eyebrows in acknowledgment. Then he turned to Jan, who was standing in the corner.

Flashing her his little-boy grin, he said, "Why don't you take a look at the test shots I took of you? They're right there on the table, and they're really dynamite. After that, be a pet and pour me a glass of champagne from that bottle, will you?"

There was an intimate caress in his raspy voice, as if Jan and he had a special thing between them. The tall blond model with the golden hair glared at Daley, then at Jan. She seemed aware that a scene was being played out for her benefit.

As if to mollify her, Daley turned and gave her the innocent smile of a choirboy.

It occurred to Jan that this was the model she had replaced that day in Daley's apartment. *"The bimbo with the hair,"* he'd called her.

Daley waited till his assistant, who had been hovering nervously about, handed him a camera. Then he addressed his models.

"Okay, you beautiful bitches, the master is now ready for you. Edith, darlin', I want you on the left. You, Brenda, on the right. The other two on either side."

He slowly pointed his forefinger at the blonde. His eyes narrowed, and his voice took on a cruel edge.

"Erin," he said bluntly, "I don't think your hair is quite right for this shot."

The beautiful blonde stared at him, as if his words hadn't registered. Then a flash of anger crossed her face.

"What's wrong with it?" she snapped. "What's with you, Daley? Are you trying to be funny, or what?"

"No, not really, Erin. Your hair is ghastly. It looks like straw—as if you're wearing a bloody can of hair lacquer, that's how it looks. This ad calls for soft, young, sexy, touchable hair."

Daley mouthed each word slowly. He seemed to be reveling in his cruelty and the power he wielded. Jan sensed an impending explosion.

"You're crazy, damn it! There's nothing wrong with my hair, and you know it."

"Well, maybe not. Let's just say that I don't have a very generous attitude toward you right now. You and I can't work together today. How's that for starters?"

Two of the models were grinning, obviously enjoying the confrontation. Brenda, who was standing closest to Jan, whispered in her Brooklynese voice. "Wow, Erin's finally getting what's been coming to her. It's about time."

Erin's eyes were blazing. She stared at Daley, her lips trembling with rage. She moved forward as if to strike him, but then seemed to think better of it. She held herself in control as best she could. When she spoke again, it was between clenched teeth.

"You know something, Daley? You are one hell of a bastard."

Daley snapped back at her. "You had your goddamned nerve coming here today after your Saturday no-show performance. Baby, you've held me up for the last time. My time is money. Just be glad I haven't decided to bad-mouth you in the business. Don't push it, or I may change my mind."

Erin glared at him, her eyes flinty.

"I couldn't care less. I intended to tell you all about it this evening. Lover, I'm through with modeling. I leave for the Coast the day after tomorrow. I'm testing at Paramount on Friday."

Her eyes clashed with Daley's; her beautiful face wore a look of triumph. Holding her head high, she turned on her heels and swept out of the studio, brushing Jan's test shots to the floor as she walked by.

Daley's face registered nothing as he muttered between clenched teeth, "That bitch'll pass a screen test when my

cock learns to walk. Now, where the hell is that goddamned hair stylist? He should have been here by now."

As if on cue, the door opened and Mark Squire casually
walked in. When he spoke, his voice had an easy, sexy purr
to it. "Sorry I'm late, but the traffic today is murderous."

Jan turned to look at him, mentally checking him out.
He had a charming smile; he was tall and very good-looking, and he seemed well aware of it. There was a strong air
of confidence about him. Since he was a hairdresser, she
wondered if he was gay—a lot of them were. Or perhaps
he was bisexual, a fence straddler, one of those who hadn't
yet made up his mind.

Jan noticed that he moved like a boxer. The weight of
his body was balanced on the balls of his feet. Staring at
her, he pursed his lips in a silent whistle, then gave her a
slow, warm smile. His eyes held an expression of honest
male admiration, which she took as a compliment.

Definitely heterosexual, she decided.

"All right, all right, is everybody ready?"

Daley's shout brought Jan out of her reverie. He arranged his models according to the chalk marks. Mark got
busy brushing, teasing, and fluffing their hair. He knew just
what to do; he managed to make them look even more
beautiful than they already were.

"Mark, sweep Brenda's hair back more—that's it,"
Daley said. "Terrific! I love it."

He began shooting, clicking his camera rapidly. He was
fast and sure; he crouched down for the close-ups. The
models slipped into one pose after another with effortless
ease. Watching them, Jan was aware of the strong chemistry between Daley and the lovely young girls.

"Hold still, Sandy," he crooned. "I want to get every
curl on the back of that beautiful neck of yours. Edith, fan
out that golden cap of hair. Marge, keep smiling, you won-

derful, pretty-faced thing. You're all terrific. We have three more sets to go, then we're done."

When the last set ended, after much cheek-kissing between Daley and the models, they left.

He then turned to Jan, who had been completely fascinated by the whole scene.

"Now I think I'd like to do some very special head shots of you."

He turned to Mark Squire. "Mark, do something wild with Jan's hair. Something spectacular, totally extravagant. They tell me you're as good or better than some of the name boys. If you're as hot as they say and we get a cover out of it, it'll earn you a credit line."

"You want a cover, Daley? You got it."

"That simple, huh?"

Mark grinned at him. "Yep, that simple. I'm with hair what you are with a camera."

He took Jan's hand in his and led her into the dressing room. His grip was firm. He sat her down in front of the small dressing table, and his eyes looked directly into hers. They seemed dark and light at the same time. Jan thought they were the kind of eyes that would reflect emotion sensuously.

As he brushed her hair, she took a deep breath. A cover! Was Daley serious? In her mind's eye she saw her face on a thousand newsstands. Daley's confidence made anything seem possible.

She followed Mark's every move in the mirror as he swiftly and confidently arranged her hair. His hands moved as if they had a will of their own, teasing, spraying, and spiking with not a single wasted motion. There was an attitude of delight about him as he worked his fingers like a virtuoso, shaping and styling with a rhythm all his own.

Finally he dug into his satchel, pulled out a can of gold hair paint, and lightly touched the tips.

Daley stared intently; his eyes missed nothing. Then a happy grin spread over his face.

"Dynamite!" he said with a look of admiration after Mark had finished. "I've gotta hand it to you. She really looks terrific. Hey, man, you're one hell of a stylist!"

Mark sought out Jan's eyes; he smiled at her as Daley yelled for the makeup girl.

"Tracy, get your ass in here and take a look. What do you think we should do with this beautiful face?"

Tracy stared. Daley stared. Mark stared. Jan felt as if she were naked on Main Street.

The makeup girl didn't say a word. She just took her palette and selected the colors. For the eyes, green, gold, and amber shades were subtly blended together. Then swift, sure strokes of black crayon were added to the corners. Foundation, powder, shading—all were meticulously applied. One slick swoop with a pencil, a dab of gloss, and the mouth was done.

Jan gazed at her image in the mirror. Was that really her face? She resembled a beautiful, golden Cheshire cat. Her hair looked like floating clouds of spun gold. The eyes she saw were huge, wild, sexy, and untamed.

"Get me that jeweled dog collar from the box of props!" Daley yelled to his assistant. "And bring me the black velvet shawl."

He fastened the necklace around Jan's neck, draping the velvet cloth around her. Then he kissed her on the tip of her ear.

"You look fuckin' incredible. Now let's get to work."

Jan tossed her head and laughed. She was ready.

Twenty minutes passed; shot after shot after shot. The studio was silent except for the clicking of the strobes.

Daley saw what he wanted, pressed the button, and that was it.

It was after midnight, and Jan couldn't sleep.

She felt too keyed up. Her thoughts jack-rabbited about, rehashing everything that had happened. It was as if someone had wired her; it was a good feeling. It had been an incredibly rewarding day.

Was it possible that she actually had a future in modeling?

Mark kept creeping into her thoughts: the wonderful things he had done with her hair. How clever he seemed! The warm sensuality about him. She especially liked the way he looked—his style, his lazy, easy saunter. He was so calm, so seemingly secure.

How very different the two men were. Daley was so volatile and keyed up; Mark was laid-back, casual, and relaxed. He seemed to be devoid of tension.

Jan was suddenly enveloped by a rush of sexual fantasies and erotic thoughts.

She fondled her breasts, her nipples hardening as she touched the tiny nerve endings. She felt a slow, sexual flame flicker, and a warm glow entered her groin. Her entire body seemed to tingle with desire—the desire to be with a man. She wanted to be engulfed by passion, to be held in warm, strong, caressing arms. She wanted the nearness of a man she could adore, a man who would fulfill her and belong to her alone, just as she'd belong to him. She was ripe and ready for love, ready to feel the hardness of a male body next to hers, a body that would be strong and lustful, yet tender and sensitive. She longed for someone she would want to share her life with—maybe not yet, but soon, very soon.

Jan smiled as she drifted into a deep sleep.

Chapter Five

Nick Tyson inched his Jag through the narrow London rush-hour streets. The traffic was slower than usual. He angrily lit a cigarette and slapped the steering wheel in frustration.

"Damn! Damn this traffic!" he muttered. "I'll never get home."

He forced himself to concentrate on something else; he switched his thoughts to his mother. He really didn't want to fly to Louisiana for her birthday. But he knew how upset Cynthia would be if he didn't come home for the occasion. He hated to disappoint her. He'd just have to make time for her party.

Nicholas Patrick Tyson. Age, twenty-five. Background, Irish-American. Born very wealthy, an only child, the apple of his parents' eyes, he was gifted with two fat trust funds, one from his grandfather and the other from his paternal grandmother.

Nick had attended all the right schools and had been thrown out of two of them. His mother had unhesitatingly condemned the schools and supported her son. To Cynthia Tyson, Nick could do no wrong. She spoiled and adored him and insisted he call her Cynthia.

Nick was a handsome young man; his eyes were as blue as cornflowers. A fraction over six feet tall, he had an air of elegance about him, coupled with a lean athlete's body. He was totally self-assured, and he radiated a quiet confidence and subtle self-esteem. Relaxed and easygoing, he had a natural gift of making people like him. It was easy to be charmed by his enthusiasm and his cheerful attitude toward life.

The Jaguar's powerful engine became more throaty as the traffic thinned out and Nick sped up.

A smile crossed his lips as his thoughts returned to his mother. Cynthia always made such a big deal out of her birthday. She loved the fuss that he and his dad made over her.

Nick frowned again. His long, tapered fingers impatiently tapped the wheel to the heavy beat of the rock music on the radio as he waited for the sudden tangle of taxis up ahead to start moving again.

His thoughts returned to home as he recalled how, after graduation, he had been tempted to remain in Tysons Landing, the town named after his grandfather. It would have been easy to accept a ready-made position in one of his father's manufacturing companies. Nick had always worked for Charles Tyson on holidays and summer vacations.

Nick adored his father and the two of them got along famously together. The elder Tyson, a brilliant businessman, had managed to quadruple the fortune left him by Nick's grandfather. He dreamed of the day when he could turn over the reins of his business to his son.

But Nick was restless, footloose, and never quite sure what he really wanted to do. He did know, however, that he wanted to succeed at something on his own. He wanted the excitement of a challenge—something new, different, and of his own choice. Much as he loved and respected his father, he wanted to march to the beat of Nick Tyson's drummer.

He had spent months bumming around the Continent, idling along, doing exactly what pleased him, trying to find himself. After a while, it became a study in tedium. The boredom grew almost unbearable.

In 1972, after a year of aimless travel, Nick settled in London. It was there that everything seemed to come together, there that he finally realized what he wanted to do.

Once the concept hit him, he couldn't get it out of his mind. He thought about it during all his waking hours and dreamed about it as he slept: a private club like nothing the world had ever seen before. It would be a floating pleasure palace for the superrich, for the most famous, glamorous, and exciting people on earth. Each of the one hundred members would pay an initiation fee of one million dollars. It would be the most exclusive club in the world, and it would be Nick Tyson's.

A smile crossed his lips as he remembered whispering to himself, "I know I can make it work."

Nick's reverie was interrupted when the traffic light turned green. He slowly increased his foot's pressure on the accelerator. The traffic was still moving at a crawl.

Again, Nick's thoughts returned to the past. How long ago was it since he had first discussed his idea for a seagoing club with Guy Monti, the manager of Promises, one of Mayfair's posh night spots?

No one knew much about Guy Monti. But one thing was certain: he himself knew everyone who was anybody in London town, and he was on first-name terms with most of them. All the beautiful people, the bored young debs, the latest trendy fashion designers and their models, the actresses, the call girls, and the colorful, unpredictable rockers—all were part of the scene at Promises, and all were part of Guy Monti's life.

Monti was twenty-six. He favored Italian-style suits with tight-fitting jackets. His silk shirts were always open at the neck, revealing a heavy gold cross. He was attractive in a street-urchin sort of way, with restless black eyes and an arrogant attitude.

Monti's slight accent gave him a certain charm; the shark tattooed on his forefinger made one wonder. His heritage was Neapolitan, although he was now a British subject. He'd married a stripper to obtain his papers; she was now safely tucked away somewhere in his past.

Nick was fascinated by Guy Monti, who seemed to grab life with both hands. He was into all kinds of fringe ventures and high-rolling deals; he had a talent for promoting anything new. So it was important to Nick to learn Monti's opinion of his plan for a seagoing club.

Monti listened silently, his eyes opening wider as he became swept along by Nick's enthusiasm. Almost before Nick finished talking, the other man slapped him on the back and proclaimed that his idea of a floating club was sheer dynamite. But where would Nick find the money for such a gigantic undertaking? The ship alone would cost a fortune. Would he go to the banks, float stocks, or what?

"No, nothing like that," Nick had told him. "My dad will arrange the financing. I'll make him my partner. He always wanted us to work together."

At last the traffic started to thin out. Nick's mood brightened as he drove past Princess Gate. Soon he'd be turning into Knightsbridge.

He took a sharp right in the direction of Brompton Mews. Down the small street to the house he had rented, and he was home.

As he turned the key in the lock, Nick knew Rusty would be upstairs waiting for him. She was a bed-smart lady; she had reluctantly left her rich lover in France after his wife had learned of their liaison. Rusty and Nick had now been together for the past three months, and their relationship was an easy one.

Nick had known quite a few women in his life. Most females adored him, but he had never given his heart to any. Somewhere in the back of his mind was the image of his dream girl. He knew she was out there somewhere— she had to be. Until he could find her he had neither the time nor the inclination to fall in love.

He observed Rusty now, stretched out naked on his bed. He stood for a while drinking her in, appraising her as she lay there looking voluptuous and wanton. Bed was one of her favorite places.

Rusty came close to being breathtakingly beautiful. There was a provocative, wild, gamine quality about her. She had untamable red hair and skin the color of alabaster.

Lying now with her milky white thighs spread open, her pubic hair like a smoldering scarlet flame, Nick knew she was savoring the effect she had on him.

With an inviting smile, she raised her head off the pillow.

"Light us a joint, darling, will you please?"

Nick lit up a toke and handed it to her. Rusty inhaled greedily, then fell back onto the sheets.

The next time she spoke, there was a carnal quality in her voice. "Do you still like what you see, Nicky baby? If so, let's have a good healthy fuck, my pet, because this will be our last time together. Louie has finally dumped his wife. He wants me to share his title and his worldly goods. I must learn to be a faithful, loving mate to him. So I'm leaving for Paris in the morning."

"Is that so?" Nicky asked incredulously as he stared at her. "I guess absence really does make the heart grow fonder."

Rusty grinned as she rose from the bed and padded over to him.

"It would seem so, wouldn't it? But let's not talk about it right now. At the moment, this is what I want."

She opened his zipper, pulled out his penis with a sudden urgency, and captured it in her mouth.

Nick felt his breath quicken as her tongue gently explored his throbbing, rapidly expanding organ. His flesh quivered under her touch. He let out an involuntary groan, and his pleasure grew intense.

Soon he too was naked on the bed. She parted her legs for him, lifting her hips off the mattress. His fingers stroked her, probed her, made her writhe with pleasure as she urged him to enter her. He was hard and ready, and he thrust himself inside her with one powerful stroke.

His lovemaking grew fast and furious—the way she liked it. They moved in rhythm, heaved up and down together in a mounting frenzy, thrashed wildly, exchanged no words. Nick suddenly forced himself to remain stockstill as she came; her soft moans turned into a scream. Then he plunged at her again, thrusting deeper and deeper inside the warm wetness until he too was totally spent.

Seconds later they lay motionless, facing each other, luxuriating in the afterglow of their own release.

Finally they hit the shower. Rusty lathered him hard again. Holding his hands against her wet, soapy thighs, he slid hungrily down and buried his head in the flaming softness between her legs.

Later, as Nick sat on the edge of his bed dressing, he turned to her.

"I'm glad for you, Rusty, really glad that the old Duke is gonna make an honest woman of you. But I'm sure as hell gonna miss you."

Chapter Six

Cynthia Tyson awoke with the sun shining in her eyes. *Damn that maid,* she thought. Alpha had forgotten to pull the drapes again.

Cynthia struggled to sit up. Her head was throbbing unmercifully. How many after-dinner brandies had she consumed before going to bed? She'd been angry at Charles last night, damned angry, when he'd called to say he'd be late again. Another lonely evening for her.

She cuddled against the empty pillow next to her—her husband's pillow. Lately he never seemed to be there. She flushed angrily to herself.

Cynthia was beginning to hate the time Charles spent in Fort Jade. What was so important about this new business venture, anyway? Certainly not the money. He had plenty of that, more than they could ever spend. Was it boredom? How could that be? He had always seemed so contented at home.

Cynthia had fallen in love with Charles Tyson the moment they met. They were married soon after, with his mother's approval. Her approval mattered to Charles, and Cynthia loved him for that. She respected his morality, his upbringing, and his family traditions. At that time she didn't dream that the young businessman she had fallen head over heels in love with was very, very rich.

Cynthia had never known her own mother, an emotionally unstable woman who had spent part of her early years in sanitariums, and who had died giving birth to her. Her father, Paul Barras, had been a weak man, a heavy drinker, and a womanizer. As a child, she had had little use for him. He was killed driving to California with his third wife. Cynthia didn't attend the funeral.

Marriage and a family of her own were all Cynthia ever wanted. Once they were hers, she guarded them passionately. She was possessive and protective about the two men in her life, excluding all others.

Even now, it still pained her to remember how Charles had broken the news to her that Nick was planning to leave for Europe. She felt the hurt anew each time she thought of it. Why did she have to hear it from Charles? Her son had always discussed everything with her before.

She would never forget the look on his face when she confronted him. He knew she was angry with him.

"Why, Nick? Haven't you even considered me? You know I shall miss you horribly. Don't I mean anything to you anymore?"

Nick paused before replying, as if weighing his words. "You know you mean the world to me, Mother. You're my number-one girl. But I'm not sure I'm cut out to work for the Tyson Holding Company. I plan to spend some time in Europe, and then I'll decide what I really want to do with my life. You can understand that, can't you?"

He had seemed like a little boy, seeking approval.

That had been a year ago. Cynthia hadn't been able to stop him; Nick had money of his own, left in trust from his grandfather's estate. At first, she felt it was just a temporary phase and was confident that Nick would soon tire of roaming and return home. But now he'd rented a house in London and had taken up residence there. Still, Cynthia told herself, it was just part of growing up. Nick just wanted to show his father that he could succeed on his own. Her heart told her that he'd eventually come back to Tysons Landing and be as close to her as before.

She clung to that hope day after day.

Sliding down into the warmth of her bed, Cynthia remembered Nick as a baby. It was her most treasured memory; they'd shared a private world together.

How she had wanted a child! Two miscarriages, and then Nick was born—the most perfect of babies. It had been important for Cynthia to be a wonderful mother.

She used to sit in the nursery just listening to him breathe. She was possessed by him, constantly marveling at the wonder of her child. She breast-fed him until he was two. Feeding him was a ritual she loved; she treasured the intimacy that they shared.

Even now she remembered the unexpected sexual high it had given her when her man-child pulled and rooted at her breast. She had such an intense, primitive feeling about it. She would sit holding him, listening to the sucking sounds he made, feeling tension build in her groin as she became sexually aroused.

A tremendous feeling of guilt would then sweep over her.

In the morning Charles would gently nibble at her swollen breasts, tasting the sweet fluid that flowed from them. It was strange, but she felt no passion toward him. In the past Charles's lovemaking had been dizzying to her—her body had soared at his touch. But after her young son suckled at her breast, it was different. Charles's lovemaking then became an intrusion to her.

At times she was sure it was a madness. It was as if she belonged only to her son and to no one else. As soon as she stopped suckling Nick, she went through a long period of deep depression. Charles was worried, but the doctor told him it was quite normal—like a second cutting of the cord, a letting go.

One day her depression suddenly left her. She no longer belonged exclusively to the male child in the other room.

Cynthia stopped her daydreaming, slid out of bed, and pressed her feet into her plush mules. Entering the bathroom, she dropped her silk nightgown to the floor.

She studied herself in the mirror. At forty-eight, Cynthia Tyson was still a very attractive woman. Her soft blond hair framed a strong yet elegant face. Her figure was firm and slim, and her skin was as smooth as ever.

Running her bath water, she poured a generous amount of crystals into the tub. Why, on this particular morning, was she so preoccupied with yesterday's emotions? She knew the reason. It would be her birthday in three weeks. Nick would be coming home.

She slid slowly into the warm, sweet-smelling water with a daydreaming smile on her face. Soon the two most handsome men in the world would be sitting at her dinner table on either side of her. How lucky she was! Lucky to have spent the last twenty-five years of her life loved and protected as Mrs. Charles Tyson, to have a wonderful husband and a wonderful son like Nick.

She had just stepped out of the tub when she heard a light knock on her bedroom door.

"Is that you, Alpha?"

"Yes, ma'am. Will you be havin' breakfast in your room? Or are you plannin' to have it with Mr. Charles in the breakfast room?"

Wrapping a terry-cloth robe around herself, Cynthia opened the door to her housekeeper.

"Mr. Charles is here?"

"Yes, ma'am"

A warm smile crossed Cynthia's face. Dear Charles! He must have come home late. Not wanting to disturb her, he'd slept in one of the guest rooms.

She dressed quickly and took the stairs down to the breakfast room two at a time. She couldn't wait to see him.

Charles was already seated at the table. Cynthia felt her heart beat faster as she looked at him. After all these years, she still loved him. Six more months, and it would be their twenty-sixth anniversary. Twenty-six years of loving each other, sleeping beside each other, giving each other comfort and joy—with rarely a moment's friction or anger.

"You should have wakened me, Charles. You know I don't mind being disturbed, dear. It would have been worth it for an early-morning cuddle. Sharing a bed in the morning with someone you love is sheer delight, one of the nicest things about marriage. And lately I miss it."

Placing one hand on his, she continued.

"What's your schedule today? How about taking me to lunch at the club?"

Charles remained silent. He seemed preoccupied, as if he had not heard a word she said. Cynthia felt a sudden concern for him. He looked drawn and tired.

"Are you all right?" she asked.

He hesitated before answering. "Yes, honey, there's nothing wrong that a good night's sleep won't cure. But I'm sorry about lunch. I have to leave for Fort Jade right after breakfast. Bill Myers, Joe Hawman, and I have to go there to straighten out a few distribution problems we've been having. We were working on them till late last night."

Cynthia's voice went flat as she sighed with resignation. "Not again, Charles! Not another weekend of work. All that driving back and forth to Fort Jade—what do you need it for?"

She felt a sudden loneliness envelop her. Charles seemed

to become more and more enmeshed in his business, and his weekend meetings always excluded her. She was feeling edged out of his life. He was always so damned busy these days—and nights.

She winced at the mental picture of herself as a brooding, jealous woman hovering over her man. Jealous of her husband's business, of his corporate responsibilities, of his outside interests, and of anything else that kept him from her. Yet she knew that Charles did it all for Nick and her. Cynthia wanted for nothing, thanks to the most wonderful, generous husband in the world.

Charles prided himself on his accumulation of wealth. He thoroughly enjoyed the power it gave him. It was his life. She couldn't fault him for that.

With a smile, Cynthia pushed all her angry feelings away. Then she kissed him tenderly on the side of his cheek.

"Okay, Charles Tyson, off you go into your gray flannel jungle. Don't care if I face a bleak, rotten weekend here without you. But next weekend is mine, hear? You're staying home so I can fuss over you. Maybe we'll stay in bed the whole bloody time and do all sorts of unimaginably sexy things. Now, don't you dare forget it. No business commitments, Mr. Tyson."

Charles reached across the table and held her hand. When he finally spoke after a moment of silence, his voice was soft, almost sad as he looked at her expressionlessly.

"I'm sorry, Cynthia. I really am."

As she walked him to his car, Cynthia was aware that Charles seemed unsettled and preoccupied. She told herself that it was due to a business problem.

As Charles turned to her, he seemed drawn and tired. When he kissed her good-bye, he held her warmly, as if to comfort her.

Her voice was tender when she spoke to him. "Why, Charles Tyson, I do believe you're going to miss me."

Cynthia's eyes were bright as she turned and walked into her rose garden. Pruning off the dead buds, her thoughts were of her husband. Poor darling—he had sounded so penitent. Cynthia smiled. Her ruffled feelings had been soothed. Of course, she hadn't really meant to make him feel guilty.

Her mind drifted toward the next weekend. She would plan something wonderful for the two of them. It would be lovely to have Charles all to herself, to make love, to talk, to share things together the way they used to do. It had been so long since they had done that.

Cynthia watched her husband's car pull away from the driveway. Her smile was warm as she waved to him. Then, after glancing around at the perfectly manicured lawn, she turned sharply on her shapely legs and reentered the house. She realized her mood was much more cheerful than before.

One last wave to Cynthia, then Charles Tyson pulled out of his driveway and headed for the highway. A wave of weariness swept over him. He was hit with another one of his strange headaches, as well as with a feeling of agonizing guilt.

Tyson drove his Cadillac at a steady speed. Only another ten miles more to go. More weariness swept over him. He'd been having these strange headaches lately—sudden spasms of pain. Fortunately, they didn't last too long. It was all guilt, he was sure.

He mulled over the same thoughts he had been rehashing for days. What the hell was he getting himself into? His affair with Maria had been going on for almost a year. It was madness, but he couldn't stop. Each time he intended to end it, he panicked. God! He'd always been a man who shied away from this sort of thing. Too time-consuming, too absurd to jeopardize a good marriage. And for what? A fast screw with some bimbo?

No, this was different. This was an enchantment, a be-witchment, a love affair. Right—a real love affair. By the end of the first month he knew it.

But how had it happened? Damn it, he'd never even made a pass at another woman! Not since the day he married Cynthia. He had been been totally faithful to her. She always came first. Without her, nothing would have mattered. She was a damned good-looking woman and a fine homemaker, and their sex had always been good. Their life-style was comfortable and easy. There was nothing about Cynthia that he could fault. Well, maybe one thing: her damned possessiveness of Nick. That was probably the reason the boy had made a break.

But now all that had changed. He swore softly to himself as his thoughts flashed to Nick. He was making love to a girl a year younger than his own son.

Why had he complicated his life this way? It was sheer lunacy, the madness of a man who would soon be fifty. Yet just thinking of Maria, remembering the sensation of her soft body yielding to his, made him tremble slightly. She was so beautiful and so passionate, such an incredible lover. He had always been proud of his virility, but ever since knowing her he had felt like a bull. She had the power to make him feel young again. It was as if she were giving him a second chance at youth.

But it wasn't only the sex. She was charming, funny, and intelligent.

He thought of the day he had bought her the shiny red Mustang. She had gasped with delight. Then she'd cried out of sheer happiness. The longer he knew her, the more he wanted to please her. He loved to indulge her, to spoil her, to do anything that would bring that wonderful curve to her lovely lips when she smiled.

As he touched the small jeweler's box in his left-hand pocket, the thought hit him, the one thought that he had been avoiding and pushing back into the corner of his brain.

I want to marry her.

It was the first time he had actually, consciously framed the words in his mind. His throat was strangely dry. He could feel tension build in his chest, then feel once more the heavy flash of guilt as he thought of Cynthia. He hated what he was doing to her. How could this have happened after a lifetime of sharing and loving together? The dull pain was building in his temple again. What would Nick think? Did it matter?

Nothing mattered. All he wanted was Maria, Maria with him always. And he wanted her now. Charles felt the excitement start to build. The throbbing in his testicles brought on a sudden ache for her. He developed an enormous hard-on. Feeling like a teenager, he hit the gas pedal, and the black Cadillac roared down the highway, heading for Fort Jade and Maria Benson.

Chapter Seven

Maria Benson was sitting in the apartment Charles had rented for her; a thick mass of curly auburn hair rippled to her shoulders. Tucked into a chair, gazing out of the window, she felt restless and uptight.

A frown crossed her lovely face. Her sandaled foot nervously swung up and down. Her normally lustrous blue eyes became flecked with shadows as her thoughts turned to Charles.

Their affair was moving in a direction that she wasn't sure she wanted. A new possessiveness on his part seemed to be taking over.

Charles had been mentioning divorce. But that wasn't what Maria wanted. She had known he was married when she started the affair. That was fine with her. She didn't love him, not in the way she dreamed of love. Still, she would never want to hurt him. She felt safe with Charles, and their sex certainly was great.

Everything had fallen into place. Her life had become comfortable. It was hard to remember how down she had been just a year before. Then Charles came along. He couldn't have been more generous. He had even insisted that she stop working.

Her mind began drifting back—back to Texas. She remembered how joyless and unchanging those years had been. So much sadness and pain. When she was thirteen, she had watched her mother die of cancer. After a year, her father had remarried, only to be felled by a heart attack twenty-four months later.

His widow was an angry, bitter woman who had resented everything about her stepdaughter. Three days later, on her sixteenth birthday, Maria had left home with her guitar and seventy-five dollars.

She hitched a ride to Nashville. To her, it was the most magical of places, the place where her dream of becoming a country singer could come true.

A year later that dream was all but gone.

Maria had hit every recording studio in town hoping for an audition. Lewd propositions had been plentiful, but no one was interested in hearing her sing. She supported herself doing everything from waitressing to vending hot dogs. She stayed with two gay decorators and dog-sat for their poodle. Finally, they found her a job as a hostess in a sleazy after-dinner spot. It was there that she had met Arnie Teller.

Teller operated on the fringe of the recording business. He was sharp, funny, and a fast talker. He seemed to know his way around. He initiated her into wild sex, drugs, and inside stories of country music. He convinced her that together they could make it; he offered to act as her manager. Then he'd talked her into marriage.

Two years later all he had done was book her as a strip singer in a local joint that ran porno movies. After that things went from bad to worse.

Teller's drug habit soon got the better of him. Without his daily fix, he began to get violent. He wanted Maria to turn tricks, and when she refused, he beat her. One night she fixed his coffee with a heavy sedative and left Nashville.

Teller was fatally shot three days later in a drug bust.

Maria drifted around the state of Louisiana, ending up penniless in the town of Fort Jade. There in the bus station she had met Paula, a girl who was leaving town. Paula had just quit her job at The Rabbit Club, an off-hours night spot, and was heading home with her dreams slightly worn.

Within the hour Maria had replaced her at the club.

She rented a back room nearby and was neither happy nor unhappy. There were moments when she'd wonder where she was heading. Mostly she knew she was just marking time, on the brink of a future clouded in uncertainty.

One night Charles Tyson walked into the club with a group of men. Taking their drink order, her eyes met his for a brief moment. As the evening wore on she was aware of him watching her. Older men had never been her bag, but he was sensational-looking, lean and handsome, and he smelled rich.

Tyson didn't act like the other creeps who felt they owed it to their manhood to try to creep into her panties. He made no pass, no move to get her into bed. That part intrigued her.

Every Friday for six weeks he dropped in for a drink. He was always friendly and warm toward her. She became more and more curious about him. Was he interested or not? Maybe he was just holding himself back. Maybe he had a fear of rejection.

One night he suggested they have dinner.

She grinned. "I thought you'd never ask."

The first time they made love, he ejaculated as soon as he penetrated her. The second time he was like a bull. From then on, he was a wonderful lover. They had sex everywhere: on the floor, on the couch, in the shower, in the tub. He seemed insatiable, like a kid let loose in a candy store.

Four months later he took this apartment for her on the edge of town.

Maria tucked herself deeper into the chair. Her thoughts jack-rabbited all over the place.

Oh yes, she had slid into this arrangement very easily. She was being fed and fucked. There were times when she felt like a whore.

Lately a flash of intuition revealed that Charles was falling in love with her. That thought worried her.

Getting up from the chair, she turned the radio to a country music station and began to sing along with Willie Nelson. Irritated when a commercial interrupted them, she clicked the radio off again.

"Damn it," she said with determination, "I'm gonna be a singer."

She repeated it again to the empty room. "Do you hear me out there? I'm gonna make it someday."

But she knew that day would have to be postponed just a little while longer. Right now she needed Charles, needed the security he gave her. She was saving every penny she got from him. Then, someday soon—

The doorbell interrupted her daydreaming. It would be Charles. Her high heels made sharp staccato impacts on the hard wooden floor as she moved to answer.

He rang impatiently. That meant he was horny. A smile crossed Maria's face as she walked naked to the door. She was ready for him.

He stood there smiling. Without a word she reached for him and pulled him to the floor. He entered her quickly, with total authority. She moved slowly, enjoying her own rhythm. She felt urgency in his body as she moved her hips. Slowly she slid her hand down to encompass all of him. She knew he would come quickly. The first time was always explosive with Charles.

The second time his lovemaking was slower, easier, and more controlled. She held him as he cried out.

Naked, they lay together, spent and relaxed. They had made love three times, she being the aggressive one. Maria had no sexual hang-ups.

Slowly, she gave a luxurious stretch. Hail the power of sex! She felt terrific, sleepy, and satisfied as she half heard Charles break into her reverie; his words drifted in and out.

"Maria, darling, I just can't handle living two lives. I want us to be together always. I'm going to ask Cynthia for a divorce. You do love me enough to marry me, don't you?"

Getting no response, he added, "Are you listening or just daydreaming?"

Maria said nothing, stunned by what she had heard. Her stomach contracted. Divorce! She took a deep breath. Why couldn't he be content the way things were?

"You can't be serious!" she said. "That's the dumbest thing I've ever heard, a really stupid move. Sure, we have terrific sex together. But don't confuse that with love."

Charles looked shocked. His face turned white. Maria could see he was numbed by her answer.

Later he begged her to think about what he had proposed. She could take all the time she needed.

The next day, after Charles left for the office, she mulled over what he'd said. She reviewed it over and over in her mind. She knew he must have gotten himself all psyched up about the divorce. But wasn't he aware that everybody's life would have to be rearranged, all because he had decided he wanted to marry her? He had no right to include her in his plans. He knew that her dream in life was to become a singer. She had no time for marriage. How could he be so selfish?

Shit! She hated this whole mess, hated that he had been testy when he left. Walking into the bedroom, she found a toke and sucked on it greedily. Smiling to herself, she thought of the time Charles had tried marijuana. She'd shown him how to do it, how to suck in the air with the smoke. How to hold it down deep in his lungs. He had giggled like a schoolboy and lost his erection for the entire evening. He never smoked it again.

Her mood changed as she continued to think about him. Why couldn't she fall in love with him? It would make her life so much easier. She'd be rich and not have to worry about the future. For a moment Maria wondered if marrying him might not be the thing to do. Then she smiled ruefully. She knew that the joint was getting to her, blurring her emotions, her logic.

When Charles came back, she would convince him to leave things just as they were.

When he did return, he seemed calmer, more relaxed. His voice was a little tight when he spoke—not angry, just tight.

"Maria, I've given what you said a lot of thought. I was making a decision without considering whether you wanted it or not. That was wrong of me. If you prefer to go on the way we are, that's fine."

Maria's face was serious as she replied, "Charles, you know I can't think of marriage. I really do want to become a singer. I can't let myself be responsible for your happiness or for anybody's, for that matter."

"Very well. If you want to become a singer, I'll help you. I love you. You know that."

A moment later Charles reached for her, pulled her toward the bedroom, and unzipped her jeans as he slid his other hand inside her blouse.

"Darling," he moaned, "you feel so good. You have one horny lover to take care of. Let's screw all night."

He undressed and pulled her close to him. She could feel his penis heavy, extended but not erect. She reached for it and brought it to an erection. He moved her onto the bed and opened her legs wide. His lips moved downward over her body. She knew he wanted to taste her warm wetness. He buried his head in her pubic mound; his tongue searched for her clitoris.

"Don't stop," she moaned as he rolled her bud.

His hands cupped her buttocks as she reached for her orgasm. She needed the release, and it was wonderful.

They changed positions. She rolled Charles onto his back. She teased him, touching all his pleasure points. Then down she went, encasing his hardness in her hands, touching the small circle of sensitivity with her mouth. His pleasure mounted. She increased the pressure of her fingers; he grabbed her hair as she slid his penis into her mouth. She could feel him reaching his climax, but suddenly he stopped. That meant he wanted to mount her, to own her, to plunge into her warm, dark cavern, to reach the paradise she could give him.

Once inside her, he was hard and pulsating. She knew he wanted to prolong the moment. A shudder engulfed him while he was cushioned in the deep, sliding warmth of her. She sensed that he wanted the feeling to last forever, never to end. Maria held his hips and worked him into her; her body came alive to him.

Moving her hips to meet each stroke, she moaned as she approached her climax. Charles thrust into her again and again, each time harder, until his body convulsed, and he ejaculated deep inside of her.

She felt him coming and coming. Then unexpectedly, he gave a hideous groan, and his body went into a fierce spasm. He thrashed and trembled in the space of a few heartbeats, then slumped heavily across her body.

"Oh, my God, my God, this isn't happening to me! Oh, no!" she screamed.

Pushing and wiggling, she forced herself out from under the dead weight of his inert body.

As she rolled him over, she saw an intense look of agony etched on his frozen features. She panicked and ran out of the room, screaming hysterically.

She stood in the hall for a moment, struggling to catch her breath. "Oh, God!" she whispered, searching for the courage to go back to help him.

His breathing was heavy and labored. His eyes were tightly closed, as if warding off some nameless horror. As she covered him with a blanket, she couldn't bear to look at the distortion on his once-handsome face. She picked up the phone; her hand shook so badly she could hardly dial. Mercifully, she reached the operator.

"Call Fort Jade Hospital. I need an ambulance. Hurry. Please, please hurry."

Maria's voice had risen to a hysterical pitch. She was having trouble breathing.

"There's a dying man in my apartment."

The voice on the other end of the phone was calm, reassuring. "Just take a deep breath, miss. Now, be sure you give us the right address."

Maria found herself clutching the phone long after it had clicked off. She sat rigid in the chair, fighting for control; a look of panic was on her face.

Mechanically, she plucked at a thread on her terry-cloth robe. The reality of what had happened hit her with full force.

She began to cry in soft mewing sobs. If she kept her eyes closed, maybe everything would go away. But she couldn't stop conjuring up the picture of Charles lying in the next room. She felt like someone in a catatonic state, incapable of movement.

Her panic grew stronger by the second. If she could only run, hide, get away, close her eyes, and have it all vanish, pretend nothing had happened.

But she couldn't run. She had to stay with Charles until help came.

Forcing herself to remain calm, she went back into the bedroom. She stood there quietly for a moment, unable to ignore the thought any longer. What if he were dead?

Then the screaming sound of sirens stopped the terror that was welling up within her.

"Thank God, thank God," she whispered to herself. "The ambulance must be here."

Opening the door, a man in a white jacket announced himself brusquely. "I'm Dr. Josephs. Where is the patient?"

He and two attendants followed Maria into the bedroom. The stricken man's breathing was heavy and labored. There was a sickly gray pallor to his twisted face. His eyes were open and staring.

The doctor pulled off the coverlet, revealing Tyson's body. Maria stared at him as he lay there, naked from their lovemaking. She could not erase the memory from her mind. He had uttered no words when the horror struck him. It had happened fast, without any warning.

She tried hard to recall how he had looked. It was as if he were already beginning to fade and vanish. This man lying on the bed bore no resemblance to the Charles she had known. She stared at his penis. An hour ago it had filled her with its power, yet now it was small and frail, looking as if its life had ended, as if it were hiding, embarrassed to be seen so small and weak.

The doctor quickly checked for pulse and heartbeat.

Maria noticed a smirk on the face of one of the attendants. It made her feel sick. No doubt he was thinking, *It must have been some fuck—she almost killed the guy.*

The doctor talked as he worked. "Pulse and blood pressure weak. Looks like a stroke to me. Get him on the stretcher, boys. Handle him gently."

The attendants moved as if they were one. In a matter of seconds they were wheeling Charles Tyson out of the room.

Dr. Josephs turned to Maria. He was a small, efficient man with sharp eyes.

He spoke rapidly, his voice cold and businesslike: "I assume you are not this man's wife."

Maria felt her stomach knot. She sensed disapproval in his voice. She felt naked, embarrassed, and angry.

"That's right, I'm not his wife. But he's a married man. We were having an affair. His wife knew nothing about it."

There was an edge of false toughness in her voice.

"Do you happen to know his wife? She'll have to be contacted. The man is unconscious and in bad shape. He's very sick. I'm not trying to pry into your personal life, but I gather his stroke happened while you two were having sex. It's a messy situation. She'll have to be told, of course."

Maria handed the doctor Charles Tyson's business card and his home phone number. As she closed the door behind him, the silence of the room seemed to suffocate her. She ran to the medicine chest and swallowed a sedative. Then she curled up in a chair and stared into the darkness outside the window. She felt edgy and restless. The pill wasn't working.

She got up. Walking to the hall mirror, she stared at herself. She looked the same except for her eyes. They were shimmering with tears.

No, she whispered to herself. *I can't worry about her. I wasn't concerned before, was I?*

But Charles's wife kept creeping into her thoughts.

How will the news hit her? What will she say? What will she do? What can she do?

She shook her head. She knew she'd have to get away. Nothing was making any sense to her right now.

Maria swallowed another pill and waited for sleep.

Whimpering, she awoke from a hideous nightmare, all clammy and weak. The memory of the night before still pounded in her brain.

The rain poured down as if it were trying to wash away the horror. She made a cup of coffee, swallowed a tranquilizer, and stared at the phone, waiting for it to ring.

Finally she picked it up and dialed the hospital. She had to find out about Charles. Then she'd make her own plans —and get away.

"But why can't you tell me?"

A curt voice at the other end of the phone replied, "I'm sorry, miss, but it's hospital rules. Only the immediate family is ever given any information about a patient."

Holding the receiver in her hand, Maria sat down on the edge of her bed. Well, she had tried. There was nothing more she could do. In a way it was a relief. It was out of her hands now. She had to concentrate on getting her own life back on course. This episode was over.

Maria packed quickly. The heavy rain continued to pour down. She closed the door behind her and hurried to her car.

Sliding into the front seat, she sat motionless for a while, just looking out of the window. She had no idea where she was going. Finally, putting the key into the ignition, her eyes fixed on a small blue box with a red ribbon wrapped around it. It was tucked inside her box of tapes.

Maria held it for a moment. Then, opening it slowly, she looked at the delicate pin flashing with diamonds. It spelled a single word: *Love.*

There was a note inside the box: "Forgive me, Maria. Don't be angry. I promise we'll go on exactly like before. No binding commitments. It's just that I love you so much."

"No! No! No!" she heard herself scream. "I can't bear any more!" She was crying again, and her tears built into hysterical sobs.

Starting the car, she pulled out of the driveway. The road stretched endlessly in front of her.

Chapter Eight

Cynthia was weeping when she reached the emergency room at Fort Jade Hospital; her breath came in long, shuddering gasps.

A nurse walked over to her, calm and reassuring, and said the doctor would see her soon.

Oh God, she thought, *let him be all right. Let my wonderful Charles not be badly hurt.* A cold panic gripped her heart as a weary-looking doctor approached her. She desperately scanned his face for information, but it was as impassive as the clock on the wall.

Reaching her side, he smiled tentatively and pointed to a small office on his left.

"We'll have a word in here," he said.

Closing the office door, he asked her to sit down.

"Would you like some coffee?"

Cynthia nodded numbly. She sipped the warmed-over brew he handed her as he studied some X rays on his desk.

"Please, won't you tell me what happened?" Cynthia asked.

"Your husband is a very sick man."

She could feel her knees shaking. She was sure she was about to fade away. She whispered her next question, barely able to get the words out.

"He's alive, isn't he?"

The doctor gave her a sympathetic smile.

"Yes, Mr. Tyson is alive. Luckily, his heart is strong. He suffered a stroke, and we have him in intensive care. We don't yet know the extent of the brain damage. But you may rest assured we're doing everything possible for him. He is being treated by the senior neurologist on our staff. Although he's unconscious, his condition is stable. I suggest, Mrs. Tyson, that you stay here at the hospital tonight. We're not yet out of the woods."

"May I see him?"

"Of course, Mrs. Tyson. Later on." Again, the reassuring smile. "But first, you and I must talk. What I'm going to say may be painful for you."

Cynthia swallowed hard.

"I'll be all right, doctor. I think I can handle sickness." Pulling on all her self-control, she faced him.

The doctor began to speak; there was a trace of hesitation in his voice, as if the words were difficult for him.

"First and foremost, we must think of the patient. He is our main concern. We're not here to sit in judgment. Your husband was with a young woman when he suffered his stroke. He was naked when brought in, and traces of semen revealed that he had just had sex."

Cynthia was oblivious to the sweat breaking out under her arms. She felt she was going to faint. The doctor's words seemed to be coming from an echo chamber, fading in and out. She had to get away from his voice. But it droned on and on; the words assaulted her eardrums in random snatches.

"The young woman in question is the one who called the hospital. We don't know who she was. But it's very fortunate that she didn't panic."

With that, he stood up briskly in one efficient motion.

"In some cases, we can prolong the lives of those who've suffered the severest strokes. Of course, he'll need care, love, patience, and understanding. We're not yet sure about his memory. He may have no recollection. We don't know how many chambers in the brain were flooded. He will be totally dependent on you, Mrs. Tyson. You must reconcile yourself to that. Time will heal a lot of your pain, and surely an indiscretion can be forgiven."

Cynthia had stopped listening. She took a long, shuddering breath as she felt humiliation, followed by anger, building inside her.

She stared at the doctor, her face ashen.

"I must go home. I'll be back later. But I must go home."

The doctor noticed the urgency in her voice.

"As you wish, Mrs. Tyson. Yes, that might be best. I'm sure this has been a great shock to you. But time is a great healer, and eventually we learn to forgive and forget."

Cynthia laughed bitterly. Forgive and forget! Couldn't he see that her whole world had flipped out of focus? Didn't he know it would never be the same again?

Walking down the hospital corridor, she thought her heart would break. *An indiscretion.* That was all he called it. *An indiscretion.* The word kept gnawing at her mind. Could she forgive an indiscretion? She couldn't find the answer.

She remembered nothing of the ride home. Once safely within her four walls, she wandered through the house, thankful that the servants were all asleep. She couldn't bear their sympathy, not yet.

It was painful for her to stay in one place. She walked aimlessly about, touching old familiar things. She looked at her wedding photographs, then at one of Charles and Nick sailing in Newport. How handsome they both looked!

Her thoughts turned to Nick. It had been difficult to phone him to tell him his father was ill. Not wanting to alarm him, she hadn't gone into detail. He was due to arrive from London the day after tomorrow.

Oh God, how she prayed she could keep the disgusting

details from him! She couldn't bear the thought of Nick finding out. Cynthia trembled as she walked from room to room, opening drawers, looking in cupboards, touching the gleaming silver, the soft linens, all so lovingly cherished, thinking how wonderful the quality of their life-style had been—or so she had thought.

She wandered into Charles's den. His briefcase was on the sofa. Force of habit made her pick it up to put it on his desk. He always left it there when he wasn't using it.

Cynthia held it close, smelled the soft leather, and remembered the Christmas she had given it to him. Tears started to spill down her cheeks.

"Oh, Charles, I loved you so. Why couldn't that have been enough for you?"

The briefcase slipped from her hand, and its contents spilled to the floor.

As she bent down to pick up the papers, she noticed a letter with the word *Maria* scrawled across the envelope.

Almost without conscious thought, she sat down on the floor, the letter clutched in her hand. Her whole life seemed to rush by. She felt frozen to the spot, unable to move. Charles must have written this letter to that girl.

Still clutching the envelope, she wrapped her arms around her knees.

She could tear it up, and that would end it. She'd never know any more about the girl. Perhaps that would be best.

But she couldn't. She had to open Pandora's box.

Maria, my beloved,

I may never mail this letter to you. But I must put my thoughts on paper. I don't know how it happened, but I'm in love with you. I intend to ask Cynthia for a divorce as soon as possible. I want to be with you for always. My body aches for you. I want you to marry me and be my wife. My love and my heart are yours for the rest of eternity. . . .

The words blurred in front of her eyes, washed away by bitter tears as Cynthia held the letter. The pain she felt was indescribable. She was almost deafened by the pounding of her heart. She found herself silently rocking backward and forward like an anguished peasant woman keening for the dead.

Charles was dead to her now.

Bile backed up into her throat. She was devastated that his betrayal had been so absolute. How had she been so blind, too blind to recognize the signals? She kept recalling his excuses. She felt shamed and reviled, remembering the nights when she had been sexually aggressive, when she had wanted to arouse him, and had ended up giving him oral sex.

She now realized that on those nights he must have come from *her*. How he must have wished Cynthia wouldn't touch him or have sex with him!

She ran to the bathroom, retching. She wished she could face him, claw at him, scream obscenities at him. For all she knew, their whole married life had been a lie. How could she be sure there hadn't been others?

Cynthia knew things could never be right again. She would have to find a place somewhere deep inside herself where she could hide.

She sat staring into space, empty, drained, her emotions frozen. It was as if her inner self were suspended somewhere else. Time passed, but she was unaware of it. She was still sitting on the floor, the letter scrunched tightly in her hand, when dawn came. She looked at the letter, then slowly tore it up, making the pieces smaller and smaller. Finally she flushed them away, watching as they swirled around the toilet bowl before disappearing from sight. They reminded her of the white confetti thrown on her wedding day. A gurgle, and they were gone—just like her marriage.

Standing up, she looked at her tear-stained face in the bathroom mirror. She stared at herself: the features were familiar, but she was no longer the same.

A chill blanket of hate had spread over her heart.

The next day Cynthia sat stiffly in the small hospital room, staring straight ahead, waiting. She heard the drone of the intercom and the endless clamor of the paging system, but none of it registered on her mind.

She was thinking, *What about my own life? Everything now is different.* She felt a wall go up around her.

Her reverie was interrupted by one of the nurses who had been attending Charles. Cynthia took an instant dislike to her as soon as she entered the room.

Nurse Kelly was heavyset, with a washed-out face. Cynthia found her voice too sympathetic, too ingratiating. She resented it that she smiled as if they shared an intimate secret.

Nurse Kelly leaned close, her ample body swaying as she spoke.

"How about I sit with you for a while? I'm not bothering you, am I?"

She riveted her eyes on Cynthia, studying her features closely as if to learn more than Cynthia's face was revealing.

"Oh, my dear, I know what you must be going through," she said.

Looking into Kelly's pale eyes, Cynthia was sure she must have learned of her recent disgrace. She seemed like the type who would eagerly feed the hospital's gossip mill.

Cynthia's voice was harsh and impatient as she answered, "Nurse Kelly, I wish you'd just go. I resent anyone being here right now."

Cynthia's one desire was to be alone, to totally abandon herself to solitude. She closed her eyes as she added, "I'm very tired. I'd really like to rest."

"Sure, I understand. Life's a corker, isn't it?"

Then with a dry laugh, the nurse moved her whalelike body out of the room.

Alone once again, Cynthia breathed deeply. She still hadn't seen Charles. Somewhere deep inside, a small part of her was wondering if she could bear to see him.

Opening her purse, she took out her pill case and absently swallowed a tranquilizer. Then, stretching out on the hospital bed, she closed her eyes and waited for the pill to relax her. But visions of the nightmare she was living prevented it from working.

An hour passed. She lay motionless on the bed, her eyes tightly closed, feeling she was in a bottomless well.

On the outskirts of Fort Jade, something seemed to compel Maria Benson to slow down and then stop as she drove past the hospital.

It was no good. She couldn't just leave this way. She had to go inside. She had to find out about Charles. Then she could be on her way.

Minutes later, while busily sorting stacks of papers on her desk, the receptionist spoke in an emotionless monotone.

"I'll be with you in a second," she said, without looking up.

Nurse Kelly was tired and in a lousy mood. She stopped at the information desk before leaving for the day.

The receptionist raised her eyes, pushing her glasses up on her nose.

"Hi, Kelly. Will you be leaving soon? I could use a lift home."

"No problem, Alice. My car's in the parking lot."

"Excuse me," Maria said. "I'm in an awful hurry. Could you just tell me how Mr. Charles Tyson is?"

Two pairs of eyes turned and looked at her.

Kelly's lips curled in ill-concealed contempt. Then she muttered inaudibly under her breath, "The little bitch. That has to be her. You wouldn't think she'd have the nerve to come here. She's the one who gave the naked jaybird his last fuck."

The ambulance attendants had filled Kelly in the night before. Every juicy morsel—and more. They were the fountainhead of hospital gossip.

"Wouldja believe the older bugger was fuckin' his heart out when it happened?"

"Hey, it's gotta be the best way to go. And the pussy was real young 'n stacked, too."

Kelly winked at Alice, turned, and walked over to a hospital phone behind a stanchion.

At the reception desk, Alice's tone was somewhat imperious. "Whom did you say you were inquiring about?"

Before Maria could answer, the phone rang at the desk. Alice grabbed it.

Maria watched her. Alice listened, smiled, and said nothing. Then she turned to Maria.

"Just take a seat over there," she said, pointing to a cluster of chairs. "I'll check your Mr. Tyson soon as I'm through with this phone call."

As Maria walked away, Alice spoke into the phone.

"What the hell is all the secrecy, Kelly? . . . No kid-din'? She's really the one? Cheeky little baggage, ain't she? Comin' in here as cool as you like.

"Okay, have your fun. I'll switch you through to room twenty-two. But make it fast. It's been a long day, and I wanna cut out of here."

Kelly pivoted her saddlebag hips into a more comfortable position as she stood holding the phone. Her gas pains were killing her. Rubbing her stomach, she let out one loud belch, then a quiet fart.

"Come on," she said impatiently as she counted the rings. Finally the phone was picked up at the other end.

"Hello, Mrs. Tyson? This is Nurse Kelly. I'm downstairs at reception."

She paused, wanting to savor the moment.

"There's a young girl at the desk asking about your husband. I think maybe it's the one who was with him when it happened. You know what I mean. Anyway, I just thought you'd like to know."

Hearing no response, she clanged down the receiver, muttering to herself as she walked away.

"Snotty-nosed broad. Her with that husband of hers humpin' young bitches like he was a dog. That'll show her she ain't so high and mighty, dismissin' me like I was some piece of shit."

Cynthia sat frozen, trying to regain a sense of balance. The phone call from Nurse Kelly had shocked her. Her pain had become unbearable.

She walked to the mirror on the wall and stared at herself, looking without really seeing. She smoothed her hair with a nervous gesture. Then she walked down the corridor and into the elevator, pressing the button for the lobby.

* * *

Maria was sitting in a chair, motionless, waiting. She was nervous—very nervous. The longer she waited, the more nervous she became. An inner voice kept urging her to get up and leave. But she couldn't.

She turned when she heard the elevator door open. The elegant woman who left the car caught her attention. As the door closed behind her, she looked around for a moment, then started walking in her direction. Maria had never seen her before, and yet she knew. . . .

This was Charles Tyson's wife.

The closer Cynthia got to the girl, the more she was struck by her beauty. God, did she have to look so very young? All Cynthia could think was, *Damn you, Charles. Damn you!*

She fixed the girl's features in her memory, filing her face away forever even as she fought for composure. She could feel her own features crumble and her mouth stretch into a thin, tight line.

The two women looked at one another. Then the older one spoke.

"Why are you here? How dare you come?"

Cynthia felt her voice rise. She fought for control and managed to lower it.

"I'm sorry," the small voice answered.

Cynthia wanted to scream, to give vent to her rage. But the words came out low, studied, and unnaturally controlled.

"You're sorry? Sorry you've changed my life? Sorry you made love to my husband? Sorry you've filled my heart with hate?"

She couldn't stop thinking how young the girl was. Her whole life was ahead of her. Cynthia's was all in the past.

Her hatred became so hot she felt it burn her. Yet when she spoke, her voice was icy, each word a stiletto.

"I feel you should know, Miss whatever-your-name-is, that my husband will be confined to a wheelchair for the rest of his life. The doctors believe his stroke has affected the right side of his brain. He will be unable to speak and will have virtually no mobility. Naturally, he'll require attendants around the clock."

Cynthia stopped. There was bitter irony in her voice as she continued.

"I know this is a ludicrous question to ask. But do you still want him?"

Maria clutched her raincoat. The knuckles of her hands were white.

Suddenly, she turned and ran. Pushing open the heavy doors, she stood trembling in the blinding rain. Then she raced to her car.

Once inside, she wept uncontrollably as she inserted the key into the ignition.

"Shit! Shit! Shit!" she screamed as the engine failed to turn over. She turned the key again. This time the engine growled and roared to life. Flooring the accelerator, she narrowly missed another parked car as she skidded down the rainswept drive and roared out onto the highway.

Cynthia stood at the window, watching as the bright red car careened out of the parking lot. Then she turned and walked back into the waiting elevator.

Maria wiped her tear-stained face, struggling with her thoughts. She had never felt as low as when she had stood there absorbing Mrs. Tyson's hatred.

She shook her head as if to erase the memory. She knew she mustn't let herself go under. She would never, never think about this again. She would put all this horror behind her and bury the pain. Somehow she'd find a way to drop a steel trap over the past.

Maria was determined to use her talent. She would become a singer. That would be her only goal. It was time she got her act together.

A small surge of assurance flowed through her. She jammed her foot onto the accelerator to get away from Fort Jade as fast as possible.

Twenty minutes out of town and driving too fast, Maria didn't see the truck until it was too late.

Frantically, she hit her brakes. The car skidded across the road. Picking up speed, it screeched down the long, winding grassy slope, tearing through the brush toward a nearby ravine.

The trucker cried out to his relief driver as he slid his heavy vehicle to a cautious stop.

"Jeeeesus! Didja see that motherfucker? Only a fuckin' asshole would slam rubber that hard on a wet road like this. C'mon, hit that damn CB and call the cops—not that there's a damned thing they'll be able to do. Whoever was jockeyin' that cannonball hasta be history by now."

Dirk Peterson had been drunk for two days, and he was drunk when he heard the crash.

He opened his door cautiously and stepped out of the little cabin that was hidden down in the heavy underbrush. Throwing a serape over his shoulders, he staggered outside. Slowly he weaved his way over to the car hanging over the edge of the ravine. As he approached it, it gave one last shudder and continued its flight to the river below.

"Holy shit!" Dirk muttered. He stood staring. The rain was finally letting up. A slight fog started to swirl mistily through the ravine. The fog made it difficult for Dirk to peer down at the murky river below.

He stood for a moment swaying, looking fuzzily around him. Then he spoke. His voice sounded harsh and whiskey-graveled as it cut through the eerie quiet.

"May you rest in peace down there, whoever you are."

Not knowing what else to do, he turned slowly away. Half stumbling, half staggering, he made his way back to his cabin.

Two hours later, old Willie was driving the highway, bringing Cynthia Tyson home from the hospital. Willie had worked for Cynthia's in-laws since he was a boy. After they had passed on, he continued working for Mr. Charles and Mrs. Cynthia.

Willie normally took the long way around to Tysons Landing. He liked the old country road. It was rarely used, except by the local folk. There he could drive the old Rolls as slow as he pleased. Willie hated to drive the highway. At his age, the white lines doubling up and angling out sometimes confused him. However, due to the recent heavy rain and the swollen river, there had been a washout. So tonight Willie took the highway.

The old Silver Dawn purred steadily along. The sky was getting lighter, and the rain was stopping. Willie squinted as he noticed the roadblock up ahead. Slowing to a crawl, he saw the sheriff's car with its flashing red light. A big transport truck was parked nearby on the side of the road.

"Willie"—Cynthia's voice, coming from the backseat, rang with impatience—"why are we stopping?"

Willie's response was laden with the slowness of old age.

"Well now, Mrs. Tyson, looks to me like there's been some trouble up ahead. Sheriff Fogarty's standing in the middle of the road flaggin' me down."

Willie approached the scene with extreme caution. A small circle of people, including a local news photographer, were staring down into Henderson's Creek.

The sheriff walked toward the old sedan just as Cynthia rolled down her window. Tipping his hat, he smiled at her. She returned his smile absently.

"I'm mighty sorry to have to stop you, ma'am. But there's been a bad accident. We're busy recording the skid marks."

Fogarty then addressed himself to the wide-eyed chauffeur.

"Just you go easy, Willie, when you ride that soft shoulder, hear?"

The sheriff pointed to the other side of the road.

"You can ride it for a few yards, but be sure to pull right on back to the highway. Then you can be on your way."

Willie clacked his false teeth.

"I knew it, Mistah Fogarty. It was bound to happen. That's why I take the back road every single time I drive Mrs. Tyson. The devil hisself musta invented fast cars. I hate drivin' these highways, passin' all those pot-smokin' kids. I'll bet it was one of them, drivin' like a fool. Ain't I right, Mistah Fogarty?"

Cynthia leaned back in her seat and closed her eyes. Fatigue was pressing in on her.

"Let's go, Willie," she said.

She had no desire to hear the gory details of the accident. Certainly not now.

Apparently not hearing her, the sheriff remained at the side of the car; his elbow still leaned on Willie's open window.

"Well now, Willie, you could be right."

Fogarty seemed to be relishing the recital he was about to give.

"But, just between you'n me, there's a real good chance we may never know who it was. Whoever was in this particular red Mustang I'm talkin' about was coming from Fort Jade heading east and must have been barrelin' along at one hell of a clip. The car skidded, hit the gulley, then wham-o! One big drop to the river below. We don't know who was in the car, or how many. But you can bet your black ass that whoever it was, they met their maker. Ain't no way they coulda survived. The car hit the river and sank like a ton of cement. I'm bettin' the current already pulled whoever was in it out to sea."

Cynthia sat back in astonishment; her heart suddenly pounded as the sheriff's words drifted back to her, spinning into her brain.

That girl. Maria. She'd been driving a red Mustang. She was heading east from Fort Jade, just as Fogarty had described it. It had to be her. There was little traffic on the highway at this hour; it couldn't have been anyone else.

The memory of their encounter just a few hours before, was still a painful, smoldering wound festering inside of Cynthia.

And now the girl was dead.

Cynthia was glad. It was so just, so right. She found herself clutching the fabric of the car seat. The sense of relief she felt was wonderful.

Willie backed the car onto the highway. Cynthia closed her eyes, alone with her thoughts. It was over. Now no one would ever know for sure what had happened. True, her self-respect was battered. She didn't know if it would ever heal. But she was still Mrs. Charles Tyson.

Now she would go back to her house and praise the gods.

Chapter Nine

There was something incredibly exciting just about being in the room. It was crowded and noisy and totally alive.

Sarah stared, taking it all in. There were actors, models, fashion designers, and an interesting assortment of trendy types—all the right people for a successful party.

And here she was, Sarah Hartley, a guest of *the* Daley Russell, even if she had gotten the invitation through Jan. Sarah was all set for an evening's fun in the big city. It was all too fucking unbelievable.

She fixed her dark, sparkling eyes onto a group of long-haired rockers. Rockers never failed to turn Sarah on. They were always so wild, horny, and raunchy.

She noticed Jan walking over to a vibrant-looking man with a tanned, craggy face. Sarah checked him out automatically. Forty, aging well, no gray in his curly black hair. He looked as if he were in terrific shape. Not too muscular—just right. He managed to look sexy and serious at the same time.

Moving his slight body closer to Jan's, he began to play with her hair.

It was obvious from the expression on his face that Daley Russell loved women. And he was obviously a hair freak. A small smile formed on her lips as she watched him casually caress Jan's ass. She wished it were hers. Her eyes lingered over his body as she fantasized hopping into the sack with him.

So that was the great Daley Russell. She could like him a lot.

Sarah continued to scan the room, telling herself to stop fantasizing about Daley and to concentrate on what was available. If nothing great turned up, there was always her trusty vibrator at home.

Her thoughts flashed back to Jan's excitement about being photographed by Daley. Daley Russell was right, of course; Jan probably could become a top model. Tomorrow she was scheduled to sign with the Adrian Dunn Agency.

Sarah studied Jan intently. How lucky could one person be? And without even trying! Sure, Jan was great-looking, with her perfect face and incredible body, legs that went on forever, and her silky yards of straight blond hair. Jan, who was always so damned nice to everyone. No matter which way you cut it, Jan Julliard had been overly blessed in the lottery of life. Now, wouldn't you just know that a glamorous career had been handed to her on a great, big, free-wheeling silver platter? Sarah wasn't even sure that Jan really wanted it.

Deep down in her gut, Sarah felt the old jealousy emerging.

She gave a cursory glance at the dwarf sitting on a high chair. He was wearing a badge almost as big as himself. He must have been some sort of funky security guard, Daley Russel's pet, or whatever.

"Hiya, doll," he said, catching her staring at him. His voice was scratchy. "My name's Goliath. Wanna get it on?"

"Get lost, little man," she retorted, swooshing past him.

Passing a mirror, she cast an appraising eye at herself. For one brief moment she saw the old Sarah staring back at her.

"You get lost, too," she said to her reflection as she busied herself with fixing her lip gloss.

Seconds later Jan walked over to Sarah, interrupting her angry thoughts.

"It's totally incredible! Daley seems absolutely certain that Adrian Dunn will want me to sign with her agency. What do you think?"

Realizing she had been asked a question, Sarah tried to dispel her hostile mood and concentrate on what Jan was saying.

"I mean, there's always a chance she won't like me, isn't there? What if she says she thinks Daley was wrong about me? What if she feels I just haven't got it?"

"Damn it, Jan," Sarah snapped, "you're just being overly dramatic, fishing for encouragement. Hell, I guess we all do that at times. You know you've got everything going for you. It'll all work out just the way you want it. It always does, doesn't it? Why should this time be any different?"

Jan detected annoyance in her friend's tone and wasn't sure how to react to it. But she was spared the necessity of a reply when Daley appeared at her side, giving Sarah an appreciative glance.

"Daley, this is my best friend, Sarah," said Jan.

His handshake was warm and provocative, Sarah thought—or was that just her imagination?

"Sarah—that's a pretty name," Daley said, still holding her hand.

She scrutinized him as he studied her with his amber eyes. Jan was right, of course. Daley Russell was one of the sexiest-looking men.

Finally releasing her hand, he gave Sarah a lazy smile, still holding her eyes with his. She idly imagined his lips and tongue teasing her flesh, and she wondered if his own thoughts were as erotic as hers.

She found Daley easy to talk to. He was totally relaxed

and interested in her every word. Almost everything she said made him laugh. Sarah felt happy that he genuinely seemed to like her. He gave her a feeling of confidence. A wonderful warmth spread over her.

Jan could see that Daley was enjoying his effect on Sarah. It was obvious that he had totally charmed her. She had never sounded cleverer or more amusing. There was definitely the beginning of a new intimacy between the two of them.

"Well," Daley said, frowning, "I hate to do it, but I'd better cut loose and make like a host."

With a grin, he winked at Sarah.

"Maybe next time we can talk some more. Give me a call when you're in the neighborhood."

Daley felt pleased with himself. He felt he could read females, and Sarah was a mighty sexy one—hot and ready for action. He was proud of his ability to sniff them out. There was always room for another like her in his ball park.

He moved away, smiling, as he touched Jan's arm.

"Next time I see you, you'll be a real live registered model."

Both girls watched him as he walked away. Then with a wide grin on her face, Sarah turned to Jan.

"Wow, I think he really liked me. Of course, I have a very strong feeling that a man like that could cause most women beaucoup de trouble. But I'd sure like a chance at him, even though I'll bet he can be a real bastard."

Sarah turned silent for a moment, looking at Jan thoughtfully. When she resumed speaking, her tone had taken on a new note of caution.

"Jan, are you interested in Daley? I mean—oh hell, you know what I mean. He certainly seems very involved in

your career. He invited you to his party, and, well, face it
—if it weren't for you, I wouldn't be here at all, would I?"

Jan's expressive mouth widened into an understanding
smile.

"No, Sarah, I'm not interested in him. Not the way you
mean, the way you seem to be. Granted, the man is charming, talented, sexy, and, as you said, no doubt a bastard. I
like Daley Russell a whole lot. I want him as my friend,
and I'll treasure his friendship. But you know me. I'm still
dreaming dreams of a great romance, dreams of a knight
on a white charger. Maybe those dreams are some sort of
safety net for me. Anyway, the field is wide open for you."

Sarah hugged Jan warmly, her dark eyes smiling.

"Well, that solves one problem, doesn't it?"

Sarah couldn't fall asleep for thinking of Daley. The last
time she looked at her night-table clock, it was after two in
the morning.

Be bold, Sarah Hartley, she thought. *Give the man a
call. What have you got to lose?*

She tossed off the covers and reached for the phone.
After the first surprised hello, he calmly invited her over.

A short time later, he answered the doorbell on the first
ring and welcomed her into his apartment.

They exchanged very few words. In a matter of minutes
they were naked and in bed.

Daley didn't rush things. He lit a joint slowly and savored the first long drag as he leisurely appraised her. After a few more puffs he finally spoke.

"You know, I was dead right about you. The first time
we met, I had you figured as a very hot little number—
ready, willing, and available."

He paused for a moment as if waiting for a reply. When
none was ventured, he continued.

"I knew you were definitely not the type who's looking for any sort of permanent relationship. No problems, no complications, right? Just a good, healthy roll in the hay, then *adios, amigo.*"

Sarah was expressionless. She studied him with her bold eyes, quietly fuming inside. How cheap he made her sound! And she had thought he liked her. Her voice was tinged with sarcasm when she finally replied.

"Are you reading me the company rules, Daley? If so, please don't bother. After all, we're both bowling in the same alley. I mean, I had you figured for a great stud, but so far you've just been all talk. You may feel you were right about me, but the jury's still out about you."

Daley winked and gave her one of his boyish grins as he handed her the joint.

"Well said. And now that that's settled, we can get on with what you came for, can't we?"

As Sarah sucked the acrid smoke into her lungs, a strange anger brewed in her breast.

The bastard, she thought. His words sounded cold to her. She was torn between wanting to leave and wanting to stay. She suddenly felt she had to say something.

"You know what I think?"

She never finished the sentence. Daley took the joint from her and placed it in the ashtray. Then, with a sudden, swift movement, he bent over Sarah and kissed her hard on the mouth, effectively stopping any further conversation.

"You know something?" he whispered. "You shouldn't think too much. That's when a person can get confused. And you don't want to be confused. Not now, anyway. So why don't we just get down to business and quit fooling around?"

Suddenly, his hands moved over her body as if they had a life of their own.

"Right now I am only concerned about the softness and smoothness of you. I've really lucked out—I didn't realize you have such a great pair of tits."

Daley's absorption was total as he circled her nipples with his tongue, sucking on them till they stood out hard and turgid. Then he moved his hands between the soft flesh of her thighs; his fingers hungrily played in the area of her wetness. Slowly, he put them inside her, exploring, probing, searching.

Sarah felt her body twist with desire. She could feel herself open up to him.

He was hard when he entered her, very hard. Their rhythm was perfect together; both bodies moved as one. Sarah needed no prompting, no guidance. Instinctively she knew all the right touches, all the right moves to arouse and inflame him. Deliberately she tightened her muscles, trapping him inside of her. Then came the release—slowly, smoothly.

Sarah experienced an exhilarating sense of satisfaction when she heard him moan. They came together, exploding in a noisy blaze of naked, animal passion.

Daley rolled over onto his back and stretched luxuriously.

"Wow, that was good."

They were the first words he'd spoken since they had started to make love. He yawned a weary, satisfied yawn as he continued.

"Goddam, Sarah, it was better than good. You, lady, are one great lay."

Then he sank into a deep sleep.

Sarah raised herself onto her elbows and studied him as he slept. She realized she had just had one of the best sexual experiences of her life. *How,* she thought, *how can I make myself more important to Daley Russell? More impor-*

tant than just an occasional one-night stand? There had to be a way, some way to reach him, to really get under his skin. Well, maybe she'd catch him sometime when he was off guard.

Glancing once more at his sleeping form, she blew him a silent kiss. Then, smiling her own secret smile, she slid quietly from his bed.

Minutes later, she opened his apartment door and left.

Chapter Ten

The weeks after Adrian Dunne welcomed Jan into her agency were incredibly hectic. There were countless additional test shots to be made and endless sessions of hair styling, wardrobe changing, and makeup adjusting.

Jan spent the rest of her time making the obligatory, never-ending calls on clients and photographers. She soon learned to take the inevitable rejections in stride.

"Too tall, too short, too blonde, not blonde enough, too round, too thin, too young, too old, too busty, not busty enough"—and so it went.

Her cover shot was not due to appear for another two months. Meanwhile, her portfolio slowly filled up with photos added each day. Sometimes, flipping through her presentation book, Jan stopped to inspect her face in the mirror. It was as if she had to convince herself that the glamorous female whose features were in the photos so carefully protected by the acetate sheets was really Jan Julliard.

Mark Squire called her for dinner twice. Although she desperately wanted to accept, she couldn't. She simply didn't have time for anything but her work.

Tomorrow, at the crack of dawn, she was leaving for the Hamptons. She and one of the agency's male models were scheduled to do a Levi's ad. They'd be shooting it on the beach.

Jan hadn't met the other model yet. Adrian had arranged for a car to pick each of them up and drive them out to Long Island together.

The next morning at five o'clock, just as Jan was starting to settle into the deepest slumber, the shrill ring of her alarm clock woke her. Groaning, she crept out of bed. Getting up early in the morning was one of her all-time pet hates.

It was all she could do to keep from yelling out loud as the icy needles of the shower stung her but made her instantly alert. Turning the faucet to the lukewarm setting, Jan mentally ticked off the things she'd need for the coming day's shoot.

As she stepped out of the shower, she pulled on her terry-cloth robe and applied moisturizing cream to her still-damp face. Minutes later, after dressing, she quickly whipped up a milk shake and added two eggs and some wheat germ. Then, slipping into a pair of khaki pants and a man's work shirt, she tied a red bandanna around her hair.

Glancing at her watch, Jan knew the car would arrive at any minute to take her to the Hamptons.

Lear Feria's mood was black as he sat in the backseat of the Buick sedan. His thoughts drifted back to the past. Why was he suddenly remembering the aching loneliness of it all, remembering the constant tension in his parents' home?

His parents' home! His mother and father had held their marriage together for social and financial reasons. His father was an austere, undemonstrative man who had married late in life. The things he valued most were money and social position. Lear's beautiful mother had been an alcoholic, hiding it as best she could, feeding her neuroses with pills. Lear's birth had been an accident. His parents had never wanted children.

Highly sensitive and so handsome he bordered on beautiful, Lear had felt different from others all through his childhood. He had constantly sought his parents' love, and he desperately wanted their approval, but they were never there for him. So at a very early age he learned to control his feelings. He hid his emotions from his parents and from the world at large.

When Lear was fourteen, his mother committed suicide. Her suicide note had been terse and cryptic: "Let no one say I was out of my mind. The one responsible knows who he is."

In some unexplainable way, during the years that followed, Lear had been haunted by an awful feeling of guilt. He felt that he himself was to blame for his mother's death.

And now, riding in the backseat of the Buick, it seemed to him that there were no fond memories in his past, only dark ones.

After his mother's death, he tried to play the role in life that he knew she would have wanted for him. When he was nineteen, his father arranged for him to be married. It was to be a merger of two distinguished families and their two large fortunes. How terrified Lear had been at the thought!

The name of his bride-to-be was Dana. She was spoiled, sophisticated, and randy. She wasted no time suggesting to him that they have premarital sex, saying that it was important to learn if they were sexually compatible. She readily admitted that she herself was no innocent virgin.

Dana had easily assumed the aggressor's role as she unzipped Lear's pants and deftly fondled his penis. He silently prayed for an erection. But nothing happened. He could still hear the derision in her voice as she pushed his hand deep into her warm pubic hair.

"What the hell's wrong with you? So okay, you've got a problem. Just relax—I can handle this."

Lear couldn't remember in exact detail what had happened, but he made some sort of excuse. The next morning he left Philadelphia for good.

His thoughts were jolted back to the present when the Buick's driver stopped in front of the building where Lear was to meet the model with whom he would be working. Turning off all thoughts of his unhappy past, Lear looked out of the window. Perhaps this would be a lovely day.

Jan took one last look around the room, making sure she hadn't forgotten anything she'd need. Then, tossing her overstuffed duffel bag over one shoulder, she locked her apartment door and rang for the elevator.

As she entered the lobby downstairs, she noticed the parked Buick. A young, elegant man had just stepped out and was pushing his way through the revolving door.

Jan couldn't help thinking how incredibly beautiful he was. Not handsome—beautiful. His face was exquisitely structured; his silken, tar-black hair hung to his shoulders. The skin on his face was golden. She was certain no razor had ever touched it. Everything about him had an air of grace. His body was slender and delicate, almost feminine.

His attire was extremely simple: black chino pants and an open shirt with a soft suede jacket. A thin, black rope bracelet encircled his finely boned wrist.

He approached her with a shy smile and spoke in a soft, velvety voice.

"Hello, I'm Lear. You must be Jan. I'm so looking forward to today's shoot."

His gestures were as smooth and languid as a fawn's, without the slightest air of self-consciousness or affectation.

Jan looked into his luminous brown eyes. Something about him seemed so innocent. Intrigued, she couldn't help staring as she tried to form an opinion of him. He was very different from any other male she had ever met. Everything about him seemed gentle and somewhat golden.

The ride to the Hamptons turned out to be very enjoyable. Jan was fascinated by Lear's naïve, almost innocent charm. He was witty, sensitive, and strangely sophisticated. They chatted easily, with friendliness and good humor. A warm bond developed between the two of them.

Lear told her that he free-lanced with Adrian's agency. He also mentioned that he earned extra money by dancing in the evenings in a Greenwich Village nightclub.

"What's the name of the club?" Jan asked.

Lear absently brushed some wisps of hair off his forehead with delicate fingers. A shadow darkened his features, like a cloud passing in front of the sun.

"Sinews." Lear raised his eyebrows in elegant curiosity. "Have you heard of it?"

Jan shook her head, still thinking how very beautiful he was. The two of them slipped back into easy, casual conversation.

"Tell me, Jan, have you been modeling long?" he asked.

"Not long at all. Would you believe, this will be my first time on location?"

"Mine, too," Lear replied with a delighted smile. It was as if he discovered something wonderfully special between them.

Reaching Westhampton's main street, the driver dropped them off at The Patio Restaurant, where a photographer was waiting to meet them.

As they entered the restaurant, Jan looked around the room. Since it was off-season, most of the tables were empty.

A middle-aged man, dressed in beat-up leather, sat drinking a cup of coffee and talking to a young man who was obviously his assistant. On the floor beside them was a jumble of camera equipment.

Seeing Jan and Lear, the older man nodded slightly and raised his eyebrows as if to indicate that he had been expecting them. Then, taking the cigarette that was hanging from his lips, he leaned back in his chair.

"Hey, kiddies, you're right on time. I'm Leonard. Leonard the lensman. Has a ring to it, eh? If you wanna do pee pee, better get crackin' now. I've got to finish this shoot before the weather changes."

With an answering smile, Jan walked into the ladies' room and quickly applied her makeup.

They left the restaurant and drove out to Dune Road in Leonard's car. There, walking over the grass-covered dunes, they reached the section of beach that he had previously selected for his location.

The beach was deserted; the sun was bright without too much glare. It was pleasantly warm for May. The only other signs of life were the small sandpiper birds patrolling the water's edge on tiny legs and the sea gulls who broke the silence with shrill squeals as they swooped and dived in their endless search for food.

The shoot went fast. The setups were uncomplicated, and there were no distractions. Jan and Lear worked well together, while Leonard had the ease and confidence of a man who had been doing his job for years.

Finally, with a nod to his assistant, he put a lens cap over his camera and turned to his two models.

"That's it, kiddies."

Then he glanced at his watch.

"Terrific, it's only two-thirty. We got all the shots we need, and they oughta turn out fine. Might as well pack up our gear and head for home."

During the drive back to New York, it started to rain.

Lear was staring out of the window as if his mind were a thousand miles away, as if he were embroiled and lost in his own thoughts. After a while, he turned to Jan.

"I'm sorry," he said. "I was off and away in my own world. That was rude of me. I want you to know that today was a really great day. There's something so very comfortable about being with you."

Jan smiled back at him.

"You know, I was thinking the same thing," she said. "It was all so pleasant, and such fun talking with you. I felt as if the two of us had been friends for years."

"That makes me happy because I don't have many friends. It would be so nice to consider you as one of mine."

Lear then turned back to the window, locked once more into his own thoughts for the rest of the drive home.

Later that day in Manhattan, as Lear was dressing after his shower, his mind was busily sorting out the events of the day.

Glancing at his watch, he saw he had time to spare before his appointment with Dr. Haas.

He ambled over to the small setup bar and poured himself a Scotch. Lifting the crystal glass, he downed the drink in one gulp. Seconds later, the liquor hit the Quaalude he had taken to soften his nerves.

Looking at his image in the mirror, a pair of sad, dark eyes looked back at him. His face seemed to swirl in shadows. He stood a moment longer, staring.

"God," he whispered, "how I hate my life."

Turning away in anger, he put down the glass, grabbed his jacket, and hurried from the apartment.

* * *

Twenty minutes later, Lear entered the office of Dr. Nathan Haas.

Dr. Haas sat benignly in his chair, exuding a quiet air of confidence and wisdom. The smile he wore had a soothing quality. He placed a small desk clock in front of him and reached for a cigarette; he offered one to Lear, who refused it. His voice was calm and relaxed when he spoke.

"Well, how do you feel today?"

Lear hesitated for a moment before speaking.

"Doctor, this is our fourth session, and I feel, as always, helpless and continually angry."

The doctor's expression didn't change. Lear paused for a moment, shook his head, and sighed deeply.

"Look, you know the problem. There's nothing more I can say. I came to you for your help."

Dr. Haas rose from his desk. He slowly walked over to the blinds and adjusted them, as if it were the most important thing he had to do.

Finally he turned back to Lear, looking at him steadily.

"These things are not as simple as they may seem. There's something I have not previously asked you. Have you ever seen a therapist before?"

He waited patiently while Lear considered his answer.

"Yes, once, a long time ago, when I was very young. My father took me to a child psychiatrist."

"Why?" The doctor's tone was noticeably casual as he returned to his seat.

"Well, I would only pee sitting down. It drove my father wild. The doctor told him I would outgrow it."

"And did you?"

"No, I didn't. I still pee sitting down."

Lear raised both his hands and pushed his dark hair away from his temples. His eyes drifted around the room, and then they came back to the doctor. He looking at him steadily.

"You see, Dr. Haas, I don't want what is between my legs. I want the operation that will let me live my life as a woman. But I can get it only with the validation of a psychiatrist. You know there are papers to sign before any such operation can be performed legally. That's the only way you can help me—by signing."

The doctor kept looking at him intently, saying nothing. The silence became oppressive. Finally, after clearing his throat, he responded in a soft voice.

"Many people have a difficult time learning who they are, getting to really understand themselves. Everyone has identity problems of some sort. Trying to solve them is often the first step toward becoming well-adjusted. I think we should set up appointments on a regular basis, twice a week. We'll dig a bit deeper and learn more about you. Altering your sex may not necessarily be the answer. It may not be what the real you wants at all. But we cannot know until we've probed beneath the surface. There may be a long road ahead. I feel there is a definite possibility that you may yet accept your maleness. Oh yes, young man, that potential most certainly does exist."

Lear wondered if his face was revealing the cold despair he felt. It was all so useless. Even this highly trained shrink —this calm, incisive professional with his impressive credentials and impeccable reputation—even he did not understand.

Looking at his appointment book, the doctor turned to Lear.

"How about Tuesday and Friday of next week, same time?"

Lear nodded without replying.

Dr. Haas's smile was fatherly as he opened the door and watched the young man walk out.

Everything looked bleak to Lear after he left the doctor's office. There was a knot of pain and despair in his stomach. Walking home, he felt as if he were living in a nightmare.

Once back in his apartment, he flung himself across the bed and broke into heartrending sobs. There seemed to be no hope, no reason for tomorrow.

Lear realized there was no one for him to talk to, no one to turn to. Getting up from the bed, he wandered aimlessly into his study and noticed that there was a message on his answering machine. He wondered who it could be as he pressed the replay switch.

It was Jan; her voice was warm and full of enthusiasm.

"Lear, I'm so excited! Adrian called and wants to see us tomorrow. You and I may be in line for a commercial. I told her I'd contact you and let you know."

As he picked up the phone to return her call, Lear's eyes suddenly seemed to come to life.

"Hello, Jan. Sorry I wasn't here when you called, but I just got your message. Could I come over and talk to you?"

"Sure, that sounds fine. We can have a drink and toast our good news. I'm on the seventh floor, apartment 7G."

"Thanks, Jan. I'll be right over."

Lear put the phone down. His heart felt lighter. At last there was someone with whom he could communicate. He had no idea how he would tell her, but he knew he had to.

As Jan sat waiting for Lear, she thought that he'd sounded troubled on the phone.

The hall buzzer interrupted her thoughts. She moved toward the door and opened it.

"Hi, Lear. I'm glad you came. Come on in. Sit down and make yourself comfortable. I'll pour the wine."

Jan noticed that Lear seemed strangely quiet. There was an odd, troubled look in his eyes. He sat down and drummed his elegant fingers nervously on the coffee table.

"I like your apartment, Jan. It's warm and cozy. You certainly have a flair for decorating."

As he spoke, Jan observed him closely. She sensed that Lear was just making idle conversation. A tightness seemed to be running through him. She watched him take a joint out of his shirt pocket and light it. He pulled on it almost feverishly, all the while remaining silent. He inhaled again, deeply. It was almost as if he had forgotten that Jan was there.

When he did speak, there was pain in his voice.

"I want to change my life."

Jan looked at him, confused.

"I'm not sure I understand what you mean."

Lear leaned back against the sofa; his elegant body sagged ever so slightly as if under some heavy burden. His voice was low as he continued talking.

"I just left my shrink. He was trying to convince me to resign myself to being a male, to having male sexuality. The man is sure that I'll eventually be able to accept it. The fool doesn't realize that ever since I was a child I knew I was really a girl. All I ever wanted was to play with dolls and wear dresses."

He gave Jan a self-mocking smile.

"Do you know what I do when I'm alone in my apartment? I dress like a woman, act like a woman, think like a woman, and sleep in silk nightgowns like a woman. I was born male, yet my every thought, my instincts, even my spirit, are all female."

Jan held herself taut, holding her breath as Lear continued.

"The worst part about it is, I know that society would consider me a homosexual. But I'm not. I don't want any part of the homosexual scene."

Tears rolled softly down Lear's cheeks. Every word he spoke disclosed the pain he was feeling.

Jan wished she knew how to respond. She decided it would be best to say nothing at all, to just listen.

Lear looked deep into her eyes, as if searching for an expected sign of condemnation. He saw none. There was only compassion for him.

Once again he fell silent. His long, tapered fingers played with the stem of his wineglass. Jan was touched by the weariness, the despondency in his beautiful face.

Then, with infinite sadness, he continued speaking, almost in a whisper. "I don't know how much longer I can go on this way. Forgive me, Jan. I don't know why I'm dragging you into all of this. It's just that, for some crazy reason, I had an overwhelming need to tell you. Thank you for listening and for not yielding to the temptation to give me words of advice. God knows I've had more than enough. There really are no more words to give."

As he started walking toward the door, Jan called out to him.

"Will you be all right?" she asked, a look of concern on her face. "Because if not, I do have an extra bed, and if you're upset you can certainly camp here for the night."

He didn't answer for a moment. Then, bending over, he brushed his lips lightly against her cheek.

"Dear, dear Jan, thank you so very much for your offer. I love you for it. You are truly one of the good guys."

He held her hand in his ever so gently, then he slowly turned. Seconds later, closing the door behind him, he was gone.

Jan flattened the pillow on her bed before sliding under the covers. She turned her TV on, hoping to catch the late news. Her eyes were fixed on the set, but she wasn't really watching. In her mind's eye, she could still see Lear's delicate features, his soft mouth, and the sadness in his dark eyes. She couldn't stop thinking about him.

A few minutes later, as she flipped the set off, she was suddenly aware of why she had felt so comfortable with Lear Feria from the beginning. It was the female in him that had reached out to her. Jan fell asleep with a silent prayer for him on her lips. She sensed the pain he must be feeling and knew that Lear Feria should have been born a woman.

Chapter Eleven

Stretching out his long legs, Mark Squire settled himself into his easy chair.

He was feeling really terrific after working out in the gym for a couple of hours, during which time he won a fast game of handball. Then he'd topped it off by spending a sensationally erotic hour with his favorite masseuse. Annie knew all the right spots to touch, and the right ways to touch them.

After the massage, they had both enjoyed what Annie called a healthy, uninvolved fuck together. She was very much the aggressor, telling him when to relax, when to be passive, and especially when to come on strong. He complied completely. It was a new experience for him, and it was great.

Yes, today was one terrific Sunday, even though Sunday had never been his favorite day.

He lounged lazily in his armchair and let his mind drift. He recalled the day Antonio Bono had closed his shop and left for Arizona. That was when Mark had gotten a job at Jerrard's. After developing an elegant clientele at that swank salon, his career progressed exactly as he wanted it to.

Stretching his arms above his head, he let his mind continue to drift. He smiled as he remembered the young hairdresser he had been hired to replace at Jerrard's. The boy had been a closet case, planning to leave for an ashram to find his identity. Mark took over his job and the lease of his apartment as well. The young hairdresser never returned from the ashram. Mark hoped he had found his identity.

The smile lingered on his face. Those had been good days. The memories were pleasant.

Then Kate Rogers had walked in. She was wealthy, haughty, beautiful, and spoiled. Mark had been assigned to do her hair. Kate was thirty-five and the darling of the tabloids. They referred to her as the year's undisputed Queen of Style.

With a look of resigned boredom, she had seated herself in the beige leather chair. Mark gently parted her dark, shoulder-length hair and slowly raised it to allow him to concentrate on her face. He studied her silently for a moment.

"Well, how do I look?" she asked.

"You look fantastic, but I think you could look even more fantastic."

Kate allowed herself a neutral smile.

"How, may I ask?" There was a slight edge of irritation in her voice.

Mark quickly piled and twirled her dark hair high on her head, holding it with a couple of pins while maintaining eye contact with her in the mirror, giving her a wide smile of confidence.

"Look at that fabulous neck of yours. It's as long and elegant as a swan's. Why hide such beauty? I'd love to see your hair short and dramatic. It should look like a feathery black chrysanthemum on top of your head."

Kate Rogers swiveled around in the chair and glanced at her profile, turning this way and that.

It was a few seconds before she replied, "Well, it certainly wasn't my intention to have my hair cut. But you're a very persuasive young man. I think I just may go along with your suggestion."

Mark nodded with a smile and started the restyling at once.

He worked silently, expertly, concentrating on every snip. Little by little, the cut began to show off her long white neck and her Irish hawk nose. When he was done, Kate Rogers was mad for it.

Later, she had the long strands of her shorn hair braided into a necklace with ivory beads. That, with the new haircut, were featured in the next issue of *Women's Wear Daily*. The credit line read, "Hairstyle by Mark Squire."

Mark finally jogged himself out of his memories. He walked over to the phone, idly thinking that he'd probably get another credit for the *Mademoiselle* hair spread he had just done. His life had certainly changed drastically in the last six months. It was moving at a wonderfully rapid pace.

Now there was one important decision he had to make. He wanted to talk it over with Antonio Bono. He knew he could always depend upon that wonderful old man for sound advice.

Mark hummed happily to himself as he dialed the number. Bono answered on the second ring.

"Hi, Antonio. . . . Sure, I'm just great. And, hey, you sound terrific! Tell me, are those Arizona dolls still crawling all over your bones?"

A grin crossed Mark's lips when he heard the hearty laughter at the other end of the line. Antonio Bono meant more to him than anybody else.

When the laughter stopped, Mark continued with mock-Oriental courtesy.

"Your most humble Number-One Barber's Apprentice wishes to speak to most honorable Number-One Barber. He asks for his wisdom in a matter close to his heart.

"What? Hell no, I'm not planning to get married. You

think I'd want to give up these wonderful liberated ladies out here who are all panting for my body? No way! You know my motto: 'Why settle for one peach when you can have the whole orchard?' "

Suddenly, the image of one particular golden-haired girl with tiger eyes flashed in front of Mark—a golden girl whose smile was as haunting as a Cheshire cat's. The vision was so vivid, Mark found himself grinning into the phone's mouthpiece like an idiot. He almost felt he could reach out and touch her. He realized he had the tenderest feelings toward her.

Strange. He couldn't remember any girl ever invading his thoughts as strongly as she. He'd have to be careful. This one could be dangerous. This smacked of possible commitment.

He shook his head to get rid of her image, then forced his attention back to the voice speaking on the other end of the line.

"Okay, Number-One Apprentice, shoot. Tell the wise one what's on your mind."

"I'm thinking of quitting Jerrard's. I want to open up my own salon with the money you gave me. But I don't know if I'm moving too fast. If you think I am, I won't do it. I just feel I've learned an awful lot during the six months I've been in New York. Working at Jerrard's has been one hell of an experience. It's an unbelievably successful operation. The man has no competition when he wields a brush and comb. He manages to cop credit after credit in all the ritzy fashion magazines.

"Hey, are you still with me out there in Arizona? Didn't you hear me say no one can give him any competition? Why didn't you disagree with me?"

Mark's voice cheerfully rose an octave.

"That was your cue to shout, 'No one except my fearless Number-One Barber's Apprentice, Mark Squire.' "

After hearing the old man say, "Go for it, you can do it. We both know you're the best," Mark put down the phone and paced the floor with excitement.

He would do it. He'd call the real estate agent. He'd rent that empty shop on Madison Avenue. He was sure he could make it big. He just had that feeling.

Suddenly he felt like celebrating. Whom should he call? One face flashed in front of him again. On impulse, Mark picked up the phone and rang Jan Julliard's number.

She took a long time to answer. For a moment he feared she might not be in. He was amazed to realize how very much he wanted to hear her voice.

"Hi," he said, finding himself grinning when she finally, breathlessly picked up the phone. "What took you so long?"

"Mark! How great to hear from you! I heard the phone ringing like crazy, but I was outside in the hall and couldn't find my damned key. Scatterbrained me—I need a keeper. I never can remember to put that darn answering machine on."

Mark's voice was light and friendly as he replied.

"What you need, Jan, is a man to sweep you off your feet, take care of you, protect you, and make passionate love to you. I just happen to be available."

Jan couldn't help smiling as she tried to imagine life with Mark. She really liked him a lot, ever since their first meeting. Her thoughts idly drifted as she visualized him at the other end of the phone: Mark, with his handsome face and high cheekbones, his changeable, deep-set brown eyes, and the cute little cleft in his strong chin. Everything about him was so very clearly defined.

Seconds later, she dispelled his image to concentrate on what he was saying.

"So, for starters, how about I take you to dinner at P. J. Clark's?"

"Yes, I'd love that. But it can't be a late evening. I have an early shooting tomorrow. Suppose I meet you at P. J.'s at seven-thirty?"

Later, over menus, Jan gaily chattered away. Mark found himself enthralled by her energy level and her enthusiasm. She was beautiful, funny, interesting, vulnerable, happy, and even sad—all at the same time.

They talked easily together. Jan asked him all about himself. He told her how happy and peaceful his early years had been, and how it had all changed when his aunt died. He told of his days in the juvenile halfway house, and how he had run away. His voice was warm and tinged with affection as he talked about his wonderful friend Antonio Bono. Jan watched little crinkly lines radiate from the corners of his eyes as he smiled. He concluded by telling her of his decision to open his own salon and of his determination to climb to the very top of his profession.

Jan listened carefully to everything he said, fascinated both by the man and by his stories.

Mark sat back and looked at her as he slowly sipped his wine. Then he gave her one of his easy, lopsided grins.

"Now it's your turn, Jan. I really don't know that much about you. Tell me everything. I want to savor it all."

Jan laughed and rested her chin on her elbow. Her jade-green eyes were large and shining. She gave Mark a teasing, sexy little smile.

"Someday, Mark Squire, I'll tell you all about my lurid past. But let's save that for another time."

God, he thought, she sure is a knockout.

"But there is one thing I must tell you. I saw our cover

photo. Daley showed me a print. It's a big close-up—just my face with your hairstyle. Utterly fantastic. They're calling it 'The Cheshire Cat Look.' Not bad, huh? Squire and me, a couple of up-and-coming stars."

Mark felt happy and lighthearted. He was aware of just how much he liked this girl. As they left the restaurant, he took her hand.

He was still holding it as he slowly walked her home.

Chapter Twelve

Maria stirred, lifted her eyelids, and winced when squares of light flashed beneath the dark velvet. She was thirsty, thirstier than she had ever been. Where was she? How did she get here? Why couldn't she remember?

Biting her lip in pain, she moved her arms and legs cautiously, as if testing every limb. There was a dull ache at the back of her head. She slowly managed to sit up.

The smell of wet foliage was all around her. She was in some sort of gulley. The bracken was dense and thick; the huge stalks were like tree trunks. It was as black as pitch and almost impossible to see. She couldn't place the scene. Her ears strained to catch a familiar sound, but there was nothing but silence. She winced again at the blinding pain that shot through her head when she moved.

Trying to blot out the pain, her thoughts became more pragmatic. What time was it? Why was it so dark? Everything was a black void. There were no safe smells around her, nothing familiar, nothing to comfort her.

How did she get to this awful place? She couldn't remember anything. The harder she tried, the more she was tortured by an agony of frustration.

She managed to stand up. Her legs were wobbly and unsure. They didn't seem to belong to her.

The slope was steep and treacherous. Trying to navigate it, she slipped and kept sliding down farther and farther till she heard the roar of the river below.

"Oh, my God!" she cried to herself in panic. She reached out and clawed at anything nearby, hung on to the shrub grass around her, and sucked air into her lungs in desperate gulps.

Exerting her waning strength to the fullest, Maria managed to wriggle her body slowly upward. Prickly dead patches of briar grabbed at her. Sharp thorns dug into her flesh. She hardly felt them—she concentrated only on survival. She was conscious of the sound of her own rough breathing as, inch by inch, she pulled herself up to the top of the ravine.

Once there, she sat and whimpered. She hunched her body forward, as if trying to cradle herself in her own arms.

"Oh, God, where am I?" she moaned.

She was in an unknown place, at an unknown time. She sat motionless and swallowed her tears, not knowing what was out there waiting for her in the darkness.

Then the pain in her head became almost unbearable, and a wave of blackness enveloped her. She let herself slide into the velvet comfort of nothingness.

How long Maria lay there in her state of semisleep, she had no idea. But then she slowly became conscious of a light shining somewhere in the distance. She wept for joy at the sight of it.

Oblivious to the thorns and brambles, she stumbled frantically toward the glow. Running with her arms in front of her to fend off the whipping branches of the bracken, she made her way down the winding road, stopping only to catch her breath. She could feel sweat pouring off her body.

Finally she saw a light in a nearby window. She stood motionless for a moment. Then her leaden legs wearily pushed her up to the lonely cabin.

Maria banged on the door and waited. No response. She kicked it with her feet.

"Oh, God, somebody has to be in there—they just have to be."

She heard the sound of a bolt being pulled; then the door opened.

"Holy shit!" the bearded young man exclaimed.

"Please help me," gasped Maria, trembling violently. She made a small mewing sound, then slid to the floor in a dead faint.

Dirk Peterson moved quickly to cover her with a woolen blanket. He could see by her shivering that she was in a state of shock. She had reason to be, he thought; he saw the cuts and bruises on her face and the multitude of scratches on her arms and legs. Her shoes were missing, and thorns stuck out of her ripped clothing. Her lovely face was twisted as if she were still in pain. She trembled even more violently.

He could feel himself break out in a sweat. *Christ,* he thought, *I sure need a drink.* His own hands were starting to tremble. Who was she? Where did she come from? How did she get here?

He considered calling the police, but he knew there would be questions. He told himself he didn't need shit like that.

Maria's eyelids flickered open for a second, then closed again. She was desperately trying to ease herself out of the blackness, to summon herself back to the surface. She slowly focused on the figure swimming fuzzily into her vision. She realized she was lying on the floor and that a pillow was placed behind her head. An army blanket was covering her.

The bearded young man who had opened the door was kneeling beside her.

"Don't be frightened," he said. "You passed out, but you're okay now." His voice was raspy and low-keyed.

"Where am I?" Maria's voice was a strangled whisper as she looked around the room fearfully. She was trying to fight back the panic building inside her. A scream caught in her throat, begging to be released. She knew she had to get a grip on herself somehow. He was speaking again. What was he saying?

"Jesus, lady, you scared the daylights outa me."

Nausea rose up in Maria. She started to retch. A hideous dry heaving shook her body. The young man left her side, and quickly returned seconds later with a bowl of water and a washcloth. A look of genuine concern was in his eyes as he gently wiped her face.

Again her head throbbed unmercifully. Her whole body was sore and aching. She closed her eyes, trying to calm herself.

"Are you okay now?"

Maria opened her eyes and looked up at him. He was tall, lean, and redheaded. His beard too was red, lightly streaked with gold. His nose was aquiline; his eyes were the color of nutmeg. There was a certain hardness to his face, although his smile was gentle. He was wearing old army fatigues.

"My name's Dirk Peterson. What's yours?"

Maria was silent, searching. She felt her throat constrict. Who was she? Why couldn't she answer him? She tried frantically to remember; a wave of panic built inside her. What was her name? *Why can't I remember my own name?* The empty void was terrifying. Once again she began to shake violently, and sweat streamed down her face. The bearded young man wiped it again with the damp cloth.

Her voice was small and scared when she finally answered him.

"I can't remember who I am. I can't remember anything

except waking up in the gulley, smothered by bracken. I crawled and inched my way out of it toward the light in your window. The rest is an awful tunnel of gray darkness. I can't remember anything before that. Nothing at all."

He furrowed his brow as if to help digest what she had said.

"Does anything hurt?" he asked.

Maria shifted her body under the blanket and gingerly tested her arms and legs. She grimaced in pain.

"Yes, quite a bit. I feel as if someone had beaten me all over with a baseball bat, paying special attention to my skull."

He gave her an easy smile; an unexpected dimple formed near his cheekbone.

"Well, you've got one hell of a bump on your head. That could have caused your memory loss. Boy, it sure is a beaut!"

"What happened to me?" she asked. There was desperation in her voice as tears rushed into her eyes and a small series of shivers rippled over her.

He stared at her silently. His voice was low and his tone was measured as he replied.

"I think I know what happened to you. Yesterday, when I was drunk—which I usually am—there was one hell of a car accident. A red sports job skidded off the road. It slid right down this gulley. The noise almost shook me out of my cabin. I came out just in time to see it balanced on the edge of the ravine. Then it dropped to the river below."

He paused as if to verify his own recollection.

"That must have been your car. By some miracle you were thrown clear. Otherwise, why the hell would you be crawling around in the gulley all banged up with your memory gone?"

Maria swallowed the lump that was welling in her

throat. She sat up, pushing back her heavy auburn hair. Her head ached unbearably.

"It's no use," she whispered. "I still can't remember. It's like someone built a wall in my brain and I can't get past it."

She edged forward as if to get up, but the effort was too much. She slid back down again; the color drained from her face.

Dirk Peterson looked at her, trying to digest what she had said.

"Hell, I'm no doctor, just an old army medic. But I don't think your amnesia will last forever. Sooner or later your memory'll come back. Anyway, you're lucky you've got no broken bones."

Dirk hesitated for a moment, as if unsure how to word his next statement. His eyes never left hers as he spoke again.

"Look, my place ain't much, but you're welcome to stay —that is, until you feel better. Or, hey, if that doesn't suit you, I can bring you to the local hospital. Maybe someone's out there looking for you."

Again he hesitated. Then after an almost audible sigh, he continued.

"You've gotta understand one thing. I drink. I mean, I'm a real heavy-duty boozer. But I ain't a violent drunk or a mean one. Hell, all I do is pass out. I'm good at that— had lots of practice. Anyway, like I said, if you wanna stay till you're on your feet again, that's okay with me. It's no sweat. After that, you can split whenever you want to, and I can go back to being a twenty-four-hour drunk again."

Maria was suddenly engulfed by a tidal wave of tiredness. Once again she felt herself drawn down into a deep, dark velvet cavern of sleep.

But even sleep brought little relief. Her dreams were

filled with terror. What was yesterday? What was the past, *her* past? Had she been running away from something, or to something?

A great feeling of panic washed over Maria and enveloped her even as she slept. She was falling, falling, deeper into darkness. In her dream she listened to her own sobs.

She awoke with a start.

It was morning. The sun's early rays filtered into the cabin. Dirk was there, slumped down in his armchair. There was an empty whiskey bottle on the floor beside him.

He was watching her.

Chapter Thirteen

Nick's stomach knotted up.

In half an hour he would be home. Then he'd pick up Cynthia and head straight for the hospital. Nick hated hospitals.

He took in a long, deep breath. The thought of seeing his father sick and helpless terrified him. His mind was full of questions as to how it happened. His mother had explained nothing to him, nothing at all. *"Just come home, your father is very ill."*

He drove past the library, the playing fields, the old oil refinery, and the general store, all of which bore the name Tyson. He thought of his father, a man of wonderful principles. There had always been an ardent love between Cynthia and him. He wondered how on earth she was going to cope with his sickness.

Parking his car, Nick entered the house.

His mother sat in the living room waiting for him. Her jaw was tense; her face was the color of parchment. Her obvious anguish distressed him and stopped him from uttering any of the usual trite remarks.

Cynthia kissed him and held him close.

"I hope you prayed for your father. He needs God's help."

Her voice sounded cold, almost unfeeling as she continued.

"It's all in God's hands now. We know that. He's always watching us. We end up paying for everything we do in life, one way or another."

Nick remembered that his mother believed in God's punishing wrath. He noticed how stiffly she held herself. She looked tense and brittle. Nick felt that if he touched her, she'd shatter.

Minutes later, driving to the hospital, Cynthia gave a long, sad sigh.

"Poor darling Nick, you must be brave, very brave. I'm here to help you through this. You and I have always been so very close. In the near future, my darling, I hope you'll come home for good."

Concern clouded Nick's face. Maybe it would be kinder to tell her now, tell her at once, that he had no intention of returning to Tysons Landing. But how could he lay that on her now? And how could he talk to Cynthia about his future plans? *Oh, God,* he thought, *it's my Dad I need to talk to.* Everything seemed so wrong.

They drove the rest of the way in silence, both wrapped in their own thoughts until they pulled up to the hospital.

Nick hung on to his courage. He had no idea what to expect or how he would be affected by what he saw. He held tight to the memory of his father, to the last time he had seen him, so hale and healthy. Abruptly, he turned to his mother.

"Would you mind if I saw Dad alone? I'm not sure how I'm going to handle it."

Cynthia looked at him.

"All right, darling, if that's what you want. I know all this is a terrible shock to you."

She put her arms around him and held him close.

As they drew near the intensive care unit, a doctor walked out. His expression looked ominous to Nick. Seeing Cynthia, the doctor brightened slightly.

"Hello there. I'm glad you're here. I'd like to talk to you, Mrs. Tyson."

She gave him a wan smile.

"Then this is the perfect time. My son is going in to see his father. He'd prefer to be alone with him."

She turned to Nick.

"Two minutes, darling. That's all the time they allow us."

Nick watched for a long moment as she walked away. What composure his mother had! What bloody control! He envied her it.

The lights in intensive care were brilliant. A never-ending hum came from the emotionless monitors that reported every vital sign. There seemed to be no sense of time here. Nick was sure everything in this room was the same whether it was day or night.

He felt a sudden constriction in his heart when he saw his father. Charles Tyson looked lost and devoid of identity. His handsome face was shrunken; his lips were grotesquely twisted on one side. Spittle was forming a rivulet, trickling down the side of his chin.

Nick forced himself to concentrate on his father's rapid breathing—anything to take his mind off the pitiful sight before him. He watched as the stricken man opened his eyes and stared helplessly at his son.

"Arrrrrrrraaa! Arrrrrrrraaa!"

The sound that came out of the twisted mouth was gibberish. A nurse quickly moved forward.

Nick felt frozen to the spot. He stood stunned, stupefied, unable to connect the man lying in bed to the memory of his father. He clapped his hands over his mouth and stared. He trembled violently. An overwhelming rush of panic and despair coursed through him. Suddenly, without a word, he turned and ran from the hospital.

Once outside, he leaned against a tree, still trembling. He felt limp and disoriented.

"Oh, God," he whispered, but could say no more because tears almost choked him. He stood white-faced and shaking and swallowed hard.

"It can't be, it just can't. That's not my father in there."

His sense of loss almost choked him. He knew in his gut that he would never again communicate with his father, never again joke with him or talk things over or even just hear his voice. It was over. His father, though still alive, was lost to him forever.

Instinctively, he thought of his mother. His own grief must be nothing compared to hers. He had to go back. She would be waiting for him.

He turned and reentered the hospital. This would be a long and tragic time for Cynthia. She would have to live each day looking at the wasted remnant of her husband. It was too unfair. It wasn't right that her life and his should have been so brutally disrupted.

During the drive back to Tyson Hall, Nick and Cynthia discussed the arrangements that would have to be made. There were nurses to hire, hospital equipment to rent, and even an elevator to be installed.

Out of the corner of his eye, Nick saw his mother lean back as if to ease the tension. He realized that not once had she broken down or cried. He told himself she must be overcome with grief, still in a state of shock. He wondered how she would ever ease her pain. He looked for the right words, the right phrases to comfort her, but he could find none.

The car turned into the long driveway that led to Tyson Hall. They drove slowly past the stables, the servants' quarters, and the apple orchards.

They pulled up near the heavy chestnut trees, and Nick stopped in front of the large Georgian mansion. Cynthia clung to him for a moment as he helped her out. When she spoke, her voice was filled with infinite sadness.

"Isn't it terrible, Nick? In a short time, our once-happy family has been transformed forever. Overnight our lives have been changed completely. They'll never be the same again."

One week later, after dinner, as Alpha removed the dishes from the table, Nick got up and followed his mother into the drawing room. He was beginning to find the house depressing and tomblike. It had a newly acquired silence, a somber pall. There was no laughter, no music, no sense of life.

Cynthia seated herself woodenly in a chair and sat perfectly still, her thoughts a million miles away. She had always looked beautiful to Nick, but since his return home, she had changed somehow. Her eyes were slightly veiled as if hiding her emotions, even from him.

He took a deep breath and glanced at his watch as he sat back in his chair. There in the room with her, he could actually feel his mother's loneliness. Tomorrow his father would come home in a private ambulance. The male nurses had already been hired, the stair elevator was under construction, and the doctors had gently taught Cynthia the best way to treat her husband's affliction.

Nick had not been able to get through to his mother during the week he had been home. She hadn't spoken to him at all about his father. It was as if the subject were taboo, as if she were trying to blot it out of her mind.

Finally he knew he had to open it up, to get her to discuss it.

"Cynthia, surely you don't intend to continue living here by yourself this way. The house is like a tomb. You'll shrivel up, and—"

Nick stopped talking. He couldn't finish.

At first she didn't answer him. She seemed to mull over what he had said. When she did reply, it was with a trace of hesitation.

"Live here by myself? I'm not sure what you mean."

"Well, you know. In the months ahead there's certain to be a void, an emptiness without Dad. Remember how you always depended on him? He had all of your love, your trust. You both lived for each other. But now—"

Cynthia stopped him with an irate glance. Her face wore a pained expression, but her voice was hard-edged icy as she answered.

"Depended on him? Oh yes, I did, didn't I? And trusted him. I lived for him, as well. But I can't do that anymore, can I, Nick? I'm alone now, except for you. But I don't want you to worry, darling. I'll manage. I'll be all right."

"I know you will. You'll come to grips with the reality of Dad's sickness. But don't you think you should ask Cousin Melody to come and stay with you after I leave? She was Dad's favorite cousin. Maybe it would make you feel better just talking to the old girl. There are sure to be days when you'll want companionship. And once you're satisfied that Dad is getting the care he needs, maybe the two of you could take a trip together."

Cynthia's eyes hardened instantly.

"A trip?" She sounded horrified. "Nick, I certainly don't want to take a trip. Nor do I want Cousin Melody hanging about. I have decided to discourage all visitors. They only come to pry, and you know what a very private person I am."

For the first time, Nick sensed anger in her voice. Then a bitter, contemptuous tone crept in.

"You see, my darling Nick, I am very well aware that the most important chapter of my life has come to an end.

All I ever cared about were my husband and my son. My family—you and Charles. Loyal and loving and always with me. But then, things never work out quite the way you expect them to. So, darling, let's not have any further discussion about my life. Fate has already dealt the cards."

Cynthia took a long, slow swallow of her brandy. Her eyes, reflecting pain, were unblinking as she looked at Nick.

"I want nothing more than to remain here at Tyson Hall. I shall stay for as long as your father lives. I know that I have your love and support, which means everything to me. Ultimately, my darling, I'm sure that one day you'll come home to stay. That will be the day you take over the reins of your father's vast holdings."

Nick felt his face tense. He became increasingly uncomfortable, almost guilty, as his mother spoke. He felt he had to get away, take a drive, unwind—anything. His nerves were like the taut strings of a guitar, pulled tight, about to snap.

Excusing himself, he left the house and walked directly to his car. Within seconds he was tooling toward the exit gates. He could understand his depression, but why was he angry as well? He drove fast and carelessly knocked over an urn of ivy at the edge of the driveway.

"Fuck you!" he yelled, feeling better for it. Driving down Main Street, he took a fast right and pulled into The Broadcasters Bar.

The saloon was a hangout for people in the music business. There, new talent was given a chance to try out. Nick usually dropped into The Broadcasters whenever he was in town. Richard Bradshaw owned the inn, and he and Nick went way back. Nick hoped Richard would be around tonight because he felt like getting drunk. Real fall-down, piss-eyed drunk. And Bradshaw was one great drinking partner.

Inside the saloon it was crowded and noisy. The jukebox was blasting away; the air was thick with smoke. As he talked to his bartender at the end of the crowded bar, Bradshaw caught Nick's reflection in the mirror. He gave a wide smile of recognition as he turned and greeted Nick; his rusty voice was filled with warmth.

"Hey, man, it's been too long."

They slapped hands, and Bradshaw continued.

"Nick, it's damned good to see you. I want you to know I was sorry as hell to hear about your dad. It's hard to believe it could happen to someone like him. He was always so healthy, so full of life. What a lousy, rotten break."

Later, as they sat across from each other in the back room with a bottle of bourbon between them, Nick described his father's recent stroke. Bradshaw sensed his friend's horror as he unfolded the narration.

"I tell you, he'll be a helpless vegetable, stuck in a god-damned wheelchair, pissin' into a bag as long as he lives."

Bradshaw groaned.

"Jesus Christ," he muttered sympathetically. "Me, I'd rather be dead."

The small scar near his mouth creased as he spoke in a low half-whisper.

"And your mother? How's she taking it?"

Nick was silent for a moment. Then, looking down at the backs of his hands, he slowly replied.

"Cynthia? No way to tell with that lady. She's keeping everything under control. If she ever cracks, it'll be on the inside. No one around her will ever know."

Taking a deep breath, he knocked back another shot of bourbon.

"But I know damned well. This whole lousy thing has completely changed her life. Changed it? Balls! It blew it away. I just hope to hell she has the strength to hang in there, with her whole world sliding down the tubes."

Slumping back in his chair, Nick poured himself another bourbon. Minutes later, softened by the liquor, he felt his mood change. The tension that had tied his stomach in knots the last few days was edging out slightly.

He drew deeply on his cigarette, speaking softly as if to himself.

"There was a business deal I wanted to talk over with my dad. It's something I've been planning for months. I couldn't wait to speak to him about it. There was nobody sharper, nobody better, when it came to making business decisions."

A bitter smile crossed Nick's face.

"And now—aw, shit, why think of it? Tell me, Richard, how's life been treating you? Still beating the talent off with a club, you lucky bastard?"

Bradshaw grinned and winked at him.

"Hey, you know me. I'm doing okay. But what about your love life? There's a great little lady waiting at my cabin. If I ask her real nice, maybe she'll have one of her juicy friends come on to you. You know, ol' buddy, life goes on. I know you're hurtin', but a real good piece might help ease the pain."

Nick knew that Richard Bradshaw used his cabin for duck hunting, deer hunting, and pussy hunting. As he considered his friend's offer, Nick realized he was very horny.

"Interested?" Bradshaw asked.

"Could be," Nick replied.

Later that night at Bradshaw's cabin, Nick looked down at the very attractive naked girl in bed with him. She was a big talker. She spoke with a slight lisp and no discernible trace of emotion.

"Sex, you see, is something I very much dig. I mean, I just happen to love fucking."

The way she said it, it sounded clinical, he thought.

"Sometimes," she added, "I get a little embarrassed because I'm always wet, and I'm always ready."

Nick's hands moved down along her body. She was right, of course. She was very wet and very ready. He could feel her excitement. The bed bounced as they went at it.

Some of the anger and frustration that had welled up inside him faded as he rammed back and forth inside her. She gasped and moaned and screamed.

"I love it, I love it!"

Nick tried to quiet her, certain that Bradshaw would come running in from the next bedroom. But apparently his friend was too occupied with his own endeavors.

After a ten-minute rest and one joint between them, they began another strenuous round of copulation. The girl was insatiable, changing positions when called for with the dexterity of a virtuoso.

The third go-round she sat astride him.

Then once again she began to fondle his limp penis. Nick was sure there was no hope for another erection.

"Just let's try one more time," she pleaded.

Leaning over the bed, she picked up her purse and took out a vial of cocaine. She took two good snorts and then gave it to Nick, who did the same. In a few short minutes it brought him back to life. They went at each other again, climaxing in an intense eruption.

Afterward, as they dressed, she nibbled on his ear, calling him a tiger. She said he was the greatest and begged him to call anytime, telling him the nights her husband worked late.

"Christ," Nick moaned, as he was dressing, "I could sleep a week."

"Sleep tight, sweetie," she said. "You've earned it."

Then she looked at her watch and left.

Nick drove straight home, marveling at how his morale had improved. Bradshaw was right—a good fuck made a man feel like he was among the living again.

But as he walked into the house, his mood slowly changed. The rooms were dark and somber, as if in mourning. He wandered into the study and touched his father's possessions, looked at his many photographs. He fixed himself a brandy from Charles Tyson's silver decanter. His handsome face clouded over as he sipped it. Once more the knowledge of his father's illness hit him. *Oh, God,* he thought, *I have to stop thinking about it.*

He knew he couldn't handle it. He had to leave Tyson Hall and return to London as soon as possible. He had to complete the project that had become the most important thing in his life: *Pleasure Palace.* He had to make it the greatest success of all. A tremor ran through him as he thought how proud *Pleasure Palace* would have made his father.

As he slowly walked upstairs, the thought of his father filled Nick's eyes with tears. Charles Tyson would never know about it. He was trapped in his own dark world forever.

Chapter Fourteen

Mark Squire stretched lazily before he got out of bed.

He felt good. It hit him that this was the very best time of his life. Everything seemed to be moving along the way he wanted it to. He yawned loudly and glanced at his clock. It was time to move—he had a full day ahead. He yanked the sheets from his body, swung out of bed, and headed for the bathroom.

As usual, he gave himself two minutes to shower, three to blow-dry his hair, and five to get dressed.

While deciding which silk shirt to wear, his mind flashed to the new salon. If things kept on the way they were, he would open another one by the end of the year.

Mark knew his star was rising. He finally had everything in his career running smoothly. Bookings were solid, and his wealthy clientele was growing every day.

He'd been shrewd about the two operators he hired. They were both gay and had total class. Korda and Rook were identical English twins. Their voices were richly theatrical; their gossip was sharp, witty, and always on target. The ladies adored them. Even his receptionist was great. Terra was black, beautiful, and incredibly exotic-looking. She brought just the right tone to Tresses. A salon's staff meant everything; it could make or break the establishment, and Mark's was the best.

He knew his name was now mentioned in the same breath as Kenneth, Vidal, and Mallory, New York's top hairdressers. He was being invited to all the fun happenings in town and appeared in all the right spots. Yes, Mark Squire had arrived.

He walked over to the window and stared outside, idly wondering who would be at Daley's party tomorrow night. One thing was certain: the guest list would include every pretty face in town. When Daley Russell threw a party in his avant-garde studio, the whole world was invited. Daley's kind of bash wasn't exactly what Mark had wanted for his second date with Jan, but she had told him Daley would be very hurt if they didn't show.

Seconds later, a frown crossed Mark's handsome face. He wondered if Daley was sexually involved with Jan. For all he knew, they might be having an affair right now. The photographer's track record with beautiful women was phenomenal. Females seemed to become amazingly vulnerable when stalked by Daley Russell.

Mark put that thought aside; he wouldn't let anything spoil his mood. He gathered up his wallet, keys, and address book and headed for the elevator. A moment later, the shiny aluminum door silently glided open. Mark winked at his mirror image and stepped inside, still smiling. It was good to be alive. He was filled with enthusiasm and anxious to face the day that stretched ahead of him.

The salon was at its busiest, a total madhouse.

Mark strongly suspected that New York was partying itself to death. Every woman in town seemed to want her hair fixed for some reason: a heavy date, a marriage, an anniversary, a divorce, or just a whim. Even the wonderful dispositions of Korda and Rook were fraying at the edges. The phone never stopped ringing.

Mark was putting the finishing touches to Kate Rogers's hair. She stared at herself in the mirror and gave him a catlike smile.

"I must admit, you have a marvelous talent. You do

know how to make a woman look beautiful. My friends tell me I look absolutely sensational since you cut my hair. Do you think I look sensational, Mark?"

She fixed her cold black eyes on him hungrily.

"Tell me, are you as wonderful with your other talents?"

As she spoke, she ran her fingers lightly over his thigh, stopping for a moment near his buttock.

It made Mark slightly nervous.

"You're not afraid of me, are you?" she added.

Mark knew she was known for her sexual switching. The gossip columns were always hinting at it. Her current lover was a powerful lady in the field of fashion. There was no way he wanted to get involved with Kate Rogers.

"That's right," he said with a smile. "Scared shitless. You got to excuse me now. I have a comb-out waiting."

Kate Rogers watched him walk away. He did have a great body.

She realized he had turned her down. That didn't happen to her often. Her reactions were mixed. She didn't like men all that much, but he would have been fun to tangle with. Something about his chemistry turned her on.

She pursed her lips, admiring herself once again in the mirror. She decided to dismiss Mark from her thoughts. After all, who the hell was he? She smiled ironically. Just the best fucking hairdresser around. Thanks to him, she had never looked better. One thing about Kate Rogers: she knew her priorities. From now on she'd keep Mark Squire in the right slot.

As he sipped a glass of wine in the Plaza's Oak Room, Mark put his elbows on the table and rested his chin on his hands. He stared at Jan with an appreciative smile on his face.

"You look beautiful," he enthused. "I like your hair

pulled back that way. It emphasizes your great cheek-bones."

Mark also approved of the short black cashmere dress Jan was wearing. It showed off her dynamite legs.

"By the way, why is Daley throwing this party tonight?"

Jan chuckled softly.

"You know Daley. He collects characters like an art dealer collects paintings. He's happiest when his studio is filled with all the 'in' people in town. But tonight is slightly different. It's sort of a farewell party."

Mark was barely listening to her chatter. He bent over and wound a wispy strand of her golden hair around his finger and kissed her teasingly on the neck.

"I wish we didn't have to go to this party," he said. "I'd like to take you home and make love to you."

Jan's heartbeat accelerated. Something stirred inside her as her thoughts raced. How marvelous it would be to have Mark make love to her!

He lifted her chin to him.

"What are you thinking?" he asked.

She smiled at him over her glass as she replied.

"Daley Russell and I are flying to London tomorrow evening."

Mark looked at her closely. She was so beautiful and seemed so happy. He was sure she had no idea that a sudden violent wave of jealousy was washing over him. Daley Russell and Jan were having an affair, just as he'd suspected. He couldn't trust himself to speak.

Jan looked up at him questioningly.

"Aren't you curious to know why I'm going?"

"Why?" Mark asked, expressionless.

"Well, Daley is going to England to shoot a cover for *Glamour,* and"—the beginning of a mischievous smile lit her face—"they want me on the cover. I'm so excited at the thought of England and being a cover girl that I could just burst. I wanted to tell you my good news because you were right there at the beginning of my career. Oh, by the way, Sarah is also going with us."

"What on earth for?" Mark asked.

"Daley's stylist quit, and he's hiring Sarah to replace her."

Jan started to laugh.

"When Sarah found out the girl was leaving, boy, did she hound him for the job! I think my friend Sarah is starting to get very involved in Daley's life. She's already decided that he's the sexiest man she's ever known.

"And," added Jan with more humor than malice, "our Sarah should know. Anyhow, she really would make a damned good stylist. She has a natural flair for fashion, and she's also tough, efficient, and smart. That lady would know how to put down an insurrection. I'll bet she'd be great for Daley. I sometimes think, despite all his hype and bluster, that Daley is actually quite a lonely man."

As Mark listened to Jan, his relief was overwhelming. It was Daley and Sarah, not Daley and Jan, who were involved with each other. There was a new note of confidence in his voice as he spoke.

"How long will you be staying in London?"

"Daley said it would be about five days—a week at the most."

"I wish you weren't going, Jan. I'm going to miss you horribly," Mark said meaningfully. "And when you do get back from London, you and I will have a ceremonial dinner at my apartment. We'll talk about life, love, relationships, and all sorts of sexy things. But right now, let's go out and party."

They both stood up and laughed. Jan was charged up with nervous energy. It was all so exciting. Mark was exciting, her new career was exciting—everything in her life had become exciting.

Daley's party was in full swing by the time they arrived. People were frenetically milling about, chatting and laughing about everything and nothing at all. Cigarette smoke, mixed with the sweet smell of marijuana, hung in the air like a blue fog as Mark and Jan surveyed the scene.

All the guests were wearing party expressions, looking bright and happy as usual. Daley had a knack for collecting celebrities, and Mark still got a kick out of mingling with them. He instantly recognized Betsy von Furstenberg, Berry Berenson, and someone who looked like an astronaut, but he couldn't place the name.

Sarah was at Daley's side, her arm possessively around him. She seemed radiant and happy. Daley's eyes lit up when he saw Jan and Mark. Sarah's own dark eyes flicked first to Mark and then to Jan. Mark thought she looked great.

Her hair was no longer straight. It was obviously naturally curly, and she had decided to wear it that way. Everyone approved, declaring that it softened her face. She was dressed in a leather-fringed jacket, tight pants and boots, and was bedecked with turquoise jewelry, Indian style.

"Hi," Daley said in his raspy voice as Jan and Mark pushed their way over. "Does Daley Russell know how to throw terrific parties, or does he?"

Before they could reply, a whiskey-soaked voice croaked out, causing them to turn.

"Come over here, you sexy bastard!"

Daley smiled and walked toward the glamorous-looking, over-the-hill singer who had been in her prime during the

1950's and who was now a little drunker than usual. It was rumored that she and Daley had once had a torrid affair.

Mark walked to one of the bars to get Jan a glass of champagne. Smiling, she watched his skillful maneuvers as he knifed through the mass of guests crowded three deep at the bar.

Then Jan looked at Sarah, who had not taken her predatory eyes off Daley. He was standing with his back to her, still talking to the singer. The woman's voice was loud and brittle above the hum of conversation in the room.

"Tell me, you heavy-duty hunk, what the fuck is this cockamamy party all about?"

Then, with studied deliberation, she put her arms around Daley and pulled him closer to her. Her manner was totally seductive; she rotated her tongue around her lips and smiled at him.

Sarah's expression grew hard as flint. She turned toward Jan, her bold, dark eyes blazing.

"Can you believe this? That old bitch has the hots for Daley, and she's actually coming on to him! The way she's looking at him, you'd think she never saw a man before. And catch how she's rubbing herself up around his crotch. She's after his cock and doesn't care who knows it!"

Then, with a tight little smile on her face, Sarah continued.

"If she thinks it's open season on Daley Russell, she's got another think coming. I'm crazy mad about the guy myself, and no one poaches on Sarah Hartley's territory."

Sarah glared at them a minute longer. Then, giving Jan a malevolent little smile, she assumed an air of studied nonchalance.

"Excuse me, Jan. I think I'll just wander over there and shake that cunt up a little."

Knowing how sharp Sarah's tongue could be, Jan felt

slightly sorry for the singer, who was still doing her utmost to get a rise out of Daley.

Seconds later, Jan lost sight of them in the jostling crowd. Mark walked over to her with a glass of champagne.

"Hey," Jan said, her eyes lighting up, "you were gone a long time, Mr. Squire. I missed you, and, what's more, you missed a very dramatic scene with our very own Sarah Hartley. She felt her territory being threatened, and she just went off to do something about it."

Mark was silent for a moment, as if carefully weighing his words before responding.

"Sarah might be okay if she didn't have so many hard edges. Just between you and me, she's just a little too ballsy for my taste."

Automatically, Jan rushed to Sarah's defense.

"Oh, Sarah's okay. There's nothing really that bad about her. I know she always tries to sound wild and depraved, but I've always felt that half the things she says and does are just for pure impact. She loves to shock people."

"You could be right," Mark said almost impatiently. "But why are we wasting time talking about Sarah Hartley? Jan Julliard's the one who makes me hear trumpets."

Jan smiled appreciatively. They didn't mention Sarah again.

Later, as the party moved into high gear, Daley Russell stood back for a moment observing the knots of people talking and grooving with each other. Everybody was so laid back and everybody looked so happy. His party was going just the way he wanted it to.

He smiled at nothing in particular. His eyes followed a woman in black leather whose bosom was nothing short of

miraculous. The 'lude he had taken was just beginning to
hit him. He felt silky; his mind smoothly drifted. Shifting
his glance, he focused idly on Jan, who was standing with
Mark.

He noticed how Mark looked at her. Daley could relate
to that look. He had used it many times himself. It was as
clear as a Colorado sunset that Mark had the hots for Jan.

Turning away, Daley's thoughts turned to the many
beautiful women he had photographed. He'd slept with
most of them. Some had been in love with him. There were
even some he had thought he was in love with. *Love*—such
an overrated word. What made people trap themselves like
that, anyway?

Then Sarah caught his eye. Daley's reaction to her was a
mixed bag. In bed she was easily one of the great lovers of
all time. He was doing some of the best basic fucking he'd
ever known. The lady was insatiable, and he had to admit
she delivered every time. Daley mostly photographed
skinny ladies, but deep down inside he was a heavy-duty tit
man, and Sarah had a pair of the best.

Still, she worried him. There was something predatory
about her. She was the type of female who wanted to stake
a claim. It was becoming too easy to rely upon her. In
some ways, she had already started to take over his life.
She brought his suits to the cleaners, had his Mercedes
washed, shopped for his groceries, and made sure his
checkbook was balanced. Most important, she soothed
things at the studio after his temper tantrums. He was
becoming much too dependent on her. How the hell she
had maneuvered him into taking her to London was a
mystery to him. And then there was tonight. He wasn't
quite sure how she did it, but she'd managed to make short
shrift of the overripe singer who had latched on to him.

He couldn't help grinning as he reached out to her. He tilted his head at a rakish angle as their eyes locked.

"Do you know what I've been thinking? You are one smartass cookie, Sarah Hartley. You're also one fantastic, world-class screwer. That's what I've been thinking. So why are we letting all this valuable time go to waste? I'm ready for action if you are."

A lush young blonde with a pretty "Today's Face" type of look was standing close by. Unaware of the preceding conversation, she blinked her myopic blue eyes at Daley and hit him with a laser-beam stare.

Sarah's face had a tight little smile on it as she whispered to the startled girl, "Don't try it, sweetie. Don't even think of it."

Giving the blonde the slightest of pushes as she edged past, Sarah slipped her arm through Daley's. There was a new possessiveness in her attitude as they walked away together.

Chapter Fifteen

As time passed, Maria's body healed.

The bruises on her face went from purple to pale yellow, then faded completely. Her aches and pains vanished along with them.

But her memory remained a blank.

Today was Monday. Dirk had gone to town for supplies. Maria was alone and felt wonderfully alive. As she sat in the comfortable old chair, she gazed around the sparsely furnished cabin and daydreamed of Dirk.

With her memory gone, he was actually the only person she knew. It was as if her life had started with him right here in this room. During the last few weeks he had been constantly at her side, always there when she needed him. She thanked God for Dirk Peterson. Without him, she wasn't sure she could have made it through her terrifying nightmares, the nightmares in which she was always falling, falling through a dark, endless tunnel. Night after night she sat up in bed with a start, frightened and bathed in sweat. But Dirk had always been there for her. He would hold her as a friend, comfort her, talk to her, and calm her fears. She relied upon him more and more and cherished the wonderful friendship he offered.

He was drinking less now. He seemed to be getting it under control. Sometimes as she watched him move around the cabin, he seemed weary and despondent, as if he were carrying a secret sorrow deep inside. But he never talked about himself, and Maria never pried. She sensed that Dirk Peterson wanted to walk a solitary path.

Maria had had the strangest feeling this morning. It was as if, in the inner recesses of her mind, something new were stirring. She felt that things were just about to pop into focus. For a split-second, a kaleidoscopic scattering of unfamiliar images flashed in front of her. But then the wall went up again, impenetrable and unyielding.

Nonetheless, a great excitement began to build inside her. Maybe things were starting to happen to her memory. Maybe she was on the verge of remembering who she was.

However, until that moment came, she suspected that her life was bounded by the four walls of Dirk Peterson's cottage.

Maria shook her head with a smile as if to clear it of all such thoughts. It was a beautiful morning. Filled with energy, she jumped up from the chair and flung open the cabin door.

Minutes later, she walked down the hill toward the river. The gully below looked lush and green, and the bracken were taller than ever. The sky above was as blue as the wild bluebells growing under the shade of the huge pine trees. She stopped to pick them and filled her arms with the fragrant flowers. All around her was the heralding of spring; the wonderful new beginning of life was starting all over again.

"Cat Bracken!" she called to the sky, her voice full of joy. "What a wonderful day this is! How glorious it is to be alive!"

The thought crossed her mind that this was the first time she had used her new name easily. It was as if it really belonged to her.

Then once again her thoughts whirled around her head and went back a few nights to a time when she had been feeling unusually disoriented due to her amnesia. Dirk, knowing how troubled she was, had tried to ease her mental turmoil. He announced that everybody needed a name and decided to find one for her there and then. He started to put together all sorts of odd names. Each was sillier than the last, and she laughed with each one.

After he had chased away her gloomy mood, he declared with mock solemnity that the logical name for her would be Cat. After all, only someone with nine lives like a cat could ever have survived such a dreadful accident.

As for her last name, Dirk had the answer to that, too. Hadn't she been saved from plunging into the river by the bracken growing near the ravine? That said it all. Cat Bracken. It was the perfect name—at least, until she could remember what her real name was.

She liked the sound of it, so Cat Bracken she became.

Cat turned and saw Dirk walking toward her through the gully. He waved to her, and a wide smile lit his face. In minutes he was at her side.

"Close your eyes," he ordered in a firm voice. "Don't peek."

She couldn't read his expression.

Then he continued, "I want you to open your eyes very quickly the moment I put the object I'm holding in your hand."

Cat was filled with strange excitement.

"I promise."

"Now," Dirk said.

She opened her eyes wide and gasped in astonished delight as she looked at the diamond brooch in her hand.

"Oh, Dirk, it's perfectly beautiful!" she exclaimed. "Where on earth did you get it?"

"Look closer," he urged her.

She focused on it again and took in every detail. Then, smiling, she raised her eyes with a questioning look on her face.

"I don't understand, Dirk," she said in a rush. Her eyes darkened. "Is it supposed to mean something to me?"

Dirk was silent for a moment as he looked at her. She was beautiful at that moment; her hair was curled around her like a saint's aureole, and her lovely face was no longer filled with anxiety. How he wanted to hold her, to put his head on her breast and love her! Not as a friend, as a lover. But first he knew he had to tell her about the loathing he had for himself, about his past and the pain inside him.

"Damn. I hoped it would mean something to you. I have a strong feeling it's yours. I found it earlier, right where your car went into the river. Are you sure it doesn't bring anything back to you? No memory jog or anything like that?"

Cat turned away from him; a faraway expression settled on her face. Then she brought her troubled blue eyes back to him again and shook her head.

"It's very beautiful, but it brings nothing to mind. Nothing at all."

Later that evening, Dirk made up his mind to tell Cat about the dark side of his life. He lit a cigarette and watched her fill the cabin with the wild bluebells she had picked. She was humming to herself; her voice was soft and sweet and full of music.

Outside, the night was warm and heavy with silence; it reminded him of those other nights.

He sat for a while and just stared into the darkness. In his mind's eye he saw himself once again in the jungle. It was like mentally watching a film. Leaning back, he imagined gunfire ripping through the quiet. Grenades exploding. Choppers buzzing overhead as they brought in the wounded. Once again he smelled the blood and heard the screams of pain from the burn victims.

He turned to Cat and took a deep breath, feeling his face tense. His voice was hoarse and choked with emotion as he started to talk to her.

"I was a first-year medical student. I dropped out and enlisted in the Marines. It probably sounds corny, but I really had a strong feeling of duty and love for my country."

Cat remained mute, her hands clasped in front of her as he continued.

Dirk's voice shook as he remembered battlefield horrors from the past.

"I was assigned to the medical corps. I'll never forget the wounded and the dying. I lived with them, shared their pain every day and every night. And the rotten names they were called—Veggies, Crispies. It was sickening.

"But it wasn't just the wounded. So many young men were scared shitless, became smack freaks, dead-eyed men. Their lives were ruined. It's always the young ones who become the human sacrifices that the old warriors offer on the bloody altar of war. I read that once before I enlisted. I didn't understand it until I served in Nam for a while. Now when I think of all those grinning, pink-cheeked kids that served as cannon fodder—"

He stopped in the middle of a sentence, was silent a moment, and then continued.

He told her about the choppers and panel vans that had moved the wounded. He recalled the boys he had worked on and the hopelessly damaged ones that were left till last in the hope that they would die before a medic could reach them, thereby saving the doctors' precious time.

Cat saw tears glisten in his eyes. She wanted to comfort this man who was her friend. But she couldn't find the words. She could only sit in silence and listen to him.

Dirk's face was tight and drawn; his eyes looked lost and brooding. His voice sounded like a dead man's.

"I fathered a son over there. He was a small, delicate, beautiful boy, full of laughter and pranks. His mother lived in a village near our base. She was quiet and gentle, full of love, with eyes like soft, brown velvet.

"The Vietcong were never far away. Their nearest encampment was on the other side of the village in the hills. One day they mined that village. There were booby traps everywhere. But I couldn't let that stop me. I had to bring rations to Mei Sing and the boy."

Dirk paused for breath. Cat leaned over and gently patted his arm as if to comfort him. She was aware that he was suffering horribly inside.

He drew on his cigarette, then stubbed it out. Seconds later, he got up from the chair and paced the cabin like a caged animal.

"As she walked to meet me, carrying our small son in her arms, she stumbled on a hidden mine. I watched, less than a hundred yards away, as they were blown to pieces in front of me."

Cat's eyes were opened wide in horror; all the color drained away from her face as she listened to Dirk. Now there was dead silence between them. The room itself took on a deathly quiet of its own.

When Dirk resumed speaking, his voice was harsh and gravelly.

"I zonked out. The doc got me three days' leave. I stayed drunk the whole time. When I returned to the base, I was told to pack my gear. I was going stateside for extra training.

"Once I was back in the United States, I knew there was no way I'd ever report to that training camp. I had been in those stinking jungles for two years. I had lived with death.

I had lost my woman and my son. It was enough. The first night home I went AWOL. I never went back."

He took her hands in his and held them tightly as he spoke to her; his voice was full of emotion.

"I took a room somewhere and stayed inside those four walls for months. My mind stopped functioning. I had been on too many alerts, been deafened by too much gunfire, seen too much suffering and pain. I was fall-down tired, both mentally and physically.

"My parents are dead. They left me a little money, and I had saved most of my army pay. So I zigzagged across the country and landed here. The old guy who owned this cabin was moving to the Coast. I paid him cash, and he asked no questions.

"I continued to drink to get rid of my nightmares. Booze was the daily pattern of my life. I became a coward with a bottle. Then the bottle took over. I was a drunk— until you walked into my life."

Putting her arms around Dirk, Cat cradled him as a mother cradles a child who is crying in pain. As she held him, she could feel some of the tension leave his body.

"Oh, Dirk," she whispered, her voice soft and full of compassion, "what grief and sorrow you must have gone through! I can almost feel your pain. But you can't let it shatter your life. You can't let these feelings of guilt keep growing and torturing you this way. I know what you're thinking. You think that in some way you're responsible for the death of Mei Sing and your son. You feel guilty because you're alive and they're dead."

Dirk gave her a sad, dismal look; his eyes reflected so much pain that it broke Cat's heart.

When he spoke, his voice sounded spent and weary.

"Guilty, yes. I feel a heavy, endless, gut-wrenching guilt.

I'm guilty about being a survivor, about the fact that many men are still over there dying."

He pressed his fingers to his forehead. It was a full minute before he continued.

"I feel so damned guilty that I was a coward, a weakling who didn't have the guts to go back."

Cat remained silent for a few seconds, searching for the right words. When she finally did speak, her voice sounded firm and convincing.

"Dirk, you have been punishing yourself much too much and far too long."

She caught the startled glance he threw her. It made her speak faster.

"No, don't interrupt. Please listen to me. You have no reason at all to feel any guilt. You're not to blame for what happened—not for any single part of it."

Having gained his attention, Cat paused for a moment, speaking distinctly, carefully, as if examining each word before releasing it.

"After you saw the obscenity, the total futility of war, both your mind and body rebelled. When they sent you back to America, it gave you a way out, an escape from all the horror you had known. It was a matter of survival, and the instinct for survival is strong in all of us. So you decided then and there that the war was over for you."

Cat's voice had now become a whisper.

"Dirk, you hurt no one by your decision. You didn't run away in the middle of battle, and you didn't desert your comrades under fire. You only did what you could to save yourself."

Dirk scrutinized her face as if he wanted to be certain she meant what she said, as if he wanted desperately to believe every word of it. If only he could make himself believe what Cat was saying! Maybe then there would be hope for him, some way to pull himself up from his well of misery.

In the next few weeks a sense of tranquillity settled on Dirk. He began to feel some of his self-loathing leave him. He stopped drinking completely. Cat saw that he was happier than he had been in months. The days drifted peacefully along for both of them.

One morning Cat convinced Dirk to shave his beard. After he did so, she grinned up at his craggy, expressive face, and her eyes lit up.

"My, my," she said. "Who knew there was such a dynamite-looking fella under all that fuzz?"

Dirk chuckled to himself as he peered into the mirror.

"Christ, it's been a hell of a long time since I saw my own face. I swear I forgot what I looked like."

He turned to Cat, who was standing very still, as if she were slipping off to another dimension. When their eyes met, a wide smile brightened up her lovely face.

"Dirk!" she cried, her voice breathless, her huge blue eyes filled with excitement. "Something happened just now. Just as you said it would."

Cat lowered her eyes and took a deep breath, trying to stop trembling. Finally the words tumbled out.

"My name is Maria Benson. I'm single. Both my parents are dead. I was on my way to Nashville when the accident occurred. I'm a singer. At least, I want to be. I was heading for Nashville because I thought that was the place to be discovered. Jesus, I remember how hard it was raining that day."

Cat stopped. The memory of the accident was suddenly sharp and clear—too clear. When she continued, her voice had taken on a more somber note.

"I remember the truck. It seemed to appear from nowhere. The road was so wet and so slippery, I couldn't stop. I was driving too fast."

She paused again; her voice was fainter and more halting.

"I remember hitting the brakes hard—too hard. Then there was an awful sensation of a car skidding out of control. I felt my head smash against the windshield. That's all I remember. I must have been knocked unconscious and thrown clear. After that, there was nothing but total blackness. When I came to, I was lying deep in a pocket near the edge of the ravine. I hung on to the shrubs and bracken for dear life. There was nothing else between the river and me. God must have been on my side because I never learned how to swim."

Dirk hadn't said a word. He just watched her, totally absorbed by her story. Now he leaned back and groped in his pocket for a cigarette. Finding one, he lit it. Seconds later, his bright, tea-colored eyes had a probing expression.

"Well, Cat, that's only part of the story. Now we know where you were going. But where did you come from? Do you remember anything before the night of your accident?"

Cat felt her throat tighten, and a small frown appeared on her face. She shook her head and blinked in frustration.

"No. I have no idea where I was coming from. Damn it, why can't I remember that?"

Dirk reached out for her. Putting his hands gently on her shoulders, he drew her close to him. He kissed her on the mouth. As naturally as breathing, Cat responded to him.

"Don't worry," he whispered. "It really doesn't matter. One of these days it will all come back to you."

That night Dirk and Cat made love. His lovemaking was beautiful. He took her both with passion and with tenderness. They held each other close all through the night, loving and laughing, each discovering new things about the other.

At one point, looking terribly serious, Cat told him that even though she had been born Maria Benson, she would be Cat Bracken, the name he had given her, for the rest of her life.

The next day they had a picnic in the woods. Cat sat hugging her knees blissfully; she looked at Dirk, thinking what a beautiful man he was and how easy it would be to fall in love with him.

Then Dirk sat down next to her, wrapped his arms around her, and held her close. After a minute he turned her chin up and kissed her gently on the mouth.

"Cat," he whispered, "I have the most fantastic idea."

Snuggling next to him, she closed her eyes, lulled by the warm sun.

"Are you listening?"

"Yes, of course I'm listening. Go ahead, tell me your fantastic idea."

"I've decided that you and I are gonna blow this town in the next few days. We're going to Nashville, just like you wanted to do before. You know why? Because we're gonna make you a singer. First I'll go into town and buy us a car. Then we'll hit the road. How does that sound to you, lady?"

Cat whirled around to face him.

"Oh, Dirk, I love you for wanting to do it, but it wouldn't be safe for you to buy a car. They'll want identification. They're sure to ask questions. I couldn't bear to lose you. Let's just take the bus."

"Don't worry, honey. Everything is gonna work out fine. I'll pay cash for the car, so there'll be no forms, no questions. Don't worry, I'll handle everything."

Once again he started to hug her, crushing her.

"I love you, Cat. You'll never lose me."

Her eyes filled with tears. But it was all right; Dirk held her close and kissed them away.

Two days later Dirk pulled into a gas station at the edge of town. The secondhand Buick he had bought seemed in pretty good condition.

He was feeling wonderful, happier than at any other time in his life. Cat had made him feel like a whole man again.

As the gas was being pumped into his car, he sat back and thought about her. Soon they would be on their way to a new life.

"Check your oil?" the attendant asked, wiping his hands on a greasy rag.

"Sure. The tires also. In fact, check everything out."

"Taking a trip, mister? If so, I'd better put some coolant in your radiator."

"Thanks, that's a good idea. You got a john around here?"

The attendant pointed the way.

A man in the street nearby was standing and shaking. The pain in his gut ripped at him; the gnawing ache made him sweat. *Christ, I need a fix!* he thought. *I got no bread, and the fuckin' pusher won't give me any more credit.* The forty-five in his pocket lay heavy and silent. Shuddering, he looked up and down the empty street.

He moved toward the service station, spotting the grease monkey under the hood of the car. He figured he could make a fast hit. If he was real lucky, the keys would be in the car.

The place looked empty. It wasn't a big, busy station;

just a small side-street two-pumper. Sweat dripped in rivulets down his body; he could smell it. How long before another car might stop for gas? His fingers curled around the gun in his pocket. It felt hot.

He moved swiftly and silently, like a predatory jungle cat. Crossing the street, he headed for the lone car at the gas pump. He reached it and prodded his forty-five into the back of the attendant; he relished the feeling of power that it gave him as the man's body grew rigid with fear.

"Freeze, you fuck, or this'll be your last breath!"

The attendant had been working at the station for only a week. He had no intention of becoming a dead hero.

"Okay, okay. Just stay cool, huh? If you walk me to the office, I'll get you whatever cash we have."

The man with the gun snarled viciously as he prodded the trembling man with his gun.

"Move your ass, and make it fast."

The attendant quickly opened the register. The gunman shoved him aside, grabbed the day's take, and stuffed it into his pocket.

"Hit the floor, motherfucker! And toss me the keys to that car you were workin' on."

His adrenaline was high. He didn't want to lose that feeling. He felt he could do anything, like blow that gas-pumpin' shit away.

"I said hit the floor, asshole!"

Rigid with fear, the helpless man dropped like a shot.

"The keys're in the ignition. Take 'em! They're yours."

All he could think was, *Oh, sweet Jesus, don't let the bastard shoot me. Hail Mary, mother of God . . .*

A sharp blow on the back of his head stopped any further thought.

The gunman moved swiftly to the car. He slammed

down the hood and slid inside. He started the engine. Just as he turned the car toward the exit, it stalled.

"Son of a bitch!" he screamed jamming his foot down hard on the accelerator. "Start, you fucker, start!"

He started to shake, jamming it down again and again. Finally the engine caught and roared to life. He threw the car into drive just as Dirk came out of the washroom.

"Hold it, you bastard!" Dirk yelled. "That's my car!"

He made a flying leap for the Buick and hung on as the sedan leaped forward. Then a hideous noise broke the silence of the street. The forty-five blasted away, and Dirk's body arched backward, fell, and hit the oil-stained concrete. Pain flooded through him. He felt cold, so cold. It was getting dark. He couldn't see. As he gasped for breath, an intense wave of sadness washed over him. Then an agonized scream of rage ripped from his throat as he called out Cat's name.

Before the scream had died away, his head rolled lifelessly to one side. Dirk's sightless eyes remained fixed on the heavens.

Chapter Sixteen

Jan still felt off-balance from the time change, so she added an extra measure of perfumed crystals to her bath water. Stepping into the oversize English tub, with its gleaming porcelain finish and ball-and-claw feet, she slid slowly down and immersed herself in the warm, soothing water. As she did, she let out an involuntary sigh of pleasure, loving the sheer luxury of it.

Jan, Daley, and Sarah had arrived in London at eight the previous evening. Daley and Sarah were out together now doing the town. Sarah could hardly believe that Jan didn't want to join them on their first evening in Blighty. How, she had asked, could anyone waste a precious night in London alone in a hotel?

But Jan was enjoying her own company in the silence of the room. Soaking in the tub, her eyes closed and she let her thoughts drift lazily. She reviewed in her mind the exciting events of the day.

As soon as they had registered at the hotel, the three of them had eagerly gone out to prowl the streets of London. They tried to sample and taste all the sights and sounds of that wonderful city.

Daley led them first to Fullham Road and Carnaby Street. He particularly wanted to check out that part of town, since he had just about decided that that was where he would shoot his center spread. However, by lunchtime he'd decided against that area. His gut feeling now opted for King's Road instead. All the while, he kept up a rapid-fire monologue, talking a mile a minute. His enthusiasm was as high as if someone had fired him up.

Daley knew exactly how he wanted to shoot the center spread. He intended to use the local color of the street: the funky little stores, the Austin taxis, the typical English passersby. It would be so ethnic, you could smell it. And Jan would be photographed amid it all, wearing the wild fashion of the moment.

She smiled at the thought as she stepped out of the tub. Everything seemed so exciting with Daley. He was talented and complicated; he was sometimes sweet, sometimes cruel, and quite often a pain; but Jan knew she would value his friendship always.

As she dried herself, thoughts of her friend Lear unexpectedly flashed into her head. She remembered the sadness in his eyes the last time she had seen him. He had seemed so depressed, so very down on life. Jan was worried about him.

She suddenly had a very strong desire to call him.

Stepping over to the phone, she dialed his number. She let it ring a dozen times, but there was no answer. Reluctantly, she put the receiver back onto its cradle and got into bed.

Sliding under the sheets, Jan made a mental note to put in a call to Lear the next day.

The next morning she was up early, feeling rested and eager for the day ahead.

The elevator of the Portobello Hotel seemed to take forever to descend to the lobby. There the concierge greeted her in his cheerful cockney voice and pointed the way to the breakfast room.

After breakfasting alone, Jan took a walk through the hotel's private garden. A small patch of grass was surrounded by a border of small, ancient rocks. Trails of creeping yellow and gold nasturtium intertwined with wild mint and forget-me-not.

Feeling tranquil and relaxed, Jan sat down on an inviting Victorian bench. She was entranced by the charm of the garden as she listened to the sweet chirping of the English sparrows as they flitted in and out of the laburnum tree. They kept up a happy morning chatter with each other.

It was there that Daley and Sarah found her.

"I am dying," Daley announced.

Sarah snapped at him. "It damned well serves you right, Daley! You were stinking drunk last night."

He gave her an angry stare.

"Boy, Sarah, you are one unsympathetic bitch. I tell you, I'm dying. Where the hell is your compassion?"

Sarah's black eyes fixed on him.

"Lover," she purred, "when you can't perform, little Sarah's compassion goes out the window."

Daley glowered at her. "You, Sarah Hartley, have no couth."

Sarah shrugged her shoulders but didn't respond.

Jan smiled as she got up from the bench. She was witnessing a familiar scene. She never took Sarah and Daley's little spats seriously; those two lovers were constantly at war with each other.

The three of them turned and walked back into the hotel. In the lobby Sarah asked the concierge to call her a taxi. She had an appointment to brief the young English photographer who would be assisting Daley.

It was still early, so Daley and Jan decided to walk to the location spot. The day was warm, and people were converging on King's Road from all over the city. The entire street looked like one big, noisy happening. They joined the crowds and were bombarded by deafening rock music that was blasting from the tiny shops.

Each store window was displaying fashions more outrageous than the next, although none were more outrageous than the clothes worn by the people themselves. There were tight pants and loose pants, caftans and jeans, hip boots and short boots, leather freaks and denim freaks. And, of course, there were the ubiquitous English nannies, primly attired in their starched, conservative grays, pushing their charges in glistening, expensive perambulators.

From one end of the street to the other, everyone and everything blended beautifully together like a wonderful living collage.

As Daley and Jan walked, they spotted Sarah outside of one of the small boutiques. A wiry young man stood next to her, laden with cameras and equipment.

Sarah aimed a forefinger at Daley; her voice was heavy with sarcasm.

"Well, well, our hung-over genius has decided to show. This must be our lucky day. We were afraid you'd forgotten where we had decided to meet. But we shouldn't have worried. After all, we've only been waiting here for over an hour."

Daley stuck his hands into his pockets and looked idly up at the sky. Then he pivoted around on his sneaker-shod feet until he was eye to eye with Sarah. When he spoke, his voice was as sweet as sugar, and his face wore a deceptively angelic smile.

"Well, it seems the lady bites. But, Sarah my pet, we're here now, aren't we? So why don't you back off and be a good girl? Don't act like a clever cunt simply because you know how valuable you are to me. I'd like you to go inside and make sure that all our props and accessories have been delivered."

Turning to the young Englishman, Daley put his arm
around him as he spoke in a voice full of charm.

"When you have your cameras ready and loaded, I'll be
ready. Then we can all go ahead and get the fuckin' shoot
over with."

An hour later, as the music blasted and the Hasselblad
clicked, Daley was in his element. He moved quickly and
gracefully, exuding confidence with every shot. Jan threw
herself tirelessly into each of the countless poses. Sarah
was swift and competent; she adjusted Jan's hair and
makeup and made sure the clothes hung perfectly. She also
handed her the many different accessories that each
change called for.

Finally Daley handed his camera to the young assistant.
Then, grinning happily, he turned and applauded everyone. The shoot was finished in record time.

The session over, they went their separate ways: Daley
to check out the film with the young English photographer, and Jan and Sarah to wander around London. There
was so much they wanted to see and so little time to see it;
they would be leaving London in only three days.

At a breathless clip they checked out the flea market at
Portobello Road and then made a quick dash to Covent
Garden. There was barely time to dress before Daley
picked them up for dinner at Mr. Chow's. After that, he
had reservations for them at London's newest "in" night
spot.

They entered Promises at ten thirty that night. Daley
had somehow managed to get them a select table. Wherever Jan looked, it was as if a big, happy, uninhibited party
was going on. Wild attire was de rigueur. From the looks
of the crowd, everybody who was anybody was there.

"Well, if it isn't darlin' Daley, my favorite demon photog."

A trendy-looking black girl had pushed her way through the crowd and greeted him warmly. Her head was shaved, and she was wearing a dress that had to have been molded to her spectacular figure. Her pear-shaped breasts were bare to the nipples.

"You should have told me you were in town, honey," she pouted. "Come on, let's shake things up for old times' sake and give the peasants a thrill."

Urging Daley up from his seat, she prodded him onto the dance floor, where she performed a wild, frenetic dance that bounced her breasts up and out of her diaphanous gown.

The evening had begun.

Nick Tyson slowly sipped a glass of champagne as he sat alone and quietly surveyed the crowded room.

Detached and brooding, his mind kept returning to Tysons Landing. It must have been the phone conversation he'd had with his mother earlier that evening. Nick didn't want to dwell on the tragedy of his father's recent stroke, but it was always with him.

Even over the phone he had sensed anger in his mother's voice. Her attitude toward his father puzzled him. Cynthia made it sound as if she herself were the victim rather than her husband, as if she had somehow suffered an unbearable defeat.

Nick had promised to return to Tyson Hall in the next month to help tide her over this dismal period. He was glad that his pronouncement made her tone sound lighter. Then they said good-bye.

He sighed to himself. Damn it, if only he could have spoken to his father. How he missed the weekly business chats they'd had! Nick knew it wouldn't be easy to discuss finances with his mother. Yet he would have to soon. The luxury ship venture, which was becoming a reality, would require a tremendous amount of capital, and Cynthia now controlled his trust funds. He'd have to find a way to convince her to release the money to him.

A loud, happy laugh shattered Nick's reverie. It came from Guy Monti.

He watched Guy, oozing charm, lead a beautiful, well-known deb and her vapid-looking escort to a number-one table. Nick smiled; Monti always placed the right people in the right spots.

Nick's eyes moved restlessly from table to table. He recognized about half the patrons, the club's faithful regulars. The others were guests and curiosity-seekers.

Unexpectedly, his attention was drawn to a girl sitting alone. She was undeniably the most beautiful creature in the room; she effortlessly out-glittered all the others. She looked like the type of girl he had long before convinced himself didn't exist.

It was exciting just to fantasize about her. He couldn't remember the last time he had felt this way; he was almost desperately eager to learn who she was. He'd ask Guy, who seemed to know everyone in the world.

Nick got up from his chair and wandered over to his friend.

"Who's the pretty lady?" he asked casually, nodding in Jan's direction.

Monti glanced over at Jan, then back to Nick.

"The lady in question, you panting predator, is Jan Julliard, an American model. There's no need to ask if you're interested; it's written all over your face."

Nick hesitated for a minute before replying.

"Know something? You're right. I am most definitely interested."

"Okay, then. Let's go meet the dolly bird, shall we?"

Guy never finished the introductions. No sooner did they approach Jan Julliard than Nick took over. Showering her with one of his warmest smiles, he held her hand firmly as he spoke.

"I'm Nick Tyson, and I have a request to make. I'd like you to cancel everything you have planned for your entire future, unless I'm part of those plans. Would you like to dance now, or should we simply fly to Paris, Italy, or Istanbul? I wouldn't even care if you just wanted to visit the London Zoo, as long as we did it together."

Surprised and flattered, Jan couldn't help laughing. He stared at her with such intensity that she felt herself growing warm.

Nick Tyson was tall and lean and disconcertingly handsome. His warm smile fashioned his lips into a soft and most inviting curve. She had never realized a man's mouth could be so beautiful. His soft, shoulder-length hair was the color of warm chestnuts, and his blue eyes were totally devastating—and they were hungrily drinking her in. Jan felt as if she were being pulled into an icy blue corridor, as if she had plunged into the bottom of an enchanted lagoon.

Nick still hadn't released her hand. He felt instantly possessive of her. His tone was warm and confident as he spoke.

"Well, now that we've resolved our future, I feel much better."

Still holding her hand firmly, he led her onto the dance floor. Jan was awash with an incredible feeling of happiness; all the while she sensed that Nick Tyson was used to getting his own way with women and took it for granted that they would adore him.

In the middle of the floor, Daley and Sarah gyrated with the best of them. Seeing Jan, they looked at her inquisitively; a funny little smile nudged the corner of Sarah's lips.

"He's gorgeous! Where did you find him?" she asked, mouthing the words quietly.

Jan gave her an enigmatic smile. Of all the couples on the floor, she and Nick were the only ones holding each other close.

That night, Jan hardly slept.

Her emotions were in a wild upheaval. Her reaction to Nick Tyson had stunned her. She'd never felt like this before. She was completely absorbed by thoughts of him.

She traced the perfect line of his nose against her pillow as she recalled the blue of his eyes and the charm of his soft southern voice. Suddenly she was filled with a wild yearning, a desperate longing to be with him. Jan knew she was hopelessly caught, filled with the stunning passion of first love. She had never known that feeling before, but she knew she would be in love with Nick Tyson for the rest of her life.

He called the next morning and asked her to spend the day with him. His lazy southern drawl sounded irresistibly sexy to her. She couldn't accept quickly enough.

But then she had a terrifying thought: What if, in the cold light of day, he found her dull and unattractive? She was certain she wouldn't be able to utter a single clever remark when they met.

Looking over her wardrobe, she realized she hated everything in her closet. Nothing looked right to her. In desperation, she decided on an antique petticoat, a paisley shirt, and her Frye boots.

She brushed her hair compulsively, put it up, then down, and finally braided it with ribbons. Then blue eye shadow, then green eye shadow—everything looked wrong to her.

Her distress reached epic proportions as she scrutinized herself in the mirror.

"I look awful, simply awful!" she moaned, slumping down into a chair.

The sound of the buzzer startled her. It was the concierge, who announced that she had a gentleman caller waiting for her in the garden.

Nick Tyson was seated comfortably on the same Victorian garden seat that she herself had sat on. Jan caught him in profile, hoping he wouldn't see her—not just yet, anyway. She just wanted to look at him. How perfect he was, sitting with a slight breeze gently ruffling his hair!

He sensed her presence. Turning, he smiled and slowly approached her. Standing close, he cupped Jan's face gently in his hands and still never took his eyes from hers.

When she felt the touch of him, her heart flipped over. For one breathless moment she was even sure it had stopped.

Nick stepped back and studied her appraisingly.

"Lady, you're even lovelier by daylight. When do you think you and I will get married?"

Bending his head, he kissed her lightly on the lips. In that single instant she knew she wanted him, and nothing else mattered.

As they held hands and wandered through the London Zoo, Jan was oblivious to everything but Nick. He leaned over and kissed her gently on the mouth.

"Let's go to my house, where I can hold you close."

The attraction he held for Jan got stronger each time she looked at him. He was everything she had dreamed of, all she had ever hoped for. Looking at him, she knew she was destined to be his, now and forever.

Nick's house in Chelsea was breathtaking. Jan was fascinated by everything in it. It was filled with wonderful antiques. Big, comfortable sofas were submerged under plump cushions. A large fur throw was tossed carelessly over an Eames chair. There were books and magazines wherever she looked.

While he opened a bottle of champagne, Jan stared curiously at an open photograph album as if to find clues to his background. One picture, of an elegant, very attractive woman, caught her eye. It was signed, "Love, Cynthia." Next to that was a matching photo of a man in a naval uniform. His eyes were the same as Nick's, and he had the same easygoing smile. Jan was sure they were Nick's mother and father.

With a start, she realized she was staring at the photographs when Nick came back into the room.

"Like 'em?" he asked cheerfully as he placed a tray with cheese and chilled champagne on the coffee table. "They're my parents. That's Dad when he was in the navy, and that's Cynthia."

Jan was fascinated by the photos.

"Your mother is lovely. Do you always call her by her first name?"

Nick shrugged. "I guess so. She always preferred it."

"And your father," Jan continued, "he's so handsome. You look just like him."

Nick stared at the photograph.

"Yes, my father and I did look very much alike."

He became silent for a moment. Then he shook his head as if trying to brush away an unhappy memory.

"Come on, let's have a glass of champagne. I don't want anything gloomy to spoil this day."

He slowly placed his arms around her and his lips on hers. As he kissed her, Jan was more certain than ever that she was in love with him. She drew back for a moment to catch her breath and ran her finger gently along his lips. They were so tender, so sweet. She moved her hands into his thick dark hair, conscious that her body ached for him.

"Will you spend the night with me?" he whispered.

She answered with her kiss.

Jan lay motionless on the bed, curled next to Nick.

His lovemaking had been beautiful. He had guided her skillfully and tenderly, and she held nothing back. Her body was filled with deep contentment, a pleasure she had never felt before.

They clung together in silence. Her heart beat on his, and their bodies merged perfectly. Everything seemed right to her. There would be other nights, she knew, but none would be as beautiful as this first time.

Nick slowly raised himself onto one elbow and looked down at her. His voice was low and husky as he spoke.

"Jan, damn it, why must you go back to New York in a couple of days? I can't bear the thought of us being apart."

His body tensed as he whispered even lower, "Don't go. Stay here with me."

Jan held him close, knowing that she would do as he asked. Nothing else in the world was as important to her; nothing meant nearly as much. She could no longer imagine a future without him.

Nick stroked her body and kissed her again and again. He was hard, and Jan was ready. The two of them had only one goal: to become one again.

After making love the second time, Nick whispered into her ear, "Do you love me?"

"Yes, darling, yes. For always and always, with all my heart."

The harsh jangling of the telephone suddenly shattered the mood.

"Damn!" Nick said.

He reached over her and grabbed the phone. Not bothering to answer it, he dropped it to the floor.

"Aren't you going to see who it is?" Jan asked.

"No need to. I know who it is. She belongs to yesterday."

Jan felt a quick twinge of jealousy. Nick must have had many women before her. She wondered if he had ever been in love with any of them.

The next day, Jan faced a wild-eyed Daley Russell.

"You're *what?*" he yelled. "You're crazy! You're kidding me, aren't you? Tell me you're kidding. If not, you're off the wall. I mean it. You've got everything going for you. It's been handed to you on a fuckin' silver platter. Baby, you need a goddamned keeper."

He paused for a quick breath; then Sarah took over.

"For God's sake, Jan, so you spent the night with somebody. So you got laid. So okay, big deal. But now you're trying to tell us that this guy is all of a sudden Mr. Right? What the hell do you know about him?"

Jan looked Sarah straight in the eyes.

"I don't need to know anything more than I do. I'm in love with him. I want him. It's that simple."

Daley clamped his teeth together angrily as he mimicked her. "I'm in love with him. I want him."

Then his voice dropped back to normal.

"You know what? You're crazy, that's what. Loving him ain't reason enough. I want to know what kinda shit you've been smoking. What sort of line did that bastard use? It hadda be a prize-winner; he deserves an Oscar. He's the nerviest son of a bitch on record. The guy wants you to quit what you're doing and play house. Why? Just ask yourself—why? What kinda prick plays around with some-one else's career? What the fuck's the big rush? Why can't you come back with us, wait a few weeks, and sort your feelings out? What happens if love goes out the window? You'll be up the creek without a paddle."

Jan struggled to keep calm, but she felt her temperature rise. She glanced over at Sarah, looking for an ally. But Sarah had an exasperated look on her face.

"Don't you see?" Jan said weakly, wishing they would understand, "I'm in love. I mean, really *in love*. Nothing else matters. After all, what's at stake here? It's not as if I'm giving up a career as a brain surgeon. Okay, so I was a model for a few short months. The world will survive my dropping out. Nick means more to me than work. He means—"

Sarah interrupted Jan, speaking rapidly, her nostrils flared in disgust.

"Honestly, Jan, as your closest friend, I consider you one heavy-duty idiot. What do you mean, you're not com-ing back to New York with us? Jesus, you have it made! You're on your way, you have Daley behind you—you can have it all. Modeling can be just the beginning for you."

Sarah paused, shaking her head.

"It's funny, I was sure you had a secret yen for Mark Squire. That guy is plain crazy about you. And he's the type who would understand your needs and priorities. You could retain your identity with him and remain a model. But I guess you don't really want a career that badly. I mean, you didn't go looking for it, did you? It just hap-pened to you, like everything else."

Jan was hardly listening to Sarah's remarks. She suddenly saw Mark's handsome face in front of her. She envisioned his laughing brown eyes and recalled his easy manner, his charming personality. Her own green eyes narrowed at the thought. Of course Sarah was right. Jan certainly had fantasized about Mark. She had been half in love with him and had enjoyed imagining him as her lover. But that was before she had met Nick.

She decided to call Mark. She owed him that; she would explain everything. She knew he'd be happy for her. Mark was always so wonderfully understanding.

She made that decision, but two pairs of eyes were still fixed on her. She turned to Sarah and Daley and gave them each a long, thoughtful look before speaking.

"You both seem so convinced that it won't work between Nick and me. But that's because you don't know him. As for me, all I want is to be with him every minute of the day and night. It's as if I've been waiting for Nick my whole life. There's nothing either of you can say that will change the way I feel."

Then Jan reached out for their hands and looked fondly at the two of them.

"Believe me, I won't lose a minute's sleep wondering if I'm doing the right thing. But I thank you for your concern."

Daley put his arms around her; his black eyes stared into hers. Then he gave her a devilish little wink.

"That means you won't change your mind, eh? No, I guess not. Well, if you ever have any trouble with the guy, just let Daley Russell know. And don't let the bastard cage you in, hear? After a while you may find you need more than his love."

Daley stepped back and turned to Sarah. He put his arm half around her shoulders, as if leaning on her.

"Boy," he said jokingly, "would you believe it, kiddo?

Jan and I never even necked. Why do I feel as if the bastard is stealing something from me?"

Sarah took his hand and led him toward the bedroom. "Let's go into the other room, lover. We'll see if I can make you lose that feeling."

Lying in the bath, immersed in bubbles, Jan lazily enjoyed thoughts of Nick. He was always in her thoughts. And those thoughts, in the weeks she had been living with him, were usually of making love.

Her desire for sex astonished her. She loved the times they had in bed, hugging, kissing, and touching each other. She was so much in love with him that it terrified her at times. She wanted nothing more out of life than to be in his arms. There was a whole world out there, but only Nick Tyson seemed to matter to her.

Nick loved to shower her with presents. He was outrageously extravagant; he had very positive, very definite tastes and an instinctive talent for knowing what was the absolute best for her. Jan was happy to let him make all her decisions. It somehow felt so right, so natural.

Whatever attracted him, he bought. His favorite scent was Joy. He bought Jan flagons of it. He loved her to wear expensive clothes and accessories, especially sleek silk dresses. He loathed anything fussy or contrived.

It was obvious that Nick also enjoyed introducing her to his friends. For her part, she loved meeting them. Tonight, she and Nick were having dinner with Jaafar al Hassad, who was critically important in a business venture Nick was planning.

Jan took a long time to dress. As she studied herself in the mirror, she knew she had never looked more beautiful than now, being with Nick.

It must be true love, she thought. She loved Nick, and he

loved her. Sometimes she felt almost numb with happiness. It was all so wonderful. Each day was more exciting than the one before.

Once, for a fleeting second, the possibility of someday being disappointed or hurt by Nick crossed her mind, but the notion was just too preposterous to think about. Jan shook the ridiculous idea away.

Jaafar al Hassad's private London sanctum was a row house, hidden behind walls like a cool oasis. The house was large and gloomy; a strong odor of sweet incense filled the air.

The dark-skinned servant who opened the door bowed from the waist. Two more servants stood at either side of an ornately carved portal. They bowed their heads respectfully as Jan and Nick, following a fourth menial, walked past them and were ushered into a richly appointed room.

The scene was one of incredible wealth. Antique porcelains, paintings, and statuary were everywhere. Eighteenth-century floor-to-ceiling mirrors hung from the ornate moldings high overhead. At the farthest end of the room, a trompe l'oeil mural depicting dark-eyed sheikhs on horseback dominated the wall.

Jan turned as she heard the soft click of a door being opened. She found herself staring at the large man who seemed to glide into the room. He was six feet tall but so obese that he looked like an advancing cloud. Fat covered his body in folds, melting into deep creases that hooped all around him. It was a disease of fat. Not even the large caftan he wore could conceal the plethora of bouncing flesh.

The handsome hawked face atop the monstrous mound had a look of arrogance, but his smile was warm and relaxed. His hands were beautifully shaped and constantly fluttered in front of him; his fingers were adorned with scarab rings of pure gold.

Most of the rumors about Jaafar al Hassad were tinged with sinister overtones. He denied nothing and ignored everything written or spoken about him.

Jaafar was the only son of an Oxford-educated Arab sheikh, a merchant prince whose holdings spanned the globe and who had conducted all his business dealings only in French. Jafaar's mother had been an aristocratic Englishwoman who died at an early age. The young heir's inheritance was in excess of six hundred million dollars; the estate was now conservatively managed by a small army of lawyers, accountants, and bankers.

Although Jafaar had been educated in the exclusive English public school system, he had a unique accent. It was neither English nor French but an unusual blend of the two. His speech was slow and precise; each word was carefully chosen and meticulously articulated. This was necessary on his part to conceal a slight stutter.

Now, standing expressionlessly in the center of the lavishly appointed drawing room, he stared at Jan with the look of one used to passing judgment on others. After a brief interval, he nodded his head in silent approval. For some inexplicable reason, she felt herself blush.

Finally Jaafar spoke: "Ah, you must be Jan."

With a slight bow he took her hand and brought it to his lips, kissing it lightly. His eyes were dark and black-rimmed. The irises seemed flecked with gold, like those of a jungle cat. His voice sounded like rich, dark chocolate. He seemed to be in his early thirties.

"What an unexpected pleasure! How very beautiful you are. I like beautiful women."

Jaafar then turned his attention to Nick.

"You'll both stay for supper, of course."

Without waiting for a reply, he clapped his hands imperiously. Almost before the sound had faded, a servant appeared, carrying a glistening gold tray with a bottle of cold champagne in a heavy silver bucket, surrounded by elegant Steuben glasses. The crest-embossed napkins were of the finest silk.

Jan was fascinated by the whole scene. She found it all very exotic. Jaafar intrigued her. She took to him instantly.

Part of his charm was his natural air of quiet assurance. Another part was the feeling that he would always obtain whatever he might desire.

Jaafar handed each of them a glass. Then he lifted his own.

"I propose a toast."

He paused, as if searching for the right words.

"A toast to Nick Tyson, my friend and partner. And to our mutual success in our new venture."

They touched glasses. Jaafar drained his.

Jan noticed that Nick's face was aglow with excitement.

"Christ, Jaafar, does this mean you've decided to sell her to me?"

"Yes, Nick. I shall sell you the ship. I made that decision last week."

Later, they had supper in a warm, intimate room that was carpeted with a beautiful Aubusson rug. The lights from the crystal chandelier reflected the pale orange marble surface of the table, set with the finest blue Sèvres celeste plates and heavy crusted silverware.

Everything was flawless. The delicate Victorian rush chairs that bordered the table were beautiful. Jaafar's own chair, heavy and ornately carved, was at the head of the table.

His conversation was witty and amusing, the food delicious, and the wine superb. But Jan sensed that Jaafar was a master of masks, showing only the part of himself he wished.

After dinner, as Nick and Jan were leaving, Jaafar escorted them through the cavernous hall, past the servants, who stood stiffly at their posts. In the doorway, Jaafar gave Nick a charming smile; his voice was pleasantly low and measured as he spoke.

"I feel one must be perfectly open in relationships. So, dear friend, I wish you to know that I now offer my friendship to your lovely lady. You complement each other beautifully."

Smiling to herself, Jan could barely conceal her delight and appreciation of the man's attitude. He was so Old World, so imperious, and yet so charmingly frank. She did her best to reply in kind.

"And I, dear Jaafar, accept your friendship and shall treasure it always."

Leaning forward, she graced his cheek with a fleeting kiss.

One of the servants escorted them out into the walled garden, bade them good night, and then bolted the heavy iron gate behind them.

Jan slipped her arm through Nick's as they walked to their car.

"God, what a fabulously interesting man! He's so flamboyant, so eccentric. I wonder if anyone ever really gets to know him."

"Well, honey, maybe you'll be the one who discovers the real Jaafar. Nobody else ever has. It's surprising the way he seemed eager to talk with you. He was in one of his gracious moods tonight. Often, under his mask of charm, he can be mighty tough. In the business world he's a predatory shark. I wouldn't want to be Jaafar's enemy. From those who work for him or with him he demands complete

loyalty and discretion. And he pays high for those quali-
ties. He's a strange one, all right. He insists on surrounding
himself with precious things and beautiful people, both
men and women.

"I'm not sure if Jaafar is queer. It's been rumored that
he might be asexual. Anyway, who gives a damn? He's an
Arab, and they're a different breed from us. I wouldn't be
surprised if his approach to sex was a lot different than
mine."

Jan wondered if, deep down, Nick really approved of
Jaafar al Hassad.

Stretched out on his bed, Jaafar lay naked under a fine
muslin cotton sheet.

His mind lazily drifted to Jan as he puffed on a thin
black reed; the sweet smell of hashish permeated the room.
No doubt she was beautiful, but more than that, there was
a fine, delicate texture to her, something that would mellow and ripen with time, like a fine wine. Men would always find her beguiling.

All during the evening, Jaafar had noticed that she ca-
tered to Nick, sought to please him, and was happy to be
exactly what he wanted her to be.

Putting the reed between his dark, full lips, he inhaled
deeply. Minutes later, the soft rapping at his bedroom door
told him Yana had arrived.

As she entered, the scent of sweet oil followed her. Yana
was tall and powerfully built; her six-foot frame was lean
and well muscled. She was an ex-guerrilla fighter, as well
as an expert masseuse. She had been on Jaafar's payroll for
ten years and was paid handsomely for her services and
her devotion to him.

No words were spoken; she silently slid the sheet from

his body. Then she gently positioned him on his stomach, moving him easily, effortlessly.

Spreading aromatic oil slowly over his back, she skillfully kneaded the folds of soft flesh. She touched each pressure point with confidence as she massaged him. Her movements were slow and easy. They were meant not to arouse but to relax. Yana's objective was to bring a feeling of peace to the flesh that hung around his body as if threatening to absorb him.

Each stroke was warm and peaceful and lovingly given. Her strong hands worked his obese body steadily and tirelessly. Every part of him was expertly kneaded and coaxed into deep relaxation as sweat poured down her face.

After his massage, she moved her hands down to his testicles, fondling them gently, first one at a time, then both together. Next she took his penis in her warm, skillful hands and milked it slowly. Finally, she placed it in the moist cavern of her mouth, even though nothing stirred.

Jaafar had been impotent since puberty. Yet Yana knew how he loved the warmth of her mouth. As he slipped into an easy sleep, she covered him, smiling down at him as a mother smiles at a sleeping child. Then, as silently as she had entered, she left the room.

Chapter Seventeen

After Dirk left the cabin, Cat thought about him.

How wonderful that they were leaving Fort Jade and heading for Nashville! She would be grateful to him all her life. It was the luckiest thing that they had found each other and needed each other's love and support.

Cat glanced at the clock on the wall. It was 1:05 in the afternoon. Time seemed to move so slowly; Dirk had only been gone half an hour. He had told her it would probably take a couple of hours to buy the car.

Trying to stifle her impatience, Cat rose from the chair and paced back and forth. Then she stood for a moment with her back to the fireplace and glanced around the room. She studied the scuffed carpet, the shabby old chair, and the plain wooden bunkbed where Dirk had nursed her back to health. Not much luxury, she thought, but she would always remember the warmth and tenderness.

She walked to the door slowly and opened it. Stepping outside, she glanced up at the sky and noticed dark clouds moving in. There was a slow rumble of thunder off in the distance.

"Damn," she muttered, an uneasy feeling taking over. "I hope it's not going to storm and delay Dirk."

She became restless and unsettled. She closed the door behind her and reentered the cabin. Then, walking over to the armchair, she curled herself into it. She sat quietly; her mind drifted. She couldn't get rid of her nervous, edgy feeling. Perhaps it was because of tomorrow, she thought

—tomorrow, when she and Dirk would set out on a new road toward a new life.

A sudden, overwhelming feeling of fatigue came over her. Closing her eyes, she fell into a deep, troubled sleep.

Later, she awoke with a start and sat up in sudden fear. A small series of shivers rippled over her from a strangely terrifying nightmare. She felt cold and frightened. The sky looked ominous and dark.

Cat tried to stem the feeling of panic that was building inside her. She glanced up at the clock; it was now nearly four.

Getting up, she nervously paced the length of the cabin. Why was she so tense? Why did she have this feeling of foreboding? Where was Dirk? Why wasn't he there? He should have been back by now.

Something must have gone wrong; that was the only answer. Taking a deep breath, Cat tried to calm herself. She knew there was only one thing to do. She had to go into town and find him.

Grabbing Dirk's old army jacket, she rushed out of the cabin and took the shortcut to town. For the first half-mile she paced herself, walking quickly but smoothly. For the rest of the distance she half stumbled, half ran, as adrenaline coursed through her.

Relief flooded through her when she finally reached the clearing that led to the village square.

She stopped to catch her breath. For a moment she was confused and disoriented. Dear God, where would the used car lot be? Where should she look for Dirk? What if he had driven home on the highway and they missed each other?

Glancing across the square, she noticed a diner. Someone in there was bound to know where the lot was.

When she got there, the diner was empty except for a

police officer and the short-order cook; both were deep in conversation. The two men looked up her as she entered.

Cat stood for a moment, her senses alert, staring at the policeman. There was no food on the table in front of him. It was obvious that he hadn't stopped in to eat. Her anxiety built even higher.

"Can I help you, lady?" the short-order cook asked.

For an instant, she had an insane notion to turn and run away, but she managed to control herself.

"Yes, you can. I was supposed to meet a friend of mine at a used car lot here in town. It's stupid of me, but I seem to have forgotten the name of the lot. I don't know where to find him."

Cat was trying very hard to control the choke in her voice.

The cook noisily scraped the leavings of batter from his griddle. Cat found herself concentrating on the sound while the officer looked at her curiously.

"There's a car lot on Forest Street, but they close at four," he said. Then he glanced at his watch. "I hope your friend had the patience to wait, because it's now four-thirty."

Finding nothing more to say, the officer turned away and resumed his conversation with the short-order cook.

Cat was beginning to feel very frightened. Her stomach was tied in knots, but she knew she had to keep a grip on herself. All she could think of was Dirk. Where was he? Was anything wrong? What had happened to him?

She found herself listening to the muttering of the short-order cook.

"Bastard! Creep! I sure hope he gets what's coming to him, and more."

He mumbled under his breath until he realized that Cat was watching him.

"Don't mind me, miss. I was just talking to myself. There's been a shootin' at the gas station. My best friend nearly had his head bashed in. He's being fixed up at the hospital right now."

Then the man made a clucking sound with his tongue.

"But let me tell you, he sure is a hell of a lot luckier than the poor young fella who was shot."

Cat felt herself gripped by a sudden internal shaking. Her hand jerked violently and spilled coffee all over the red counter. She stared at it in fascination. It suddenly looked like a pool of blood.

Turning to the officer who was nearby, she spoke to him in a choked, hesitant voice.

"The young man he's talking about, the one who was shot—is he still alive?"

"No, he died at the scene."

Cat shuddered at his words. She broke out in nervous perspiration, feeling numb, nearly paralyzed with fear. She swallowed huge gulps of air to stop herself from fainting.

The officer was looking at her with interest and sudden comprehension.

"Miss, do you think you know the young man who was shot today? Could he be the friend you were supposed to meet at the car lot? If you could help identify him, it sure would be a great help to us because he had no identification on him."

The officer paused for a minute as he scanned her face.

"The only thing in his pocket was a handwritten receipt for a 1963 Buick."

Cat's heart pounded. What was happening just couldn't be. She must be dreaming. When she awoke, everything would all fade away.

Her knees buckled and she slid to the floor in a dead faint.

* * *

The morgue was cold and reeked of death.

The officer put his jacket over Cat's shoulders. She couldn't stop shivering.

She felt detached, outside her own body. She had an overwhelming feeling of déjà vu. It had happened once before; now it was happening again.

She gripped the officer's arm and squeezed it hard as the container slid from the wall.

"Take a deep breath, miss. A quick glance—that's all you have to give," advised the morgue attendant.

Cat looked. She saw blood still on Dirk's head. She shut her eyes and stumbled back. There was a sharp *click* as the container slid back into place.

"Do you know him?" the officer asked.

The scream in her throat would not come.

Her mind went blank for a moment. She just stood motionless, helpless. Then her face crumpled as tears came. They were silent tears, painful, uncontrollable tears. The reality hit her, and she didn't think she could bear it.

The officer looked at her.

"I'm sorry, miss. Perhaps we'd better leave now. I'll drive you home. I don't think you're in any condition to come down to the station. Tomorrow you can give us all the details."

As the officer reached for her arm, Cat experienced a terrible, sickening loneliness. She bit her lip and shook her head; a trancelike expression was on her face.

"I won't go home. I want to do it now. I want to get it over with."

Minutes later, an impassive desk sergeant took down the report. Then, moving as in a trance, barely aware of what she was doing, Cat made arrangements for the undertaker to collect the body. Dirk would be buried in a small cemetery on the outskirts of Fort Jade.

When she returned to the cabin, Cat closed the door behind herself and threw herself onto the bed. She sobbed uncontrollably, trying in vain to blot out the image of the dark, horrible morgue and the cold, gray slab that held Dirk's lifeless body.

She was inconsolable. Grief washed over her in waves. She cried and keened as if her heart were breaking.

Later, when there were no more tears to shed, Cat rose from the bed and paced the cabin, trying desperately to sort out her thoughts.

Once again she would have to start her life anew. It was no good looking back; there was no one there for her.

As she began to accept the finality of Dirk's death, Cat felt a cold calmness come over her. She knew what she had to do. She would travel the same road that she and Dirk had planned to travel together. There was no other choice. But now she'd have to do it alone.

The next day Cat took Dirk's army fatigue cap, the one he always wore, and put it on her head. Then she carefully placed all his possessions into a neat pile in the middle of the floor. Her brow was furrowed by intense concentration, as if she were performing the most important task in the world.

Next, she lit a match and tossed it into the middle of the pile of clothes, papers, and books. She silently watched as the fire took hold. It seemed vitally important to her that no one ever pry into Dirk Peterson's life.

As she walked away from the cabin for the last time, Cat looked back over her shoulder and watched flames take hold of the wooden frame.

Minutes later, walking along the back road to Fort Jade, she heard the shrill scream of fire engines in the distance.

At the cemetery, Cat's blue eyes were wide and dark and filled with infinite sadness as she stood quietly in the grove of cypress trees. She was alone except for the gravedigger.

"Good-bye, my darling," she whispered, a bunch of bluebells in her hand; her eyes were awash with tears.

She placed the flowers on the coffin and touched her fingers to her lips in a silent kiss.

Then she slowly turned and headed for the highway.

A large, heavy van trundled noisily along the road. The sign painted on the side read THE WORD OF GOD TRAVEL-ING MINISTRY. JIM BOYD, PASTOR.

The van's interior was clean and tidy and contained all of Jim Boyd's earthly possessions. His large, flat hands held the wheel with ease. Reverend Boyd was of average height and fair-skinned, with pale, deep-set eyes. His nose was prominent; his head was large and covered with faded ginger hair touched with gray. There was a touch of weakness to his chin that fell away in soft folds above his Adam's apple. He looked older than his forty years.

As a small boy, Jim Boyd had traveled the Bible Belt with his daddy, Reverend Dawson Boyd, selling Bibles up and down the South.

Early in their marriage, the elder Boyd's young wife had run off with a draper, leaving their three-year-old son, Jim, to be reared by his father.

Dawson Boyd had been a God-fearing man. He read the Bible to his son a dozen times, from beginning to end, before the boy was sixteen.

Young Jim's formative years were punctuated by a never-ending series of revival meetings. There he would sit wide-eyed, hypnotized by the impassioned fire-and-brimstone sermons and miracle-healing ceremonies. He'd study the faces of the people in the crowded tents and saw, even in his teens, that they responded emotionally to promises of heaven and threats of hell.

When he reached his twentieth birthday, Jim Boyd's father died of a massive heart attack. The day Reverend Boyd was buried was the day his son, Jim, started preaching. He never stopped. The evangelical life was as natural to him as breathing.

Knowing Scripture by heart and gifted with a flair for oratory, the self-ordained young pastor criss-crossed the Bible Belt, thundering, threatening, cajoling, promising, and preaching to anyone who would listen to him.

When Jim Boyd was moved by the passion of the gospel, his voice became fired with seething intensity and sweat poured from his body. Energized by his own excitement, his charisma was sometimes only a little short of electrifying.

After particularly enervating sermons, the young reverend often felt a need for a woman. He preferred them eager and active. He was no stranger to the local whorehouse of every town he stopped at.

Jim Boyd had never been in love with a woman, nor had he ever made a genuine commitment at any time in his life: not to another living soul, and not even to his Lord. The only thing Boyd loved was the power of the pulpit, the power of knowing how easily he could play upon the emotions of his congregations, and how easily he could manipulate them with visions of God and the devil.

The Reverend Jim Boyd glanced at his watch, then squinted down at the roadmap on his lap. He had fifty more miles to go before he would turn off the highway and into the town of Tysons Landing.

No sooner had he put the map back into the over-crowded glove compartment than he noticed a young woman walking along the soft shoulder just ahead of him.

Hearing the sound of his engine, she turned and waved at him, hoping to flag him down.

Boyd applied his brakes and pulled over to the side of the road. His curiosity was piqued as he watched her run over to the van. He wondered where she had come from. She was alone, carrying no luggage, nothing.

When he opened the van door and took a closer look at her, he saw that she was quite beautiful. Tendrils of auburn hair escaped from under the army fatigue cap she was wearing. As her large blue eyes studied him warily, he saw that her face was pale and drawn.

When he spoke, his voice was pleasant and bland; his tea-colored eyes were warm and friendly.

"Welcome to God's caravan. If I am heading in your direction, you're certainly welcome to a lift."

She paused for a moment and looked back along the highway as if trying to remember something. Then, in a voice that sounded small and strangely wistful, she replied, "Well, I'm heading away from here. So I guess your direction suits me just fine."

With an almost imperceptible shrug, she entered the van and seated herself on the only available space—the faded plastic seat cover alongside Jim Boyd.

He reached over her to make sure the van door was securely closed, then maneuvered the vehicle back onto the highway.

"My name is Jim Boyd. I'm a preacher."

"Mine's Cat. Cat Bracken."

Boyd peered at her closely.

"Are you in trouble?" he asked. "The way I see it, you must be. What are you running from? You mustn't be afraid—we all have our devils. Sometimes it can be helpful to talk things over with a man of God. It might ease your burden. Remember, the Lord has great mercy. He has un-bounded compassion for a repenting sinner. You can speak freely to me, sister. The Lord works in mysterious ways. Maybe it was ordained that I give you this ride in order to set you on the true road to righteousness."

Jim Boyd enjoyed the sound of his voice. He was pleased at how easily the words came together, built, grew, and filled the van with religious fervor.

"Truly, each of us has sinned. How many times I have told my flock—"

Cat cut across him, her voice chipped with ice.

"Forget it. I'm not one of your flock. I'm not one of anybody's flock. All I want from you is a lift, not a ser-mon."

Jim Boyd gunned his engine and burned up the high-way; there was a look of rigid disapproval on his face. He didn't like the way the bitch had spoken to him. Maybe he'd just dump her, kick her out of the cab right now.

No sooner were her words out of her mouth than Cat was aware of his anger. She decided it would be wise to lighten up the atmosphere in the van.

"Look, I didn't mean to be rude. I know you're in the business of saving souls. You were just doing what you thought was right. I'm sorry for what I said, and I'm really most grateful for this ride."

His foot lightened on the accelerator, and his expression softened. She continued speaking, trying to inject as much friendly interest as possible into her voice.

"It must be very satisfying doing the Lord's work. Tell

me, what kind of a minister are you? In which church were
you ordained?"

It's a good thing the wiseass little bitch changed her tune,
thought Jim Boyd. When he replied, it was as if the un-
pleasantness had never happened. He took a deep breath
and spoke in a low voice.

"I'm not an ordained preacher, not in the actual sense of
the word. But then again, neither was our blessed Lord
Jesus. I merely follow in His Way, going among the people
to preach His Holy Word to all who will listen, to save
their souls, to show them The Way."

Boyd paused for a moment. A reflective look came into
his eyes. Then he spoke with deep conviction, as if to himself.

"It hasn't been an easy life. I picked a hard row to hoe.
But things are gonna be different from now on. No more
tents. No more moving from one town to another. No
more sleeping in my van. Now I've got a chance to have
my own church."

The sun was slipping down toward the horizon when
Jim Boyd pulled his van into The Broadcasters Bar. He
wanted to find a bathroom. He had to pee real bad.

After relieving himself, Boyd decided to have a cup of
coffee before checking out the vacant church in Tysons
Landing. He invited Cat to join him.

As she sipped her coffee, she looked idly around. A sign
on the wall caught her attention: WAITRESS WANTED,
MUST BE ABLE TO SING.

The girl who had taken their coffee order was bright and
perky and had a friendly expression on her face. Cat
leaned over the counter excitedly and asked her how to
apply for the job.

"Gee, honey," the girl said sympathetically, "I'm sorry.
Dumb me, I forgot to take the sign down. The boss just

hired someone yesterday. But he's standing right over there if you want him."

Cat turned to Jim Boyd.

"Excuse me," she said, "I have to talk to that man."

She walked slowly over to a tall, heavyset man who was leaning against the bar. She was aware that he had been looking at her.

"I like the way you move," he said as she approached him.

"Do you? That's what I call a real good start."

Her voice was silky; her large, turquoise eyes were fixed on his. *Think positive,* she told herself. She was determined to sell Cat Bracken to him. She focused all her attention on the man.

She moistened her lips deliberately before speaking again.

"My name's Cat Bracken. I want that singing waitress job. I want it real bad. I know you've already hired someone else. But I'm telling you true, she can't be as good as me."

Richard Bradshaw, a great admirer of women, scrutinized her carefully. Her turned-up nose was pure Celtic. Her skin was like satin. She was definitely beautiful, with a provocative aura of sensuality about her. Even in her beat-up jeans and with her tousled red hair trying to escape from under the old army cap she was wearing, he could see that she was a dazzler.

"Have you had any experience?" he asked. "Done any late-night waitressing or bartending? How about the mean drunks that are sure to come on to you—will you be able to handle them? And what do you sing? Can you do ballads and sexy torch songs? I want someone who can make the guys cry when they've had a snootful and then make 'em feel like ordering a snootful more."

Cat didn't take her eyes off him all the time he was speaking. She nodded her head affirmatively to all his questions. She knew she had a shot at it. She remained silent, waiting for his next remark.

"Well, I'll say one thing about you. You're mighty damned sure of yourself. A real super somebody. Right?"

Cat grinned up at him.

"Not yet, but I will be someday. Just try me. Give me that job. I promise you won't be disappointed."

Bradshaw said nothing. He reached for a cigarette, lit it, and he continued to stare at her as he puffed thoughtfully, blowing a series of smoke rings.

Cat watched them curl slowly around his head.

When he spoke again, his voice was gruff.

"Lady, I like your confidence. I also like the way you look. A man would be a damned fool not to take a chance with you. I'll give you a tryout tonight and see how you do. If you're as good as you say, you got yourself a job."

Cat felt a little whirlpool of happiness build inside of her. Maybe Lady Luck was at last looking her way.

Chapter Eighteen

His hands gripped the steering wheel, ready for action. The cabbie asked, "Where to, man?"

"Club Sinew, Greenwich Village."

The cabbie was about thirty. His porcine face was pockmarked, and his dank, greasy hair hung down to his shoulders. A half-chewed toothpick dangled from his puffy lips. His face took on a nasty look as he turned to Lear.

"Hey, that's a fag joint, ain't it?"

"I suppose it is."

The cabbie turned away with a disgusted grunt.

Lear was too depressed to care. He had been walking the streets of New York, dejected and lonely. Wherever he looked, everyone seemed to be living some sort of a life, while he was just existing.

As he leaned back in the seat and closed his eyes, his thoughts turned to Jan. How excited and happy she had sounded when she phoned from London yesterday! Her voice had bubbled over as she told him that her wonderful Nick and she were more in love with each other than ever.

"Maybe it's not real," she said. "Maybe it all happened too quickly. Maybe it won't last at all. But I don't really believe that. I feel too marvelous, too special, and I love him so. I really, really do. He is all I've ever wanted, all I've ever dreamed of."

Lear had been feeling dejected and was going through an agonizing emotional blizzard of his own when Jan called. But bouyed by her happiness, he'd put on a cheerful front. The conversation had ended with Lear telling Jan he would miss her very much.

Now, in the backseat of the cab, he smiled ironically as he realized how true that statement was. In the short time they had known each other, Jan Julliard had added balance to his life. She would never know how important she had been to him.

The cabbie drove like a shark in turbulent waters, switching from lane to lane. Finally, as he pulled up to the club, he rose in his seat, did a full turn, and fixed his small, baleful eyes on Lear.

"Hey, my meter's broke. But I figure this ride's gonna cost ya ten bucks even, plus tip."

Lear sighed. The last thing he wanted was trouble.

Getting out of the cab, he pulled a twenty from his pocket and placed it silently into the outstretched hand that reached through the open window. The cabbie stuffed the bill into his pocket, uttered an epithet under his breath, and sped off into the night.

Entering his dressing room, Lear started to apply his makeup. He was only half-listening to the other chorus boys as they snapped at each other.

"For God's sake, can't you hurry, Thomas?" asked Bryce Greeley. "I swear, darling, you look an absolute mess! You didn't need that quickie in the men's room. Now wipe your mouth, you horny bastard. Honestly! You'll be the death of me yet."

Tom Pace's smile was insolent as he turned to Greeley and kissed him on the lips.

"But, ah, my carping cavalier, you loved every minute of it."

Then his expression changed.

"Darling, I'll positively expire if I don't have a snort. In fact, Greeley, I'd sell my soul for a heavy line. Without one, I'll simply never make it because you, you irresistible little faggot, have unquestionably sucked my energies dry."

Greeley giggled.

"I take that as a compliment, Thomas. There's always more where that came from. Thank God, nature provided us with an inexhaustible supply."

Attaching extra glue to his false eyelashes, Greeley spent the next few seconds combing his pageboy wig. Then a fast flick of gold paint on his eyelids, and he was ready. He stopped, snorted, and rubbed the remaining coke on his gums as he turned to Tom Pace.

"Wow, that was all I needed to perk me up!"

Greeley beamed at his reflection in the mirror as he blew himself a noisy kiss.

"Okay, world, I'm ready. Ready for all those humpy young dudes. I'm horny, hot, and, as anyone can see, primed for passion. Isn't that just gorgeous?"

Unexpectedly, Greeley turned to Lear.

"Not as madly gorgeous as you, sweet thing. But then, you still don't know what fence you're straddling, do you? Don't fight it, darling. Let go. Abandon yourself to our faggot life-style. Believe me, sweet thing, I can vouch for it. Fucking and being fucked—that's what it's all about."

There was a rap at the door, and a stagehand called out, "Two minutes to go. You're on next."

With a flurry of feathers and sequins, the two chorus boys swished out of the dressing room, leaving Lear alone.

He remained motionless and stared at himself in the mirror, haunted by Greeley's remark.

Who was he? What was he, really? Where did he fit? Where did he belong?

As if in a trance, he pulled his long hair back into a ponytail. Taking a makeup brush, he shaded his cheeks, accentuating the planes of his face. He painted the curve of his full, sensitive mouth and added more mascara to his heavy, dark lashes.

There was something strange, almost surrealistic about the whole tableau. It was as if he were watching himself in a dream.

He reached for his carrying bag, aware that he was trembling. He took out a pair of stockings and pulled them over his long, slender legs. Next came soft silk lingerie, a simple black silk dress, and silk shoes. He clipped on a pair of rhinestone earrings but decided they were too garish and took them off again.

Finished at last, Lear stared at himself in the full-length mirror. He felt a chill of pleasure as he admired the beautiful woman in the glass—the woman he so desperately wanted to be.

The loud banging on the door startled him.

"Hey, move your ass in there!" a voice called out. "You got thirty seconds before you're on."

Lear ignored the call. Throwing his camel-hair coat over his shoulder, he walked to the club's rear exit. In seconds, he was on the street outside.

He walked slowly, lost in his own thoughts. He walked past sushi bars, movie theaters, massage parlors, pizza stands, and, finally, a singles' bar. He stopped and stood for a moment, then went inside.

He was aware of the enormity of what he was doing. A small panic gripped him, but he pushed it away.

Bob Cawdy, seated alone at the bar, looked up.

"Well, hello there, gorgeous. Where have you been all my life?"

Lear tried to walk past him. Something about the man frightened him.

"Hey, don't be shy, sweetie. You're just my type."

Bob Cawdy was a hardhat, a construction worker for the city.

"Come on, doll. I'll buy ya a drink."

Without waiting for an answer, Cawdy pulled Lear onto the barstool next to him. He insinuated sexual intimacy as he put his arm around him and touched his bottom as if by accident.

"Whoops, sorry about that, doll," he said with a foolish smirk on his fleshy face.

Lear could feel his fear mounting. Jesus, he had to get out of this. He had only wanted to walk into the club as a woman to play out his fantasy, to have some man look at him as a woman. That was all. But now he felt disgust for himself, despising what he was doing.

"Hey, what's the matter, doll? You shy or somethin'?" Cawdy asked. "You act like you're scared shitless. Hell, I ain't gonna bite you. But I sure gotta hand it to you, lady. You are one hell of a knockout. Most of the broads that come in here are just dogs, y'know, and over the hill at that. They ain't got nothing. Spending a night with one of 'em would be like screwin' your own mother—know what I mean?"

"Hi, Cawdy," a voice behind them said.

The beefy man turned to face a sad-eyed, middle-aged blonde.

"Aw, fuck off, Mavis. Can'tcha see I'm busy?"

Turning back to Lear, a look of suspicion crossed his face. His pale flat eyes peered into Lear's.

"How come I ain't seen you here before? I'm a regular. And how come a classy dame like you hits a place like this, anyway? It don't figure. Someone with your looks—you could go anywhere."

Lear felt caught up in an awful, nightmarish game. The pounding of his heart was so strong, he was sure the other man could hear it. It was all he could do to stifle the wisps of fear in the back of his mind. He knew he had to stop this masquerade, and soon. It was wrong, and it was becoming dangerous. He had to make some excuse, any excuse, to get out and get away.

Cawdy's eyes again flicked over Lear. He placed his heavy hands together and cracked his knuckles.

"Hey, you always so quiet?"

Lear had a feeling something terrible was about to happen. He felt wretched, full of shame and fear.

Swallowing hard, he started to speak. He spoke disconnectedly; his voice sounded naked to him.

"I must go home. I shouldn't be here. I'm sure you feel I owe you an apology."

"An apology, huh? How come?" Cawdy's eyes narrowed.

Oh, God, why had he said *apology?* He knew his voice must have sounded much too frightened.

"You see, I came in here looking for a friend. And I don't see him. So I really have to leave."

Cawdy leaned closer; a flash of resentment crossed his face.

"Don't hand me that bullshit, lady. Give it to me straight. I ain't your type, right?"

"No, you don't understand. That's not it at all. I've enjoyed talking to you. I'm sure you're a very nice, warm person. But I really must go."

As Lear stood up, Cawdy positioned himself in front of him; the smell of whiskey was on his breath, and cheap cologne on his body. His male ego made him want to believe what Lear had said.

"Okay, babe, I read ya. I knew you wanted to come on to me, but you was too shy. Hell, anyone coulda seen that. So just gimme a number where I can call ya, 'cause you light my fire, know what I mean? Face it, a guy who knows the ropes like me could show you a real hot time."

He punctuated his little speech with a crude, knowing wink.

Lear felt claustrophobic, but he forced a smile on his face. He wrote down a phony number on a matchbook cover.

"Okay, let's go," said Cawdy. "I'll walk you outside. I could do with some air."

He reached for Lear's hand. Lear tried to pull away, but Cawdy held it tight as he pushed through the crowded bar, past the back entrance, into a dimly lit alley.

Once outside, he stood facing Lear, swaying slightly. He was a little drunk. Slowly he moved closer and pressed his body to Lear's.

"Shit, doll, I don't even know your name."

Lear pushed him away. His mind was churning. He felt disaster all around him.

Cawdy sensed Lear's growing panic.

"Hey, what're you so uptight about? Someone would think ya never scored before."

A wave of pure fear descended on Lear as Cawdy grabbed him and pressed him tight.

"Please don't do that. Please. I—I don't want you to."

"Aw, come on, what's a little good-night kiss?"

Cawdy thrust his hand up along the inside of Lear's thigh and pushed it deep between his legs.

Suddenly he pulled back; there was a look of shock and disbelief on his face. Lear watched it turn to disgust and loathing. Naked hatred seethed in his eyes.

"You fuckin' faggot! You dirty, filthy, walkin' piece a shit!" he snarled through gritted teeth.

Fists clenched, Cawdy rushed at him with an angry roar. Lear tried to sidestep but stumbled and fell to one

knee. Then, faint and trembling, he buckled and pitched
forward.

Cawdy looked down at him, frustrated in his rage. With
an oath he turned to go but suddenly stopped. Almost as
an afterthought he stood over Lear.

Lear heard the sound of a zipper being opened, then
smelled the strong odor of urine as it gushed over him.
Through it all, he heard Cawdy's voice shouting with pent-
up hatred, "Thought ya put somethin' over on me, huh?
That's how ya get yer kicks, huh? Okay, pansy, this is how
I get my kicks—by pissin' all over garbage like you."

Then he turned and ran off into the darkness.

Lear had no remembrance of how he got home. All he
could think of was how to end his life of shame and fear.
He longed to sink into nothingness and never know such
degradation again.

He barely remembered opening the medicine chest. He
swallowed every prescription pill he could find and washed
them down with vodka. Then he fell into a drugged sleep.

If his cleaning lady hadn't arrived early that morning,
Lear would have died.

He woke up at Bellevue. They had pumped his stomach
and told him he needed psychiatric help.

Returning to his apartment, Lear packed a bag and
pinned a note on his medicine chest that read FUCK PSY-
CHIATRY. Then he taxied to the airport and boarded a
plane for Paris.

Lear checked into a small nondescript hotel on the Left
Bank. His French was just good enough to get by on.

The first two weeks he barely slept. He brooded constantly but came no closer to solving his problem.

One night he remembered that Greeley and Tom had

talked about a Club L'Accord where they had danced. He decided to go there the next day. He couldn't stay all alone in his tiny room any longer. It was beginning to close in on him.

The next night he walked into the club with an air of bravado and self-assurance that was all false. His stomach churned inside as he faced the smooth, gleaming bald pate of the somewhat menacing man in front of him.

Pythias had been bald since age sixteen. He smiled at Lear, displaying sharklike teeth framed by his full, sensitive lips. His white face and coal-black eyes gave him the look of an ambulatory skeleton. He was dressed in black leather, and each wrist had a heavy gold bracelet with a different name spelled out in diamonds. One read DAMON; the other PYTHIAS.

Despite his forbidding appearance, the eyes that appraised Lear were friendly. Until the age of nineteen, his name had been John Belton. He had adopted the name Pythias in London, when he took his first and only lover, a man named Damon.

They were active participants in London's sexual underground. They put together a theatrical act. Dressed in drag, they were aggressively obscene and wildly amusing. Onstage they flaunted and parodied their sexual proclivities as outrageously as possible. By working at numerous demimonde clubs, they developed a widespread cult following.

One night a French talent scout caught their act. He booked them into a failing club in Paris for a two-week stint. They were a smash hit. That was fifteen years ago. Club L'Accord became one of the most popular boîtes in the city. Damon and Pythias owned it now.

Looking at the extraordinarily beautiful young man in

front of him, Pythias could sense Lear's nervousness. He sought to put him at ease.

Pythias's voice was warm and appealing. It carried traces of a lower-class Midlands accent. Lear felt soothed by his nonthreatening tone.

"Good evenin', luv," the club owner said. Pythias called everybody "luv." It was part of his personality, part of his natural warmth.

"So you've come to look at the naughty end of Paris, 'ave you?"

"No, not at all. I was hoping to find work. I'm a dancer, and I can also sing."

"Can you, now? Is that a fact?"

An amused smile crossed Pythias's face.

"Forgive the tacky question, luv, but are you one of us?"

Lear's voice took on a hard edge.

"Am I a homosexual, is that what you mean? A brother faggot? One of the guilty, the cursed, the damned?"

Pythias looked hard at the young man. Lear's face had a gentle but suffering look about it, as if he had recently gone through a trauma. Pythias sensed the pain in him. He wondered if he was just out of the closet, or still hesitating, still looking for the courage to change his way of life. One thing was certain: he was bloody marvelous to look at. He was one of the most beautiful boys Pythias had ever laid eyes on.

As he stared at Lear, Pythias's brain ticked over. He was one entertainer short tonight. Queen Reggie had taken off with an Arab from Tangiers. The promiscuous bastard should have been back an hour ago. He was probably holed up somewhere, smashed on Moroccan hash.

Instinctively, Pythias snapped his fingers at Lear and said, "Follow me, luv."

He walked him through heavy, red-velvet, tassled curtains, past the bar festooned in satin, under the silver sequined balls hanging overhead. A gold candelabrum sat atop a white, Art Deco baby grand piano.

They continued past the stage and out through a side door, until they were in the semidarkness of the wings. Then they entered a dressing room.

Lear gasped at the profusion of glitter that faced him. On poles at either side of the room hung dresses of silk, satin, velvet, and sequins, a potpourri of vibrant colors. Feathered boas, glittering shoes, and boxes of costume jewelry were scattered carelessly about. Furs and accessories were evident in every corner, and a row of beautifully coiffed wigs stood on a huge faux-marble table.

After studying Lear's reaction for a moment, Pythias spoke.

"I'm not sure why I'm doing this, luv, but I'm going to give you a chance. It might be confusing for you to dress like the most flamboyant, outrageous female in all of Paris. But tonight I want you to take Reggie's place. We'll see if you can pull it off with class."

With a wide, sharklike smile, Pythias winked at Lear.

"Cross-dancing can be fun, luv. Who knows? You might get to like it."

Lear was silent for a moment. He stared at Pythias with no expression in his dark eyes. Then he began to laugh deliriously. It was as if he were laughing at himself—but not enough to wipe the sadness from his eyes.

After a few seconds, the laughter stopped. Facing the mirror, Lear moved quickly. He knew exactly how he wanted to look. Not like a drag queen, but like a gorgeous, desirable woman. If he couldn't be one in real life, he'd play-act as one. Fuck the world. Lear Feria was not getting off it after all.

Carefully, he applied a small amount of makeup. Then

he slid into a white satin dress and reached for a short platinum-blond wig. Next, he rummaged through the box of paste diamond jewelry and added earrings and armfuls of bracelets. Finally he grabbed a white feathered boa. Lear was ready.

Pythias looked at him with unconcealed approval and smiled through his full lips. He motioned for Lear to walk around the room. Lear's steps were measured; his pace slow and easy. He tilted his head and gave Pythias a wide, trembling smile full of vulnerability. His every gesture was delicate and totally feminine.

Pythias sensed that this was no dizzy queen he was looking at. There were no infractions, no false moves in the fantastic masquerade. The young man had simply assumed another identity—perhaps his true identity.

The words came out before Pythias could stop them: "Bloody marvelous. We'll put you center stage tonight."

He rehearsed Lear all afternoon.

That evening, as the stage lights went on at L'Accord, Lear stood in the wings. He watched the fun as the chorus boys, all in drag, screeched out, "Don't put your daughter on the stage, Mrs. Worthington."

The whole ambience was warm and friendly to him. It was as if this had always been his home, as if they had always been his friends. For the first time he felt safe and sheltered. He would make this his world. From here, Lear Feria would plan his future.

He felt a gentle prod on his shoulder.

"Time to get into position, luv. If you're 'aving stage fright, not to worry. By this time tomorrow, all of Paris will be talking about you and wondering who you are."

The house lights dimmed, and the stage shifted. After entering from stage rear, Lear took his position. The set panels slid backward to form a staircase. On each rung stood a statuesque Ziegfeld-looking chorus "girl," each dressed in an outrageous costume.

The music beat out "Diamonds Are a Girl's Best Friend," then dropped to a softer pitch.

The lights dimmed once more. A single spot shifted to center stage.

Exotically positioned on a red velvet chaise sat an exquisite blonde. As the music dropped to a softer pitch, she yawned, then stretched her body in a sensuous, feline gesture and looked out at the audience.

Taking a black velvet gunny sack from the floor, she pulled out a handful of glittering diamond jewelry. Languorously, she slipped rings and bracelets onto her fingers and wrists. Then she started to sing; her voice was low and husky, with an Eartha Kitt growl to it.

Suddenly she tossed the empty gunny sack into the wings and uncurled herself from the divan, trailing the white feathered boa after her. Every gesture she made was slow and teasing as she moved across the stage in rhythm to the song.

Lear worked his way deeper and deeper into his new persona. In some inexplicable way the pretense became reality.

He ascended the stairs; his back was to the footlights, and his body moved slowly and seductively. Upon reaching the top step, the chorus joined in with him.

As the final note faded, he turned to face the audience. There, bathed in the glow of the spotlights, he blew them a kiss as a cascade of diamond confetti started to fall, framing him in a myriad of lights.

Posing sensuously atop the stairs, he let the endless waves of applause wash over him. Obscured by confetti, no one noticed glistening tears trickling down his cheeks.

Chapter Nineteen

Nick looked handsomer than ever to Cynthia as he approached the breakfast table. There was something different about him, but she couldn't quite tell what it was. She only knew that it was heaven having her son home with her, even if only for a short visit.

He idly picked at the food on his plate for a moment or two; then his blue eyes peered directly into his mother's.

"Cynthia, I've met a girl in London who is indescribably perfect. I never thought anyone could make me feel so happy. Within minutes after our meeting, she changed my whole life. I'm seriously thinking of marrying her."

Sitting in her straight-back chair, Cynthia Tyson's posture stiffened ever so slightly.

"It was the most fantastic thing. I knew I was in love with her the moment we met. Not only is she incredibly beautiful, but she's warm and gentle and loving."

As Nick talked, his face glowed with excitement, as if he were reliving the joyous time they spent together.

"She's an American who was working as a model over there. Would you believe that Jan is giving up her career just for me? The next time I come home to visit, I'll be sure to bring her with me. It's important to me that my two favorite ladies meet. I know you'll be as crazy about her as I am."

The room suddenly seemed very still to Cynthia. A surge of angry emotions rushed through her. She didn't want the thought to surface, but it did: *Nick is going to leave me.* Once again she felt the aching pangs of loss. First she had lost her husband, and now she was about to lose her son. This girl—this model, this utter nobody—was trying to seduce Nick into an early marriage! Couldn't he see she was after his money? In a few short years he would have control of his grandfather's largest trust fund, a sum well in excess of fifty million dollars. Then, at age forty, there would be his grandmother's fund, plus the balance of his father's estate when he died.

Cynthia was unsmiling as she looked at her son, her jaw set tight. She knew it was up to her to protect him from this obvious fortune hunter.

"Nick, you sound serious about this girl. Tell me, have you known her long?"

She watched her son slowly trace the rim of his coffee cup with his finger.

"No, I guess we haven't known each other all that long. But it's been long enough to know that we love each other."

Cynthia moved her hands nervously to her hair. She was getting one of her horrid headaches.

Seeing his mother's expression, Nick's face sobered slightly, but he tried to keep his tone light.

"Hey there, you don't seem to be happy about my news."

Cynthia forced a note of cheerfulness into her voice, trying hard to keep it steady.

"Well, darling, I must admit it's all a bit startling to me. Since your father's illness, I've felt so very much alone. My only real comfort in life is knowing that I have you to depend on."

As she looked at her handsome son, her thoughts spun around in her head. *Oh Nick, why did you have to tell me your news today? It's going to spoil all the time you and I have together! It's so wrong of you to think of marriage at this time!*

As Nick studied his mother's face, it seemed as if her mind were a million miles away.

"Cynthia, Cynthia!" he called, his voice teasing. "Come back to me, wherever you are."

There was a long, unusual silence before Cynthia answered him.

"Nick darling, I'm so happy for you, but promise you won't marry that girl until I meet her. I mean, she's not pregnant or anything like that, is she?"

Nick raised his hand to stop his mother's words.

"Of course she isn't pregnant. And I certainly won't marry her until you two get to know each other. I'm sure that Jan would feel the same way."

Nick's blue eyes were happy again as he smiled at Cynthia.

"Thank you, my darling," she said with enormous relief. Then she bent over and affectionately kissed her son on the cheek.

Minutes later, Nick left her and went upstairs to visit his father.

As she sat alone with her thoughts, the breakfast room felt strangely empty to Cynthia. She welcomed the emptiness and privacy. There was so much to think about. She knew she would always be there for Nick, to protect him and guide him. A sad, soft smile crossed her face. Once in her life she, too, had been protected and loved. But that was before . . .

A swift, mean spasm of hate filled her. Nick would never know the desolation she felt, nor the deep, gnawing hatred she had for his father, a hatred that had become very familiar to her. It was always there, along with the loss she lived with every day of her life.

The voice of Alpha, her housekeeper, interrupted Cynthia's thoughts. She glanced up with a startled expression on her face.

"Yes, Alpha, what is it?" she asked impatiently.

"Mrs. Tyson, ma'am, the Reverend Boyd is waiting in the vestibule."

"Oh dear, not now. Send him away. Tell him I'm not here."

Alpha'a black face was stubborn as her lips folded into a thin line. She replied in a voice both whispery and indignant, "No, ma'am. 'Tain't right to ask me to lie to a man of God. I can't do that."

Cynthia's expression was impatient and angry.

"You're becoming impossible!" she said as she stormed out toward the vestibule.

Alpha followed Cynthia Tyson with her eyes for a moment, then walked back to the kitchen, muttering somberly to herself.

"You poor grievin' woman. I know about your misery, jus' like I know what you been hidin' in your linen closet and how you been nippin' alone night after night. I see the brandy bottle tucked away with all your fine linens. You need the preacher's help, for sure. Maybe he'll be the one to get the happiness back on your face, to help you get into the Lord's graces again."

Entering the kitchen, Alpha shut the door behind her and reached for her Bible.

Walking through the long hall toward the vestibule, Cynthia Tyson's thoughts went to the man waiting there.

She had met the Reverend Jim Boyd about six months before, on a stifling hot and humid Sunday. Willie was driving her to the back pasture, for a reason she couldn't recall. They were about ten miles from the main house and were just passing the small church that had stood on the property for years, even before it had been purchased by the Tysons.

Old Man Tyson had stipulated that any God-fearing preacher could use the church as long as it was kept in repair and a token rent was paid to the estate.

Cynthia normally paid little attention to the gossip of her household help. She had, however, heard murmurings about the new evangelist who had come to town and who was filling the church with his hellfire, tub-thumping style of preaching.

Just as they came abreast of the church on the old country lane, the Rolls had sputtered and wheezed and the exhaust had belched smoke. Then, with a bang from the engine loud enough to wake the dead, the car came to a stop.

Willie stomped down on the accelerator and muttered to the car. The overwhelming smell of gasoline filled the air as he vainly pumped the pedal.

Willie turned to Cynthia. Beads of perspiration were on his brow, and embarrassment and frustration showed in his yellow-tinged dark eyes.

"Looks like there ain't nothin' gonna get this car movin' again. We're gonna need a heap o' help from the good Lord himself to get this old girl goin', Missus Tyson. She sure is actin' mighty persnickity."

Seated in the back of the stalled sedan, Cynthia closed her eyes with a sigh of resignation. Her clothes were sticking to her body due to the oppressive heat.

And then she heard someone speak.

"I think you've flooded her."

The voice was soft, with a nasal, rhythmic twang to it, as it continued pleasantly.

"Just let her cool down and rest awhile. She'll start up again."

Cynthia opened her eyes and looked through the open window at the man who was talking to Willie. He glanced at his watch, turned, and opened the back door of her car. Smiling, he faced Cynthia. His eyes seemed strangely flat.

"How do you do, ma'am? May I introduce myself? I'm the Reverend Jim Boyd. My flock's inside, and by my watch it's preachin' time. I heard the noise from your car, so I came to see if I could help. May I offer you the cool sanctuary of my church? After services are over I'll see that your car is taken care of."

Cynthia remembered allowing herself to be escorted into the church by the preacher. People were pouring in. She slipped into a pew in the half shadows at the back of the chapel.

She recalled thinking how absurd it was for her to be sitting there. The Tysons were members of St. James's, the fine old church on the hill, although Cynthia had long ago given up her needs for communion and worship.

Out of the corner of her eye she noticed some of the local townspeople who made up the congregation. They sat in their pews, silent and respectful, waiting.

The voices of the choir rose sweetly behind Jim Boyd. He stood at the pulpit with his arms outstretched. He held a Bible high in one hand, and his head was devoutly bowed.

As the choir finished, he walked down the center aisle, staring at the congregation. His flat, pale eyes darted from one worshipper to another. Back and forth he prowled, holding his Bible high.

The shuffling of feet seemed to be his cue to start preaching.

"Jesus says, 'Ask unto us and ye shall be forgiven,' " he roared. "What did I say?" he demanded, cupping his ear.

"Jesus says, 'Ask unto us and ye shall be forgiven,' " they roared back at him.

His voice dropped down to a whisper.

"Tell me, what is the unforgivable sin?"

"Unrepentance!" the congregation cried out in one voice.

Pivoting on his heels, Jim Boyd held the Bible high and talked with fanatical rapidity, as if in the grip of an emotional frenzy.

"Jesus says I want you! Jesus says I want you!" he repeated over and over, striding back and forth in front of the altar. Then, clasping his hands, he looked down at the worshippers. His voice dropped to a low pitch again as he pointed at the faces of those in the pews and spoke the words again with fervent conviction.

"Jesus says I want you. Shout it out, ye who have sinned! Tell Him, tell Him now, tell Him loud, tell Him true, purge yourselves before the Son of God! Purge the Judas from your souls. Deny Him not. Deny Him not. Deny Him not!"

The congregation took up the chant, building and feeding on their mounting fervor.

Cynthia had watched him rail against them and whip them to a peak of virtual self-hatred. She could sense his power, the power to arouse these people in the name of God.

"Brothers and sisters, Heaven is there for all of us to share. How many souls are we going to bring to the light of God today? How many sinners among us are ready to confess? I can feel the evil, the sin, that is lurking all around us."

He slowly raised his head upward and stretched his

arms in a dramatic gesture to form a cross. His voice was deep and resonant as it rolled around the church.

"Oh Lord, we want to dedicate our pitiful selves unto Your holy care. We want to sin no more."

"Amen and hallelujah!" the congregation answered in unison.

Then Jim Boyd silently bowed his head, as if to gather his thoughts. Finally he raised his eyes and continued.

"Today, my good brothers and sisters, I'm going to talk about another of the Lord's commandments and of those who break it. Yes, I'm talkin' about the evil adulterer, the wrecker of homes, the whoremaster and the harlot incarnate, the sinner who steals another's mate."

His voice was dry as he rasped out the words; his finger pointed straight ahead.

"Which of you God-fearing people sitting among us has known such an adulterer? Which of you has been touched by the son or daughter of the devil? Whose life and loved ones have been split asunder by the home wrecker's evil? Brothers and sisters, show such sinners no mercy! Shun them as you would the devil. Fight their evil ways, destroy them with your power, the power deep inside you, the power of God Almighty, for they are surely the hell-spawns of Satan."

Cynthia absorbed his words with rapt fascination. She felt her breath come in sharp gasps. It was as if his sermon were being addressed directly to her. It took effort for her to control her feeling of panic and her desire to run, to get out of his church.

After the service ended, as the congregation rose and slowly filed out, Jim Boyd walked up the aisle and stood next to her.

He escorted Cynthia to her sedan. The sky had clouded over. There was a rumble of distant thunder, and heavy raindrops began to fall. People scurried into their cars and drove from the parking lot.

Though the rain cooled things off a bit, the heat was still oppressive. When Cynthia and the Reverend reached the Rolls, Willie was dozing in the front seat; small beads of perspiration trickled down his forehead.

He awoke with a start when he heard Jim Boyd speak to him.

"If you move over, brother, I'll see if I can get this car started."

Pumping the gas pedal rapidly, twice in quick succession, he succeeded in bringing the ignition to life. The engine responded and purred like a kitten.

"The Lord be praised!" said Willie. "And thank you kindly, Reverend."

Jim Boyd felt tension in his neck as he waited in the vestibule of Tyson Hall. He tapped his prayer book and his pale eyes squinted; a thoughtful expression was on his face. He wondered if he should hit Cynthia Tyson with a request for another church donation today. He had to be sure not to move too quickly. She'd been mighty generous with the last one.

Boyd's eyes wandered through the open French doors, past the flower gardens and manicured lawns. He pulled his attention back into the vestibule and glanced at the fine paintings hanging from the high, ornate ceiling. As he studied the lavish, magnificent surroundings, he smelled the sweet scent of money all around him.

A reflective look came into Boyd's eyes. He reminded himself that he must tread very carefully and make no mistakes. His lips curved into a smile that somehow didn't reach his eyes. Renting the Tyson church might prove to be his luckiest move. He had rented the plain, white-frame church for a dollar; it sure as hell had a big pot of gold attached to it. It was going to be mighty important for Jim Boyd to gain Cynthia Tyson's complete confidence.

What he wanted above all else in the world was to be an evangelist superstar. He longed to take his place with the most successful practitioners in his field, the multimillionaire preachers on TV. He knew he was as good as any of them. Hell, once he got going, maybe he was better. He was a fuckin' spellbinder, that's what he was. Why shouldn't he be as rich as they? Why shouldn't he have his own church, his own limousine, and his own airplane? Why shouldn't he have their fame, their glamour and their power—especially their power?

His smile broadened, and his pale eyes shone with excitement. Mrs. Tyson, with all her money, might just be the one to make it all happen.

At that moment Cynthia Tyson entered the vestibule.

Jim Boyd stood up and fixed his pale eyes on her as he rose from the chair, his hands extended in greeting.

Cynthia greeted him coolly.

"What can I do for you, Reverend? What brings you here?"

Boyd cocked his head to one side, and his eyes narrowed with sudden suspicion. Cynthia Tyson seemed very self-confident today, much more so than the last time he had seen her. When he responded, his voice was deceptively soft.

"Do I judge by your tone that I'm not welcome, Mrs. Tyson?"

"No, not at all. It's just that my son Nick came home for a visit, and I'm afraid I have no time for anyone but him. It was very kind of you to pay me a call."

There was definitely dismissal in her words.

"Another thing," she added quickly, her voice almost

snappish. "I'm sure you are aware that we are members of
the Church of St. James and have been for generations."

It seemed to Jim Boyd that he was being put in his
place. He managed to keep his voice calm and devoid of
anger. Giving her a soft, sad smile, his tone remained
warm and casual as he spoke.

"Dear Mrs. Tyson, I hope you haven't mistaken my mo-
tives. I simply came here today to extend my help and to
offer the hand of friendship if ever you should desire it."

Seeing her expression soften a bit, he looked deep into
Cynthia Tyson's eyes. He paused for a moment before continuing, as if to give his next remark great importance.

"You know, from our very first meeting I could sense
the kind of woman you are. A good woman whose whole
life has been devoted to her family. The kind of moral
woman who has always been surrounded with love and
faith and trust. A woman who, if she ever came face to face
with the devil, would stand and do battle with him."

He stopped, casting his eyes downward in a gesture of
humility as he wrapped his large, flat hands around his
Bible. It was time to study the effect his words were having. He noticed a small nerve twitch under her left temple
and a flat, bitter smile flit across her face. Cynthia Tyson
had a wounded look in her eyes. Her lips trembled imperceptibly; her posture stiffened.

Jim Boyd surmised that his words had hit a part of her
life that was painful to her, but his expression gave no hint
of it. He determined to find out sometime just what it was
that Cynthia Tyson was hiding from the world.

Boyd smiled inwardly. For some reason he now felt in a
much stronger position of power with Cynthia Tyson.

"Well, I'll be going now, Mrs. Tyson. I do hope you'll
find the time to visit my church again. The kind donation

you gave will do so much toward spreading the word of God."

As he turned to leave, Jim Boyd noticed Nick Tyson leaning leisurely against the rich paneling of the vestibule and staring at him.

"Nick darling!" Cynthia called out to her son.

He smiled warmly at his mother and walked over to her with an easy air of self-assurance. Looking at her with warm affection, he casually put his arm around her as he spoke.

"So here you are, Cynthia. I went down to the barn looking for you. Well, are we going to exercise the horses, or have you changed your mind? I hope not, because it's a great day for a ride down to the beach."

Jim Boyd studied the scene carefully. He noticed the expression on Cynthia Tyson's face as she looked at her son. She gazed at him with such an expression of possessive love that it seemed to consume her. It was the look a woman usually gives her lover, or the man she wishes would be her lover.

Finally she pulled her eyes away from him. Her voice was light and youthful as she replied, "Reverend Boyd, I'd like you to meet my son, Nick."

Boyd felt a pair of cold blue eyes pinpointing him. There was no trace of a smile on the young man's face.

"Reverend," he said, stretching the word out with a sarcastic twinge. "Are you from around here? Or have you taken over the rectory at St. James?"

Although the voice was politely interested, there was a cutting edge to it.

Jim Boyd answered with a laugh, "No, young man, I didn't take over St. James. I rented the small, plain church on your father's property."

"Really?" The icy blue eyes of the young man gazed

over him. "We've had quite a few preachers do that in the past. None of them ever lasted very long."

The voice took on a taunting quality; the cool edge was still very much in evidence.

"This part of the country gets a lot of itinerent preachers passing through. They're mostly hellfire and brimstone, saber-rattling pulpit-thumpers. They put on a good show. You no doubt have lots of competition."

Boyd knew he had to remain calm no matter how much white-hot anger rushed through him. This rich, cocky bastard was making fun of him.

Throughout the exchange, Cynthia remained silent, content merely to observe. *How strange,* she thought. *It's as if Nick, who is always so gracious, has taken an instant dislike to the preacher for some reason.* She attributed it to his natural protectiveness toward her. It only made her love him more. What bliss it was going to be to have him here with her for the next few days!

Turning to Jim Boyd, she gave him an almost wintry smile and addressed him quite primly.

"Thank you again for paying us a call. My son will see you to the door."

As the door shut behind him, Jim Boyd raged inwardly; his thoughts pinballed around in his brain. Those bastards had dismissed him as if he were one of their nigger servants!

His jaw tightened as he stormed over to his van. *What the fuck was all that "dear, darlin' Cynthia" shit, anyway? Why can't the prick call his mother "Mother" like everyone else? Someday I'd like to punish that smirking smartass and take something of his away.*

Searching in his pocket for his keys, Boyd speculated about Cynthia Tyson. *She looks at her son like he's some sort of fuckin' idol!* Well, he'd just have to put her on the back burner for now. Later, when her charm boy went back to wherever the fuck he came from, he'd plan his next move.

As he climbed into his van, Jim Boyd suddenly thirsted for bourbon. He was ripe for a night of debauchery and a tight little cunt to go with it. He could always tell when the devil called: it was when his balls started to ache.

He sat quietly in the van; his large, heavy hands were pressed to his lips in a position of prayer. He had promised himself that he would make no careless moves in this town. But even as he cautioned himself, he knew what he was going to do. He was going to call Dolly and tell her to send over that new redheaded whore of hers. He'd never met a gal quite like her before. Even thinking about her made him shiver. He knew it would be dangerous to bring her to the church; there was always the risk of being found out. But in a way, that danger was the best fuckin' part of it.

Later that morning, the sun-warmed air caressed the faces of Cynthia and Nick Tyson as they rode their horses along the water's edge.

As they turned into the cove of their private beach, Nick looked around at the familiar scenery. There was the beach cottage, tucked among the clump of wind-twisted pines; its once-dark exterior was bleached by years of sun and wind. As lonely as ever, it hugged the beach, basking in the sun like a sleepy old dog.

Nick's head filled with thoughts of his father. There were so many wonderful memories here, memories of the past, of their once-happy family. He recalled his first time on water skis; his father had been at the wheel of the family speedboat. How carefully Charles Tyson had maneuvered the boat, and how proudly he had observed his young son's skill on the skis! He remembered the picnics and the barbecues, the horseback rides and the sailing races. Every memory of his father was a happy one. A shudder ran through him as he thought of his father now.

Today when he had visited him, Nick had been stricken with heartache; the gnawing pain had rushed through him again. He had had to fight to hold back tears as he looked at the withered figure hunched over in his wheelchair. How difficult it was to accept that his father was unaware that his son was at his side! Charles Tyson sat like an empty shell, a merely physical presence in the darkened room; his shattered brain stumbled along strange and lonely paths, and he lived in his own shadow world, oblivious to life around him.

Nick glanced over at his mother and admired her regal air as she sat astride her mare. He wondered about her. It was impossible to comprehend the nightmare she must now be living. Today more than ever, he was reminded of how she had adored his father. Their love had been so apparent to all who knew them.

Nick was filled with admiration for her. He was amazed at how well she seemed to cope with the heartbreak that he knew must be consuming her. Certainly in the privacy of her room, there must be many times when she'd broken down and wept, times when she could no longer restrain her grief. But always in private—only in private. Cynthia Tyson was a very private person and prided herself on keeping her emotions in check.

As he looked at her, Nick wondered if she was remembering the happy times of the past, as he was. Or was she bitterly decrying the cruel blow fate had dealt her? Her husband was still alive, but he had been taken from her forever.

As they came to the end of the cove, they turned their horses in unison and headed for home. Cynthia broke the silence between them.

"Nick darling," she said, a questioning tone to her voice, "why did you take such an obvious dislike to Reverend Boyd?"

Nick looked at her, puzzled.

"The preacher man? Is that who you mean, Cynthia?"

He paused for a moment. She nodded. He carefully considered his words.

"Well, you must admit he doesn't come across like a class act. Let's just say I couldn't warm up to the guy. Everything about him was smug, condescending, and patronizing. To me, there was something phony about him. I'll bet Dad would have felt the same way. Tell me, how did you ever meet him? What made him think he could come calling on you?"

"Actually, Reverend Boyd was most kind to me one day when my car broke down. He invited me into his church. You know, he's really quite a charismatic preacher. I remember giving him a donation. The man seems to be totally involved with God's work. Surely, darling, you don't mind if a man of the cloth comes to pay his respects?"

Nick fought back his feeling of resentment.

"Of course I don't mind. I just hope you'll remember that I'm always here to sort out any problem you may have."

Cynthia smiled to herself. Her son was feeling male. He was being protective and letting her know he felt responsible for her.

Later that evening, after his mother retired, Nick desperately missed Jan. He needed to hear the sound of her voice, so he decided to call her.

Minutes later, tapping his foot in impatient frustration, he listened to the echo of the distant rings.

"Come on, Jan. Where are you?" he muttered. He felt a sharp stab of irritation when the answering service picked up. Disappointed, Nick left no message and replaced the receiver.

Flopping down into a chair, Nick felt angry that Jan wasn't home. He chain-smoked a couple of cigarettes and wondered where she could be. Then he restlessly prowled the house and decided he had to get out, take a drive, unwind somewhere.

Chapter Twenty

At eleven o'clock, Nick walked into The Broadcasters Bar. Cat Bracken was on the small stage, her head bent forward; she was tuning her guitar and getting ready to perform. As the lights dimmed, the buzz of conversation in the crowded room came to a halt. Then Cat began to sing.

Her voice sounded like liquid gold to Nick as he stood leaning against the bar. When the song was finished, she stood in the spotlight for a moment and smiled seductively at the audience while acknowledging their applause.

Nick stared at her. Her beauty was as striking as her voice. Her wide, almost insolent smile and her tousled hair, piled high on her head, somehow made her look sexy and innocent at the same time.

Nick followed her with his eyes as she walked offstage. Then, just as he was making a mental note to learn who she was, he heard his name called. Turning, he saw his friend Richard Bradshaw beckon to him to join his table.

"How goes it, Nick? How long have you been in town?" Bradshaw asked.

Nick reached for the bottle of bourbon on the table, twisted the cap open, and poured himself a shot. Making a silent toast by suspending his glass in the air, he drained it in one sip. Then, feeling loose and relaxed, he replied, "Not long. How's it going, Richard? Who's your latest hobby—the new songbird with the honeyed pipes?"

Bradshaw looked knowingly at Nick, and a slow grin crossed his usually poker-face features.

"You noticed her, huh? Hell, you'd have to be blind not

to. Yeah, I have my eye on the lady, but I think her head is somewhere else."

Leaning back in his chair, Bradshaw crossed his arms over his chest and called out to Cat, who was bringing a round of drinks to the next table.

"Hey, sweetheart, come on over here. I want you to meet a pal of mine."

Seconds later, Nick was looking into a pair of blue eyes that seemed almost transparent. Cat stared back at him as if trying to bring him into focus.

She had a distinct sense of knowing him. A flutter of memories seemed to kaleidoscope in front of her; patchwork, hazy, with no details attached to them. She scrutinized his face as she spoke.

"Despite how it sounds, this isn't a come-on line, but I have a strange feeling that we've met before. You don't happen to remember me from anywhere, do you?"

Nick smiled at her. It was a warm, easy smile.

"No, can't say I do. I'm sure I would have remembered someone as lovely as you. Tell me, how did you ever learn to phrase a song the way you do? You're good. I mean, really good."

Cat acknowledged the compliment with a smile.

"Thanks, I needed that. But I've still got a long way to go. My breathing's way off. With more study I know I could do much better."

Nick replied quickly, almost without conscious thought, "Hey, I may just be able to give you what you need. Tell you what—how about having supper with me after you're through working?"

She hesitated as she looked at him thoughtfully. Then she nodded.

"Okay. You're on."

"Good. I'll be waiting at the bar."

* * *

It was nearly three A.M. before Cat returned to her rented room.

After dinner, she and Nick had talked the night away; they had effortlessly fallen into easy friendship and relaxed conversation. She told him what little she could remember of her past, mostly about Dirk and her desire to become a top-flight entertainer. Talking to Nick was easy; it was as if they had known each other for a very long time.

Cat was also a good listener; she seemed to hang on to every word. Nick enthusiastically went into great detail about the ship he planned to buy. Warming up to his subject, he described *Pleasure Palace* and explained the lavish way he planned to decorate it. He grinned boyishly as he admitted it was still just a vision in his mind, a big, floating dream waiting to be transformed into reality. But sooner or later he would turn that dream into a seagoing palace, a private club limited to one hundred members—those who could afford the one-million-dollar membership fee.

His eyes gleamed with excitement as he told how the selected one hundred could, if they wished, actually live aboard *Pleasure Palace* for a period of time and use her as a floating second home. The ship would have tickertapes, telexes, closed circuit TV, a telephone switchboard, satellite communication, a gambling casino, a helicopter—every conceivable modern convenience.

Cat knew from his tone of voice that she wasn't listening to a pie-in-the-sky daydream. Nick Tyson meant every word he said. As he spoke, his excitement seemed to feed upon itself.

Drawing a crude map on the tablecloth, he told her how the ship would cruise from Palm Beach to the southern coast of France, then on to Italy, Greece, or any other desired port of call. He then discussed the hundred staterooms, telling how he planned to make them more lavish, more ornate, and more sybaritic than any hotel suite in existence, using the finest marble, crystal, and wood. And of course the walls would be adorned with the most coveted works of art. He explained that he had already contacted one of the finest decorators available, giving him carte blanche to create the most mind-blowing adult playpen on earth. In short, *Pleasure Palace* would simply be the golden yardstick against which all other regal accommodations would have to be measured.

Finally Nick paused. He smiled almost sheepishly, as if he realized he had gotten carried away with his own oratory. After a few seconds of silence Cat asked him about himself and his family. Nick touched briefly on his background but seemed hesitant, as if he preferred to keep his private life private.

However, in answer to Cat's question about whether he was involved with anyone, he became almost rhapsodic. He confessed to being hopelessly, wildly in love with Jan Julliard. He said that he was counting the hours till he returned to London, where Jan was waiting for him.

Later that night, Cat stumbled into bed with her mind still focused on the events of the past few hours. Her excitement was so high that sleep eluded her.

She sensed that meeting Nick Tyson could be the most momentous thing that had ever happened to her. She had no idea why someone as wealthy as he would be interested in managing her career, but of one thing she was certain: she trusted him implicitly. Never had anyone raved that way about her singing. She still remembered the words he had used, words like *captivating, innocent, enthralling, talented,* and, most wonderful of all, *star quality.*

Cat glanced at the clock on the nightstand. Would the morning never come? Tomorrow she was to audition for a man named Pete Brody. Nick had arranged the whole thing, telling her that Brody had coached some of the very best.

Pounding her pillow, trying to turn off her thoughts, Cat finally willed herself to sleep.

It seemed only a matter of minutes before her alarm rang, waking her from a short and restless sleep.

After showering and dressing, Cat slid into her well-worn jeans and scuffed cowboy boots. Then she pulled a man-size sweater over her head and turned toward the mirror. Pushing her hair back from her face, she inspected the strands of silver that flecked her auburn curls. "Damn it," she murmured under her breath. They seemed to be multiplying. Soon she'd have to start coloring her hair.

For a long, quiet minute she looked at her reflection, her thoughts far away.

"Dirk darling," she whispered softly, "wish me luck."

Then Cat's soft, full mouth curved into a smile. Somehow the mention of his name seemed to reassure her.

She wrapped the raincoat belt tightly around her waist and slung her bag over her shoulder. Then, reaching into her closet, she took the old army hat from its peg and tucked her mop of curls under it.

Once again she stared at her reflection, this time winking at herself almost defiantly. Then she turned and opened the door of the small room. Feeling eager and confident, Cat walked out into the street.

One hour later she was in a darkened studio in downtown Fort Jade, together with Nick, Pete Brody, a musical director, and a sound man. They were all waiting to hear her sing.

Brody scrutinized Cat, trying to visualize the best on-stage image for her. She certainly had a great little body,

and her hair was dynamite. He even approved of the gray
in it. Of course, she ought to make it all silver and wear it
wild. Turquoise jewelry—yes, that would be terrific on her.
It would match the color of her dazzling eyes. Nope, there
would be no problem making this lady look like a star.

The only question was, could she sing? Only one way to
find out.

"Hit her with a single strobe!" Brody yelled to one of the
lighting technicians. Then he turned to Cat.

"Okay, me darlin', we're all set for you. Now let's hear
those pipes of yours."

Cat nodded and licked her lips. They felt strangely dry.
Her throat was tight and tense. Taking a deep breath, she
made a false start.

"Sorry," she whispered.

Brody's smile was encouraging, his voice coaxing.

"Nervous, darlin'? Sure, it's natural. But no need for it
here. We're all with you, so let's just take it again."

As he turned away, Brody muttered under his breath to
one of the musicians.

"Shit, I hope we're not wasting our time with some
Nancy-No-Talent just because Nicky-boy has the hots for
her. A broad with a voice like a frog can sound like Strei-
sand when a guy has a hard-on."

Meanwhile, Nick smiled a smile at Cat that gave her
confidence. As their eyes met, a flow of adrenaline rushed
through her. She knew she wouldn't screw up this time.

Minutes later, her throaty voice was filling the studio.

As soon as Brody heard her range, he relaxed. Her voice
was warm and rich. It seemed to sensually caress every
note she sang. Oh yes, the lady had potential to spare.
Listening to her was like an emotional roller-coaster ride.
Brody's private test for singing talent was, Did it give him
a certain horny feeling? Well, he was sure feeling it now.

Her voice slid in and out of the speakers like golden treacle. The way she held her notes for one extra heartbeat was electrifying. Then she'd slide down to velvet undertones that wrapped themselves around the room and everything in it.

Yes, oh yes, the lady could sing. The pro in him knew she could use some sessions in phrasing and maybe breath control. Also, she'd need time to develop her style, work with an audience, let herself grow as a performer. But Brody was certain that Cat Bracken possessed star quality, that indefinable something that entertainers were either born with or not.

After the final notes, there were a few seconds of silence, and Cat looked questioningly around the room. Then applause rang out from everyone in the studio, from everywhere at once, from all the cynical, jaded professionals, and from a triumphant-looking Nick Tyson.

Cat let the sound wash over her. It was probably the most glorious moment of her life.

Later, in Brody's office, he and Nick engaged in a serious discussion about contracts and percentages. They also pondered the best musical group to provide Cat's back-up and the best vocal coach for her. Nick told Brody to spare no expense; he would foot every bill.

Wrapped in whirling thoughts, Cat paid little attention to what they were saying. Her nervousness and tension had been replaced by a warm and comforting sense of euphoria. She had absolutely no doubt that fate was about to give her everything she had ever wanted.

Beaming with approval, Nick turned and smiled at her. Cat lazily focused on his deep blue eyes—eyes that more than ever seemed strangely familiar to her. Beneath her grateful smile her thoughts ran wild. How dramatically her life had changed in the short time she had known Nick

Tyson! Their chance meeting had given her the break she needed. Cat Bracken was now on her way, and this time she was ready. Nothing could stop her from reaching the golden ring now.

Chapter Twenty-one

Mark Squire could hardly believe that nearly a year had gone by since his arrival in Paris.

Luckily, he had been able to give Korda, Rook, and the other staff members a bonus generous enough that he didn't have to worry about the running of his Madison Avenue salon while he was gone.

But he still wasn't happy. He couldn't shake the depression that had come over him when he learned that Jan wouldn't be returning to New York. Mark had never been in love before, although he had known dozens of women. But this time had been different. He was in love with Jan Julliard.

He kept asking himself, Why her? What was this hold she had over him? He had lost his heart the first time he laid eyes on her, and he still felt the same. He couldn't stop thinking of her jade-green eyes, her perfect mouth, and her indescribably graceful figure. Jan was the only girl he'd ever met who affected him this way.

Why couldn't she feel the same about him? There was a time, back there for just a moment, when he was sure she did. But the mood was fragile; the timing had been off.

The practical side of Mark Squire knew how pointless it was to bemoan the fact that the lady loved somebody else. There had been a brief period when he had hoped that she might fall out of love as fast as she fell in. But she didn't.

That was why Manhattan had palled on him. Without Jan, there was nothing to hold him there.

The remedy seemed obvious to Mark: He would get

away. He and Antonio Bono had often talked about expanding his horizons, going abroad, seeing the world. So after a long, soul-searching conversation with the old man, that's what Mark decided to do. They decided that France was the logical destination for someone in the hair salon business.

Mark was lucky. Shortly after his arrival in Paris, he met Pierre Gravet at a hair-styling show.

Gravet was well-known in the European beauty trade. A man of great charm and proven talent, he hit it off beautifully with his American counterpart. It wasn't long before the two men decided to pool their talent and open a salon in the shadow of the Eiffel Tower.

And then Mark had his second stroke of luck. He learned that his new partner's father was a chemist associated with some of the most prestigious international cosmetics firms in the United States and abroad. It seemed to Mark that fate was making amends by dealing him a winning hand. In Paris, with his new-found partner, he would do what he had always dreamed of doing: launch his own line of hair and beauty products.

Their chic salon, which they named Tresses, was an instant success. Geared to the life-style of the on-the-go socialite, its fame spread throughout the city. Staffed with the finest hairdressers money could buy, its brilliant haircuts and its sophisticated approach to tone and taste made Tresses the most sought-after beauty salon in Paris.

Mark and Pierre were already planning to open additional salons in Cannes, St. Tropez, and Monte Carlo. Their hair and beauty products, now being formulated in the laboratory of Pierre's father, would be marketed under the name Tresses.

Today Mark was preoccupied as he stared out over the

rooftops of the Left Bank and listened to tiny French sparrows chirping happily in the blooming chestnut trees.

With a sigh he turned from the window and sat down at his desk. He looked idly over some of the layouts scattered on his desk. He studied them for a moment without really seeing them and drummed his fingers absently on his desk.

Hearing the door to his office open, he pivoted around in his black leather swivel chair. Mark's smile was wide and warm when he saw that his visitor was Pierre Gravet. Waving him to a chair, Mark spoke without waiting for the usual pleasantries.

"Hi, good old partner. You couldn't have come at a better time. I was just thinking that we have one small problem. You and I still haven't decided how to get our products out to the public. We'll be using your dad's concoctions in our salons here and in New York. But that's small potatoes compared to the worldwide market out there. I want shopgirls in Seattle, nurses in Norway, housewives in Holland—I want females all over this whole damned globe to be panting for tins of Tresses. I don't want a bored, couldn't-give-a-shit distributor to dump our products on dealers' shelves and hope someone finds them. I want every beauty-seeking mother's daughter to clamor for it."

Then Mark leaned back in his chair and clasped the nape of his neck in both hands. He seemed to be trying to find the right words for what he wanted to say. Finally he just grinned and continued talking.

"Pierre, if it's okay with you, I want to represent our company. I want to be the spokesman, the barker, the guy who talks it up. Maybe I've got a hunk of the huckster in me, but I don't want to let anyone else handle it. I want to buy TV time for us, get a dynamite ad campaign going, and plan the marketing."

Mark stopped to catch his breath as he leaned forward and searched his partner's face for a reaction.

"Well, say something, will ya? What do you think of the idea?"

Pierre's soulful brown eyes rolled upward in an exaggerated expression of sheer delight.

"Fantastique! You will make me a very rich man, *mon cher partenaire."*

Mark grinned and drew in a quick breath as he experienced an instant high. He had known there would be no problem with Pierre. How lucky he was to have such a terrific guy for his partner!

"Well then, if it's okay with you, Pierre, let me tell you the rest of it. I contacted a friend of mine in New York. His name is Daley Russell. He's dynamite when it comes to filming commercials. He is numero uno in his field—the absolute best. Right now I'm waiting for his phone call."

Pushing his chair back, Mark turned toward the telephone as if willing it to ring. Both men sat silently for a few moments until the private line's red light lit up. Mark reached for it with a knowing smile.

"Hello? . . . Yes, I've been waiting for your call . . . You will? Fantastic! I'll leave this weekend and be in your New York studio early Monday morning."

Mark hung up the phone.

"Wow, Pierre, it's hard to believe that so much has happened to us in such a short time. We're really on a roll. I feel as if nothing can stop us."

Pierre laughed.

"You Americans are ingenious the way you decide things and move so quickly. We French ponder matters for a long time. Being associated with you has been most exhilarating to me. Your enthusiasm makes mere business seem like an exciting adventure. So I, for one, will be delighted to share in your coming triumphs—or should I say *our* coming triumphs?"

Mark poked the Frenchman playfully in the ribs.

"Hey, partner, you ain't seen nothin' yet."

Feeling pleasantly jubilant, Mark poured each of them a drink as his thoughts whirled around in his head. He couldn't wait to start work on the Tresses campaign. He was sure that he could create a unique and compelling ad campaign, and Daley Russell's powerful photographic style would certainly give it the impact it needed. He knew the two of them would be a good team.

And if he lost himself totally in his work, perhaps he'd be able to forget about Jan.

Pierre's rich, Gallic tones interrupted his daydreaming. "And what is next on the agenda, my friend?"

Smiling at him, Mark reached for the phone again.

"This calls for a celebration. We'll have champagne, Beluga caviar, and a night on the town. I'll book a table at L'Accord. I hear the club's been bought by an Arab billionaire who's tearing it down for God knows what reason. This will be their last show, so tonight they're sure to go all out. Just think—the end of L'Accord and the start of a new era for us. It's kismet, my friend."

Sarah Hartley walked naked into the bedroom of Daley Russell's New York apartment. Daley, lying lazily on the bed, was also naked. He had just hung up the phone; his mind was still full of his conversation with Mark Squire.

Stretching across the plump eiderdown, Sarah cuddled next to him.

Then she rolled over on the bed and reached for a joint. Lighting it, she inhaled deeply and let her head fall gently back onto Daley's navel. When she spoke, it was in an exaggerated, low, sexy tone.

"Let's get laid."

"I can't believe you," Daley replied, shaking his head as he appreciatively scanned the lines of her body. "Don't you even have any curiosity about who I was speaking to in Paris? I mean, it can't be more than a half-hour since our last session. I'm beginning to think you could screw all day long."

Sarah smiled her best fuck-you smile and langorously stretched her legs.

"You've noticed, have you? Well, it so happens my taste runs to carnal-type activities."

As she spoke, she ran her hand slowly over his chest and pulled gently on the short, dark hairs clustered in the center. Then she handed him her joint.

"So tell me, who was the mystery man on the telephone, and why should little Sarah care?"

She moved her hand down until it reached Daley's thigh and at the same time blew in his ear with her warm breath.

"Don't make it too long a story, lover," she whispered. "I'd like to get laid while I'm still young enough to enjoy it —that is, of course, if you can still raise the mast. After all, twice in one hour can be tough for a guy over forty."

Daley calmly placed his arms over his naked chest and strove for as much dignity as possible under the circumstances.

"In case nobody ever told you, you're about as funny as a fever blister, lady, and nearly as welcome."

Sarah smiled up at him, impudently.

"Oh, Daley, you're so sexy when you get angry! Come on, baby, I was only teasing. I'm dying to know who phoned."

Daley rolled over onto his side to find a more comfortable position. Then he looked expressionlessly into Sarah's bold, black eyes.

"Cut the crap, Sarah. I'll tell you anyway. The guy on the phone was Mark Squire."

"Mark Squire? You're kidding!" Sarah said, a new note of interest in her voice.

"I kid thee not," smiled Daley proudly. "Who else but Dashing Daley Russell, the Demon Photographer, could shoot the kind of glamorous, glitzy commercial that Squire wants?"

"Commercial? What kind of commercial?" asked Sarah, flexing her tummy as she did her pelvic thrust exercises.

Daley answered slowly. Focusing on his own words required a conscious effort because he was already occupied with the new project in his mind's eye. He could almost feel himself looking through the lens of his camera and filming the commercial.

Shaking his head as if to clear his thoughts, he replied, "Mark wants to be the on-air spokesman for his own products. He intends to become a *muy* big maven in the hair and beauty game. Me, I know how to capture him on film. He's got the kind of look girls dream about. And he's got the voice and the smile to go with it. There's a lot of romance in the guy, and I'm the shutterbug who'll see that it comes out on the screen. I'll make women wanna kill for him. Hell, at the very least I'll make them buy his products!"

As he talked, Daley put his arm casually around Sarah. She cuddled up close and tickled his feet with her own. Then she let her own thoughts lazily drift by.

She knew how important her relationship with Daley had become to her and how much she enjoyed it. She wondered if she was falling in love with him. If so, she also knew she was one very stupid female.

Sarah sighed heavily. Of course she knew what kept their relationship going. When you came right down to it, the glue that bonded them was sex. They were great in the sack together.

Nothing else between them had really changed. Still, Sarah had a feeling that Daley's infidelities had been tapering off of late. But for how long? Time and again she had thought to herself that he would always be a cheater.

Sarah's thoughts suddenly leaped ahead. In two months Daley would be leaving for London, where Jan was now living, and then on to Wales. That was where he was scheduled to film his first movie.

Without quite realizing it, Sarah began an internal dialogue with herself.

Oh, God, how I hope he takes me along.

Hey, come on, Sarah, don't be so insecure. Of course he'll take you. You're the very best assistant he's ever had. You're one of the few people who can control his explosive temper tantrums. You keep everything smooth and organized in his life. Even though the idiot may not be aware of it, he would be totally lost without you. You have definitely become an oasis in the desert of Daley Russell's life.

Sarah's thoughts were interrupted by Daley's erection rubbing against her flesh.

He said nothing. He just slid his fingers slowly, deeply into her and made her squirm under his touch. In Daley's lovemaking there was always crazy urgency—to which she inevitably responded. There were never any love words between them. Daley never made promises.

He just happened to be one hell of a lover.

Chapter Twenty-two

There was great excitement at Club L'Accord.

The night spot was jammed with the crème de la crème of French society. No one who mattered in the social whirl would dream of missing the last performance of the beautiful Parisian mystery lady.

Flashbulbs and strobes caught everyone in sight. Russian caviar was served as casually as potato chips, and bottles of Dom Perignon popped at every table.

Standing in the wings, Pythias looked out over his crowded club. He knew that this would be a memorable party, the last one ever for L'Accord. And that was exactly what he wanted. None of the revelers had the slightest suspicion that their entire tabs would be picked up for them at the end of the evening.

Noticing a contingent of society publicists sitting at one of the front tables, he smiled to himself. They were all here: the ones from *Women's Wear Daily*, *Le Temps*, *Vogue*, *People*, *Stern*, *Rolling Stone*, *Tatler*. All the right publications, eager to record the last performance of his star.

His mind went back to the day she had walked into his club. Ever since that first performance, he had always thought of Lear Feria as "she." Her first performance had launched a major new career. Curiosity about the electrifying beauty had begun that very first evening. *Why is nothing known about her personal life? Where did she come from?* Questions about her were on everybody's lips. Pythias had managed to keep her identity a secret.

Soon, outrageous gossip filled the columns. The press pounced on every rumor and wrote elaborate stories about her. Pythias savored every word of every write-up. When questioned about her, he'd merely shrug his shoulders and answer tolerantly. But the questions never stopped.

Who is she? Where did she come from? Is it true that she is the illegitimate daughter of an ex-President of the United States? Or the banished daughter of a British nobleman? The ex-mistress of a Greek tycoon? Admit it, Pythias, isn't she a harlot you found on the streets of Paris?

Pythias laughed knowingly, showing his shark teeth. Then he added tidbits of his own, telling of her endless gifts of fabulous jewels, her offers of marriage from the world's wealthiest men, the countless suicide threats made by those she had rejected.

And now they were all here to catch a last glimpse of the beautiful mystery lady, the gorgeous enigma whose name and background were still unknown. All this time he had kept her secret.

Pythias turned and saw his glamorous star walk toward him.

"Hello, luv," he exclaimed in his soft cockney voice. "Are you all right? You won't be doing this act much longer now, will you?"

Lear's eyes were warm with affection as he looked at his beaming friend.

"I want you to know, Pythias, that I don't think I could ever have made it this far if not for you and Damon."

"Come on, luv, don't go laying any trips on yourself. You're a bloody winner, a great star, and that's for sure. You're starting your new life at the top of the bloody 'eap. Listen, luv, all the glitterati are out there waiting for you to knock 'em dead. When they yell and holler for an encore, don't give 'em one. Leave 'em wantin' you, pantin' for you, hungry for more. That's the way to say good-bye."

Lear's large mahogany eyes were moist as he smiled at Pythias. There was no one in the whole world for whom he felt such deep affection. Pythias and Damon had been his friends, always there for him. Yet after tonight, he knew they would never meet again.

His voice was calm and gentle as he spoke.

"And you, dear Pythias, what will you do? Where will you go after tonight's show?"

An amused expression crossed Pythias's face, and he rubbed his skull-like head.

"Well, luv, Damon and I might just retire to the south of France. Maybe we'll buy a villa in Monaco and spend the rest of our lives sailing up and down the Côte d'Azure in a bloody big yacht, just like the idle rich. Why not? Considering what we were paid for the club, we've become one of them. However, Damon fancies Australia, so that's where we'll probably end up."

He let out a loud cackle.

"Maybe we'll open another L'Accord down under and bring a little culture to the Aussie masses."

Then he gave Lear a ribald wink.

"After all, luv, I 'ear they're just starting to come out of the closet down there."

As they both laughed, Pythias's face took on a strange, sad look.

"All right, luv, time to smile and get ready for the photographers. They're all out there waiting for you."

Lear checked his makeup and stepped toward the wings for his final entrance. But he turned to look again at Pythias.

"Good-bye, dear friend. I thank you from the bottom of my heart."

Parting the red velvet curtain, he stood motionless for a moment, a nonchalant look on his beautiful face. Then he languidly moved to center stage and picked up a sequined mike. With an enigmatic smile, he softly whispered into it.

"Tonight I feel hot, naughty, and outrageous."

The husky voice was low and seductive as he moved down into his audience. He threaded his way among the crowded tables, pausing at every single one. The silver rhinestone Bob Mackey dress he wore was ablaze with light as the spot followed his graceful figure.

Sitting with Pierre, Mark Squire was fascinated by the performer.

Finally Lear reached their table.

"Hello, gorgeous," crooned the soft voice, flirting blatantly with him. "I'll be sure to remember you when next I fantasize."

Then Lear returned to the stage, teasing and tantalizing, the ultimate seductress, the sex goddess of every man's dreams.

When it ended, the applause was deafening. It threatened never to stop. The revelers shouted, stamped their feet, and pounded on the tables with cries of "More! More! More!"

But Lear simply blew them a kiss, and pivoting on stiletto heels, he vanished into the wings for the last time.

Minutes later, a black-windowed Mercedes limousine glided up to the stage entrance of Club L'Accord.

The chauffeur let the motor idle. He sat motionless, staring straight ahead. An armed bodyguard rose from the front seat and slowly left the car. He looked appraisingly around him. Then, with a catlike tread unusual for one so powerful, he walked to the stage door, where he stationed himself and patiently waited.

A short time later, a sable-clad woman in a turban and dark glasses walked into the waiting car, escorted by the burly, dark-skinned bodyguard.

The chauffeur kept his eyes glued to the road ahead as the softly purring limousine glided through the traffic to Orly Airport. Reaching their destination, he made a sharp right turn and stopped at a guarded gate. The car was speedily cleared by security. He continued driving about five hundred yards onto a private runway. There he pulled alongside a sleek silver-hued jet whose twin Rolls-Royce engines were idling, ready for takeoff.

Within seconds the woman was aboard.

She wandered through the luxuriously decorated lounge and threw her sable stole carelessly over a gold velvet chair. Then she walked into the bathroom, sat down at a gold-mirrored makeup table, and removed her dark glasses and turban.

As her rich black hair cascaded to her shoulders, she gazed at herself thoughtfully in the mirror. Her beautiful face took on an amused smile as she whispered to her image, "After all these years of never fitting in, of never really belonging, I've finally made my choice. Pythias was right. I'm starting all over again. But this time I'm where I want to be."

Moments later, the plane was airborne.

Chapter Twenty-three

Jan gasped for breath after the last exercise.

Beads of perspiration trickled down her face. Just ten more minutes, and the class would be over. She was enjoying it, even though her muscles ached and her legs burned.

"Okay, me pretty birds, one more time," Scotty, the instructor, called out.

"Bend the torso, grab the ankles, tuck in the arse, suck in the pelvis, and breathe. Yes, breathe, me lovelies. One, two, three, four—up we come. Slowly, luvs. Stretch. Up with the arms, reach for it. You're all bloody marvelous! Now hit the floor and reeeeelax."

Stretching his own superb torso and twitching his tight little ass, Scotty moved over to the phonograph and switched the music off.

"Fuck this!" said Sarah, collapsing onto the floor. She grabbed her towel and wiped the sweat off her brow.

Jan stretched out, breathing slowly, trying to relax every muscle. Then she stood up and looked at her colorful reflection in the studio mirror. The orange leotard looked great with her taffy-colored hair. Her bright pink leg warmers were stretched over aqua tights. She viewed her body critically. Her figure looked pretty good. Her waist was tiny; her tummy flat. Her "arse," as Scotty called it, could be a mite tighter. Next class she'd talk to him about it and really work on it.

Jan and Sarah walked to the locker room and grabbed large, fluffy towels from an Indian attendant. They showered in the clean, scented stalls. Then, wrapping their towels around them and carrying their toiletries, they walked into the white, Spanish-style pool and sauna area of London's most elegant exercise club.

Colorful Mayan birds and parrots squawked loudly from their perches as the girls passed sunken pools filled with trailing exotic plants. Then down a short flight of stairs to a tiled courtyard bedecked with potted orchids. Finally into the dry heat of the sauna.

They were lucky today. They had the sauna all to themselves.

"God!" Sarah groaned, stretching out on her towel. "Now, this is what I call sheer heaven. I could stay here all day. How I totally despise exercising! I always did. I'll never know how I let you talk me into this, only two days after a transcontinental flight. Of course, on the other hand, I must admit, fantasizing about Scotty makes it almost worthwhile. He sure is cute. I'll bet he's some great lay. Imagine the control a physical instructor like him would have!"

She rolled onto her stomach.

"Can't you just hear him in the lovemaking department?" she asked, laughing mimicking Scotty. " 'In, out. In, out. Now you're getting the 'ang of it, luv. Lock in the pelvis, suck in the arse. Squeeze those loverly thighs together. Look out, dolly, 'ere comes the mighty pelvic thrust.' "

Sarah thrust her crotch into the towel and gave her best version of an exaggerated, passionate groan.

"Can't you just picture him moaning, 'I'm coming, dolly, I'm coming'? His orgasm would probably shake the walls."

She looked up at Jan with a salacious smile on her face.

"Now *that's* the kind of exercise little Sarah could really get into."

Jan sat up laughing. Then she took a large pot of Astral cream and smoothed it over her body.

Sarah also took some of the cream and massaged it into her face. After that, she settled back on her towel and let out a deep sigh of pleasure.

"All I need now is a joint, and I'd be in heaven."

They were both silent for a moment. Jan sensed Sarah's mind shift gears as she broke the silence.

"Jan, tell me something. You and Nick—is he still the one for you? Are you still deliriously happy doing whatever the man wants? I mean, does your every mood still fit in with his? Don't you ever have any regrets about giving up your career for him?"

With a quick glance at Sarah, Jan shook her head and smiled.

"Nope, not even the slightest, tiniest little regret do I have."

"Then why the hell don't the two of you get married?"

Jan's eyes flicked to Sarah's, then down again.

"Come on, Sarah, you know why. I've certainly mentioned it enough in my letters to you. I've told you how very involved Nick is with that new business venture of his. He wants to make it a great success, and it takes up almost all his time. Marriage is simply not on our minds right now. But don't lose any sleep over it. I can assure you that Nick and I will marry as soon as the time is right."

Sarah's eyes were bright and brittle as she replied, "Well, I guess the two of you know what you're doing. I hope so, anyway."

Silence filled the sauna as both women luxuriated in the

heat, each occupied with her own thoughts. It was Jan who next broke the silence.

"And you, Sarah?" Jan asked with the slightest touch of impatience in her voice. "Do you know what you're doing? I mean, are you still infatuated with Daley? And is he still, as you used to say, the best lay in town?"

Sarah nodded her head.

"Absolutely, positively. I can say that without reservation. If he were a movie, he'd get a four-star rating. The man is sexually insatiable, just like me. But I also know his bad points. He'll never be a one-woman man. But who cares? Let him complicate his life with little seductions if he must, just as long as he keeps coming back to me. What he does when little Sarah isn't around is his business. The important thing is that, when we're together, he sees to it that I have no complaints."

For the next few moments, Sarah seemed to forget that Jan was in the sauna with her. It was as if she were lost in contemplation, alone in a shadow world with her thoughts of Daley Russell. Then she began to speak again, half to herself.

"In our relationship, I have to always guard myself against becoming the complaining bitch—that is, if I want a happy ending."

Sarah drew a quick breath.

"Putting any pressure on Daley Russell would be the surest way to lose him."

Jan knew that Sarah's flippant attitude was merely a subterfuge that hid real pain. Sarah had always discredited the merits of romantic love. But she hadn't been the same since she first laid eyes on Daley Russell. It was obvious that he affected her more than any other man ever had.

Sarah suddenly laughed out loud.

"Well, enough about me. Let's change the subject. Did

you know that Daley shot a fantastic commercial for Mark Squire just before we left New York? I was there, working as the stylist on the set. Mark arrived with the most beautiful model. And were they ever cozy! Of course, for all I know, he may be that cozy with all his models. Anyway, he was on-camera himself as the spokesman for his new cosmetics company. Let me tell you, the man is a natural: smooth, easy, dynamite-looking. He could sell ice to an Eskimo."

Sarah wrapped her towel around her and poured more water on to the hot coals. Then she turned back to Jan, who was lying supine on her towel.

"Boy, Daley really outdid himself when he photographed Mark. Granted, he had a great subject to work with, but he made him look sincere, friendly, boy-next-doorish, and terrifically sexy-looking at the same time. Daley knew just how to shoot him. It was as if they'd been working together for years."

Jan sat up and wiped her face with her towel. Sarah's dark eyes met hers, as if waiting for a reaction to her words.

Swift memories of Mark surfaced. Jan recalled the first time they met. She could always picture him easily. He never seemed blurred to her. Mark was the kind of man she had thought she wanted.

Of course, that was before she'd met Nick.

Jan smiled softly and felt quite pleased as she turned to Sarah.

"It sounds like it was a wonderful session. I'm very happy for Mark. But then, I'm not surprised that he was good on-camera. I'd expect Mark Squire to be sensational at anything he did. He's bright, charming, talented, and attractive—one of the most together men I've ever known."

She rose to her feet and reached for a towel.

"If we stay here any longer, we'll melt away."

Back home again, Jan stripped off her exercise clothes, showered, and rolled her long hair in rag rollers. Tonight she wanted to look totally outrageous because she would be meeting Nick later at Promises. Friday was always the club's most exciting night.

Reaching for a couple of magazines, she stretched out on the bed to relax awhile.

She opened the thick, glossy issue of one of the more stylish European magazines. As she idly scanned the society gossip column, reading the usual overblown tidbits of scandal, one name jumped out at her.

"Our spies inform us that Jaafar al Hassad, one of the Middle East's superrich oil barons, was married today in a private ceremony. The identity of the bride, who was heavily veiled and gowned in traditional Arab dress, is still unknown."

Jan's thoughts were on Jaafar as she dressed. He was so different from anyone she had ever known. At first she had found him terribly imposing, but she had come to like him more each time they met. She wondered whom he had married. Had the wedding been arranged? Was it a girl who'd been pledged to him from childhood? Or was it an affair of the heart? She hoped it was the latter. She wondered if Nick knew about the marriage.

Minutes later, as she ran her bath water, she dismissed it all from her mind. Soaking lazily in the tub, she started to think about what to wear to the club tonight.

Promises was crowded when she walked in with Nick.

Jan made a dramatic entrance with her long hair all frizzed out. She wore a short Ossie Clark red silk jersey and armfuls of deco plastic bracelets. There was a haughty sensuality about her. She knew she looked terrific by the glances shot at her from admiring males and females alike.

With studied deliberation, Nick pulled her close to him. The implication to the room at large was crystal clear: This lady was Nick Tyson's woman.

Later, seated at their table, Nick held up his glass to make a pronouncement. Jan almost missed his first few words as she stared at him tenderly, marveling at his beautiful profile.

"Next week, honey, I have to fly to the States. I want to bring you with me to meet Cynthia. It's important to me that she learn to love you as I do."

He took a sip of champagne. Then, reaching across the table, Nick gently cradled Jan's hand in his.

"Then, darling, you and I will get married."

As Nick's words took root, Jan went weak with happiness, and her mind went spinning. They had been living together for over a year now. Marriage was what she had really wanted, what she had always dreamed of.

Yet it was such a serious business. It was the most important single decision a woman could make, one that had to last forever. *Forever.* That was the only way she would have it. Yet were they both ready for such a commitment? It seemed they were still learning about each other.

A tiny frown crossed her beautiful face. There was a small, niggling worry, one little thing that she couldn't forget as she ran Nick's words over in her mind.

He had mentioned how important it was to him that Cynthia love Jan. Well, what if she didn't? What if they didn't hit it off? Would that stop Nick from loving her? Would it stop the marriage?

She shook her head impatiently, as if to push that foolish thought from her mind. It was ridiculous to dwell on such a thing. Why on earth wouldn't she and the mother of the man she loved hit it off?

Hearing no response, Nick squeezed Jan's hand.

"Jesus, honey, why the worried look? I didn't think you'd take so long to answer. If you're contemplating a change of heart, forget it. You're mine now, lady. Now and always. It's just you and me. In case it slipped your mind, we love each other."

Then Nick leaned closer; his expression was serious. She wondered what he was about to say as he slowly whispered in her ear, "And, hey, don't we fuck beautifully together?"

That did it for her. It broke the pensive mood. It banished the gathering doubts. Relieved and lighthearted once again, Jan burst out laughing.

Pleased at her reaction, Nick touched his glass to hers as they continued.

"Baby, here's to us. You and I belong together. There are no problems, no pitfalls ahead—trust me. The two of us are one great team, and our life is gonna be sensational. Guaranteed."

It was all Jan wanted to hear. She would go to Tysons Landing to meet Nick's mother. And, as Nick said, their life would be sensational.

Guaranteed.

Chapter Twenty-four

Cynthia Tyson walked into the drawing room, coldly aware of its sheer perfection; everything glistened, everything was perfectly tended and cared for. Her smile was humorless. At one time this sight would have pleased her. Now it was just a room full of yesterday's memories.

Sometimes a distant thought, the remembrance of a happy occasion, came to mind. But Cynthia would push it away. There was no room in her heart for tender memories.

She sat in a straight-back chair and thought of her son. She glanced at her watch, then moved her hands nervously to her hair. She rose, walked over to a brandy decanter, and poured herself a double shot, which she quickly downed.

Returning to the chair, she sat down again and waited.

It was cool and quiet inside the room. A soft summer breeze fluttered the curtains.

The wheels of a car crushing the gravel in the driveway told Cynthia they had arrived.

Walking over to the window, her whole body tightened as she silently peered through the curtains.

Nick was coaxing a slim, long-haired girl out of the car. They stood for a moment laughing about something.

Cynthia forced her eyes away from the window. Then, hearing the peal of the doorbell, she counted old Willie's steps as he shuffled down the hall to open the door and welcome them.

She sat in her room waiting and heard the chatter of

voices. A few seconds later, Nick was standing silhouetted against the high arch of the doorway.

Smiling, he said, "Cynthia, you look just beautiful!"

Cynthia felt tears flood her eyes. How could she ever let anyone take him away from her when she loved him so?

Then she turned to look at the young woman standing close to Nick as if he were her security. The girl was taller than she had expected and really quite lovely to look at. But her heavy blond hair and full generous mouth were a little too sensuous for Cynthia's taste.

"Cynthia, this is Jan, the girl I want to marry."

She forced herself not to wince at the words. Instead, she smiled and concealed her feelings as if wearing a mask.

"Hello, Jan. Welcome to Tyson Hall."

The girl stared at her for a second. When she spoke, her voice was soft and husky.

"I want you to know I love your son very much, Mrs. Tyson. I hope we will have your blessing."

Cynthia nodded quietly.

"Yes, I see. I quite understand."

Her tone was courteous but detached and reserved. She put her arm through her son's with an air of studied possessiveness.

"Nick darling, I've arranged for tea in the gazebo. Do come along, Jan. Just follow us."

An elderly black lady put her arms around Nick. The white uniform that covered her ample frame was as starched as a nun's wimple. Alpha Brown's whole life had been spent serving the Tyson family. She had walked the floor with Nick when he had the colic as a baby and had chased away his nightmares when he was a toddler. When Nick introduced her to Jan, a warm smile stretched across her face. It was a smile of approval for Mr. Nick's young lady.

Minutes later, while clearing away the tea tray, Alpha turned to Mrs. Tyson.

"Will that be all, ma'am?"

"Yes, Alpha. Now I would appreciate your showing Miss Julliard to her room. You can help her unpack."

Jan's room was spacious, with high ceilings and tall windows. Nothing in the house seemed to be in current fashion; everything had a timeless look to it. Seating herself in a small slipper chair, her eyes wandered around the room. The walls were covered in a romantic floral fabric. Two fat, round armchairs in faded rose-colored velvet sat in front of a carved marble fireplace. Jan felt it was a room for daydreaming.

She was fascinated by the speed with which Alpha unpacked her belongings and hung her clothes in a large, airy closet that smelled of lavender.

"Thanks so much for unpacking for me," she said, smiling appreciatively. "I guess this is what they mean by southern hospitality."

Alpha's round face beamed.

"That's right, miss. It's jus' the only way we know. Now, you go right along and get yourself settled in, hear? There'll be cocktails at six in the sun parlor, same as always. Then you'll be meeting Mr. Nick's daddy."

Alpha made a clicking sound with her tongue. Then she talked as if to herself, shaking her head from side to side.

"That poor, poor Mr. Charles." Her voice was full of sorrow. "It jus' don' seem right what happened to that fine gentleman. No, ma'am, the Lord ain't done right by him. This used to be such a fine, happy house. Then, after Nick's daddy had his stroke, everything changed. Jus' like the devil hisself took over. That nice personality of Mrs. Tyson, it plain flew out the window. It was like she been punishing herself for what happened to him. All the joy jus' up and left her."

Alpha blew her nose loudly.

"I do declare, I don't know why I'm ramblin' on so."

Smoothing her apron, she smiled at Jan.

"There's a back stairway to the garden, miss, if you feel like going on a discoverin' walk."

Then, with a gentle rustle of her starched uniform, she left the room.

Jan walked to the window and looked out across the rolling lawn. Nick and his mother were strolling together arm in arm; their laughter floated up through the open window.

Jan's green eyes clouded slightly. She sensed that she was being left out and didn't quite know how to handle it. She felt uncomfortable and insecure—or was she just imagining things?

Then she started a mental conversation with herself.

Should I go downstairs and join them?

No, that wouldn't be wise. They might think I'm pushy. Cynthia Tyson obviously wants to be alone with her son. I have a very definite feeling that I was dismissed after tea. Even when we met, she was only minimally polite and quite detached—even brittle.

Jan sighed. She was beginning to feel apprehensive. She had a strong feeling that Mrs. Tyson simply didn't like her.

Taking off her shoes, she stretched out on the bed like a lazy cat. Absently counting the roses on the wallpaper, she quietly dozed off.

Jan awoke to someone tickling her toes. It was Nick. He held her close and kissed her.

"Oh, Nick," she said, "I love you so!"

"And I love you, too. Now move your ass—it's time to

dress for dinner. Cocktails are at six sharp. If there's one thing Cynthia hates, it's tardiness. And, honey, wear the blue Cacharel dress. It's pretty and feminine. Pull back your hair, and go easy on the makeup. Cynthia loves a natural look."

Jan had wanted to be nurtured; she was feeling insecure. Growing hostility began to sweep over her. She had a strong desire to grab Nick and yell at him, "Fuck what Cynthia likes! I'll wear what I want to wear. There's nothing wrong with my taste!"

But before she could say anything, he was gone.

She smiled weakly and pulled back her hair. She knew she would do what Nick asked. She always wanted to please him. She put on the blue Cacharel dress and stared at her image carefully. She hoped Mrs. Tyson would like the way she looked. Then a frown crossed her face. She wondered nervously how the evening would progress.

Telling herself to relax, Jan went downstairs to meet Nick and his mother.

Minutes later, the three of them walked to the west wing of the house. Jan noticed an open elevator on the side of the staircase. It was a grim reminder of the tragedy that had befallen the Tysons.

The room they entered was dark. The draperies were drawn, and the heat oppressive. She could just discern the silhouette of a man sitting motionless in a wheelchair. A shiver ran through her at the unmistakable scent of sickness that hung in the air.

Cynthia spoke crisply, with an edge of distaste in her voice: "Turn up the lights, Madison. It's too dark in here."

"Yes, Mrs. Tyson. Mr. Charles was just dozing."

The black attendant, whose soft, fat body exuded an odor of jungle gardenia, flicked on the light switch.

For the next few seconds, the silence was so oppressive that Jan feared she might giggle out of sheer nervousness.

Nick held her hand tightly as he walked over to his father with Jan at his side.

"Hi, Dad," he said.

The eyes that greeted them were blank, devoid of expression. Charles Tyson seemed to be frozen in time. He looked incredibly old; his body was bent like a withered tree. His left hand was grotesquely gnarled and was curled in an unnatural position, as if in anger. His facial muscles were pulled down in a permanent grimace; drool continually dribbled onto the linen napkin around his neck. His breathing was strained, with long pauses after each inhalation, as if the next lungful of air might be his last. The plastic bag attached to the wheelchair was continually filled with the steady drip of urine.

Cynthia walked to the balcony window and stared out as if to detach herself from the scene.

Joining her at the window, Nick took her hand. His face registered deep concern for his mother.

"Are you feeling all right? Is it one of your headaches again? I know how these visits affect you. Seeing Dad this way must be almost unbearable."

For a moment there was no response from Cynthia. She sighed a soft sigh and took Nick's hand in hers. She smiled at him. There was a touch of weariness in her voice as she replied, "Yes, darling, I'm so glad you understand how difficult it is for me. But today I have you to lean on. Whatever would I do without you?"

Jan stared at Charles Tyson, feeling her eyes flood with tears. The entire scene had moved her tremendously. Waves of sympathy and compassion swept over her.

Then Cynthia's voice called out almost contemptuously,

and her eyes seemed to flash with annoyance as she watched the young girl stare at her husband.

"Come along, Jan. I'm sure this is a depressing sight for you."

Walking downstairs, a disturbing thought ran through Jan's head. Had there been an undercurrent of anger in Mrs. Tyson's tone, or was it her imagination?

She tried to be fair, to put herself in Cynthia's place. It must be living hell for Nick's mother to have to watch the man she loved turned into a helpless vegetable. Maybe she needed a measure of smoldering anger. Maybe it was the only thing that enabled her to face her pain and survive. What a heavy, tragic burden she had to bear! Jan shuddered, turning her thoughts away.

The next morning after breakfast, Nick stood smiling in the doorway.

"Ladies, I'm heading down to the stables to saddle the horses. It's a perfect day for a ride to the beach. Jan, I can't wait for you to see the cottage. But till I come back, you two can discuss the sheer wonderfulness of me."

No sooner had he left than an uncomfortable but polite tension settled between the two women.

"More coffee?" Cynthia asked stiffly, a coldly polite expression on her face.

She appeared to thaw slightly as she filled Jan's cup, but only for a moment.

"Nick seems to love you, my dear, and yet I hardly know anything about you except that you and he want to get married. Tell me about yourself."

Jan's first reaction was annoyance. There was something in Mrs. Tyson's tone that irritated her.

"Exactly what would you like to know?"

"My dear, there's no need to be defensive. You must understand, I'm only asking as any mother would."

Jan hesitated for a moment, then replied quietly, "Yes, I understand that. I thought Nick had already told you about me. My parents are dead, and I had just begun modeling when I met him. I was on assignment in London, but meeting Nick changed all that."

Jan paused for a moment, tense under the other woman's cool stare. She wondered if Mrs. Tyson would ever like her. Then she continued.

"Nick and I fell in love. I couldn't go back to America without him, so I gave up modeling, and we stayed in London together. I love him very much."

Cynthia clasped her hands. Her voice was as cool as chipped ice.

"Love," she murmured. "Oh, yes, I'm sure you are both convinced that you're deeply in love. You have been living with my son in his house in the Mews?"

Cynthia shifted slightly in her chair, then continued without waiting for a response.

"I must admit that some of the young women of today"—she paused, as if searching for the right words—"are very different from those in my time."

Suddenly a stern expression crossed her face.

"I am referring, of course, to today's morals. I for one do not understand them. To put it bluntly, I disapprove of them."

Jan felt her throat tighten. Mrs. Tyson had made one thing crystal clear: She did not welcome Jan Julliard with open arms.

At that moment Nick came into the room.

"Well," he asked, a broad smile on his face, "how are the two of you getting along?"

Cynthia rose and walked over to him.

"Just fine, darling," she said, taking his arm and leading him toward the open French doors and onto a small patio.

As Jan watched them walk away, she had that feeling of being left out again. She tried to tell herself that Mrs. Tyson had the right to be concerned about the woman her son was marrying. It was wrong for Jan to be so sensitive, so filled with doubt. Still, Cynthia Tyson was an extremely difficult person to warm up to. She was a cold, angry woman. *Oh, to hell with her!* Jan thought as Nick smilingly beckoned for her to join them.

Standing outside, Jan smelled the air, which was rich with the scent of roses and pines. A soft breeze brought whispers of the sea so close at hand.

She was still tense from her conversation with Nick's mother, but she had made up her mind about one thing: As long as she was at Tysons Landing, she'd take it one day at a time.

As Jan and Nick walked toward the stables, he impetuously bent and kissed the top of her head.

"I hope that you and Cynthia had a nice chat," he said.

He waited as Jan wondered how to respond.

"Well, I guess so. We were both very polite, extremely civilized, and . . ." Her words trailed off as she looked deep into Nick's blue eyes.

"Oh, damn it, Nick, the truth is, I don't think your mother likes me."

Jan glanced at him, waiting for his reaction.

Nick was silent as he helped her mount the mare. Then, as he secured the picnic basket behind his own gelding, he tilted his head as if examining her. There was concern in his eyes. His mood seemed quite serious.

Finally, as if carefully weighing his words, he spoke. "Honey, I'm sure you're wrong. You're just imagining things. Jesus, I'll admit that Cynthia can be very difficult at times. But you've got to remember, she's still terribly distraught about my dad. I wouldn't be surprised if she feels she's somehow losing me. You know how mothers are with their sons."

Jan wasn't sure that she did know. She certainly hoped that Cynthia Tyson wasn't typical. But she listened attentively as Nick continued.

"You know how important it is to me that Cynthia likes you. Tell me you'll try your best to make it work between the two of you. Tell me you'll make every effort to be nice to her."

Right now what Jan needed most was to have Nick hold her. She desperately wanted him to tell her that he loved her, that no one could ever part them, not even his mother. When she replied, there was an edge of bitterness to her voice.

"Nice to her? I couldn't have been nicer. I'd give anything for her to like me, for us to be friends. That's what I was hoping for."

Nick flashed one of his I-love-you smiles.

"That's what I wanted to hear. I know it's only a matter of time before the two of you become very close. Tomorrow, honey, I'm asking Cynthia to take the family engagement ring out of the vault. I want to put it on your finger, and I want you to wear it forever."

Suddenly, all the frustration of the past few hours was erased from her mind. At this particular moment, Jan's heart soared with happiness.

As Nick turned the key in the lock, the door of the beach cottage swung open.

The interior seemed to welcome them. Jan instantly fell in love with it. The sun touching the windows made everything look golden to her. She wanted to become familiar with every part of it so she could pull it from her memory at any time in the future.

After lunch, they walked the secluded beach and listened to the screeching of the gulls. Jan picked up an old fishing basket and filled it with a myriad of seashells she found along the shoreline. Warm and relaxed by the big yellow sun, they wandered back to the cottage, where Nick lit a joint and they finished a bottle of wine.

They made love in a glow of sunlight. Every emotion, every sensation seemed heightened and more sensual than ever before. Their bodies entwined as they climaxed in a sweet, lazy joining of passion. Jan's world was perfect again.

She felt relaxed and contented. The tension of the past couple of days slipped away.

Cynthia Tyson sat under a large magnolia tree's huge natural parasol in ladylike composure, surrounded by loneliness, her soft eyes wore a strangely lifeless, almost unfathomable expression.

Deep down, Cynthia was experiencing a growing fear. The full impact of Nick's situation was beginning to hit her. Her son seemed bent on marrying this Jan person.

A burst of laughter floated in the air.

Cynthia watched as her son and the girl walked from the stables toward the house. Their voices floated vaguely over the lawn, but the words were only murmurings to her.

Nick noticed his mother and waved to her. She could see the girl looking at her. Then she saw her turn back to Nick and say something to him.

"Today has been such a lovely day, darling," Jan was saying. "I'm going to soak in a warm tub and rehash it all over again in my mind. Why don't you go and visit with your mother? I'm sure she'd enjoy it."

Nick kissed the end of Jan's nose.

"That's a very good idea, honey. I'll see you later."

His face wore a sober expression as he walked over to Cynthia. He wondered if this was the right time to talk to her about releasing some of his trust funds.

Cynthia smiled at her son; her eyes searched his.

"Nick darling, you look so serious. I suspect you want to have a meaningful discussion with me."

Nick laughed.

"You know me so well. You're right, of course. I want to talk about money. Lots and lots of money. Cynthia dear, I sure would appreciate it if you'd release some of my trusts."

His mother sat perfectly still, her hands folded in front of her. Her eyes were fixed on her son.

"Are you telling me that you need still more money?"

"Yes, I do. My ship is becoming the most indescribably magnificent seagoing palace you've ever seen. But she is also outrageously expensive to outfit. If I'm to remain an equal partner with Jafaar, I need all the money I can lay my hands on to share in the financing. After all, we want to make her fit for royalty. One thing is certain: I plan to devote myself to this project totally and completely. I'm determined to make it the greatest success imaginable. There's just no way I'll let it fail."

Cynthia's voice was soft and relaxed when she answered, "Honey, every business venture of yours has been successful. Ever since you were a little boy, you always knew how to turn a dollar. But now, Nick, you're talking of millions. I know it's unlikely, but what if your venture does fail? If it does, do I want to be the one responsible for letting you lose your inheritance? I'll have to think about it very, very seriously. Perhaps you and I can discuss it again after dinner. Let's go in now, shall we?"

As Nick walked her back to the house, his mother's mood was strangely happy. Taking her son's arm, she smiled at him warmly. It was wonderful to know that she had the power of decision in regard to his trusts. Maybe this was the answer she had been searching for. As she looked at his serious face, she pictured Nick wondering if she would turn him down. She tucked her arm in his, feeling in a rare, exultant mood.

Cynthia could have given him the answer then and there. She knew exactly what her decision would be.

That evening a midsummer thunderstorm left the air sweet with the smell of wild honeysuckle. The beardlike moss that hung from the aged oaks was greener than usual from the rain.

In the spell of the evening's darkness, which was punctuated by sparkling lightning bugs flying in and out among the branches of the trees, Nick took Jan for a walk around the grounds.

After drinking in the sheer beauty of the moment, Jan looked up at the man she loved and whispered to him with a luxurious sigh, "What a wonderful night, and what a truly enchanting place this is. It's like something out of a storybook."

They walked in silence for another few minutes. Then Jan stopped. She turned to face Nick; her eyes were probing and serious.

"Tell me, darling, have you discussed our marriage with your mother?"

He hesitated for a moment before answering.

"No, not yet. You see, I'm hoping she'll release one of my trust funds to me."

Jan stopped walking and turned to face Nick.

"That's a strange answer. What on earth do your trust funds have to do with our marriage?"

She kept her eyes directly on his, waiting for him to say something. The silence between them grew awkward.

Unexpectedly, Nick put his arms around her. He held her close and kissed her lightly on the lips.

"Let's go inside, darling. I promised Cynthia I'd play cards with her. You've got to leave it to me to pick the right time to discuss our marriage plans. Trust me, honey."

Jan didn't reply. She was too confused. She couldn't accept the idea that there was a right or wrong time to discuss their wedding. She struggled to fight back feelings of resentment, to brush aside negative thoughts. But they kept surfacing, stronger and stronger, until she almost feared that Nick could hear them.

Damn it, I was right. Cynthia Tyson doesn't want her son to get married. Not to me, certainly, and probably not to anyone. She wants him all to herself.

Seemingly oblivious to Jan's musings, Nick unlocked the front door, and they walked inside.

Cynthia's voice sounded warm and friendly as she called out from the game room, "Is that you, darling? I'm waiting in here."

Nick walked in to his mother, put his arms around her, and gave her a kiss.

She had been shuffling a deck of cards. A brandy decanter and two glasses were on the table. Once again Jan felt Cynthia's eyes studying her.

"Do you play cards, Jan? Would you like to join us in a game?"

"No thanks, Mrs. Tyson. I'm afraid I don't." Jan's voice was cold. "I seem to have developed the most horrid headache. If you'll both excuse me, I think I'll retire for the night. I'm sure that you and Nick have many things you want to discuss."

The room was suddenly filled with an oppressive silence. Jan's eyes were steadily fixed upon Mrs. Tyson's, returning her stare. Each woman's face was impassive.

Nick was the first to break the silence; he spoke solicitously to Jan.

"Darling, I'm so sorry about your headache."

Jan tried to muster a smile as she replied, "It's nothing to worry about, Nick. I'll be fine after a night's sleep."

Cynthia Tyson echoed her sentiments.

"You're quite right, Jan. The sensible thing to do with a headache is close your eyes until it passes."

Though the headache had been merely an excuse to leave, Jan's head actually did throb with the beginnings of a genuine, intense headache when she walked into her bedroom.

Downstairs, the room was silent for a moment after Jan had left. Mrs. Tyson's eyes never left her son as he poured them both a brandy and then smiled warmly at her.

"Cynthia dear, I'd like us to talk about Jan. Now that you've met her, how do you feel about her? She seems to be unsure about whether you like her or not."

His mother moved ever so slightly in her chair; there was a look of injured surprise on her face.

"Why, honey, you know how much I love you. And you must know I'd also love any girl who loved my son."

Nick gave a small sigh of relief.

"I was sure you'd feel that way. Jan and I would prefer a small wedding here, if that's acceptable to you, and then a reception in London."

"Are you quite certain that the girl is not pregnant?"

Nick laughed.

"No, mother, of course she's not. I'm light years away from thinking of a family. No way do I want to be tied down. Kids are definitely not for me—not for a long time, anyway."

Cynthia's voice was controlled and cautious as she spoke.

"If you're not planning a family, then why do you need to get married? Jan seems quite content just to be living with you."

Nick detected that a quiet edge of disapproval had crept into his mother's voice. He didn't know how to reply.

Cynthia tamped a cigarette against her hand. Moving quickly, Nick reached out and lit it for her. She inhaled slowly before speaking again.

"You know, darling, I have been thinking very seriously about releasing one of your trust funds. That is, if you would just proceed more slowly with your marriage plans. It certainly can't hurt to wait a little longer. I'm sure you'll agree that you simply won't have time for a wife and marriage until your private club has been successfully launched."

Nothing registered on Nick but the news that his mother was releasing his trust fund.

Cynthia could almost read his thoughts. She knew that her son would go along with her wishes for the time being. She knew how badly he wanted that money and how necessary it was for his project.

At this moment, she felt closer than ever to Nick. He was such a wonderful young man, and she was so very proud of him. As she sat looking at him, she wondered if he would ever understand how very much she loved him. He was now the hub, the very center of her life.

* * *

The next morning, Jan and Nick were sitting together at the pool house. He was being unusually attentive to her. In fact, he was so charming that it almost bordered on parody.

Jan smiled to herself. Sometimes Nick could be so transparent. She knew there had to be a reason for his sudden display of undiluted adoration. She sensed that he wanted to talk about something but was finding it difficult to begin. Well, he'd get to it in his own good time.

She leaned back and let the sun warm her face as she listened to the songbirds high in the magnolia tree. Tomorrow she and Nick were scheduled to return to London. Later this afternoon they would visit a local recording studio. Nick wanted her to hear his new discovery, Cat Bracken, cut a record.

Gently he urged her closer to him and put his arm around her waist.

"I love you, Jan Julliard."

"I love you, too, Nick. In fact, I feel so beautifully contented right now."

He turned silent again as he sat holding her hand. When he finally spoke, his voice was low and easy.

"Honey, would you mind if we postponed our wedding for just a little while? Cynthia suggested that we give her a little more time, you know, to get used to the idea. It didn't seem like much to ask, especially after all she's doing for me."

He began to speak more quickly, as if he were trying to get all the words out while he could.

"She's releasing one of my trust funds. I can't tell you how much that means to me. I'm damned grateful to her— and she did it with absolutely no hassle. She might have made it very difficult for me if she'd wanted to."

Jan said nothing. She just studied him, focusing on the small worry lines that furrowed the corners of his eyes.

Encouraged by her silence, he continued.

"I don't think Cynthia is all that well emotionally. What with my father being so sick and all . . ."

Nick paused again and waited for Jan's reaction. Getting none, he kept talking, as if he didn't want to deal with a period of silence.

"You can just imagine how awful her life here must be— how empty and lonely. And now I think she feels she's losing me, too. It wouldn't be right for me to make things too difficult for her if I can help it. All she needs is a little more time. We can give her that, can't we? I just knew you'd understand. That's why I told her we'd wait."

Jan looked down at the ground for a few seconds as if studying her shoes. Then she slowly raised her eyes to his.

Suddenly she was irritated by the sound level of the songbirds. Their singing had become a shrill irritant in her ears. She wished she could shut them up.

She was simmering with rage. She knew that as far as Mrs. Tyson was concerned, she didn't exist and she never would. It was obvious that Nick's mother was the power in his life. He needed his money, and Cynthia controlled it— it was that simple.

She couldn't think of the right words to say to Nick, but at that moment she hated him and she hated his mother. She couldn't wait to leave Tyson Hall.

Her pounding thoughts were interrupted by the sound of Nick's voice.

"Hey, don't look so somber. Everything will be okay, you'll see. We'll still live happily ever after, as planned."

Then he glanced down at his watch.

"C'mon, honey, it's almost time to leave for the studio. We'd better hurry, or we'll miss Cat's singing."

Jan finally found her voice.

"That's it? Just like that—off we go to listen to somebody sing?"

Her voice sounded cold and bitter.

"You act as if nothing has happened. Tell me something, Nick. Do you want to marry me? Because if you do, I don't think your mother is ever going to agree to it. Ever since I've been here, I've had this feeling that she thinks of you as a surrogate for your father. You're his replacement in her life, and she'll never let you go."

As she spoke, Jan felt that she was becoming unstrung. She forced herself to stop.

"I can't believe what I just heard," Nick snapped back; his face was dark with anger. "You sound like a spoiled, peevish child. It's as if you're jealous of my mother. Well, you've no cause to be, and you know it. I love you, damn it! How many times must I tell you? You're trying to make it sound like I'm choosing Cynthia over you. That's the craziest thing I've ever heard. She's my mother. Am I supposed to apologize for loving my mother?"

Jan could feel tears brimming in her eyes.

"Oh, to hell with it! Why don't you just go and listen to your lady singer? I'm not in the mood. I don't happen to feel all that musical right now."

"If that's how you want it!"

'His eyes blazing, Nick turned on his heel and walked away.

Cat's greeting was warm and full of affection. Her voice was charged with animation as she introduced the group she was cutting the demo with. Then, adjusting her headphones, she tossed Nick a smile and started to sing.

He felt intensely proud of her as her vibrant tones filled the studio. She was really great, he thought. Brody had brought her along beautifully. He'd succeeded in getting rid of all the rough edges.

During a break, Cat walked over to Nick.

"You have been wonderful for me, Nick Tyson. You happened along just when I needed you most."

Then Cat looked at him and frowned.

"You're alone. I thought you were bringing Jan with you. I'm anxious to meet her."

Nick's voice turned suddenly cold.

"Forget Jan. We had a damned stupid hassle. She's pissed off at me, so I came alone."

"Okay, so she's forgotten," Cat replied easily. As Cat saw Brody approach, she seemed to remember something else.

"By the way, did Brody tell you I'll be leaving for London in three weeks? I'm so excited, I could die. I've been booked into The Round Table. It's the break I've been waiting for!"

After a few more takes, the demo was finished and Nick drove Cat back to her apartment.

"Come in," she said quietly.

He followed her inside. For a moment neither of them spoke.

Nick watched her and appraised her thoughtfully. As their eyes met, he thought of Jan. She suddenly seemed far away.

"Well, Cat," he said softly, "it's getting late. Perhaps I'd better go."

He made no move toward the door.

She put her hands to his lips as if to quiet him. Nick pulled her to him and kissed her gently. Holding her by her shoulders, he stared with great intensity into the corridors of her turquoise eyes. Then his searching tongue pried her lips apart. Cat returned his kiss and felt her nipples harden through her silk shirt.

She began to shiver.

"Baby," he said, "what I feel for you has nothing to do with how I feel about Jan. But I'd sure as hell like to sleep with you."

Cat stretched her lissome body and focused her attention on Nick.

"It's been a long time," she said. "I'd almost forgotten how great it can be."

As Nick slid quietly off the bed, Cat appreciatively studied his lean, muscular body. Her thoughts grew increasingly erotic. She found herself becoming excited again; there was a throbbing, aching need for him between her legs.

It would be easy to become emotionally involved with Nick Tyson. But that would spoil everything because it would be only temporary. Cat knew that the one lasting emotion, the greatest satisfaction of all, came when she was on a stage performing. An audience, rather than just one man, embracing her with its love—that was the true reality for her. That was the most important thing in her life.

Without a word Nick placed his body on top of hers and traced her breasts with his tongue. Her legs parted immediately as she awaited his next move.

He entered her with one long, smooth thrust. As he rode her, she felt herself tremble; her breath came in short, sharp gasps. He brought her close to orgasm and then away. Cat rocked with his rhythm. Nick was giving her just what she wanted.

Finally, after the delirious sensation of her orgasm's

small afterwaves, she noticed that Nick still had an erection.

"Satisfactory?" he asked.

"Terrific, but I felt you were holding back."

Nick winked at her. "I'll just sleep on this one."

"What a waste!" she said as she rolled over and shut her eyes.

Nick patted her ass, then moved off the bed and headed for the bathroom.

Before showering, he looked at his reflection in the mirror. He wondered if at any time in the past few hours he would have changed the course of tonight's events if he could have. Here he was in love with Jan, and yet he had cheated on her.

Well, after this he'd close the book on Cat Bracken forever.

Yet even as that thought whirled around in his brain, there was still a conflict in his heart. Cat Bracken was one dynamite lady.

The next morning Nick and Jan were packed and ready to leave for London.

Cynthia walked them to the car. As old Willie opened the door for Jan to enter, Nick hugged his mother close. Then, as she watched the Rolls drive away, Cynthia politely returned Jan's good-bye wave. When the car was out of sight, she turned and walked back into the house.

Once inside, she made her way upstairs, where she entered her bedroom and closed the door. Putting her hand in her pocket, she pulled out the faded blue jeweler's box.

She opened it and removed the ring that lay centered inside. Cynthia held it and looked at the delicate mounting. The pale, tea-colored diamond caught the light, and the soft violet amethysts surrounding it reflected their own rich color.

The ring had belonged to Enid Tyson, Nick's grandmother. And to Enid's mother before that. Cynthia herself had worn it as a bride and had always loved it. When Nick was born, she had carefully put it away. Perhaps it was foolish sentiment, but the ring was to be handed down to future Tyson brides.

She frowned as she noticed the trembling of her hands. Walking into the bathroom, she opened her linen closet and reached back among the rows of fleecy towels. She brought out a bottle of brandy. She opened it and tipped it to her lips.

She walked slowly back to her bedroom, the bottle of brandy in her hand. As she slid down into the pink satin slipper chair, she heard the pounding of her heart.

She sat quietly for a while, then slipped the ring onto her finger. Unexpectedly, she felt a swift surge of emotion, and she found herself blinking back her tears. Then, pouring a large jigger of brandy into a glass, Cynthia waited for the numbness to settle in.

Chapter Twenty-five

From the moment Cat Bracken walked onto the London stage, she was a hit, a winner. It was as if she had come to claim what was rightfully hers. The audience loved her. She was vital, exciting, and unpredictable, and she seemed determined to give them her all, and more.

Jan sat with Nick in the front row of the theater watching her, entranced by her. She felt she had never seen anyone so alive, so vibrant.

"I told you she was great," Nick whispered.

After the show it was party time. Nick threw a private bash for Cat at Promises. All the beautiful people of swinging Mayfair showed up.

After Nick introduced Cat to Jan, he moved Cat off to meet his other guests. Jan quietly observed that Cat effortlessly charmed everyone with her warm, easy manner.

She heard a familiar voice and turned to see Sarah Hartley approaching her. Sarah's eyes were wide with interest.

"That is one great performer!" she said, casting a quick glance in Cat's direction.

"She certainly is," Jan answered.

"And you could bottle her charm and sell it by the quart," added Sarah, studying Cat Bracken quizzically.

She was really curious about the entertainer. Jan had told her how Nick had helped Cat with her career. Sarah wondered if that was all he was helping her with. There was always the possibility that they were having an affair. She watched Cat toss off a bright smile to one of the patrons, then return her attention to Nick. There was an easy familiarity in the way she touched him. The two of them seemed totally comfortable with each other.

Sarah knew something about cheaters. She could sniff them out a mile away. She was always questioning and was never fully able to put away her suspicions. But not Jan. Jan had no idea of infidelity. She loved and trusted Nick completely. She was the kind who would take it the hardest if Nick ever cheated and she found out.

Sarah drew a quick breath and fastened her eyes on Jan, who stood watching Nick and Cat. Jan's beautiful face was calm. She exhibited no sign of jealousy, no trace of concern. She looked at Nick with the moon and the stars in her eyes.

Sarah tapped her lightly on her arm.

"Come on, Jan, let's go out in the garden and have a good old chat. Daley's not with me, so I can relax tonight. He flew to New York with his producer. I expect he'll be gone for about three days. He tells me they're going to need another million to complete the film, so you can bet he'll be out there charming the money men again. That damned movie is all he seems to care about these days. I've become a combination mother, friend, whipping boy, and anything else Daley Russell might need. What a selfish bastard that man is! Yet I can't imagine life without him."

Then Sarah's voice turned mildly sarcastic.

"Of course, there's always the chance I'll have to. Daley has never given me any feeling of permanence or security."

"Sarah, whether you admit it or not, I believe you're in love with that man."

There was a note of frustration in Sarah's voice as she replied, "Love? What is love, anyway? I, for one, sure as hell don't know."

They were both quiet for a minute; then Jan spoke softly, as if to herself.

"I think love, real love, is when two people realize that they're absolutely essential to each other."

Sarah let out a short breath.

"Do you realize what would happen if I did love Daley? I'd never get any return on that investment. If you want to know the truth, Jan, the very idea of such a situation scares me to death. So let's change the subject. It's making me nervous, fidgety, and more than a little apprehensive. I'm going over to the bar. I need a very dry martini."

After Sarah left for the bar, Jan stood still for a minute and quietly took in the room. The party was now in full swing; almost everyone was gathered in intimate little groups and clusters.

Jan looked for Nick and saw he was still talking to Cat. When she caught his attention, he waved to her and beckoned for her to join them.

When she walked over, Nick put his arms around her.

"I love you," he whispered in her ear.

Cat stood a little apart and smiled at Jan, who couldn't help thinking how striking she was. She admired her easy grace and the way she acknowledged people as they came to pay court. She was sometimes sexy, sometimes earthy, usually humorous, and always flirtatious, independent, and very sure of herself. Watching her, Jan was convinced that Cat could never look embarrassed or ill at ease about anything.

Cat suddenly turned to Nick with an enthusiastic smile on her face.

"Isn't this wonderful, all the attention I'm getting? I hope it lasts forever! Nick, you were just the dearest thing to throw this party for me."

Her voice was filled with gratitude, and her eyes were wide with affection as she looked at him.

"I'm having a truly sensational time, but it's getting late, and I'd better head for home. I have two shows tomorrow, plus an early morning rehearsal."

She gave them each a dazzling smile and headed for the door.

Nick's arm circled Jan's waist as he watched her leave. Jan's eyes were shining as she looked up at him. There was no trace of envy in her heart. Cat Bracken might be tomorrow's newest and brightest star, but Nick Tyson and Jan Julliard belonged to each other, and they would be together for the rest of their lives.

Late the next morning, Jan and Nick woke up and made love.

They savored the nearness of each other, their limbs sensuously entwined. But Jan sensed that Nick's mind was elsewhere as he moved his fingers gently through her hair. They had not even discussed the party.

Finally, Nick kissed the top of her head; then he got up and lit a cigarette.

"Jan, I think I've decided on an interior designer for *Pleasure Palace.*"

Relaxed and sleepy, Jan listened with a lazy smile on her face.

"Now that she's been overhauled and outfitted, we're ready to move forward. Jafaar tells me she's all set to leave Le Havre and sail to her permanent berth in England. It looks like my dream is at last becoming a reality. When she arrives, the decorators and their staff can start to glamorize her interior immediately. Honey, it's the greatest feeling! Everything is moving along just as smooth as silk."

Jan lifted herself from the pillow and leaned on her elbow as Nick enfolded her in his arms. Brushing her face against his, she murmured into his ear, "That's terrific news, darling. I'm so very happy for you."

She pressed her nakedness next to his and listened to the rhythmic beating of his heart. As he held her close, she concentrated on every line of his body. Then she looked up at his perfect profile and finally gazed deep into his wonderful eyes.

Nick bent down to kiss her. His lips made her neck tingle as his hands slid down her hips.

"Let's make love. Just one more time," she whispered.

He grinned at her.

"I don't know. That's very short notice, baby. But with a little help from you, maybe it can be arranged."

Chapter Twenty-six

An hour after Cynthia called her son to ask him to come home, Charles Tyson died.

She had not been in the room when it happened. Madison tapped on her bedroom door and gently told her the exact time that Charles expired.

She studied Madison silently. His eyes were running with tears as he wiped sweat from his shiny black face. It was obvious that Charles's death had upset him. Madison had been with her husband every single day of his affliction, watching over him and talking to him all that time.

Actually, it had often irritated her. It seemed so stupid; Madison knew full well that Charles Tyson could never reply to anything that was said to him. Cynthia knew it was just a habit of Madison's, a habit of treating her husband as if he were a functioning human being instead of the vegetable he had become.

Tears kept running down Madison's face.

"Poor Mr. Charles. Poor, poor Mr. Charles. He mus' be with the angels now."

Cynthia hardly heard what he was saying. She was telling herself she must make sure to give Madison a glowing reference and a large severance check when she dismissed him tomorrow.

Later she stood by the hospital bed and looked down at her dead husband. He looked peaceful and composed. His face was relaxed, almost handsome again. His lips were shaped in a soft smile, as if anticipating something that he alone could foresee.

Cynthia wanted to cry, but tears wouldn't come. Her eyes were empty as she walked back to her own room.

Before he left, Madison told Alpha and Willie that Mr. Tyson had actually tried to talk just as the end came. But all that came out had been a croaking gargle.

"Mar! Mar! Mar!" he called out, Madison said, before sighing and falling back on the pillow. Seconds later he was gone.

Blowing her nose hard and wiping away her tears, Alpha answered Madison.

"I'm bettin' I know who he was calling. Jus' like the preacher says, jus' before you die, you get your first look at Heaven. And where is Mr. Charles's mama now? In Heaven, that's where. He saw his own mama, and that's who he was callin'."

She quickly crossed herself before continuing.

"Well, he's with her now, that's for sure."

"Praise the Lord," the three of them said in unison.

The next morning, Cynthia waited for Nick to come home.

The death certificate had been written. The undertaker had come and gone. The hospital bed was dismantled, and the wheelchair removed. Madison had left.

Cynthia stared critically at herself in the mirror. Her eyes looked faded; her skin sludgy. She had aged incredibly in the last few years. Her trembling fingers told her she needed a brandy.

Walking to the bar, she poured herself a measure. She planned to stop drinking, but not today. Maybe tomorrow.

Right now, she didn't seem to be able to get hold of her emotions. For the first time in months, she knew her spirit was free—free from the despair that had entrapped her for so long. Now perhaps she could pick up the pieces of her life and get a new start, somehow rejoin the living. It was up to her. She'd talk it over with Nick. He would help.

But was her spirit willing to let go of the hatred she had cherished for so long? It had been her friend, her constant companion, her only comfort all through the long ordeal.

Her face was pensive as she sat alone and looked hopelessly around her. Beneath her show of calm she was trembling. She seemed to be in the throes of delayed shock. She continued to stare expressionlessly at the wall until, finally, wrapping her arms around her body, she began to rock back and forth, as if she were trying to get in touch with herself, to find some part of the old Cynthia while seeking the relief of tears. Then at last they came, running silently down her cheeks.

"Dear God," she whispered out loud, "maybe now I can forgive him."

The funeral was private and brief. Charles Tyson was buried next to his parents in the Tyson family plot.

His son Nick did not attend.

Nick's connecting flight in New York was grounded for seven hours due to a violent electric storm that was blanketing the area. Even after the long-delayed takeoff, bad luck continued to dog the flight. Trouble developed in the right engine, and the pilot announced to the passengers that he was returning the plane to New York.

The day after the funeral, Cynthia locked herself in her room with her brandy bottle. She stayed in bed most of the day.

She finally dozed off, silently slipping into one of her faraway places.

Sometime later, after dreaming that she was being damned by God, she awoke with a start. Her heart pounded in the stifling heat, and her body was wet with sweat. The last rays of sun were staining her room red.

She heard a knock at her door, then a voice.

"Mrs. Tyson, ma'am," the voice called.

"What is it?" Cynthia asked, coming out of her deep, black void.

"Mrs. Tyson, ma'am," the voice persisted, "it's the Reverend Boyd. He's waiting downstairs. The good man's come to give you comfort."

Cynthia tried to sit up. The pain in her head was unbearable.

"I don't think I can see anyone right now."

"Ma'am, everybody needs a man of God at times like this. I'll have tea fixed for him, so you jus' freshen up and come on down whenever you're ready."

Cynthia got up and washed her face. Next, she cleaned her teeth and gargled with peppermint. She hid the half-empty bottle of brandy high atop her closet. Then she absently chose something to wear. All the while, the house seemed strangely still and empty.

Walking to her dressing room, she picked up her hairbrush. She paused to wipe the sweat from her palms. Her dream was still heavy on her mind.

How could she face Reverend Boyd? She had a vicious hangover, and the dull pain in her head was still with her. All she wanted was to be alone till Nick got there. He was due to arrive later that day.

Surveying herself in the mirror, Cynthia saw that she looked pale and drawn. Her features appeared blurred and indistinct to her. The feathers of gray in her blond hair seemed more pronounced than ever.

She soaked her handkerchief in cologne and pressed it against her forehead. The heat was oppressive, and the pain between her eyes was unbearable.

Outside, a summer storm was brewing; the tall poplars swayed wildly in the breeze. Far out toward the ocean, she saw black clouds piling high in the sky. A sudden vivid flash of lightning startled her as it illuminated the room.

The rattling of china on a tea trolley interrupted Jim Boyd's thoughts. Alpha carefully rolled the cart, heavily laden with a Georgian silver service and delicate porcelain, into the drawing room.

Watching her maneuver the luxurious trolley, Boyd gave her a soft, sad smile.

She poured and handed the Reverend his tea, then quietly took her leave.

Cynthia felt strangely unsettled as she walked downstairs; she paused outside the drawing-room door. Her eyes again blurred, so she closed them and leaned back against the door for a moment. Finally, with an inaudible sigh, she opened it and walked in.

Inside the drawing room, the first thing she saw was the Reverend Jim Boyd, comfortably seated sipping his tea and completely at ease. Something about his manner conveyed that he felt he belonged in the room. Cynthia hesitated and felt as if she were the visitor, about to intrude.

"My dear, dear Cynthia," he said, putting down the china cup, "you have been in my prayers."

Her face was expressionless. She had a strange sensation of being asleep with her eyes open.

Jim Boyd rose from the chair and walked toward her. He took her hand and guided her toward the sofa.

"My dear lady, I can truly sense your pain."

Reaching out, he touched her hand gently. His smile conveyed great sympathy. Then, with a soft, understanding smile, he motioned for her to sit down. Cynthia continued to feel uncomfortable as he looked at her with intense eyes.

"It's very kind of you to be concerned about me," she said, her voice barely a whisper, "although all I really want is to find a quiet corner somewhere."

Jim Boyd nodded understandingly.

"I can certainly understand that, my dear. After the death of a husband, a woman sometimes wishes she could assume the power of invisibility."

Cynthia didn't respond. She leaned farther back into the sofa and felt her hand tremble. She could tell that one of her migraine headaches was coming on. In a matter of minutes she knew that the full force of pain would hit her. She pressed both of her palms against her head.

"I . . ." She couldn't finish. She turned to Boyd, imploringly.

"What's the trouble? Are you in pain?" he asked.

"I feel one of my dreadful headaches coming on. Sometimes I'm ill with them for days."

He fixed his tea-colored eyes on her.

"I worry about you, Mrs. Tyson. You are not taking care of yourself, and it seems to me that nobody else is looking after you, either."

Without hesitation, Jim Boyd walked over to the bell pull and yanked at it ferociously. Then he returned to his chair.

A few seconds later, Alpha walked in and glanced uneasily at the Reverend and at Mrs. Tyson. A heavy silence seemed to fill the room, broken only by the ticking of the clock on the mantel. Cynthia concentrated on the rhythmic beat.

Jim Boyd sat very still and squeezed his large, flat hands together. Then, as if he felt the time was finally right, he calmly extracted a small Bible from his pocket. Holding it in one hand, he smiled slowly at Cynthia.

"With your permission, dear lady, I would like to pray that your headache will soon leave you. I want you to trust me. Because, you see, after I pray, I shall lay my hands on your head, and in the name of God I will seek to rid you of your pain."

Cynthia wasn't listening. She couldn't even muster up anger or humiliation at the position she found herself in. She could only feel pain throbbing inside her head. It was burning and relentless.

She sat rigidly in the chair and held her breath. Thoughts faded from her mind. She fought desperately not to faint. If she could somehow just hide back behind the darkness, she was sure she would feel all right again.

"In the name of our Lord Jesus, remove the pain from this, Thy child. We, Thy children who revel in Thy love, ask you in His name."

Jim Boyd's voice was rhythmic and punctuated by devout sighs.

"Let us pray. Let us pray to Him, our Savior. Let Him put His power into these hands. Let this willing servant of the Lord remove a sufferer's pain, in Jesus's name, in Jesus's name. For ye that believeth in Him shall be eternally blessed. Amen and amen."

"Amen," Alpha murmured, rocking back and forth on her feet.

Jim Boyd rose and walked over to Cynthia. He stood for a moment behind her chair. Then, looking upward as if in silent prayer, he placed his hands firmly upon her head.

She felt an instant reaction, as if the pain in her head got lighter. The voice that droned above her seemed to carry her weariness away with it. A velvet blackness gathered, an engulfing sense of peace, followed by comforting darkness all around her.

Cynthia awoke on her bed.

She hovered a moment on the edge of wakefulness. Images swirled in her mind. As she opened her eyes, she saw Nick peering at her.

"Cynthia," he said with concern in his voice, "are you all right?"

"Nick darling, when did you arrive?"

"I got here just as you passed out. You looked as if you were in some sort of trance. I was scared to death. Alpha helped me get you upstairs. Christ, Cynthia, my father was just laid to rest, and I come home to find this crazy quack preacher holy-rolling all over the place like a goddamned circus is going on."

Cynthia remained silent. She didn't want to say anything that would make Nick angrier than he was. She was trying hard to pull her thoughts together, but everything was vague in her mind. She could recall nothing after Jim Boyd's hands had touched her.

Her eyes welled with tears as she looked at her son. She knew how difficult it would be to explain the situation to him; she herself was not sure what had happened. All she knew was that her headache was gone and that her mind and spirit felt different, somehow more uplifted.

She smiled weakly at Nick.

"Honey, can we talk tomorrow? I feel so very tired. I'd like to go back to sleep now. Please make sure I'm not disturbed."

As Nick walked out of his mother's bedroom, his jaw was tight and his dark eyes were black with anger.

Once outside, he slammed his hand hard on the banister rail. What the hell was that son of a bitch doing hanging around his mother? As he walked downstairs, he speculated about Reverend Boyd. The old bastard had probably set his sights on the Tyson money.

Nick shook his head as if to dispel the thought. He was worried about his mother. She was so innocent, so vulnerable. In no way did he want anyone like Jim Boyd involved with her. Nor did he want any part of his own personal world to change. There was only one answer: Cynthia had to get away from Tysons Landing and do some traveling.

The next evening after dinner, Nick took his mother's hand.

"Cynthia darling, I want to talk to you. You and I have said our good-byes to Dad. His love for you and your memories of him will stay with you forever. But now I really think you should get away from those memories. You can't stay here forever, chained to the past. You need a rest, a change of scene. You need to get away from any responsibilities, any decisions. Mostly I don't want to think of you here all alone."

He paused for a second. Cynthia started to daydream.

How wonderful! Nick is going to ask me to come to London to live with him! Or perhaps a lovely long holiday, just the two of us. Come to think of it, he hasn't even mentioned Jan this trip. Maybe it's all over between them. Maybe things will start to brighten up now.

Then the serious tone of his voice broke into her thoughts.

"I'm also very worried about your health, Cynthia. Alpha tells me that you take to your room quite a lot."

She clasped her hands to stop their trembling. What had Alpha been discussing with her son—her drinking? That was nobody's business but her own.

When she responded, her voice was cold, and a sudden anger flashed through her.

"Nick, since when do you listen to the prattling of servants?"

Nick stared at his mother. Her skin was so pale, and her face so strained. He had never seen her features look so puffy before. What could be wrong with her?

"For God's sake, Mother, Alpha is more than just a servant. She's been with our family since she was a girl! She was with you the day I was born. She's just plain worried about you, that's all. Who else would she talk to but me?"

"Forgive me, darling. You're right, of course. You know how I feel about Alpha. It's not important enough to bicker about. When would you like us to leave for London?"

Nick looked slightly startled, but he managed a smile.

"Cynthia . . ."

He hesitated, his voice gentle.

"I didn't mean . . ."

His voice trailed off again.

His mother was silent as the full impact hit her. Nick had never asked her to go to London with him. He had never intended for them to live there together. How foolish her fantasies had been! She was annoyed at her own stupidity.

The next day Nick returned to London.

After he left, Cynthia strolled through her rose gardens. It had been years since she had tended them personally. None of the gardeners had her touch with flowers. They looked neglected to her, as if they were growing wild.

Her mood was thoughtful as she walked back to the house and turned some decisions over in her mind.

She knew now that it was impossible to cling any longer to Nick, despite her all-consuming love for him. After

Charles's death, she had taken it for granted that her son would want her to be with him. But he was too busy in his own world, with his own life.

The sound of an approaching car made her stop and turn.

The Reverend's van was coming up her driveway.

She felt strangely excited, almost elated at the thought of seeing him. And yet she was also a little ill at ease.

"Hello," he called to her, getting out of his van. "How are you feeling today? And your son—how is he?"

There was a slight edge of mockery in Jim Boyd's voice when he mentioned Nick. *The smartassed little bastard,* he thought. *The nerve of him showing me the door the other night! It'll take a lot more than young Tyson's temper to stop Jim Boyd from getting what he's after!*

Cynthia looked at him with sadness in her eyes.

"Oh, Nick left for London hours ago."

Jim Boyd smiled; he figured this would be a good time to stir her up about her son. He fixed his pale, flat eyes on her and spoke in his warmest, most sympathetic manner.

"Oh my, I had no idea his stay would be so short. He's leaving you so soon after your bereavement! I must admit I'm a little shocked."

Then he made a clucking sound with his tongue.

"I simply don't understand young people today. They can be so thoughtless, so cruel. They seem to lose sight of where their duties are. They so often ignore family ties, and they lack the courage to face up to their responsibilities. Yes, my dear, I'm afraid they tend to live very selfish lives."

Then Boyd took her arm quite firmly.

"Let's you and I walk awhile. It's truly one of God's fine mornings, for sure."

As they walked around the inner gardens, Cynthia

opened up to him. She told him about Nick and how he had wanted her to travel, leave Tysons Landing.

"What do you think of that suggestion, Reverend?"

Boyd was consumed with a feeling of numb despair. Just when he thought he had a chance at the golden ring, Cynthia Tyson was planning to leave! His dreams would float away with her. He told himself to go very carefully and not to screw up, but he felt like a crock of shit.

He forced a wide smile onto his face as he replied,

"Why, that sounds like a fine idea! Get away and clear all the sad thoughts from your mind, then get on with the business of living. The good Lord sure hates a wasted life."

Boyd sighed heavily as they continued walking.

"The truth is, I shall miss you. It's not very often I meet a woman like you. I do so admire you."

His voice was soft and gentle, hypnotically persuasive.

"I hope I won't offend you if I tell you about a vision I had. It was a vision of you and me working together in the service of the Lord."

He watched her closely. As she looked at him, he noticed a soft blush on her face. He was getting to her—he could feel it. He had gambled that she was as vulnerable to flattery as anyone else.

She stopped and stood very still, shaking her head slowly.

"I'm not sure I'm worthy of such an offer. But I would like to help by contributing in my own way. Would you accept a donation of fifty thousand dollars, payable to you? It could go for any of God's good works that you deem worthwhile."

Boyd was dumbfounded. His mind whirled. He had thought her last gift—five thousand dollars—was unbelievable. But fifty thousand! And made out to him! The sum staggered him. He knew he mustn't show it. He thought to himself, *How stinkin' rich she is, what the fuck does it mean to her?*

Bowing his head slightly, a warm and compassionate expression on his face, he let his eyes well with tears as he looked at her. Then he stepped forward and took hold of Cynthia's hand. He held it firmly; his tone was slow and measured as he spoke.

"Bless you, bless you, bless you, my dear Mrs. Tyson. How can I even begin to thank you? It's people like you who keep the spark of faith alive in a believer's heart. Whatever lies ahead of you, I hope you soon return here."

Cynthia studied him thoughtfully. When she spoke, there was an unfamiliar note of shyness in her voice.

"I really haven't yet decided where I'm going or what it is I'll be doing. I've made no definite plans at all. But in any case, I'm sure we can continue our friendship."

Boyd smiled, satisfied. Suddenly everything was going his way. The plum was there for the taking—he would bet his sweet ass on it. When he replied, his voice was soothingly gentle and rich with appreciation.

"That would surely be my pleasure, Cynthia, and an honor as well. I hope, dear lady, you don't mind my taking the liberty of calling you Cynthia? I would consider it a great privilege."

He paused. She smiled in acquiescence. Relieved, he continued.

"I want you to know, dear Cynthia, that I shall pray for your swift return."

Chapter Twenty-seven

Two weeks had passed since Nick left Tysons Landing and returned to London.

Cat's party was in full swing by the time he arrived. He had reluctantly agreed to go without Jan, who was at home nursing a cold.

This particular party was being thrown to celebrate Cat's success. The demo she had cut in the United States was creeping up the charts. According to *Billboard,* it was a phenomenally successful single and a good bet to make it to the number-one spot. Also, her six-week engagement at The Round Table was being extended indefinitely.

Nick watched her move through the room of well-wishers; a cameraman followed, clicking pictures nonstop. Catching sight of Nick, Cat smiled a wide, happy smile and put her hands on his shoulders.

"Nick, it's so good to see you."

She tossed back her silver hair and combed it with her delicate fingers. She leaned close to Nick, almost as if he were a prop. Then he noticed the photographers; their flashbulbs rapidly popping away.

Tensing, he muttered under his breath, "God, how I hate those bloody bastards."

"I understand how you feel," Cat whispered back to him, "but people like me need them. When they *stop* snapping me, that's when my problems will start."

As Nick looked into her warm, expressive eyes, he felt a stirring in his groin. He rememberd the last time they were together. Damn it, why had he come to the party without

Jan? He knew it was dangerous for him to be alone with Cat. She always seemed to strip him of his self-control. Deep in his gut he knew he desired her.

Almost without conscious thought, he bent down and kissed the soft corner of her mouth, feeling horny as hell. He was suddenly oblivious to the photographers, who still clicked away, taking endless photographs.

Sarah Hartley leaned against the banquet wall and watched Cat and Nick. She turned to Daley, who was standing next to her, and spoke in a low, purposeful voice.

"I'll bet you anything those two end up screwing each other royally tonight—that is, if they haven't done so already."

Daley gave her a throaty chuckle.

"You couldn't give me big enough odds to take that bet. Usually, baby, a guy just follows where his cock leads him."

Sarah looked up at him.

"Do you know something I don't know?" she asked.

"Nope. All I know is what I'm looking at right now."

Without taking her eyes off the two of them, Sarah thought back to the last time she saw Cat and Nick together. Even then she had been sure that they were playing a little nooky. But later she had convinced herself that it was just her overly suspicious nature.

Glancing at Daley, she noticed that his eyes were glued to Cat. The expression on Sarah's face hardened as she thought that the bastard was no doubt thinking he'd like to shtup her himself.

"Well, are they or aren't they?" she asked angrily.

Daley gave her a slow, salacious, yet meaningful smile.

"You want an answer? You'll get an answer. I'll lay odds that the two of them are involved with each other—and that that particular involvement has nothing to do with business."

Sarah was tempted to call Jan then and there and tell her to haul her ass over on the double. She tried to envision how Jan would react. How would she handle it if she learned that Cat and Nick were having an affair? Jan was so crazy in love with the guy that there wasn't a pedestal high enough for him.

Cat closed her eyes and wriggled her warm, soft, naked body next to Nick's.

"What time is it, lover?"

"It's almost two in the morning. Time for me to go," Nick answered.

The room was heavy with the odor of perfume and sex. Cat ran her fingers through her hair sensuously, and he got out of bed slowly, keeping his eyes on her.

"I should be blushing with shame, the things I do with you," she purred; her satisfied smile never leaving her face.

Carefully buttoning his shirt, Nick felt gnawing pangs of guilt as the image of Jan's lovely, adoring face crossed his mind. He knew how much he loved her. She was everything he wanted. So why the hell was he putting that love in jeopardy? Why was he fucking around with Cat Bracken? How many more times would he end up in Cat's bed, foolishly risking the wonderful relationship he had with Jan?

Watching Nick dress, Cat noticed he was preoccupied with his own thoughts. Nick, suddenly aware that her eyes were on him, gave her a lazy smile and started to reach out for her but stopped.

"Go to sleep," he whispered, blowing her a kiss. Then he was gone.

As the door closed behind him, Cat snuggled down under the covers and pulled the quilt over her head. It was obvious to her that Nick had been feeling guilty. She knew that he really and truly loved Jan, and she was happy for him. She knew he would soon work Cat Bracken out of his system; their affair could only be short-lived. After all, she had a dazzling career ahead of her. Nick would certainly marry Jan, *Pleasure Palace* would be a roaring success, and everyone would live happily ever after.

Smiling a fuzzy little smile, Cat closed her eyes. In a few seconds she was fast asleep.

The next day, Sarah Hartley phoned Jan. Finding Jan home, she invited herself to lunch.

As they waited for lunch, sipping a glass of chilled wine, Sarah studied Jan carefully.

"How's the cold?"

"Much better, thanks. I went to bed early and slept the whole night away. Today I feel marvelous. I want you to tell me everything about Cat's party. Was it fun? Who was there, and was I missed?"

Sarah casually played with the sapphire and diamond ring on her pinky. When she spoke, there was a faint trace of pity in her voice.

"I would say it was a very successful party. Everybody was slightly sloshed and merrily stoned. Cat was as charming as usual, and she looked bloody terrific."

Sarah's mouth tightened slightly as she continued.

"Were you missed? I honestly don't know. But I do know that Nick and Cat left the party together. It was rather early on in the evening, at that. What time did he get home?"

"I've no idea, Sarah. I was fast asleep. And I haven't seen him this morning at all. He left before I got up."

"Are you sure?"

"Of course I'm sure. The housekeeper fixed breakfast for him."

Jan refilled Sarah's glass, trying to sort out her feelings.

"Maybe I'm dense, Sarah, but I have a distinct feeling that you're trying to tell me something."

Sarah slowly brought her wineglass up to her lips. A sudden high-voltage silence filled the room. Jan felt ruffled and uneasy as she watched her friend.

"Jan, I don't know how to say this . . ."

"Just say it, Sarah."

"Well, I think Nick and Cat are having an affair."

Jan was stunned. She had suspected that that was what Sarah was leading up to, but now that the words were out, the shock was no less enormous. She felt stunned, depleted, and hot with rising anger.

The green eyes that faced Sarah were like chips of ice.

"You're totally wrong, of course."

Sarah shrugged.

"I hope I am, Jan, but for God's sake, check it out. Ostriches who keep their heads in the sand end up with nothing but sandy tonsils."

Jan felt her hands tremble. Could there be any truth in what Sarah had told her? She felt as if she might break into tears at any moment—especially when she remembered that Nick's birthday was the day after tomorrow.

Nick's birthday. Jan so wanted to do something special with him.

The thought was too much for her. She pushed her chair away from the table.

Sarah looked up at her.

"Hell, Jan, maybe I should have kept all this to myself. But the thought of Nick playing around right under your nose was too much for me—playing around, I might add, with a woman you seem to admire and consider a friend. I just had to tell you."

Sarah took another sip of her drink, then continued.

"You're my best friend, Jan, and I didn't want you to be the last to know. Cat Bracken has everything going for her. She's so fucking independent, and a celebrity to boot. She thinks she can do whatever she damned well pleases."

"Sarah, I know I should feel grateful to you for telling me this. But right now all I feel is a numbing sense of outrage. Let's cancel our lunch for today."

Sarah stood up, looking very unhappy. She finished the last of her wine, kissed Jan briefly on the cheek, and walked toward the front door.

After Sarah left, Jan felt limp and exhausted.

She walked slowly upstairs to her bedroom and made an effort to stem her tears. Propping three big pillows against the back of the bed, she stretched out and tried to will her shoulders to relax. But she couldn't stop her nerves from tightening. Her whole world seemed to be crashing down.

She couldn't get her thoughts into focus. *Nick and Cat! It can't be.*

She felt defeated, drained. Almost aimlessly, her eyes wandered around the room. Nothing had changed, yet nothing felt the same. Nick had been unfaithful to her.

Mounting fury welled up inside of her. Her thoughts grew more bitter, more explosive. Jan Julliard, the dreamer, the romantic sucker! All this time she had believed herself to be the one essential, most important element in Nick Tyson's life—Nick, to whom she had given her heart, her trust. She felt as if her insides had been shattered and broken. She had lived with someone all this time and hadn't even known him.

The hurt grew stronger when she realized that her romance with Nick was the consuming passion of her life. Jan knew that she had not been given that part of him which she had counted on—his abiding love and eternal loyalty.

Her thoughts were interrupted by the sound of his key turning in the lock. She listened as he raced up the stairs, taking them two at a time. The bedroom door opened, and there was Nick in the doorway, smiling his wide, provocative smile. He looked so clean, so handsome, and so innocent—not at all like a broken idol.

As Jan stared at him, an overwhelming sadness crept over her. Her heart was broken, and yet she couldn't weep.

Nick gestured toward her with his forefinger.

"Know something? You look beautiful."

As he bent over to kiss her, she pulled away sharply.

"Rough day, baby?"

"Shitty," she answered.

Expressionlessly, she stared at him. Nick's face wore a puzzled expression.

"If this is a game of Twenty Questions, I'm not in the mood to play."

Taking off his jacket, he walked over to the televison set and turned it on. He settled himself in his chair, and his attention was immediately fixed on a soccer match on the big screen.

Jan had a strong urge to scream, but she kept her voice calm.

"Nick, please turn the set off. There's something I want to discuss with you."

With a look of resignation on his face, he rose from the chair and reached for the TV. Jan spoke quickly, fighting for control.

"Sarah told me at lunch that she thinks you and Cat Bracken are having an affair."

As Nick slowly switched the set off, she noticed the slight tensing of his shoulders. When he turned to look at her, his confidence faltered for just a second. Then he sat down angrily on the edge of the bed.

Damn him, thought Jan. *He cheated on me. What the hell gives him the right to look so hostile, as if he's the injured party?*

They eyed each other like warriors. Nick moved toward her: she put up her hand to stop him. Something in her eyes made him back off.

Part of her was hoping, hoping there would be a wonderful, easy explanation, one that would make everything all right again.

Nick remained silent, as if at a loss for words. Jan felt her heart plunge down to her toes. There was a terrible constriction in her throat as she realized there would be no wonderful, easy explanation.

The more she stared at him, the more panicky the look in his eyes seemed to get, as if he were wondering whether to tell her the truth or try to get away with some lie.

Finally the words came.

"Jan, I love you. Only you. You've got to believe that. I don't know how it happened, but Cat and I, we sort of just drifted into it."

His voice was surprisingly calm, almost soothing.

As she listened, Jan ached inside. She hated him. The more she hurt, the stronger her hatred grew.

"Jesus, Nick. Tell me, who else have you been sneaking around with? How long have you been a player, a skirt chaser?"

Nick drew his breath in sharply.

"Jan, listen to me. The thing with Cat was nothing. It had no meaning. Believe me, it was nothing."

She looked straight at him, unblinking. Her eyes were

dry, with no hint of tears. When she spoke, her voice held just a hint of barely controlled rage.

"Please, Nick. Don't give me the worn-out excuse that it was nothing. To me, it's everything. I thought you were special, but you've turned out to be a typical cheating bastard. Damn you! When I think how stupidly romantic I was! I actually believed I was the most important thing in your life."

The words came faster. She didn't know how long she could keep her tears in check.

"I see things clearly now. It's time for me to get out into the world, time for me to grow up. Damn it, Nick, don't stand there! Why don't you just go to her?"

"Jan, please—"

"Please nothing! I can't play according to your rules, and I wouldn't if I could. So let's just end it. Our so-called love affair has just been a crazy fantasy, a dumb storybook romance. Well, it's over now. The game's been called on account of a foul. Maybe I can pick up where I left off a couple years ago."

Nick started to reach out to her, but something in her eyes made him draw back. There were still no tears on her face. Tears he might have been able to handle. But her stony resolve was a wall he couldn't breach.

When he finally spoke, his voice was softer, less assured. He knew this was his last chance, and that the odds were overwhelmingly against him.

"Jan, honey, all I want is to have you with me, to let things be the way they were before. You know that. You're blowing this up out of all proportion."

"Maybe I am," she answered sadly. "But right now I don't want to return to the way things were. I could never be comfortable with that again."

She glanced down at her watch.

"I'll go pack my things and leave."

Nick's expression grew desperate. His words tumbled over themselves as he looked at her imploringly.

"Jan, I love you. I've never stopped loving you. Please don't go! We can get married right now."

She smiled at him mirthlessly, her voice full of sarcasm.

"We can, Nick? Haven't you forgotten something? You don't yet have your mother's consent."

As he looked directly into her cold green eyes, it was obvious he had lost her. There wasn't a trace of compassion on her face, no sign of relenting. His own blue eyes were dark with despair; his voice was full of pain.

"Honey, please stay. Give me another chance. You're more important to me than anyone or anything. Don't you understand? I love you."

"I'm sorry, Nick. You've told me that before. I'm not sure I could ever trust you again. I'm not sure we can ever go back. Right now, all I want is my own space."

By the time Jan walked downstairs, her knees were weak and her thoughts were scattered. Nick had called a limo for her, and he was proceeding to get very drunk.

She walked to the hall phone and slowly dialed a number. After three rings Sarah picked up.

"Well, Sarah, you were right. Nick and Cat were lovers, right under my nose. I want you to be the first to know that Jan Julliard is no longer an ostrich. I am walking out on Nick Tyson."

After a short pause Sarah replied, "Jesus, I'm sorry. Now I wish I hadn't told you. Daley's furious with me. He said, So okay, now you know they fucked. He said there isn't a man in the world who won't cheat if he had the chance. So his advice to you is forgive and forget because Nick doesn't love Cat, he loves you."

Jan took a big, deep breath.

"Daley's just the sort of person who would rationalize cheating. I remember way back when he told me that nothing lasts forever. Well, right now I feel scarred, deep down inside me. I'm going to leave, to get out into the world and reconstruct my life. It'll be very hard for me, Sarah, because you see, I'm still in love with Nick. And I probably always will be."

Sarah's eyes swam as she stood for a moment holding the phone. She held it long after Jan had placed the receiver back on the hook.

After Jan's departure, Nick sat and stared into space.

He felt awful. He couldn't remember when he had ever felt so miserable. He wondered if he'd ever get over this feeling of loss. He knew the house had never felt so empty before.

Rising from the chair, he walked into her bathroom and caught the scent of her perfume, remembered the fragrance of her body. He still couldn't believe she had really left him.

A short time later, Nick pulled his car up to Cat's apartment building. He sat for awhile before he pulled his keys from the ignition. Then, getting out of the car, he walked inside. With an almost imperceptible shrug, he rang her doorbell.

Seconds later, Cat opened the door.

"Oh, Nick!" she said, giving him a sudden grin. Her eyes were bright with excitement. "Come in, come in. I have the most wonderful news to tell you. I was just going to call you."

Nick shut the door quietly behind him.

Then Cat saw the expression in his eyes.

"Is anything wrong, Nick?"

His voice sounded shattered.

"Jan just left me. She found out about us."

"Oh, my God, I'm sorry. I know how you cared for her. And I can guess how she must have taken it. Right now she's probably feeling wounded and betrayed. But after a while, when the hurt eases, she may come back again."

Cat half-closed her eyes and silently analyzed her own feelings. The thought of Nick and Jan breaking up because of her sent her into a panic. She had already made up her mind that it was time to disconnect with Nick. They'd had fun running the rapids; it was great making love with him with no ties, no commitments. It had been the perfect arrangement for her. But now, fun time was over.

Cat gently stroked his face and looked into Nick's beautiful blue sorrow-filled eyes, eyes that always reminded her of someone. But she had never been able to figure out who it was; maybe it was someone she had met in a dream a long time ago.

"Nick, please go and find her, for my sake. The two of you belong to each other."

"I will. I will," he murmured.

She watched him walk to his car. He didn't even turn and look back. As she closed the door behind him, her own eyes grew moist.

Two hours later, Cat sat in the back of a limousine, asking herself if she was making the right decision.

It wasn't like her to doubt herself where her career was concerned. She had been asked to take over the lead role in a movie that was in trouble. The temperamental female star of the film, who'd been drinking heavily, had walked off the set. Daley Russell was doing his best not to let the project fall apart; he had recommended Cat to his producer. But Cat knew that the movie had many other big problems; even with all her talent, it could still turn out to be a disaster.

She had wanted so much to talk it over with Nick, whose advice she valued tremendously. But today had not been the right time to discuss anything with Nick Tyson. He had been absorbed in his own problem.

The following morning, Nick awoke with a dull ache pounding inside his skull. His limbs felt like lead weights. He slowly lifted one flickering eyelid and cringed as the burst of light pierced into his throbbing brain. His hangover was horrendous.

He tried to focus his thoughts, to think back to the night before.

After leaving Cat's apartment, he had desperately tried to learn where Jan was, but to no avail. She had simply vanished from sight. So there had been nothing for him to do but continue drinking, and now his head felt like an army was marching through it.

He got up from the bed with a groan and held his temples as he stumbled to the bureau to pick up the remains of a joint. All he could think was, *Christ, I need a toke to help blow this headache away.* Holding up the crushed joint, he lit it and sucked on it greedily. After a couple of deep drags, the throbbing stopped—or at least he was no longer conscious of it—so he put down the joint and stretched himself out on the bed.

With his eyes closed, Nick let his mind drift. Without Jan, there was a void in his life; his loss grew more oppressive with each passing minute. And he alone was responsible for the mess he had gotten into.

Damn it, if she was gone, she was gone. Wishing wouldn't bring her back. He'd have to stop thinking about

her before the men in white jackets came to haul him
away, he realized.

He'd think about *Pleasure Palace* instead.

The ship would be his refuge. He would now be able to
devote all his attention, all his energies to her. He'd make
her the crowning triumph of his life, and his success would
be a dramatic tribute to Jan.

Damn it! He was thinking about her again.

Well, so what?

After his triumph with *Pleasure Palace*, he'd catch up
with Jan somewhere, somehow, no matter where she was.
She was an unshakable part of his life. He knew they were
meant to be together. Neither of them could bear to be
away from the other. But right now he'd have to put her
on the back burner of his mind.

Suddenly Nick felt pleasantly relaxed, as if he had
crossed an invisible line of demarcation. And having
crossed it, he was sure that everything was going to work
out just fine.

Chapter Twenty-eight

The slight drizzle blanketing Paris perfectly matched Jan's mood as she landed at Orly Airport.

Driving to the Ritz Hotel, she felt the pain of Nick's unfaithfulness more acutely than ever. Yet she knew she was still in love with him. That was why she had to get as much distance between them as possible.

The most important thing for her to do was to find a way to stop thinking of Nick Tyson. Otherwise each day would be filled with torment. She had to be strong enough to erase the awful feeling of loss that threatened to engulf her.

Of course, there were moments of self-doubt. Perhaps she had acted too hastily. Perhaps she should have been cooler about the whole situation. But she cast those thoughts aside. She didn't want to spend her life playing games. How could it be love if you had to mask your true feelings? Okay, perhaps she had no right to expect anyone to be a hundred percent faithful, but she had been so sure about Nick, so secure in his love.

Luckily she had the inheritance her parents had left her and her passport. She was beholden to no one. Jan Julliard was free to do whatever she wanted, and right now what she wanted most of all was to get Nick Tyson out of her system.

So here she was in Paris.

She had told no one where she was going, not even Sarah. As far as Jan was concerned, they could all think she had vanished from the face of the earth.

* * *

At the hotel reception desk, Jan noticed that the lobby was filled with happy-looking couples, and she felt a vast loneliness settle in.

She got the registration over with as soon as possible and took the elevator to her suite. After tipping the porter, she walked over to the French doors and pushed them open. She took a deep breath as she looked out over the rooftops of Paris. Even lightly coated by the drizzle, it was still unmistakably Paris, the city of light. For some reason, the thought depressed her.

Walking back into the room, Jan noticed the welcoming bottle of champagne on the coffee table. After her third glass, she began to relax and released some of the tight grip she had been holding on herself.

Without bothering to remove her clothes, she stretched out on the bed and told herself she would forget all about Nick Tyson. She'd find herself a new lover—maybe more than one. And this time she'd have better control over her emotions. This time she'd be tougher, wiser, and a lot less trusting.

After finishing the bottle she ordered another one, then tumbled back into bed, where she soon slid into a deep and dreamless sleep.

The next morning Jan woke up with a pounding headache. Her throat was burning, and her stomach felt queasy. She decided that getting drunk was not the answer to her problems.

After a bath and some hot coffee, she began to feel better. The ache in her head was still fierce, but she was determined not to let it keep her from the legendary streets of Paris.

The soft drizzle of the night before had turned into a warm, soggy downpour.

Undaunted, her umbrella held high, Jan slowly toured Avenue Montaigne, the Rue du Faubourg, and Rues St. Honoré and Victor Hugo. Attracted by the colorful, striking window displays, she peered into the windows of Chanel, Givenchy, Cardin, Yves St. Laurent, and Karl Lagerfeld. But her thoughts strayed back to London.

At the Jardin des Tuileries, she absently wandered through the famous gardens. Ignoring the weather, she sat down on one of the ancient iron chairs, where she watched the ever-changing clouds move across the gray Parisian sky. The day perfectly matched her own bleak mood.

Two days later, Jan's bags were once again packed.

From Orly Airport, she flew to Monte Carlo. There she checked into the Hôtel de Paris and spent her first few hours idly watching the yachts steaming into the harbor.

That night, her first evening in Monte Carlo, Jan had dinner alone in her room. Later, too restless to go to bed, she decided to take a walk.

The warm sea breezes were sweet and balmy, and the temperature not too hot for August. Jan mingled with the casually dressed tourists who packed the streets and walked aimlessly along in a seemingly endless procession. Moving leisurely along with them, she eventually found herself outside the famed Casino of Monte Carlo.

She debated whether to continue walking or to return to her hotel. Since neither prospect particularly appealed to her, she decided that she might as well visit the Casino.

Inside the building Jan was fascinated by the ornate architecture, the intricately carved moldings, and the high, painted ceiling. They seemed to belong to another, far more elegant era, one at odds with the casually clad wash-

and-wear tourists who were noisily playing the slot machines.

Having no particular interest in gambling, Jan watched for a few minutes and then turned to leave. But before she could make her way through the crowd, the imposing figure of Jaafar al Hassad sailed like a schooner through the doors of the casino.

He caught sight of Jan, recognized her instantly, and made a beeline in her direction. Though slightly out of breath by the time he reached her, he bent and kissed her on the cheek. Then he stepped back a pace, took her hands, and stared at her. There was undisguised curiosity in his black, probing eyes.

Having caught his breath again, he spoke in his low, rich, halting voice.

"My dear, dear Jan." He paused for a moment, and then said, "How lovely you look. What a wonderful surprise bumping into you like this. May I ask where you are staying?"

Before she could reply, Jaafar answered his own question.

"No matter. Wherever it is, you will leave and stay with my wife and me at our villa. I am so eager for you to meet my young son."

Jaafar's eyes left hers for the first time when he suddenly looked around the room.

"Now tell me, where is Nick? Has he ungallantly abandoned you for the roulette tables?"

Taken aback for a moment, Jan was uncertain how to reply. Seconds later, she made her voice as light and frivolous as possible.

"Oh, Nick's not with me right now. He's so busy with his ship that he couldn't come. So I left him in London. You see, Jaafar, I feel neither of us should be a burden to the other. I've always believed in being an independent person."

Jaafar looked at her with undisguised disbelief in his eyes. But his smile was warm and understanding as he replied, "Well, I think independence is a most admirable state of being. So if you're here all alone in this gaudy pleasure dome, do come along with me. You can be my luck for tonight."

Without waiting for a reply, he took Jan's arm and sallied forth across the room. The stern-looking man who guarded the entrance to one of the the private salons gave him a welcoming nod of recognition as Jaafar, with Jan in tow, walked past the velvet rope.

Inside the softly lit room, Jan took stock of the elegant men and beautifully gowned women who were playing roulette.

Jaafar obtained fifty thousand dollars' worth of chips from the cashier as casually as if he were buying a newspaper.

She was fascinated as she watched him play. His nonchalance was incredible, and yet it was obviously quite genuine. It really seemed to make no difference to him whether he won or lost. Within twenty minutes he had gone through most of his chips. A slight nod to an attendant caused a new pile of chips to be placed on the table in front of him instantly. This time his luck improved. He won four times in a row. Yet his attitude didn't change in the slightest. Jan saw that the money meant nothing to him. Jaafar al Hassad was simply killing time.

A few moments later he stopped playing. Scooping his remaining chips off the table, he slid a few across to the croupier. Then he nodded to Jan.

"Come along, my dear. Let me get you a glass of champagne. This must all be very boring for you."

A faint sigh rose from those in the crowd who had been betting with Jaafar during his roll. To them, it was incomprehensible that anyone would leave while on a winning streak.

The next morning, Jan sat in her hotel lobby waiting for Jaafar. She smiled at the thought that he was certainly the most persuasively charming man she had ever known.

Her first impulse had been to refuse his invitation to stay with him and his wife at their villa. However, Jaafar had easily won her over and had effortlessly brushed away all her reasons not to go.

When Jan finally accepted his invitation to stay a few days, she admitted to herself that her decision had been influenced by the fact that she was very curious to learn who Jaafar had married.

After driving about twenty minutes in his sleek, silver Bentley, they arrived at a private airfield. From there, Jaafar's waiting helicopter flew them to the picturesque landing pad at the edge of his villa, La Casa della Bellezza, where they were greeted by respectful, uniformed attendants and a pair of savage-looking guard dogs.

Jaafar told Jan that lunch would be at twelve.

His wife did not put in an appearance.

A housekeeper, fluent in English, appeared with a bevy of servants, who were also multilingual. They escorted Jan to a suite overlooking luxurious tropical gardens. As a housemaid unpacked for her, Jan pushed her sunglasses back to the top of her head and stepped out onto the terrace to view her surroundings.

As far as she could see, the hills were ablaze with wild flowers. A huge pink bougainvillaea graced one wall of the terrace; its dropped petals formed a carpet on the floor.

Masses of orange nasturtiums created a blaze of color; they crept and trailed through the latticework as if part of the sun had fallen down.

Jan was entranced by the lush beauty of the place, by its green lawns and its gardens filled with luxurious plantings. Tropical birds and tame parrots perched in the trees, while full-tailed peacocks strutted across the lawns with smug, proprietary airs. The ten-acre compound was like a hidden corner of paradise.

Later she walked the grounds.

The pool was built into a grotto beneath a cascading waterfall. Parts of the estate had been left wild, with magnificent stone and terra-cotta sculptures placed in strategic spots. They blended with the terrain as if nature itself had placed them there. Looking around her, Jan realized how enormously rich Jaafar al Hassad had to be.

She was excited at the thought of seeing Jaafar and meeting his wife. Since it was nearly twelve and time for lunch, she turned and headed back toward the house.

The imposing figure of Jaafar al Hassad glided toward her across the lawn.

"Do come inside so you may meet Leancia. I expect that you and my wife will become very good friends."

He led Jan through a succession of huge, airy rooms that were lavishly furnished with sofas and chairs in vibrant colors. The walls were adorned with modern art and paintings by many of the nineteenth-century masters. Every ceiling was skylighted, filling the rooms with sunshine.

Jaafar and she walked until they entered an enclosed garden. There the rush of a waterfall filled the air as it cascaded into the aqua pool.

Standing near the pool was a woman with her back to them. She was slender, tall, and barefoot; she wore a large sun hat and a full-skirted white cotton dress.

Jan knew this must be Jaafar's wife, Leancia.

A small, beautiful boy was in her arms, resting easily on her hip. The child laughed with glee as the water rushed into the pool.

The woman turned, as if suddenly aware of the presence of others. For a few silent seconds her dark eyes held Jan's. Then, turning her head, she called out in a voice unusually soft and musical, "Yana. Yana, where are you? It's time for Brian's nap."

A tall, powerfully-built woman walked into the garden. Leancia handed the child to her. Yana swung the laughing boy astride her shoulders with effortless ease. Leancia's delicate features were filled with love as she watched her son being carried away by the muscular, Slavic-looking woman until they were both out of sight.

Jan was struck by the striking resemblance between the beautiful woman and her child.

Jaafar broke the silence.

"Ladies, please excuse me. There are a few business calls I must make. Why don't you go ahead and have a cocktail before lunch? It will give you an opportunity to get to know each other."

He then moved off in a princely fashion.

Leancia removed her hat with a gesture of infinite grace and slowly walked toward Jan. She studied her with her large, dark, heavily fringed eyes. She swung back her long, glistening hair, and her full lips curved into a warm and gracious smile. It was as if she were smiling at a secret all her own.

Jan experienced a feeling of confusion. The longer she looked at Leancia, the more certain she was that their paths had crossed before.

When Jan finally spoke, she knew her words might sound vague and confused.

"Do forgive me for staring so, Mrs. al Hassad. You must think me very rude. The fact is, you remind me so strongly of someone, and yet I simply can't place who it is."

Leancia laughed a tinkling, musical laugh.

"Dear, dear Jan. You're quite right. I do remind you of someone. That's because you and I have met before. And now our paths have crossed again."

Seconds later, it hit Jan with numbing impact.

"Lear!" she whispered. "It is you, isn't it?"

Even before she received an affirmative nod, Jan knew that, no matter how incredible it seemed, Lear Feria and this lovely wife and mother were one and the same person.

Later after lunch, Jan and Leancia sat in the quiet of the garden talking.

Leancia started to talk about her previous life in Paris, especially her career as the star of L'Accord. She told of Damon and Pythias and of the unselfish friendship they had offered her.

As they spoke, servants kept appearing out of nowhere with iced drinks and bowls of chilled fruit. But the refreshments lay untouched; Jan listened, enthralled. At one point she eagerly interrupted the other woman's narrative.

"I can hardly believe it, Leancia! I remember reading about your exciting performances. The columnists seemed to love writing about you. They referred to you as an exquisite enigma, as the ravishing rage of Paris."

"Yes—blond wig, silver-sequined eyepatch, outrageous attire, madness and mystery. All of it hid the real me from the world, the real me that was locked up, held captive, and never really able to break free."

Leancia paused for a moment and selected a mango from the bowl of fruit. Her mind seemed a million miles away as she rubbed her long, delicate fingers over its smooth surface. Then she continued speaking.

"During the afternoons, I was Pythias's private secretary. No one ever guessed that it was me. My clothes were understated, and my eyes were hidden under heavy designer glasses. My own hair was slicked back in a severe bun. Keeping my identity hidden was Pythias and Damon's idea, and it was simply amazing that nobody ever guessed. I suppose people only see you as they want to see you. They only see the image you convey to them. No one ever put the two of us together—except for one person."

Her voice became softer; her brown eyes seemed to fill with memories. She spoke the word as if to herself: "Jaafar."

At the mention of his name, Jan saw Leancia's face change. Her expression became suffused with love. There was passion in her voice as she spoke of him.

"He came to the club and . . . oh, I won't go into all the details, Jan."

She smiled to herself, as if at a private joke.

"When we first met, I remember not liking him at all. You know, it's sometimes difficult to see past Jaafar's enormous bulk, his great flamboyance, and glimpse his true nature."

It seemed to Jan that Leancia's thoughts had suddenly turned elsewhere. As she spoke, her tone became distant, as if she were caught up in a secret reverie.

"But, oh, his kindness, his understanding, his concern! I came to trust him completely. I realized there comes a time when you have to make a commitment, when you must put your fate in someone else's hands. I did that with Jaafar. It was the most wonderful decision I ever made."

Leancia paused.

"And now, as you can see, I am so very happy. It was

Jaafar who arranged everything. He took total control. He had truly fallen in love with me. Not with Leancia the performer, but with the real me.

"My operation was handled in a private clinic in Mexico. There were no problems. When it was over, I had no regrets, sensed no loss. I finally felt free. We need each other, Jaafar and I. I imagine poeple would be hard put to understand our strange relationship. You see, there is no sex between us, not in the sense of physical copulation. My husband is impotent. But that doesn't matter because there is love. Oh yes, there is beautiful, bountiful love between us."

Leancia paused; her dark eyes were soft and glistening.

"And there is our son, of course, our wonderful son. Jaafar again took care of all the arrangements."

"He handled the adoption?" Jan asked.

Leancia smiled knowingly, her eyes full of merriment.

"Brian is not adopted."

There was a moment of silence as Jan stared at her in disbelief. When she finally spoke, her voice was barely audible.

"Leancia, what do you mean?"

The other woman tilted her head back and shook her hair loose. Her smile grew wider; then she broke into a laugh.

Jan found that she too was laughing. It was as if they were laughing at a secret joke known only to them. Finally Leancia took a breath and continued.

"Well, dear friend, two months before my operation, sperm was milked from me and stored in a sperm bank. Then a surrogate mother was chosen with the greatest care. The beautiful child you saw today truly is my son. the son of my own seed."

Jan felt tears coming, but she shook them away. There

was no need for tears. Her heart was filled with happinesss
for Leancia.

Jan's stay at La Casa della Bellezza was a joyful one.
Leancia was attentive, witty, and fascinating. She and
Jaafar managed to keep Jan busy with a breathless schedule. They visited the small Mediterranean island of
Cavello, and from there they flew to Spain to attend the
bullfights. After that, they spent a week at Jaafar's villa in
St. Moritz, then on to Germany for a deer hunt before
returning to Monte Carlo. They seemed to genuinely enjoy
taking Jan everywhere, showing her everything of interest.

Nothing marred her pleasure except the recurring memories of Nick. But whenever he crossed her mind, Jan
forced herself to will his image away, hoping against hope
that she'd forget him in time, that her heart would somehow heal.

The gloriously sunny days drifted into weeks.

Each time Jan decided to return to London, Leancia
convinced her to stay just awhile longer. The time had
gone so fast that she could hardly believe she'd been away
from London for almost six months.

One night at a local party Jan met an exceptionally attractive man. His strong sexual magnetism and his charming manner so appealed to her that she ended up in his
bed. After him came a French ski bum, then a German
tennis player, followed by a very proper English lord. All
were very compelling, totally attentive, and quite eligible,
but none affected her heart. Now more than ever, Jan was
convinced that she would never fall in love again.

The day before Jaafar planned to leave for London, Jan
decided it was time that she, too, bade the villa farewell.
Having made up her mind, she announced it to Leancia as
they were having tea after a shopping spree in Monaco.

"I really must return to London now. I've loved every minute I've spent here with you, but it's time for me to plan what to do with my life. You and Jaafar have pampered me so; if I stay any longer, I know I'll become hopelessly spoiled."

"It's still Nick, isn't it?" Leancia asked in her soft, breathy voice. "You feel the loss of him keenly, don't you? You know, Jan, perhaps a new love is what you need."

"I know, Leancia," sighed Jan. "I tell that to myself a thousand times a day. If only it were that easy."

She paused for a moment, as if searching for the right words.

"I loved Nick very deeply. I just don't seem able to take that love and transfer it somewhere else. I know it must sound mad, but since my split with him, I feel unsure about who I really am. I thought taking lovers might be the answer, as long as I kept my head numb and empty. But it's all so meaningless, such a trivial bore."

Leancia's eyes were warm with compassion as she looked at her friend. Her voice was soft when she spoke; her tone was gentle and soothing.

"Dear Jan, you yourself are the only one who can choose your future. Perhaps the right course for you would be to return to Nick and forgive him. I'm sure that's what your heart wants. If you could just forget the hurt of the past, think how you would treasure a new beginning."

Jan turned her head away, but she needn't have bothered.

Leancia had already seen the tears.

Chapter Twenty-nine

As the makeup man worked on her face, Cat stared at herself in the mirror and barely listened to his idle chatter. Over the sound of his voice she heard angry footsteps thundering down the hall.

Daley Russell stormed into her dressing room like a supercharged whirling dervish.

"Balls! I need a drink. Where's that goddamned bottle of booze? We'll have to do the fuckin' shot tomorrow! A whole day wasted. Sunrise! Why did I hafta go for it? I know it's a bitch to capture. That shitty English fog blew the whole damned shoot. With just a little luck we could have wrapped everything up this morning. And I was planning to catch the early flight tomorrow for L.A."

His eyes blazing, he turned his attention to the makeup man.

"This is turning into one pig-shit kind of a stinkin' day. You might as well fuck off. Go on—lose yourself somewhere, for Christ's sake, and take that tight-ass assistant of yours with you."

The makeup man and his startled young helper gave Daley a look of utter contempt and left the room.

Cat reacted to Daley's yelling as she always did—by saying nothing. She just let him scream his emotions out.

He shoved his hands into the pockets of his black leather jacket; his moody face was a symphony of scowls. Finally he sat down next to her.

He was silent for a moment, sipping Scotch out of the

bottle. Then, as if suddenly aware of her presence, he turned to her.

"Jesus, I don't see how you do it, lady! Here you sit, as calm as a freakin' clam in the heart of a hurricane. Okay, I'll admit I don't give a flying fuck about anybody but me at the moment, but I sure expected a little temper from you, too. After all, weren't you planning to hightail it back to London tomorrow, right into the arms of lover-boy Nick?"

Cat's big blue eyes appraised Daley calmly.

"No. What gave you that idea? That wasn't my intention at all."

"Well, well, whaddaya know?" Daley asked. The booze was starting to relax him.

He stared at her for a moment and raked his fingers through his tousled gray-streaked hair. His legs were tossed over one arm of the chair as he dangled his sneaker-shod feet. Daley's black eyes took on a lazy-lidded look. He cocked his head to one side and gave her one of his infectious grins; his voice was reflective as he spoke.

"Well, you sure fooled me. I figured you and Tyson were a hot, heavy item. 'Specially when the word around the set was that you've been real unapproachable—no sleeping around or anything. Hell, I figured you were being Little Fanny Faithful, saving it for ol' Nick."

Cat didn't reply. Her eyes were expressionless as Daley warmed up to his subject.

"So you weren't planning to head back to Nick's waiting arms, huh? Know somethin', Cat? You're a lady after my own heart. Tell you what. While we're here, how about trying on my arms for size? Hey, it doesn't make sense to waste a chance like this."

Cat seethed inwardly. She slowly removed the terry-cloth turban she had been wearing while her makeup was being applied. Then, combing her long, silver hair with her delicate fingers in an angry gesture, she glared at Daley in the mirror through narrowed, turquoise eyes.

"Maybe my idea of what makes sense is different from yours, Daley."

He stretched and stood up.

"Look, baby, leave us not forget who gave you the chance to try out for the part of Jessica. You're lookin' at him, right? And now hear this. The big brass at the studio are crazy about you. They're sure they've got a hit. In fact, they're already talkin' sequel."

"You mean it, Daley? Why didn't you tell me?"

Thrilled by Daley's news, Cat's anger faded away. She flashed him a grateful smile and settled herself more comfortably into her chair. The words tumbled out of her.

"That's absolutely terrific! Wow, to tell you the truth, I was beginning to feel a little shaky! I wasn't too happy with the way those last rushes looked, even though I must admit you made me look gorgeous the way you shot me."

Daley sat down again near Cat. He was glad her mood had turned more mellow. She smiled at him as she continued.

"You're right, of course. If not for you, I'd probably never have gotten that audition. But I hope you won't hold it over me forever."

"Hey, lady, I never intended to. You know that. Just didn't want you to forget about it, that's all. Now, how about dinner? We really should talk some more about your career. Anyway, I wanna get to know you better. Much better."

"But what about Sarah? Aren't you and she—?"

"Look," Daley cut in, "Sarah knows just where she stands with me."

Cat thought for a moment, then nodded understanding-
ingly.

One week later the movie was completed. All that remained was the traditional wrap party.

The next morning Daley stretched, turned over in bed,
and tapped Sarah on the shoulder.

"It's seven-thirty—time to get up. It's your turn to make
breakfast today."

Sarah sat up but seemed to have trouble getting out of
bed. She fell back and burrowed her head deep into the
pillows.

"I feel blehhhh," she said.

"Tell me something new," Daley snapped. "The way
you sound, you'll never make the party tonight. Hell, it
doesn't even look like you'll make it through the day.
What is it with you, anyway? You've been acting like death
warmed over for days."

Sarah mumbled back at him, "Thanks, Daley. I love
you, too."

"Skip the sarcasm. I wanna know what the fuck's wrong
with you. If you're not dizzy, you're nauseated. If you're
not nauseated, you're groaning—unless you're whining. I
might add, lover, that living with you lately has been as
much fun as a broken leg. Today you go get your ass to a
doctor. You're probably walking around with the goddamned flu or something."

Sarah didn't answer him. She didn't need a doctor to tell
her what was wrong. She knew what it was.

She was pregnant.

She had missed two periods, and her breasts ached like a
son of a bitch. For the last few days the only thing on her
mind had been how to break the news to Daley.

She decided that right now was as good a time as any.

She tried not to gag as she sat up in bed.

"I'm pregnant, Daley."

For a second or two she thought her words hadn't registered. Daley just stared at her. Then his expression
changed. He looked like he was about to explode.

"You're what?"

Sarah didn't see any need to repeat herself. She waited
for his next outburst.

She didn't have long to wait.

"You've gotta be kidding! You can't mean it! How could
it happen? You can't do this to me! Look, you know this
kinda thing isn't my scene. I never bargained for this. If
it's true, don't just lie there, damn it! You've gotta get rid
of it."

"You louse!" was all Sarah had time to scream as he
stormed out of the room, slamming the door behind him.

Trembling with anger and frustration, Sarah got out of
bed. She reached for the phone book and quickly found the
number of her gynecologist.

Concluding his examination, the doctor told Sarah she
was two months pregnant. He gave her some prescriptions,
and she stopped at the pharmacist to have them filled.

Later, as she walked aimlessly down the chilly London
streets, oblivious to the damp March drizzle, Daley's cruel
reaction insinuated itself into her thoughts. Sarah felt
alone, angry, and frightened. She was suddenly seized with
an attack of nausea and threw up her guts in front of
Harrods.

It was almost six o'clock when she returned to the apartment.

Daley wasn't there. She swore softly to herself. The son

of a bitch must have left for the wrap party without giving her a thought.

Exhausted, Sarah ran a warm tub, hoping it would help soothe her frayed nerves.

As the comforting warmth enveloped her, her eyes filled with tears. She didn't want to have an abortion, and yet she knew she would have to. Damn Daley Russell! Damn the heartless cruelty of that bastard! How was it possible for her to hate him so and yet to keep loving him at the same time?

She had to put him out of her mind for a while or she'd scream. She had to think of something else—anything. The image of Jan Julliard flashed before her. How she missed her! How she wished Jan were here so she could talk to her!

After Sarah stepped out of her tub, she wrapped her terry-cloth robe around her and flopped down onto the chaise. She was angry at the world and very, very angry at Daley. As she sat moodily thinking about him, she knew deep in her gut that Daley had never played any games with her. Never once had he ever said that he loved her or that he wanted anything permanent in his life. She knew he didn't want the responsibility of a child. That would really blow his mind.

"Yes, little Sarah," she whispered to the empty room, "you fucked up this time."

So, okay, she would get rid of it, like the man said.

But the more Sarah thought about having an abortion, the more she wanted to reject the idea. Deep down in her heart she was opposed to it. She was in love with Daley Russell. She had been for a long time. She wanted Daley's child.

Sarah conducted a mental conversation with herself. *Lots of unmarried females have babies. So why not me?*

Sure, it would be a lot to handle, an enormous commitment.
Could I manage it all alone?

Well, I do have money of my own, money my grandpa left
me. It isn't a fortune, but my baby would want for nothing.

For the first time that day, a smile crossed her lips. She
knew what she was going to do. Sarah Hartley was going
to have her baby with or without Daley Russell. And she
was going to be one hell of a mother.

After making her decision, all Sarah's anxiety left her.
She felt terrific—relaxed and renewed.

The phone rang, and she reached for it. The sound of
the familiar voice made everything perfect.

"Jan darling! Is it really you? You're here in London?
Well, it's about time you came back. Boy, have I ever
missed you!"

"I missed you, too, Sarah. How's Daley? Have you settled him down?"

Sarah's voice had a cutting edge of anger to it as she
replied, "Give me a break, Jan. Does a leopard change its
spots? Daley is the same as ever. He'll never settle down.
But I think I have. Yes, Sarah Hartley has definitely settled
down."

Then her voice took on a pleading quality.

"Jan, won't you please come over? I have so much to tell
you, and I want to hear everything that's happened to you,
too. Then, later, on, you and I are going to Daley's wrap
party. His movie is finally finished and in the can."

Sarah hesitated for a moment.

"Nick will be at the party. I'm sure you know that Cat
and he are no longer together. I don't think they ever really were."

Jan fell silent; her mind raced. Nick had been in her
thoughts all day. She had been wondering what it would
feel like to actually face him again. She'd wanted to call

him, but each time she'd picked up the phone, something had stopped her. If Cat had answered, she wouldn't have known how to handle it.

Oh God, here she was, still in love with Nick Tyson without knowing whether he still cared for her anymore. And why should he, when he had all of London at his feet? Every magazine she picked up on her travels had seemed to contain an article about the handsome, oh-so-eligible Nick Tyson. His life-style was constantly being glamorized in print, with colorful photos of the interior of his fabulous ship, soon to become the most exclusive club in the world.

Sarah's voice cut into Jan's thoughts.

"Mark Squire will also be there. He's been in London for a couple months now. Did you know that Nick hired him to design *Pleasure Palace*'s salon? It's amazing when you think of it. Here are Nick Tyson and Mark Squire— two of the most successful bachelors anywhere, and both of them were in love with you."

Jan let that observation slide by. She addressed herself to her friend's previous remark instead.

"Sarah, I don't know if I'm really in the mood to meet Nick right now. You see, I only just arrived in London this morning."

"What the hell has just arriving got to do with it? Stop stalling, Jan. Now is as good a time as any for you to meet him, grab him, and claim what's yours—that is, unless you happen to have changed your mind. I mean, who knows? Seeing Mark again—well, maybe he'll be the one you want to grab. Either way, I'm giving you one hour to make yourself look outrageous."

Without waiting for Jan's response, Sarah hung up the phone with a satisfied smile on her face. She had a feeling that everything was going to work out fine for everyone.

* * *

Later that evening, a preoccupied Mark Squire was driving toward the outskirts of London. He was heading for the sprawling Shepperton Studios, where the wrap party for Daley's movie was being held.

His mind was on Jan. He had been thinking about her for the entire week, and he was still thinking about her now. He realized that he was still in love with her and probably always would be. As the miles sped by, he found himself idly wondering where she was and if he would ever see her again.

After reaching his destination and parking in the assigned lot, a guard directed him to the large sound studio where the party was being held. Mark heard loud music, noise, and laughter coming from within.

The party was in full swing.

Cigarette smoke hung in the air, mixed with the sweet smell of grass. A strikingly beautiful woman with wonderful eyes was standing by the door, a half-smoked joint held limply between her fingers.

Turning her full attention on Mark, she pointed a long, graceful finger at him. Then, with a lazy smile on her pastel-colored lips, she spoke to him in a stoned-out, spacey voice.

"I know you from somewhere, don't I? It's the telly, I'll bet. Yes, that's it. I've seen you on the telly. You're always going on about soft, bloody gorgeous hair. I'm right, aren't I? That is you."

Mark grinned at her.

"Close, but no cigar. That happens to be my twin brother. He's the one in show biz. People are always getting us mixed up."

Mark always felt a little embarrassed when people recognized him from his TV commercials.

"Wow!" she said, puffing greedily on the smoldering roach. "You could have fooled me! You're a dead ringer for him."

Mark smiled at her, shrugging his shoulders in apology. Then he turned and pushed his way through the tangled crowd to the bar. He couldn't help but notice that most of the people in the room, both men and women, were unusually attractive. It was apparent that Daley Russell personally had chosen the guest list.

After getting a drink, Mark looked for Daley.

The room was so crowded, it was difficult to maneuver. While trying to edge away from the crowd, he suddenly was transfixed by a glimpse of a face that stood out from all the rest. A pair of heavenly jade green eyes pinpointed his.

At first Mark stared blankly ahead, speechless. It couldn't be her! But it was. She was standing with Sarah in a tight group of celebrants.

In seconds Mark was at her side.

"Jan, I can't believe it's you! It's been so long. You look more beautiful than ever. How are you?"

Mark's warm brown eyes radiated happiness.

Jan threw her arms around him.

"Oh, Mark, it's just wonderful to see you!"

They stood for a moment looking at each other. Both silently mulled over their private thoughts; both were momentarily oblivious to Sarah's presence.

Mark was the first to speak.

"Do you know that you stayed on my mind for months when you left New York? In fact, you were the reason I hightailed it to France. Life in the Big Apple just wasn't the same without you."

Mark paused for a moment, as if he realized he was

baring his emotions too much, making himself too vulnerable. His conversation quickly took a lighter tack.

"Anyway, it all worked out for the best. Here I am, the undisputed caliph of the hair salons, the arbiter supreme of woman's crowning glory, the sultan of styling and prince of perms! What McDonald's is to burgers, Squire is to hair."

As Sarah moved off, Jan studied Mark as intently as his dark eyes studied her. She couldn't help but notice how wonderful he looked. His face had matured in a most attractive way. His clothes were more casually elegant than ever. His beige jacket seemed molded to his slender frame; the color and texture suggested the finest custom fabric, and his slim, slightly pleated trousers fell to just the right length over his soft Italian shoes. He wore a cream-colored silk shirt open at the neck, devoid of adornments. His hair was styled differently from what she had remembered; it was winged back from his face, giving him a princely look.

Suddenly aware that she'd been staring too long, Jan hastened to reply to his last ebullient remark.

"Oh, Mark, even though you said it lightly, I know how successful you've become. I think it's simply fabulous! Not a week went by that I didn't read some glowing tribute to you and your salons, no matter where I was. I'm so very proud of you."

Mark heard her words, but his thoughts were a million miles away. Looking down at her lovely face, he knew he was still crazily in love with her.

His thoughts raced back over the past couple years. He realized he could barely remember any of the women he had been involved with. None of those affairs had lasted any length of time; none had really meant anything. He had constantly moved on from one to the other, as if hoping to find Jan somewhere at the end of the line.

Knowing that something had happened between Jan and Nick and that they were no longer together, Mark's mind kept zeroing in on one thought: Was this the time to tell Jan that he loved her? He wanted to say it so badly that it hurt. And yet something deep inside stopped him. Deep in his gut he felt that Nick Tyson still had the inside track. A primeval instinct told him that Tyson was still unfinished business.

As Jan looked into his eyes, she detected an expression in them, a mood behind a mood. Then Mark took her hand. There was something safe and secure about having her hand in his as he spoke.

"Hey, it just occurred to me—what about Nick? He's supposed to be here tonight. How long has it been since the two of you split? Is it permanent, or what?"

Still holding his hand, Jan had a feeling that Mark was waiting for a confirmation of her breakup with Nick. For a moment her lovely face clouded over. Should she confide in him? After all, he was more than just an acquaintance, more than just a friend. Mark Squire was someone she loved very dearly.

Jan closed her eyes for the space of a heartbeat.

Her mind raced; her head was full of images—snatches of an old song, a dress of hers that Nick had liked, a vivid picture of Nick holding her tight after making love.

Her words slipped out of their own accord, her voice down to a mere whisper.

"I'm still in love with Nick. I've never stopped loving him. I don't think I can. I don't know if he still loves me, but that doesn't change my feelings for him. It's as if there's nothing I can do about it. I can't stop loving him."

Jan was so deeply involved in clarifying her own feelings that she was unaware of the pained look that swept over

Mark's handsome face. She was also unaware of the fact that he had very gently released her hand.

He stared at her for a long, long moment. And then, with his voice level and controlled, he said the one thing he knew he shouldn't say.

"I love you, Jan. I've loved you since that day we first met in Daley's studio in New York, a thousand lifetimes ago."

He paused and took a deep breath before continuing.

"I don't know why I'm telling you this now. I know how insane it is. If you think about it, it's like some mad, cosmic joke. I love you—the way you love Nick Tyson."

Jan opened her mouth to reply, but before she could say a word, Mark touched his finger to her lips and continued talking.

"Don't say anything, Jan. There's really nothing you can say. In some strange way I feel better for having told you. I know it can't change anything; I didn't expect it to. But I think I'd have suffocated if I'd kept it in any longer."

The smile on Mark's face was loving, compassionate, and, in some strange way, forgiving.

"And now, my next move is to head straight for the bar and get myself pleasantly sloshed."

"Mark," Jan said, her voice barely audible. But he was already beyond earshot.

Her eyes filled with tears as Mark's words sank in. Suddenly the room seemed to be whirling around her much too quickly. She was having a difficult time handling her emotions as she watched him walk away.

Minutes later, as Jan sat in the ladies' room fixing her tearing eyes, Cat Bracken walked in.

The silence was almost a solid thing as the two women locked eyes in the mirror.

Oh God, Jan was thinking, *what now? How do I handle this?*

Unexpectedly, Cat smiled at her. It was a warm, friendly smile. Jan didn't quite know how to react. Her throat was dry, and her legs felt like lead weights. She stood up and turned toward the door, anxious to leave.

"Don't go," Cat urged softly. "Please stay a moment."

"Why?" asked Jan, her jade-green eyes smoldering with anger.

"Well, perhaps we could sit and talk awhile."

If Jan could have read Cat's mind, she'd have seen her dilemma. Cat wasn't sure quite what she wanted to say, but she knew in some strange way that she had to say something, that she had to square things somehow. She knew that it was because of her that Jan had split with Nick. She had harbored guilt feelings for a long time because of that. She genuinely liked both Jan and Nick, and she knew that they truly loved each other. She was human, opportunistic, and perhaps selfish, but rarely intentionally. And now, she was wondering what she could say to Jan that would make her understand. She finally decided simply to tell her the truth, and, in so doing, she hoped she wouldn't sound too much like a complete idiot.

Jan seated herself back on the stool in an angry motion as the two women's eyes searched each other.

Jan was curious as to what was going on inside Cat's head. Obviously she wanted to discuss something. Was it guilt she was feeling? Was her conscience bothering her?

"I know this is crazy," Cat said, groping for the right words. "I don't quite know why I have this need to talk to you, but I obviously do. Jan, I'm really not a person who hurts others, although I know you were desperately hurt when you found out about Nick and me."

"Really?" Jan asked, unable to keep the bitterness out of her voice.

Cat shook her head as if to clear any confusion away.

"Please listen to me, Jan. I want you to know that everything that happened was my fault. It was all my fault. Nick never really loved me. It was always you he loved. He was involved with my career—that's all. Okay, we had a brief fling, but it was unimportant, it was meaningless. It wasn't love. It had nothing to do with love. It was totally isolated from his relationship with you, from his life with you."

Seeing no reaction on Jan's part, Cat paused for a moment and wondered if she was reaching her. The silence grew oppressive, so she continued talking.

"Damn it, Jan! Don't you hear what I'm saying? You and Nick belong to each other. The kind of love the two of you have for each other doesn't come along every day. Can't you see I'm trying to help you? I'm telling you to forgive and forget, to give Nick another chance. It isn't me he loves—it's you. It's always been you."

Jan's head was spinning as a rush of thoughts flooded her mind. Cat's words had dredged up old hurts, old wounds, old heartbreaks. And yet they somehow seemed to bring things into focus. Of course, the unresolved conflict was still torturing her: Could she ever simply rationalize Nick's affair away?

She shook her head. Why wasn't she being honest with herself? It wasn't even the affair; it was the cheating that she hated. She had no doubt that she loved Nick Tyson. But she did doubt that she could ever trust him again. How could she be in love with someone she couldn't trust? Yet wasn't she much wiser now? Hadn't she changed, grown, matured?

She noticed that Cat was still watching her and no doubt

found her silence unnerving. She was probably aching to learn what Jan's reaction would be. Then Cat turned away and glanced down at her watch as if dismissing Jan from her thoughts.

"It's late," she said. "I have to go."

Jan listened expressionlessly as Cat told her that a limo would be picking her up in ten minutes. She was catching the evening flight to Los Angeles. It seemed that every script in Tinseltown was being offered to her. Cat would be doing radio and TV promos in Los Angeles for the movie she had just completed, Daley Russell's movie. Best of all, the producer of the film would be traveling with her. A soft smile crossed Cat's face as she told Jan how much she liked the producer and what a very powerful man he was in Hollywood. Her tone grew confidential as she said that he was also warm, friendly, and crazy about Cat Bracken. She was sure that when the time came, he was going to be an easy, relaxed lover in bed. Her eyes, still riveted on Jan, were glowing with anticipation.

Then, turning to the mirror, Cat studied her reflection. She combed her hair with her fingers, tugging and pulling at it till fell around her lovely face like a silver cloud. Next, she touched her lips with gloss and her nose with powder. Finished at last, she stood up and made a final inspection of herself in the mirror, obviously pleased by what she saw. Jan could see why: Cat looked vital and alive. Her career was moving forward just the way she wanted it to, and her life was becoming more exciting and unpredictable each day.

As the two girls faced each other, Jan knew she should hate Cat, and yet for some unaccountable reason she felt a certain admiration for her. Maybe it was the gamesman cool that Cat possessed. She was a female who would always take what life had to offer, the good or the bad, and turn it to her own advantage.

Once again, Cat flashed her a wide, somewhat theatrical smile as she headed for the door.

"Good-bye, Jan. Please don't think too badly of me."

Then she was gone.

Jan felt she had witnessed a great performance. She was almost tempted to applaud.

Walking away from the back-lot corridor, Jan was happy to return to the warmth and noise of the party.

From the looks of things, the festivities had begun in earnest. Everyone seemed to be in a festive mood. The three bars were jammed. Voices everywhere praised the cast's performances, especially Cat's. There seemed to be no doubt about it, thought Jan as she moved through the crowd. Daley's movie was certain to be a smash success.

But where was Daley? This was his night to howl, and he was nowhere in sight.

Unable to catch a glimpse of Daley in the crowd, Jan headed for the buffet table when she heard a voice call out to her.

"Hi, there. I couldn't help but notice you. You're an actress, aren't you? I figured you must be. I thought I caught a glimpse of you in the film."

She turned to face a beautiful young man with dazzling teeth who managed to display virtually every single one of them as he spoke.

"Some outa sight party, isn't it? My name's Barry. I'm an actor. But, hey, you musta guessed that. In fact, I came with my producer; that's him over there. He drags me to all the wrap parties. You may not recognize him, but he's a big man in Limeytown. In a way he's kind of a creep, but what the hell, as long as I work. Who'd you come with?"

THE PLEASURE PALACE 339

"A friend."

Jan was in no mood for a lengthy conversation. She was about to move on when a smirking man with lecherous eyes walked over to them.

"So there y'are, Barry sweetheart. 'Ow about introducin' me to the darlin' bird? No, don't bother, luv. I'll do it meself."

Jan was instantly repulsed by his too-familiar manner, to say nothing of his squat, unappealing body, his overpolished fingernails, and his badly capped teeth. Even the scent of his cologne was vulgar and overpowering. It was obvious that he'd been drinking far too much.

The coarse little man patted her arm possessively and started to speak, cocking his head thoughtfully to one side.

"You," he mumbled, "look bloody familiar, ducky. Ever do porn? You've got the look, y'know. I can always tell. I produce 'igh-class pussy movies out of Spain."

Jan could hardly believe what she was hearing. This had to set a new high—or low—for party small talk.

"I'm one bloke who 'ardly ever forgets a face, and I don't never forget a body."

He lowered his voice, and his tone grew conspiratorial.

"I don't know if you 'eard, but I don't do the real 'ard porn anymore. Too much 'assle doin' X, don'tcha know? I'm concentratin' on the soft stuff, the bloody respectable R-rated shit. Family stuff, y'might say. I'm big on cable and in cassettes."

He puffed up like an adder.

"Hey, seems t'me you got classier-looking since the last time I saw you. Y'know, I just got an idea. Ideas come to me bloody fast. I'm thinkin' you and Barry would look super doing it. He's a new find of mine. Take it from me, dolly, the boy is really hung. And a bird like you—you've seen the best, right?"

Thoroughly repulsed, Jan tried to pull away, but he took her arm as he edged even closer. The odor of his cologne almost stifled her.

"The minute I saw you talkin' to Barry, I was dry-fuckin' you in my head, just like I always do. Remember how I love tall, classy-lookin' eatin' stuff? Look, sweetie, this is your lucky night. You bloody well got t'me. I just made up my mind. You 'n me are gonna 'ightail it to St. Tropez for the weekend."

Then, belching loudly, he grabbed Jan's hand.

"So what did y'say your name was? You wouldn't want me t'call out the wrong name when I'm comin', wouldja?"

Jan strained to keep her teeth from grinding.

"I didn't say," she replied, her voice like flint. "And what's more—"

"Yeah, yeah, I'm listening."

He wasn't. His mind had wandered off into a wild, erotic fantasy. He'd add spice to the weekend by letting Barry watch him and the new bird make it together. He'd also set things up so the hidden cameras could roll. He'd make sure to have a good supply of coke on hand, and he might even bring in that young black piece from the beach who wanted to be a star. Yes, it promised to be a bloody perfect weekend.

As the images faded, he realized Jan was speaking. By now the liquor had mixed with the coke, and his mood was turning ugly. He squinted his eyes to focus better as he grunted at her, "What the bloody hell are you saying?"

"I repeat, you unspeakably loathsome toad, we have never ever met. We never could have met. And we most certainly will never meet again."

His hooded eyes blazed with alcohol-induced rage as his voice became a throaty snarl.

"Lady, you ain't even grounded. I should 'ave spotted you for a bloody dyke the minute I saw you."

His tone became loud and nasty. His face grew redder. He sputtered for a few seconds, visibly trembling in anger. Finally he spat out the only two words he could think of: "Fuck you!"

Then he turned to the dazzling young man who had impassively witnessed the scene.

"Know somethin', Barry? You're a bloody king-size asshole. With all the stuff around, you pick up a creepy lesbo to talk to. That pussy-eatin' cunt wouldn't know what t'do with a real man if she 'ad one."

Jan was surprised at her sudden fury. Her cold green eyes shot the man a look that would have stopped a charging rhino. She knew she had to do something, anything, to take this nightmarish abomination down.

Before he could make another move, as he smirked at her, she kneed him squarely in his testicles.

He expelled his breath like a punctured balloon, and then he seemed to freeze in place. His face went ashen. His eyes bulged. Finally, he reared back, screaming and clutching at himself in pain as he dropped to his knees on the floor.

"Holy shit!" cried Barry, bending down to aid the stricken man.

Jan saw that everyone nearby had turned to see who had caused the violent outcry. She grimly stood her ground, returning stare for stare, and concentrated on the voice of Marvin Gaye pulsating through the sound system.

Her anguished victim was still crouched on the floor, wide-eyed and moaning. Then, after catching his breath, he snarled at Jan, "You bloody, crazy, 'omicidal cunt! I'll get you for that."

Nick Tyson had just arrived at the party. Hearing the

commotion, he caught the final moments of the outrageous scene. He reached Jan's side in a couple of strides.

The porn producer was almost on his feet. He was heading for Jan with his fists clenched, his eyes blood-red, his mouth spewing obscenities.

That's when Nick swung at him.

He hit the floor with a thud.

Seconds later, seeing the look on Nick's face, he didn't try to get up again. Nor did he utter another word.

Nick put his arms around Jan.

"This, my love, is one hell of a way for you to come back into my life."

Sarah and Mark watched silently as Nick and Jan walked off together, oblivious to everyone else in the room.

Sarah emptied her glass of wine.

"Well," she said, "I suppose that's that. It seems as if the lovers have found each other again."

Then her eyes slowly misted over.

"It's a shame that you and I haven't been that lucky with the ones we love."

Mark made no reply. Sarah stood for a moment biting her lower lip. Finally she turned to him with a look of resignation.

"Would you mind giving me a lift back to town? I've decided this party is a disaster. The host didn't even bother to show."

They drove most of the way in silence, wrapped in their own thoughts.

When Sarah finally spoke, she again expressed her amazement at Daley for not showing up at his own party.

Mark nodded sympathetically and listened to Sarah without actually hearing anything she said.

Again, they lapsed into a period of silence. He drove down the narrow roads without regard for the speedometer. Sarah absently turned her attention to the window and watched a thick, heavy fog start to roll in.

Suddenly Mark swerved to miss a driver who was careening along, hugging the center divider. It happened so quickly that it was over almost before Sarah realized that their car had veered off the pavement. They landed with a crunch in a nearby ditch.

"Christ, Sarah!" Mark cried out. "Are you all right?"

The night was cold, and she was shivering, mostly due to shock. Mark's eyes were bright with concern as Sarah put her hand gingerly to her neck, which had snapped forward when the car hit the ditch.

"I'm okay," she said, bringing Mark into focus.

Mark turned his attention to the car. He turned the ignition key and restarted the engine. Then he tried rocking the car, hoping to move it out of the ditch. It surged forward, then slid back again. He tried once more, but he saw it was hopeless. The ditch was too deep; the ground too soft.

"I'm afraid we need help, Sarah. I have a distinct feeling that we may not make it home tonight."

Sarah let out a deep sigh.

"Well, we'll just have sit it out until the fog lifts. Let's hope someone comes by to help us."

The sun was just coming up when Mark managed to flag down a morning milk truck. Once he and Sarah reached London proper, they left the truck and hailed a taxi. After dropping Sarah off, Mark headed back to his own apartment.

Daley opened the door; his black eyes were flecked with anger.

He grasped Sarah's shoulders and pulled her inside. Then he pushed her down into a chair.

"Where the hell have you been?" he shouted.

As Sarah stared at him, something fast and furious flashed between them. Her smile flickered; her dark eyes were flirtatious. She gave an arrogant toss of her head.

"I spent the night with Mark Squire."

Daley looked at her blankly.

"Damn!" he said in his gravelly voice. Then he paused, his expression softening. He smiled at her with a wry, ironic smile.

"Is that supposed to be funny, or what? You're kidding, right?"

Next, he paced back and forth across the room. Sarah wondered what the hell was on his mind.

Then he started to talk as if to himself.

"Just between us, I discovered something about myself tonight. I tried to rationalize it away, but I couldn't. I had the sudden feeling that you set me up, and any gal who can outsmart Daley Russell can't be all that bad."

"Well, that's nice to hear," Sarah said with feigned enthusiasm in her voice.

"Just sit there and shut your face, woman! I'm not finished. Daley Russell, who could always get off at any station and just let the train roll by, can't do it anymore. It's a fuckin' shame, but that's how it is. I'm damned well trapped."

Sarah looked at his craggy face, at his body so filled with nervous energy, but she didn't reply.

"After I left you this morning, I went to the studio. From there I went over to Cat Bracken's apartment."

Sarah tried hard to keep a steady grip on her emotions. *Here it comes,* she thought. *He wants to tell me about Cat. He can't wait to tell me.*

"Yep, I went over to her apartment. Now pay attention 'cause you'll never guess the punchline."

Daley chuckled, as if enjoying the memory of that moment.

"I couldn't get it up. You listening? On account of you, I couldn't raise the mast!"

He gave Sarah a wry sidelong glance.

"I'm waiting," she said, looking directly at him.

"Well, I figured maybe my timing was off. So I drove to the studio and stopped off at the pub on the back lot. A couple of hot little numbers with figures that wouldn't stop came on to me, but, wouldja believe, something was still wrong? Any other time I coulda shtuped them both. They were primed for it, all set for a little afternoon nooky. But again—nothin'. I let it pass.

"The ol' pecker just wasn't interested. All I saw was you. You kept coming back at me in flashes. I just kept drinkin' and figurin' that maybe I was a moron, maybe I was throwin' away the best thing I ever had. So I went lookin' for you. But by the time I got to the wrap party, they told me you had left with Mark. I felt so fuckin' hollow, like my whole world was shattered."

Daley looked at Sarah and waited for her to say something.

Her heart was beating so hard, she could only stare at him. His words were so unexpected that she felt the color drain from her face.

Daley swallowed slowly and took a deep breath. Finding his voice, he kept it carefully steady.

"Look, I know I've been a real shit. I'm not even sure I'll be able to change. But I wanna give it a try."

Sarah's tone was so low, he had to strain to hear her.

"What are you trying to say, Daley?"

He looked at her for a moment.

"Okay, here goes. Let's not play any more games. I'm gonna ask you something I never thought I'd ask anyone again. Let's get married. I want you to have our kid."

They stood staring at each other for a moment as the full impact of his words sank in to her.

"Say it, then," she said. "Damn you, go ahead and say the words!"

Daley grinned at Sarah. Then he rubbed his nose against hers, Eskimo style, as he growled theatrically.

"What words? You mean like, *I love you?* Like, *I can't live without you?* Like, *forsaking all others?* You mean those kind of words?"

Kissing her gently on the lips, Daley pulled her to him and enfolded her in his arms. As he held Sarah close, there were tears of happiness on her cheeks.

"Oh, Daley," she whispered, looking up at him, her voice filled with laughter, "I love you so, you unpredictable bastard, you. I'm not sure what I'm getting myself into by marrying you. But you know something? I'll reform you yet."

Chapter Thirty

Melody Anderson opened the door of her New York apartment and hugged her cousin with great warmth and excitement.

"Come in, dear Cynthia, come in! How wonderful to see you after all these years!"

Melody was small and round, with eyes the color of bright blue agates. She smelled of talcum powder and English lavender. Although fifty-eight, her unlined face had a tranquil, youthfully innocent look. She had never married but had always managed to live very comfortably due to the sensibly invested trust fund her father had left her. Utterly without guile or malice, Melody Anderson was beholden to no one, and envied no one.

She was surprised to notice how tired Cynthia looked, how drawn her once-lovely face was, and how strained with tension. But Melody said nothing. She fussed over Cynthia from the moment she arrived.

Melody's apartment was a warm, comfortable haven, and within minutes Cynthia found some of her tension fading.

The only other members of Melody's household were the cats and dogs who roamed the apartment freely. If Melody was fanatical about one thing in life, it was pets. Protecting and caring for God's creatures was a perpetual crusade to her.

Every day she took a walk in Central Park. Once there, she had walnuts for the squirrels and bread for the pigeons, and she always kept her sharp eyes on the lookout for lost dogs or abused cats.

While Cynthia unpacked, Melody walked through the apartment, calling out in a scolding voice, "D'Oyly, D'Oyly, we have a guest! Cousin Cynthia is here. Where are your manners? Come and say hello, you little villain."

D'Oyly Carte, one of Melody's favorites, came to her side. He was an old, decrepit-looking mongrel, bad tempered and asthmatic. Melody had rescued him from the dog pound years before. His legs were like a bloodhound's, always turned out in first position like a ballet dancer. His enormous tail stood up like a plume and curled high over his body; it seemed to propel him along like the sail of a ship. His coat was the color of rusty Brillo, short and prickly. D'Oyly had only one eye; an animal of the homo sapiens species had poked the other one out when he was a puppy.

The irascible old dog waddled into the room, gave Cynthia a baleful look, broke wind, and then retired to his bed in the kitchen.

"Shame on you, you naughty boy!" Melody cooed to him as she sprayed Guerlain's Potpourri around the room.

That evening after dinner, the two women settled themselves in facing chairs for a chat. Cynthia was the subject of a close inspection by Melody.

"Are you well, dear?" asked her cousin.

Something in Melody's tone made Cynthia tense again.

"Oh, I'm all right, I guess. I just have to regain more of my strength. You see, Melody, so much has been taken from me. . . ."

She paused and momentarily lost her train of thought.

The room was peaceful and still, yet through the wall she heard the occasional opening and closing of doors in neighboring apartments. She could also discern voices at the elevator in the hallway outside. She was conscious of the scream of brakes as trucks and taxis swerved in the street below. In some crazy way she felt as if the noise of the entire city were being sucked up into Melody's apartment. A sudden feeling of being trapped, of being caged in, swept over her. She longed for the space and airiness of Tyson Hall.

Pulling her thoughts together, Cynthia turned to her cousin.

"Nobody," she continued, "can know what it is like to lose—"

Melody cut in.

"Oh, my poor dear, how you must have suffered, watching that beautiful man of yours helplessly trapped in a wheelchair! How he loved you and lived for you! If ever there was a man utterly without sin, it was Cousin Charles. The two of you had such an idyllic, perfect marriage. Every so often I'd open the wedding book you sent me those long years ago; it's always been a source of pleasure and inspiration to me. You were such a beautiful bride. Look, here it is right on the coffee table."

Cynthia heard her voice drone on as if in a dream.

"There's Charles in his uniform. Look, there you are cutting the cake, and there are the two of you dancing together."

Melody became immersed in the well-thumbed leather-bound album and commented on each and every photo as she turned the pages.

Meanwhile, motionless in her chair, Cynthia felt her face grow hard, and she silently wept deep inside. She wept from the fury that raged in her heart whenever she remembered the indescribable pain of Charles's betrayal.

Then, just as Melody put the book down, Cynthia

backed away from it and thought of Jim Boyd instead. Cynthia heard a little gasp from her cousin as Melody noticed tears in her eyes.

"Oh, my dear, please forgive me! Here I am distressing you with memories from the past. That's terribly thoughtless of me. We should be talking about the future and all the wonderful promise it holds."

Melody took Cynthia's hand in hers.

"Tell me, dear, what do you plan to do now? I can imagine how lonely it must be for you without Charles, and with Nick so far away. Still, I'm sure there must be many options awaiting you."

Cynthia had a faraway look in her eyes.

"To tell the truth, I haven't really given much thought to the future, although I know I should. I keep pushing it away in the hope that I won't have to make a decision, though I know I'll have to pull my life together sooner or later. If only all my thoughts didn't center on Tyson Hall! It's as if life begins and ends there for me. But never fear, darling Melody, things have a way of resolving themselves eventually, don't they?"

During her second week in New York, Cynthia suggested that Melody join her for a trip to London to visit Nick.

Melody's face was a picture of confusion.

"Oh, Cynthia, I'm no good at all when it comes to traveling. How could I possibly leave my darling pets? Poor D'Oyly gets so confused when I not here. He's never learned to accept a dog-sitter, even though I've tried time and again. That's why I never visited you and Charles all these long years. And what about those poor, dear animals of mine in the park? Who would look after them? Please, Cynthia dear, tell me you understand."

Cynthia's features softened when she saw the sincere, almost vulnerable expression on her cousin's face.

"I suppose I do understand, in a way. All these creatures you care for are really your family, aren't they, Melody?"

Melody beamed back at her.

"Oh yes, they are. They really are."

The next day Cynthia called her son at his office in London.

They had a very bad connection. Nick sounded impatient over the phone. Cynthia gathered from his tone of voice that he was very busy and that she had interrupted a meeting. He did tell her that *Pleasure Palace* would be sailing for the States right on schedule, and when it arrived he planned to celebrate by holding a lavish charity ball aboard the ship. After that, *Pleasure Palace* would be officially turned over to its members as their private floating club.

Cynthia tried to keep her tone light as she replied, "I understand, darling. I can see how impossible it would be for anybody to compete with that wonderful ship of yours for your affection."

Cynthia gave a tight, bitter little laugh as she hung up.

Later that evening, in the privacy of Melody's guest room, Cynthia felt particularly tense as she sipped her snifter of brandy.

A feeling of tension usually came over her just before she dived headlong into one of her awful headaches. The memory of her last agonizing headache swirled around in her mind and made her think of Jim Boyd.

Jim Boyd. She wrapped the blankets more tightly around herself as she decided it was time to return to Tysons Landing. Then she dozed off.

* * *

On the flight home, leaning across the empty seat next to her, a flight attendant removed the lunch Cynthia hadn't touched.

"Will you be needing earphones? We have a very good movie on this flight."

Cynthia shook her head.

"Just another brandy, please."

Pushing her seat back to a reclining position, she let her thoughts flow free.

Perhaps the Reverend was right. Maybe it would be right for her to help him. She could easily afford to give some of her time and money to his cause. Nick certainly didn't seem to want her around. Perhaps a godly man like Jim Boyd could help her find a new reason for living.

She swallowed the last of her brandy and rang for the attendant to bring her a blanket and pillow, hoping to sleep away the rest of the flight.

As she waited for old Willie to retrieve her luggage at the small airport, Cynthia was glad to be back in Tysons Landing.

Driving to the house, Willie chattered incessantly, but she was too busy with her own thoughts to pay much attention to him.

She told herself that she must stop drinking. Even now she was aware of a slight shaking of her hand. Taking a small flask from her handbag, she sat in the back of the vintage Rolls-Royce and sipped the brandy that she needed to compose herself.

Although distantly aware that Willie was still droning on, Cynthia's thoughts centered on Nick and the last conversation she'd had with him. He had seemed so different to her then, almost as if something were transpiring that he didn't want her to know about. It was probably just her imagination. Still, because of her love for him, she had always been extremely sensitive to his moods.

As they approached the house, she fussed with her hair and sprayed her mouth with peppermint just before Willie opened the car door for her.

The first face she saw was Alpha's, beaming at the front door with a wide, welcoming smile.

But as she entered the house, Cynthia was surprised to see Jim Boyd inside, waiting to greet her.

He stood in the doorway, totally at ease, as if he belonged there. He took her hand and led her into the drawing room as Alpha went to fetch the tea service.

"My dear Cynthia," he said, "I cannot tell you how happy I am to see you."

As they faced each other over tea, Cynthia frowned. She asked how he had known she was coming home today.

Jim Boyd stared at her through his flat, tea-colored eyes.

"Why, my dear Cynthia, I have been a constant visitor to this house since you've been gone! I took the liberty of caring for your rose gardens. The Lord and I tended them for you as best we could. You'll see a grand difference, I think. The blooms are so perfect that, if I may say so myself, we could win a prize."

His large heavy hands opened and closed as he spoke.

Cynthia was filled with an emotion she had not felt for a very long time. It was a warm, sweet feeling. As she looked around her beautiful drawing room, she thought how pleasant it was to be there talking to Jim Boyd.

She studied him with a thoughtful expression on her face; then she gave him a wan but gracious smile when she realized some response was expected from her.

"You are too kind, Reverend Boyd. The care you lavished on my gardens must have kept you from your own work."

Boyd raised a reassuring hand.

"Think nothing of it, my dear. It was my pleasure. Now, if you will excuse me, I don't want to take up too much of your time. You must be tired after your journey, so I shall be going. The Lord's work is never done, you know."

Cynthia extended her hand to him, and Jim Boyd held it for some seconds longer than necessary. He kept a warm, syrupy smile on his lips and gazed intensely into her eyes.

After leaving the palatial Tyson home, Jim Boyd was charged with a new enthusiasm and vitality.

He would have laid odds that the stupid old cow had been nipping from her brandy bottle all day long. Well, so what? If he could get to her, make the right moves, maybe even marry her if he had to, he could have the fuckin' world in the palm of his hands. Yep, with a little luck and some cautious maneuvering, he might end up lord of the manor. And, what's more, he could also be TV's next big-time preacher.

But a sudden frown crossed the Reverend's face when he thought of her son, Nick. That snob bastard would do his best to throw a monkey wrench in Boyd's plan. Yes sir, young Tyson had made it very plain that he didn't want this preacher man sniffin' around his darlin' mama.

Well, Nick Tyson was just another problem for Jim Boyd to wrestle with. He was sure the Lord would show him the way.

After Boyd left, Cynthia went into the gardens to look at her roses. As the Reverend had said, they were truly beautiful. The garden was ablaze with color. What a lovely gesture that had been on the part of Jim Boyd! The roses made such a beautiful welcome-home present.

Her thoughts were interrupted by Alpha, who told her that Nick was on the phone.

"And how is my beautiful mother today?" he asked. "I just wanted to make sure you had gotten home safe and sound."

Nick's voice was cheerful and buoyant. Cynthia was glad his mood was upbeat.

"It was wonderful spending time with Melody, though I'm glad to be home again. I don't think I'll want to take another trip for a very long time."

Then, with great excitement in her voice, she went on to describe the beauty of her rose gardens. In bubbling tones she told Nick how wonderfully Reverend Boyd had tended them while she was away, and that Alpha had told her what a blessing and a joy the good Reverend had been.

Much of the lightness went out of Nick's voice.

"So that damned preacher is still hanging around you, is he?"

"Hanging around me? I'm surprised at you, Nick. A man like Jim Boyd can't be referred to as 'hanging around.' You really don't know the man at all. I should think you'd be very pleased that I have someone to lean on at a time like this. He happens to be a kind, caring human being who is quite concerned about your mother."

There was an oppressive silence over the phone. Nick's words were measured and cool as he slowly replied, "Concerned about you? What does he have to be concerned about? Look, Cynthia, you're right, I don't know the man. And I'm pretty damned sure that I don't want to. Tell me, has he asked you for any money yet?"

It was all she could do to fight back the resentment that welled up within her at her son's words.

"I'm not sure whether you have any right to ask that question, Nick."

She tried desperately to keep her voice under control as she continued.

"But I will tell you this. Whether Reverend Boyd asks me for money or not, if I choose to give him any, it is mine to give."

She virtually snapped the last few words but felt much better for having said them.

Nick sighed into the phone and took a deep and weary breath before replying, "Of course it's yours to give, Cynthia. There's never been any question of that. I know you have the right to do whatever you want to with your money. But, damn it all, you're my mother. I happen to love you very much. I don't want anyone trapping you into anything or taking advantage of your trusting nature."

Nick paused, desperately searching for the right words. Cynthia remained silent until he continued.

"You know, darling, Dad was always there for you, always loving you and taking care of you. What would he think of this oddball preacher? If only I weren't so far away from you. Cynthia, I'm sure that preacher is either a con man or a nut case. I'm betting he's a little of each."

When Cynthia replied, there was a bitter edge to her voice.

"Nick, I'm really surprised at you. I almost can't believe this conversation. Those things are easy for you to say. After all, your whole life has been smooth sailing. But have you really tried to visualize my position? You've been so involved in your own activities that you haven't had any time for me. That's perfectly natural, and I certainly don't blame you. You're young; you have your own life to live. But it was Jim Boyd who convinced me I should get out and join the living. And it is Jim Boyd who, in some way, seems to be helping me fill the awful, empty void in my life."

Once the words were out, Cynthia felt better. Up until this moment, she had never indicated even to herself how important the kindly, moral Jim Boyd had become in her life.

She turned to the phone once more.

"Anyway, dear, enough about me. Did you call to tell me anything special?"

Again, Nick's voice turned eager and enthusiastic.

"I sure did. All the invitations have been sent out for the gala charity party on *Pleasure Palace*. The ship should reach its port of call in San Diego two weeks from tomorrow. She's gonna have the most spectacular launching ever. The whole affair will be a media bonanza. I wish you could see her, Cynthia. Each and every stateroom is a wonderland. Believe me, there's not a ship afloat that can match *Pleasure Palace* for sheer opulence. And the members are the crème de la crème. I tell you, the launch will be awash with titles, tiaras, and tycoons. Then to top it off, some of the greatest names in show business have promised to appear and entertain. The whole trick was to announce that the evening's proceeds would go to help starving children around the world. Who could refuse? It'll be a night to remember, and the bottom line is—I sure hope you're planning to be there."

Cynthia hesitated for a moment. When she replied, her voice was regretful but firm.

"You know how I hate crowds, darling. I think I'll just stay here and read about it in the papers. I know everything I read will make me tremendously proud of you."

Nick expressed disappointment at her decision and then hung up. He felt somewhat guilty about his true reaction.

Hearing that his mother would not to attend the festivities had filled him with an enormous sense of relief.

He hadn't been able to bring himself to tell her of his forthcoming marriage to Jan. He didn't want to face any suggestions that he postpone the wedding for whatever reasons she might invent.

Everything had been arranged for their wedding on board ship the night of the launch. They planned to honeymoon in Rome; then Jaafar's private seaplane would whisk them away to his secluded villa at Porto Ertcole. After the honeymoon, Nick and Jan would return to Tysons Landing and surprise his mother. Nick was certain that once Cynthia accepted Jan as his wife, she would come to love her as he did.

The guilt feeling soon left him. His thoughts once again turned to *Pleasure Palace.*

During the following week, Cynthia decided to clean out Charles's room and get rid of everything.

She hadn't been able to do it until now. His files and personal possessions had remained intact ever since his death. She knew that going through his effects would cause the pain to return once again, but it had to be done.

As she opened the door to his room and stepped inside, her thoughts turned bitter. She had devoted most of her adult life to the man who had lived in this room. She had loved him with all her heart—and he had betrayed her.

Wearily she began her depressing task. She started with a dresser and went through drawers of socks, shirts, and sweaters. She made separate piles of different items so that Alpha could box them for the various charities.

Her eyes narrowed when she came across a photograph hidden in the back of one of the drawers.

"Oh, no," she moaned. A look of anguish came over her face as she stared at the offending picture.

It was a snapshot of Charles with his arms around Maria Benson. Both were smiling happily into the camera.

Cynthia felt a moment of mounting rage as she looked at the two of them, loathing them. Remembering her betrayal once again, she felt a new throbbing in her head. Once again she felt victimized by them; once again she was at their mercy, even though they both were dead.

There were tears in her eyes as she walked downstairs, oblivious to Alpha, who was dusting the staircase.

The picture still in her hand, Cynthia's heart was pounding. The house had suddenly become a lonely tomb; it stifled her with its heavy, oppressive silence.

She needed a drink badly.

Walking into her den, she poured herself a large brandy from the decanter and downed it in one swallow. Then she poured another and sat in a chair to drain the glass.

She tried to focus on the snapshot, but she only noticed that it was turning brown at the edges.

The distant ring of the front doorbell vaguely penetrated her consciousness. There was a soft murmur of voices, then footsteps in the hall. A soft, soothing voice, pleasant and casual, floated her way.

"Is everything all right?"

Her eyes dumb with misery, Cynthia turned to see Jim Boyd standing in the doorway. She clasped her hands together.

"Oh, Reverend," she murmured, her voice slurring ever so slightly, "please come in, and do shut the door."

Then she gestured for him to sit down next to her.

"I must apologize to you," she said; her voice sounded conspiratorial. "I've been drinking."

He raised a hand as if he understood.

"I don't mean to intrude on your privacy, dear Cynthia. I came merely to prune the roses. Alpha met me at the door and seemed concerned about you. She said you looked a mite distressed when she saw you coming downstairs."

Cynthia hesitated for a moment. Finally she clenched her hand around the empty brandy glass and handed Jim Boyd the photograph.

"Do you know who those two people are?" she asked quietly.

There was a long silence as the preacher studied the picture. He knew that the man was Charles Tyson; he had seen photographs of him around the house. But the good-looking girl next to Tyson intrigued him. He'd seen her somewhere. But where? Where the hell did he know her from? He never forgot a face. He knew it would come to him.

Then suddenly he had it. She was the hitchhiker he had picked up near Fort Jade a long time ago, the wise little bitch he had dropped off at The Broadcasters Bar.

Pleased with himself, he smiled inwardly. But he remained silent as Cynthia probed him with her eyes.

"I want you to know, Jim, that the photograph you are holding is a picture of my late husband, Charles."

Cynthia paused for a moment. When she continued, her voice had a curious, slow-motion quality to it.

"And the girl with my husband was his lover. He was planning to leave me for that smiling whore. But the Lord didn't let that happen. He saw to it that Charles had a stroke while they were engaged in one of their filthy acts together. And the Lord's damnation followed them both. Now Charles is dead, and so is his whore."

She closed her eyes for a few seconds. She seemed to

have forgotten the preacher. It was as if she were speaking to herself.

"For a long, long time there has been no love, no joy, and no forgiveness in this house."

Unexpectedly, Cynthia laughed a bitter laugh.

"I have lived only with smoldering hatred as my constant companion."

As Jim Boyd listened in silence, a patient expression on his face, his mind raced ahead. *So that was it! Her old man had been humpin' that young bitch when the stroke hit him. Holy sufferin' shit! That sweet young pussy did him in!*

Cynthia turned her ashen face to the solemn-visaged preacher. She swallowed slowly and took a deep breath.

"Now that I have finally spoken the words, now that I have finally told someone, a godly man like yourself, well, maybe the hate will be over at last."

Jim Boyd's eyes were on Cynthia Tyson, but his thoughts were still on the girl in the photograph. He was sure he'd seen a picture of her recently. But where? It nagged at the back of his mind until he remembered: it was in one of the weekly tabloids. His attention had been caught by an article about Nick Tyson's floating palace. There had been a photo of Tyson with a girl, this girl. He remembered feeling at the time that he had seen her before. The thought had haunted him.

Boyd probed his memory and tried to recall the caption under the photo. What had it said? Slowly, bits of it came back until he had it.

"Millionaire Nick Tyson and glamorous actress/singer Cat Bracken seen together at Promises, London's hottest night spot. It's been rumored that an early marriage between the two of them is imminent."

That's it! Boyd felt like laughing out loud. *What a great, fuckin' piece of luck!* It was crazy, insane, but this was the piece he needed to grab the brass ring. Maria Benson was alive! And unknown to Cynthia, her precious son was banging her; he was banging the woman Cynthia hated most in the world.

Boyd felt like cheering. Now he'd have his revenge on that snotty Nick bastard. He'd make Tyson's mother hate the damned sight of him! Jim Boyd clenched his teeth to stop himself from grinning.

Finally, his expression relaxed. He managed a sad, soft smile, took Cynthia's hand, and gently patted it.

As Cynthia stared at her empty glass, the Reverend smilingly refilled it for her. She knew she was getting drunk; her head was beginning to ache. But she wasn't through talking. She wanted to explain to Jim Boyd that she had started to drink only after she found out about her husband's whore. She wanted to tell him that her only happiness was the time she spent with her wonderful son, Nick. She wanted him to know how much she loved Nick, how possessive she felt of him. Cynthia wanted him to know all those things before she joined him in doing God's work. It was important for him to understand.

Her eyes blurred as she looked at Jim Boyd. She thought he looked uncertain, apprehensive. She couldn't imagine why.

Boyd leaned back in his chair and closed his eyes, wondering if this was the right time to break the news to Cynthia that Maria Benson was still alive. It would be interesting to see how she handled it.

With a sigh he sat upright and took Cynthia's hands in his. As she looked at him questioningly, his eyes were moist with tears. Then he shook his head.

"I don't know how to tell you this, dear Cynthia."

He glanced around the room.

"It's so difficult for me. You've been through so much

pain already. But, dear, dear Cynthia, you must be strong. I fear there is still more pain ahead of you."

Cynthia felt her mouth tighten. She didn't understand what he was talking about. His words made no sense to her. Yet she was suddenly terrified. She could feel her heart pound.

"It's about the girl in the photograph," said Boyd.

"What about her?"

"She's alive."

Cynthia paused as if gasping for breath. She swayed in her chair. Her breathing was labored; her face was strained and white.

Boyd stared at her with his most professionally compassionate expression. He hoped she wasn't having a heart attack—not yet. It was too soon. He needed her. She was the key to his plan. He looked deep into her eyes.

"Are you all right?" he asked.

"Tell me . . ." she said. Then she paused for breath, to muster enough strength to finish her question. When she finally continued, her voice sounded hoarse and strange to her.

"Tell me how you know she's alive."

She dreaded his answer.

Boyd pondered a moment and relished the situation and his new-found feeling of power.

"It all happened some time ago. I saw that girl hitchhiking just outside Fort Jade, and I gave her a lift in my van. She asked to be dropped off at The Broadcasters Bar, where, I later learned, she got a job as a singing waitress. The next thing I knew, I was seeing photos of her in the newspaper under a different name. It seems she went on to become a very successful singer, calling herself Cat Bracken."

Cynthia sat as if frozen in time; a swirling mist of anger

surged through her. She had been sure that Maria Benson
was justly punished by death when her car went over the
cliff at Henderson's Point. But she was alive and pursuing
a successful, glamorous career, untouched by the suffering
and anguish she had caused.

Cynthia realized that Boyd was still speaking. Suddenly
she was afraid to hear anymore, afraid that he would say
something that would destroy her world completely.

Keyed up and sweating, Boyd took a deep breath. He
couldn't stop now. He just hoped that he wouldn't blow it
when he told her about Nick.

He placed his hand sympathetically on hers; his voice
was barely above a whisper.

"I cannot tell you how much it hurts me to bring you
these unhappy tidings. I've sat here with a heavy heart,
listening to the sorrow you've endured, and tried to fit the
pieces of this tragic puzzle together. Finally I see the picture clearly—and a shocking picture it is. I'll never understand how a son could do such a thing to his own wonderful, loving mother."

Boyd stopped talking and wiped his brow with his handkerchief; he never once took his eyes off Cynthia.

She sat stone still and stared at him mindlessly. What
had he said about Nick? It didn't make sense. What could
her beloved son possibly do that would hurt her? How
utterly unspeakable it was of Boyd to drag Nick into this,
just because Nick disliked the Reverend!

As Boyd continued, his voice grew more urgent, more
insistent; a note of near hysteria crept into his tone.

"Cynthia, my dear, we cannot hide from the truth, no
matter how painful it might be. There is no easy way to tell
you this: Your son is in love with Maria Benson."

For a moment of stunned silence, Cynthia looked at
Boyd in mute disbelief. Finally, she replied in a voice weak

with tension and fear, "What are you talking about, Reverend? You're not making sense. My son—and that whore! It's simply impossible!"

Holding his hands as if in prayer, Boyd raised his eyes to the ceiling.

"You'll never know how it grieves me to say this, my dear, dear Cynthia. I know how difficult it is for you to accept, but your son and Cat Bracken, the woman who was your husband's lover, plan to get married on that new ship of his."

So intense was her pain that Cynthia's mind went blank. She just sat motionless.

"I really had no alternative but to tell you. I'm glad that I was the one who brought you the news. Painful though it has been, I thank God for letting me be the one. For it now falls to me to comfort you and look after you, with the Lord's help."

Cynthia felt her eyes glaze over. She was suspended in an abattoir of agony. She couldn't move or speak or think. She just sat motionless.

Boyd drummed his fingers nervously on the arm of his chair. As he stared into Cynthia's blank, expressionless eyes, he wondered if his words had sent her into a state of shock.

"I think I should leave you now. I'll ring for Alpha," he said. "She'll take you to your room. You must get some rest."

The sad-eyed little housekeeper bustled into the room, her starched petticoats rustling. She clucked like a mother hen and assumed that Mrs. Tyson was having another one of her headaches.

"Lordy, how this poor child does suffer!" she muttered as she helped Cynthia upstairs.

A triumphant smile on his face, Jim Boyd watched quietly as the two women walked the long staircase up to Cynthia Tyson's bedroom suite.

Tonight he had laid the groundwork for the destruction of Nick Tyson in his mother's eyes.

Lighting a cigar, Boyd casually sauntered through the many rooms of Tyson Hall. His eyes took in the beautiful furnishings and priceless antiques. At the entrance to the elegant dining room, he paused. Then he turned. With confidence in his stride, he reentered the foyer, opened the heavy oak door, and stepped outside into the night air.

Later, walking across the parking lot to his church, he was filled with excitement that bordered on unbridled elation. Everthing was going even better than he had planned.

It was cool and dark inside the chapel. The light was on in the basement downstairs, where Jim Boyd lived. Then he saw someone leaning against the partially open door at the bottom of the stairs. It was redheaded Cory Jones. She stood looking at him insolently; her lips were slightly parted.

Boyd looked back at her; his own mouth was tight. He felt a stirring in his groin as he studied her slight, slim figure with its full breasts. Every feature of her catlike face and form seemed to shriek of sex and seduction.

He wanted her. His tea-colored eyes lustfully devoured every line of her body. For a brief moment he felt a flash of caution, but he pushed it away.

"What the fuck are you doing here?" he growled. "I didn't send for you."

Cory licked her full lips and tossed her ginger curls in a gesture of careless defiance.

"I know that, but I ran away. I don't want to work in a whorehouse no more."

Boyd walked slowly down the stairs. His whole body

rode a tide of excitement, and he grabbed at her, pulled her to him and took her warm mouth in his, sucking it hungrily. He thrust his hand inside her bra and squeezed her erect nipple. She was soft and pliant; she giggled as he fondled her and sighed as he rubbed his large, flat hands over her pelvis.

As he carried her to his bed, her small, childlike hands undid his belt buckle. She stripped him as his fingers penetrated her. There was no resistance on her part. She smiled and moaned with pleasure. When she finally exposed his penis, she took it hungrily between her lips. Down it slid, deep into the warm tunnel of her mouth.

It was dark when Cynthia awoke.

She wondered how long she had been in bed. She seemed to have been in and out of sleep for hours. She had a hazy recollection of speaking to the Reverend about something.

She tried to recall, to bring back the conversation. She took a deep breath and thought very hard. There were many patches of it she couldn't remember.

She tried to get out of bed, but her body refused to obey. She looked at the illuminated dial of her bedside clock. Her vision was blurred. It was still dark outside.

Slowly she pulled the room into focus; it was fuzzy from the brandy she had consumed. She edged herself to the side of the bed and stood up. She heard the sounds of the night outside her window. Then the whole house shuddered with the renewal of her pain as Cynthia remembered what Jim Boyd had told her earlier that evening.

Sitting on the edge of the bed, clasping and unclasping her hands, it all came back to her. As tears rolled down her face, her uncontrollable sobs filled the room. Was there never to be release from the unbearable agony that engulfed her?

Nick, my son, my beloved Nick! How could you do this to me? You, whom I have always loved and protected. You, to whom I have devoted my entire life. What sickness is there in you? What perversion has possessed your soul? What monstrous insanity could make you want to take your father's filthy whore for your wife?

Reaching out with trembling fingers, she snapped on her bedside lamp and caught a glimpse of herself in the mirror. Naked hatred was deeply etched in every line of her face.

"Perverts, all of you! Ugly, dirty, godless perverts!" she shrieked and cursed at the empty room.

Back and forth she paced, distraught, disoriented, and filled with burning rage. Her bitter thoughts jackrabbited around her brain. She would disown her son, disinherit him, destroy him! She'd take away his trust funds, leave him penniless! No court in the world would dispute her; no woman in the world would condemn her.

Jim Boyd was right. She would use her money for God's work. That was the only thing that counted, the only thing that would never betray her. She must go to him, tell him, and commit herself to him.

Cynthia dressed quickly. She left the house and ran across the sand-packed lane toward the church; her mind was filled with thoughts of her son. Nick as a child. Nick as a young man. Nick. Nick. It was always Nick. His name surged through her mind.

Suddenly breathless, she stopped running and stood still, taking deep gulps of air. A floodgate of memories broke open in her mind. A silver ray of light penetrated the dark rage that had engulfed her. All at once she knew.

Nick was innocent of betraying her.

He had known nothing about Maria Benson, nothing

about his father's shameful betrayal. How could he have known? Cynthia had kept everything secret from him.

She was on the verge of hysteria when she realized that her blessed, wonderful son was innocent of any wrongdoing. But lust for vengeance still blazed through her as she thought of Maria Benson.

Her body shook as she entered the church. She had to talk to Jim Boyd.

A crack of light shone through the basement door. Cynthia descended the stairs.

She heard Boyd's voice, as soft and silky as ever. For some reason, she counted the steps. One more step, and she would be inside the room.

The preacher had heard no footsteps on the stairs. He was unaware that someone had entered the room. He was unaware of anything except Cory Jones sitting astride his penis, riding it with great gusto.

Cory was just about to edge Jim Boyd into paradise when her gyrations came to an abrupt halt. When she found her voice, her tone was shrill and mocking.

"Who the fuck are you?"

Boyd turned to look just as Cory contracted her eighteen-year-old vagina, locking him in like a male dog on a bitch in heat.

Cynthia Tyson stood rooted to the spot; her flesh prickled. Almost soundlessly she whimpered to herself; her labored breathing turned to agonized moans. Then, with a tortured wail of pain, she slid limply to the floor.

"Holy fuckin' shit!" cried Boyd, pushing the giggling girl off his rapidly shrinking organ.

"Sister," he said, "let's move ass!"

Pulling a wooden box from under the bed, Boy stuffed the thousands of dollars he had milked from Cynthia Tyson into a leather case.

Cory Jones watched silently as he moved with frantic speed, sobbing and cursing to the empty air.

"On accounta you, I blew millions!" he screamed at her.

Her own reedlike voice was controlled and emotionless.

"Screw that, preacher man. We got all we need. You an' me, we're gonna do just fine. Wherever you're goin', I'm goin'."

Hitching up her skirt, she proudly displayed her naked thighs. Her young face wore a provocative, ageless smile.

"You already got lots of money, but here's somethin' that's better than money. Now, ain't that right?"

In one bound Boyd was at her side. He grabbed her hand, and together they ran past Cynthia's body. Up the stairs they raced, out of the church, and into the van.

Jim Boyd burned rubber all the way down the quiet country lane. As they pulled into the highway traffic, he had one hand on the wheel and the other between Cory's thighs.

The ginger-haired girl made an obscene gesture toward the town as they sped away.

"I'm gonna be good for you, preacher man, you'll see. When you were drunk at the whorehouse, preachin' up a storm, I'm the only one who listened. You speak God's words real good. Maybe I don't understand most of it, but I want ya to teach me to be a preacher lady. I wanna be all dressed up in white, lookin' like an angel, talkin' real pretty to everyone, tellin' them how you saved me from the devil. I also got me a real sweet singin' voice. You'n me, preacher man—we could be a real fine team, preachin' in the daytime and sinnin' all night long."

Jim Boyd felt a surge of joy bubbling through him. His ambition was still intact; his mind was acutely alert. With Cynthia Tyson's money and this child-woman as his disciple, the miracle might still happen. Holy shit, the media loved a repentant sinner! His dream of being up there with the big TV preachers might be closer than he thought.

Humming his favorite hymn, "Amazing Grace," Jim Boyd drove across the border into the next state.

Cynthia opened her eyes.

Her first conscious thought was, *Dear God, don't let them still be here watching me.*

When she saw she was alone, she forced herself to concentrate on one thing: getting to her feet.

She smoothed her dress mechanically with unfeeling fingers; the blood pounded in her ears. A pulse beat in her head like an overwound clock. She felt as if a plumb line had been dropped down the center of her spine and was anchoring her to the floor. She couldn't rise to her feet.

Her body started to heave as she retched again and again; a gush of warm bile spewed from her mouth.

Finally she sat back, drained.

As the room and its furniture slowly came into focus, she began to weep. She wept for the fool Jim Boyd had made of her. What an easy, stupid victim she had been!

"Oh, Nick darling," she whispered, "you were right all along. The man was perverted and evil."

An overpowering sensation of unbridled hatred coursed through her body and blazed through her veins like red-hot lava. All her mounting rage, all her seething fury centered on one person and one alone: Maria Benson.

Minutes later, after the trembling stopped, Cynthia knew she couldn't stay in the filthy basement any longer. She had to get up, she had to get away, back to the security of her house.

But there was one thing she had to do first.

She had to purify the church.

* * *

The next morning, the hard core of anger still seethed inside her.

She had lain motionless on her bed all night. She couldn't remember if she had slept or not. It really didn't matter. Nothing mattered to her anymore—nothing but the hatred.

Slowly she got up and made her way to the bathroom. In the tub she scrubbed herself so violently that her skin turned red and her arms began to ache.

Later, back in her bedroom, she barely heard Alpha's chatter when the housekeeper entered with her breakfast tray.

"Mrs. Tyson, ma'am, I swear I don't know how you managed to sleep through all that commotion last night. All those fire engines racing around till early mornin'. Had to be somebody crazy, somebody wicked and sinful to burn down the Lord's own house of worship. Sheriff Fogarty told my Willie it was arson for sure. The mos' peculiar part of it is, wasn't no sign of the preacher anywhere. Looks like he jus' up and vanished."

Alpha attacked the bed pillows as she spoke, fluffing them up and pummeling them in rhythm to her words.

"Lordy, I sure hope that God-fearin' man came to no harm. I never knew a man who had such a gift for preachin' the Word. He made me feel like Jesus Himself was right at his shoulder."

Cynthia felt she would scream if Alpha uttered another word. Her voice shaky, her eyes sullen, she snapped at the surprised housekeeper, "Forget about him. He's gone. He left town. He won't be back."

Then she turned to face the window. Her voice was so low, it was almost inaudible.

"I never want his name mentioned in this house again. Never—do you understand?"

She turned back from the window; her fingernails dug into the palms of her hands as she strove for control.

"Now, take my breakfast tray away. I'm not hungry."

Alpha stared blankly at Mrs. Tyson for a moment. Then, without a word, she picked up the tray. She made angry clucking sounds with her lips as she carried it downstairs.

"Dear Lord," she muttered to herself, "that poor soul is gettin' meaner and sicker every day that goes by. Now she's nourishin' a hatred for the good preacher. Seems like no love or mercy can penetrate that grievin' heart of hers no more."

The minutes turned to hours, and still Cynthia Tyson remained in her bedroom, staring unseeingly at the wall in front of her.

Finally she walked over to her desk and picked up a beautifully embossed envelope. She held it for a moment, then took out the invitation that Nick had sent her. The text was beautifully scrolled over a magnificent painting of *Pleasure Palace* rendered in oils by a prominent artist.

She could barely keep her eyes from blurring as she tried to focus on the date. The gala event would take place in two days.

Then one name jumped out at her from off the card.

Cat Bracken.

The line read, "Cat Bracken, the fabulous Queen of Song, will be Guest of Honor."

But all Cynthia Tyson saw was the name Cat Bracken.

Cat Bracken—who used to be Maria Benson. Cat Bracken—the woman who had ruined her life.

Trembling, her head spinning, she dropped the invitation.

She knew what she had to do.

She opened her large closet and reached deep inside. She unlocked the drawer of a small, narrow dresser at the back of the closet. From the drawer she took out a gun.

She opened a cartridge box and slowly inserted six bullets into the chambers.

Charles had gotten her the gun years before for protection. Sheriff Fogarty had taught her how to use it.

As Cynthia packed her suitcase, she felt as if she were caught up in some unreal dream, some unendurable nightmare. Her mouth was dry. Her hand was shaking.

She was on her way to commit a murder.

Chapter Thirty-one

Sitting in Nick Tyson's stateroom aboard *Pleasure Palace,* Jan thought it was indecent for anyone to be as happy as she.

In just a few short hours she'd be married to the man she loved.

The last few months in London had flown by swiftly—almost too swiftly. Living with Nick once again in his wonderful house in the Mews, each day she found more heavenly than the one before. The hours they spent together had been wildly romantic and insanely exciting. It was as if their love had grown stronger than ever because they had come so close to losing it.

There was only one small cloud on Jan's horizon: She was genuinely sorry that Sarah and Daley couldn't be with her on this very special day. Jan had attended their wedding at the church in Covent Garden. But poor Sarah was having a rough pregnancy, living with nausea most of the time. The last place she wanted to be was aboard ship.

A happy grin crossed Jan's lips as she thought of Daley. Daley, whose outrageous behavior in the past had brought people to the very brink of cardiac arrest. Daley, the enfant terrible, who had surprisingly turned out to be a protective and loving husband. And Daley, who was so thrilled by the prospect of his impending fatherhood that he tended Sarah's needs as gently as he nursed her through her constant morning sickness.

Yes, Jan would miss them both. But Leancia was to be

the matron of honor, and Jan was very happy about that. Leancia was due to arrive momentarily.

Having left Jan in his stateroom, Nick Tyson wandered once more through the interior of his ship.

Creating that interior had been a prodigious task for his crew of decorators. By dint of hard work and the expenditure of large sums of money, they had succeeded in giving him the opulence he wanted. Art and antiques were everywhere, in a variety of styles that embodied decades of memories of other times and many places.

Nick was pleased by everything he saw in the main salon. There were tables in dark green velvet skirts; the intimate dance floor, whose stage was a sweep of pale pink marble; the subtle, pastel-hued lighting, designed to give every female the complexion of a rose; and the specially commissioned paintings, portraits of beauties from past eras, in heavy gold frames that hung suspended from antique cords and tassels.

He went down to the next deck to check out the disco one more time. There everything was being readied for the evening's festivities in accordance with his own detailed specifications.

Next, he inspected the kitchens, the theater, the pool, the lounge areas, and finally the stateroom suites. Everything was impeccable, luxurious, and sybaritic. The entire ship was abuzz with activity; every crew member was thoroughly trained and eager to serve.

The media would be out in full force to give the year's biggest gala saturation coverage. Then, the next morning, after the last guest had gone, *Pleasure Palace*'s one hundred members would remain on board and sail with the ship on the afternoon tide. Their destination would be

Porto Ertcole, the exclusive millionaires' retreat on the Italian coast.

In the purser's office Nick checked with Thaddeus Johnson, his chief security officer. After that, there was nothing more for him to do. In one hour the evening's activities would begin.

Finally he allowed himself the luxury of thinking about his bride-to-be. He savored the memory of their lovemaking. In his mind's eye he could see her beautiful face grinning up at him, hear her whispering, "I love you, Nick Tyson."

They belonged to each other; he knew that now. They would be together, where they belonged, for the rest of their lives. Soon the woman he loved would be Mrs. Nick Tyson. This was surely the most exciting evening of his life.

Soon the ship would be alive with celebrities of every type, from every field. Nick watched the guests as they were brought aboard until, glancing at his watch, he saw it was time to go downstairs to the disco. He wanted to make sure that everything was set for Cat's performance.

On another part of the ship, Cynthia Tyson stood in a crowd of boisterous, jostling celebrants.

She felt hemmed in, trapped, and suffocated as they moved her forward with them. Cynthia didn't know where they were going or how to find Nick. She had never imagined that his ship would be so large.

Her silk evening bag clutched close to her side, the dark object inside hardened her heart against any weakness. She was here for a purpose. No matter what the consequences or the sacrifice, nothing must dissuade her.

When she finally managed to break away from the crowd, Cynthia's demeanor caught the attention of a

young officer standing nearby. She seemed strangely
harassed to him. Something about her reminded him of his
own mother, who had recently died. He wasn't supposed
to leave his post, but he elbowed his way through the
crowd. Reaching Cynthia, he took her arm and gently
ushered her toward a quiet deck, where, by taking deep
breaths, she regained some of her composure.

Her face was expressionless as she stood at the young
man's side, waiting for him to speak. He observed her carefully for a few seconds, then smiled.

"May I help you, ma'am? Are you looking for someone?
This ship, with all its decks, can be confusing to someone
here for the first time."

The young officer's voice was warm and sincere. Cynthia
swallowed hard.

"Thank you. You're very kind. I must admit, that horde
of people had me quite confused. Would you be good
enough to tell me where I might find Nick Tyson? It's
quite important that I see him."

The officer nodded politely.

"It may take me awhile to locate him. Let me find you a
comfortable place to wait."

He led her toward one of the lounges and continued
speaking.

"I'm afraid this is a very busy night for Mr. Tyson,
ma'am. He's hosting the entire evening's festivities. The
entertainment begins in about half an hour, when Cat
Bracken will be performing in the downstairs disco. We
even have a shipboard wedding scheduled. This is going to
be quite a night. As a matter of fact, the people you were
crowded in with were heading for the disco."

Cynthia's head was spinning. She needed time to think,
time to plan the most important act of her life.

Suddenly there was a beep on the young officer's walkie-talkie.

"Excuse me, ma'am," he said, putting the receiver to his ear. "I've got to go now. I'm wanted by the chief of security. Will you be all right here for a few minutes?"

Cynthia nodded.

After giving her a comforting smile, the security officer was soon lost in the crowd.

She stood for a few seconds, momentarily confused. Then she decided that the best thing to do would be to follow the crowd down to where the security men in evening dress were admitting them through black velvet ropes into the dark red, womblike chamber of the ship's disco.

As she approached the disco, Cynthia stood back a moment. The deafening sound of rock music filled her ears. The din was so penetrating, so loud, that she felt her head would burst. Almost mesmerized by the noise and the flashing colored lights, she felt strangely disoriented, unable to focus her thoughts.

Then, propelled forward by the motion of the crowd, she soon found herself at the black velvet ropes. She opened her evening bag and presented her invitation, nervously chewing her lower lip.

Once inside the ropes, Cynthia carefully slid her revolver into the pocket of her beaded jacket.

The gun felt cold to her touch.

Hesitantly, she stepped into the disco. The noise was even more deafening inside the glittering room. Standing by herself, she silently watched the dancers. On the crowded floor they all seemed to move to some primitive beat. The very air vibrated with sexual tension. It wasn't like dancing; it was as if they were all making love, gyrating their bodies in lewd, frantic foreplay before thrusting themselves at each other to the urging of the music.

The crowd grew. Photographers walked back and forth, snapping pictures endlessly. Everyone seemed to be smiling and waving at everyone else.

Cynthia stood among clusters of noisy revelers. The gun in her pocket was still tightly clenched in her trembling hand.

Suddenly the lights dimmed. The music dropped to a softer beat, and the dancers left the floor. The crowd surged forward, Cynthia with them.

She stared unblinkingly at the small stage with its single spotlight. Every fiber of her being was waiting for someone. She couldn't control the trembling of her body; she didn't even try.

Then her heart began to pound like a trip-hammer: she caught a glimpse of her son.

Nick was standing close to a woman whose back was turned to Cynthia. He had his arm through hers. They were laughing happily; their bodies were touching.

As beads of perspiration trickled down her cheeks, Nick's mother stood rigid, unaware of the twitch that slightly twisted one side of her face. Standing motionless, as if frozen in time, she saw the woman turn and sweep her long silver hair to one side. She saw her throw her arms around Nick in a warm, spontaneous gesture.

A quiet moan slipped from Cynthia's lips. The woman's face was now full center in her line of vision.

It was the face that she had locked away in her memory. The face that had never stopped tormenting her in a dark corner of her mind. The face that she had cursed and damned to hell that nightmarish day in Fort Jade Hospital.

And now, that face was looking with adoration into the eyes of Cynthia Tyson's son.

She stood half-hidden in the shadows until she saw the two of them separate with a brief, affectionate kiss. Then she insinuated herself through the sea of bodies moving closer and closer to the footlights. She watched the woman walk to center stage, watched her blow another kiss to Nick.

Then the show began.

TV cameras prepared to film the event.

As the audience applauded, streaks of strobe light flew across the room. The blinding flashes and shattering sounds bounced off the walls and covered the crowd with a living, raging crazy-quilt of rhythm.

Cynthia saw the faces in the audience transfixed by the strutting, sexual movements of the performer. As a sensuous drum roll started to build, the flashing lights painted her moving body in blinding colors of red, blue, orange, and green.

The crowd broke into an explosion of cheers. She twirled about, flirting shamelessly with her audience. Cynthia watched as if hypnotized.

Then, with arms outstretched, bathed in a spotlight of silver, Cat stopped strutting and picked up the sequined microphone. She slowly snapped her fingers. On cue, the music moved to a softer beat. She started to sing.

Cynthia flinched when a flashbulb went off at her side, startling her. She heard the singing as if it were coming from deep within a dark, black tunnel. It sounded distorted to her ears. She hated it. She hated the singer. She couldn't stand much more.

The people around Cynthia started to crush even closer to the stage. In a frenzy of enthusiasm and affection, they called out to the performer, "Cat, Cat, Cat! Go for it, Cat!"

More flashbulbs popped. White rings of light were blinding Cynthia's eyes. She couldn't focus. Everything was a blur. She became conscious of the thunderous drum rolls, the deafening clash of cymbals, the incessant screaming of the electric guitars. The music reached a deafening crescendo, and the sound cut through her brain.

She reached deep into her pocket and felt the cool metal of her revolver.

As the strobe lights flashed on and off, Nick stared at the stage from inside the glass-walled deejay's booth. He thought what a terrific performer Cat was—and what a wonderful lady, as well. She had kept her promise to him. She had said she would perform at the charity bash, and here she was.

When Cat was onstage, it was as if she were fired up by an inner power, some super energy source. Her magnetism brought everyone into her shining circle. She soon had the entire audience on its feet, cheering.

Nick glanced out at the crowd; his gaze idly traveled back and forth. Then, for one startling instant, he froze.

Unbelieving, he stared in horrified fascination. He was looking directly at his mother. But something was wrong —frighteningly, horribly wrong. The Cynthia he saw was a Cynthia he had never seen before.

As exploding flashbulbs illuminated her, a look of madness burned in her eyes. They flashed with naked hatred at Cat Bracken.

Then Nick saw the gun in Cynthia's hand pointing straight at Cat.

"Oh, God!" he whispered to himself.

Without conscious thought, he started for the door, wondering if he were trapped in some horrible nightmare, or if his whole world were going mad. What was Cynthia doing here—and with that gun? He had to reach her, talk to her.

With Herculean strength, he pushed his way through

the human wall of spectators. The lights flashed on and off
as confetti fell from the ceiling. The smoke machine filled
the stage with a ghostly silver fog.

The next few seconds ticked away in a mad, slow-motion tableau.

Cynthia stared at the stage with unseeing eyes. She felt
herself dissolve and crack open.

As the music pounded relentlessly and the fog swirled
around, the gun shook in her hand. From somewhere in
her head a voice whispered, "Such is the way of an adulterous woman who saith, 'I have done no evil.' "

At that moment, when Nick reached the stage, saw
where his mother's gun was pointing, and pushed Cat
Bracken to the floor, Cynthia fired.

She fired and fired and fired until the gun was empty.

"Holy Mother of Christ!" shouted Thaddeus Johnson,
the head security guard. "What's happening down there?"
He dimmed the lights instantly. Next, he hit a switch
that brought the heavy red velvet curtain down to form a
dome over the stage.

There was one frozen moment of silence. Then someone
in the crowd cried out, "What the hell's going on?"

Thaddeus flicked the strobe lights on again, and at the
same time he hit the automatic switch that flooded the
room with canned music. He grabbed a microphone and
started to speak; his voice was calm and soothing.

"Ladies and gentlemen, we have a temporary technical
problem onstage. We'll have it fixed as soon as possible. In
the meantime, please follow the officers into the grand ballroom. You'll find another performance about to begin."

Confused and puzzled, the audience moved toward the
velvet stairway leading to the ballroom. Cynthia moved
along with them. As they cleared the disco, a few of the

curious looked back, trying to see what had happened on-stage. But the curtain effectively hid the scene from view.

"What's happening?" whispered elfin Brenda Fairchild, Hollywood's newest teenage idol, to the young male model with the million-dollar smile.

He answered in a low, intense voice, "Know something, Brenda? I felt really bad vibes in there. Let's have a toot as soon as we hit the ballroom. That'll blow them all away."

"Oh, my God," moaned a drunken Randy Tallon, star of one of TV's most macho detective series. "I swear, Ambrose, if this crowd moves any slower, I'm gonna piss right on the floor."

His bored, fat agent ignored the actor's complaint as he casually responded, "The food here'll probably be shitty. You can't get a good meal anymore now that the whole fucking world's on a diet."

The big-breasted anchorwoman in the angora sweater smiled her toothy grin at both of them as she launched into her familiar machine-gun chatter.

"Very baffling, isn't it? I wonder what's really going down. Of course, it's not to worry. We'll know soon enough. In fact, just tune in to my newscast. Whatever went on up there, you can bet my cameraman got it. He was on the scene filming Cat Bracken. What a talent that girl is! She gets better all the time."

Even as Ambrose returned her big flashy smile with one of his own, he was thinking what a tacky broad she was. *So fuckin' fascinated with herself.* If the head anchorman at her station wasn't into big tits, she'd still be earning two bills a week in the secretarial pool.

Nevertheless, Ambrose held his smile and turned on the charm. As a Hollywood agent, he knew better than to offend any member of the media, especially one with dynamite gazebos.

"Talkin' about talent, Dallas honey, lemme tell ya you're the best damned thing that ever happened to that news spot."

"Ambrose, you're an absolute love—kiss, kiss," she cooed. Her eyes met his with a flirtatious glint. After all, he was one of the town's top agents, and she didn't want to be an anchorwoman all her life.

As the crowd of TV personalities, columnists, movie stars, myth makers, and celebrities of every persuasion shuffled through the ship's thickly carpeted corridors, Cynthia Tyson moved along with the human tide.

Minutes later, after everyone had been shepherded into the grand ballroom, they greeted the sight of the lavish decor with a chorus of oohs and ahs. Talk of Cat's performance and the crazy hassle on stage was already beginning to wane as the celebrants concentrated on getting high again in one way or another.

*Darling*s and *wonderful*s peppered every conversation. Gowns were admired, and jewels were envied. The more drinks were sipped, marijuana smoked, cocaine sniffed, and 'ludes swallowed, the more everyone relaxed and agreed what a fabulous party it was. Any moment now, Raider Bell and his hard-rock group would rock them to glory.

It promised to be a night of unsurpassed fun and gaiety.

Leancia hurried down the stairs and headed for Captain Dudley's quarters. The door opened, and there was Jan. Her green eyes were tremendous in her pale face; her voice was shaky as she spoke.

"So there you are, darling! Come in, come in. I was just about to have a glass of champagne. Please join me. I'm developing a case of the jitters. The captain and I have been waiting for Nick. Have you seen him?"

"No, darling," Leancia answered in her husky voice. "I just came down from my quarters. Jaafar will meet us here. But don't worry, Jan, the place is a madhouse upstairs. Nick is probably having trouble making his way through the crowd."

Before Jan could reply, an excited ship's officer rapped frantically on the captain's door, then burst in before anyone inside could open it.

"Sir, there's been some trouble in the ship's disco," he addressed the captain.

"Trouble? What kind of trouble?"

The officer's voice dropped to a whisper.

"The head security guard told me to keep it very quiet and report to you alone. There's been a shooting."

Captain Dudley's eyes widened.

"A shooting? What the hell do you mean? Speak up, man! What's it all about?"

Jan stood transfixed, unable to move. It was as if all her nerve endings had surfaced, as if she could hear her own heartbeat. Her first thought was that something had happened to Nick—something so horrible she couldn't or wouldn't let the image form in her mind.

She rushed past the captain and ran breathlessly down the corridor to the disco. She had to find Nick. Her love for him was a physical thing; it threatened to stifle her with its intensity. He was all she could think about.

Let him be all right! Dear God, let nothing have happened to Nick.

Once outside the disco she hesitated momentarily, afraid to go in, afraid of what she'd find. But she had to enter. She had to know.

Making her way slowly forward, she saw a luminous mist rising from under the dome onstage. She heard the somber murmuring of voices from behind the curtain. Her

whole body trembled. She was awash with an awful feeling
that she couldn't pin down. Reaching the stage, she moved
the curtain ever so slightly and stood back in the shadows.
Then she peered behind the billowy material.

Jan froze with horror when she saw a sheet-covered
body on the marble floor.

Standing next to the body, his eyes wary, was Thadde-
ous Johnson with two of his guards. He spoke disapprov-
ingly to Jan.

"Sorry, miss. This area is off-limits. You shouldn't be in
here."

Johnson had gone through scenes like this before. These
wacky broads got their rocks off looking at tragedies.

As he spoke, his voice was curt and full of authority.

"I'm afraid you'll have to leave! The entertainment
you're looking for is in the main ballroom."

Jan stood white-faced; her eyes were wild. The tragedy
in this room involved her—she sensed it, she knew it. She
could almost touch her feeling of fear as she stared at the
pool of blood that was forming beneath the sheet on the
marble floor.

"My God, what happened?"

Johnson moved toward her. Jan felt hysteria building
inside her as the security officer took her arm.

"Come along, now. All I can tell you is that there's been
an accident. I'm afraid you'll have to leave."

At that moment, she heard a rustle at the stage curtain.
Turning her head, Jan saw Jaafar standing there. He
seemed to dwarf the stage. His black eyes were fixed on the
shroud-covered body, and his deep, rich voice broke
through the sudden silence.

"Why? In God's name, why?"

Jan shook her head helplessly. Her sensation of fear, of
mounting panic was growing stronger. She moved swiftly,

before anyone could stop her. Kneeling down beside the body, she lifted the sheet just enough to see the face.

Agonizing pain ripped through her. The air was rent by a tortured scream that filled the room, like the scream of a wounded animal, suspended in time.

Somewhere, far in the distance, Jan heard the scream fill the room as if it were a thing apart. She turned to Jaafar and tried to speak to him, but her tongue seemed frozen. She wanted to die. *Oh please, God, let me die,* she thought. *If only I could shut my eyes, never to wake again.*

Strong hands seized her. They were carrying her somewhere. She felt like a little girl again.

She was in a quiet place—except for the sobbing. Who was sobbing?

There was a blur of faces. Hands were patting her, soothing her, holding her. Then the delicious feeling of nothingness.

The pain was going far, far away.

"She'll be all right, Mr. al Hassad. The shot knocked her out."

The ship's doctor snapped his bag shut.

"What a night. I've got to leave now and tend to Miss Bracken. One of the bullets grazed her forehead. She's a lucky girl—all she got was a powder burn."

Chapter Thirty-two

Cat Bracken rested in the captain's quarters while the ship's doctor checked the powder burn on her head.

Captain Dudley, his brows raised, had asked her many questions.

"Miss Bracken, what actually happened up there on that stage? Do you have any idea who fired those shots?"

Cat swallowed hard and took a deep breath. She felt she was going to be sick at any moment. The horror of the evening kept replaying itself in her mind. She couldn't blot out the sight of Nick slumping to the floor and clutching at his chest, or the sound of his voice when he cried out.

Her lovely face contorted in pain as she remembered. Her large blue eyes were red-rimmed from crying. Her brain was spinning; her thoughts whirled. She couldn't answer questions yet. She had too much to think about, too much to remember. Oh God, she desperately needed to talk to someone. She couldn't tell what she knew until she had talked to her lawyer, her agent, her producer—somebody.

She turned to the captain.

"Please don't ask me any more questions. There's nothing I can tell you."

After the captain left, Cat was alone with her thoughts.

She slowly unpinned a small diamond pin from her dress. It was a silly habit; she wore it as a lucky charm every time she performed.

She held it now in her hands, remembering the day Dirk had found it on the grassy slopes of the ravine at Henderson's Point. She hadn't remembered then who gave it to her, but now she did.

She looked at it for a long time, holding it tightly in her hands. She saw the light reflected by the four letters spelling *Love*.

Then she hid her face in her hands and began to cry softly.

"I'm so sorry," she whispered to the empty room.

She felt herself sink into a deep pit of pain. She knew the bullet that had killed Nick had been meant for her.

For a split-second she had seen the face of the woman in the audience. She had felt the overpowering hatred that blazed in her eyes as she pointed the revolver straight at Cat.

Then, in that traumatic instant, as she hit the floor, it had been like a crazy slow-motion rerun of a movie. A montage of pictures flashed in front of her eyes—everything she had blocked out. Everything her brain had kept hidden because it was too painful to remember rushed back into focus.

She now remembered the past—all of it.

She now knew that Charles Tyson had been her lover when her name had been Maria Benson. It was he who had given her the Love pin. They had been making love when his stroke occurred. Cat now recalled her painful meeting with Mrs. Tyson at the hospital and the raging guilt she had felt as she drove away from the scene. She relived the car accident, that additional horror. She was aware that temporary amnesia allowed her mind to remember just what it wanted to and to blot out all the rest.

The memory that had returned that day with Dirk had been only a partial return. It still had blocked out the painful images she hadn't wanted to face.

Now at last, Cat had the many parts of the puzzle sorted

out. But there was still one piece that eluded her, that defied her understanding: She could not comprehend the depth of Cynthia Tyson's hatred.

She held her breath as tears began to flow freely. She was reliving the moment when Nick Tyson had pushed her blindly to the floor. Nick, whom she had loved in her own way. Nick, who was the son of Charles Tyson, her earlier lover. Nick, who had saved her life.

Now he was dead. And his mother was the murderess.

Then Cat's thoughts flashed to Jan, and she felt herself dissolve and start to cry and whimper like a small child.

"Oh, my God!" she wailed out loud as tears ran down her face. Her breath came in short, shallow, panting gasps. She wept as if she would never stop.

Dear, dear God, how could she live? How could she cope with all the tragedy she had caused? It seemed as if diabolical fate were playing a morbid, horrible joke on her.

Her heart ached with grief and remorse as she paced the room. Then, she stopped abruptly when she caught a glimpse of her now-famous face in the mirror.

As she silently contemplated her reflection, unconsciously combing her delicate fingers through her hair, she thought of her dreams and longings throughout the years, of how they were now all starting to come true. She thought of the movie roles that were being offered to her, of the public that loved her.

She realized that it would take a long time to put all the ghosts behind her, a long time to recover from the anguish of the past. But she had to get on with her own life, to be true to her own destiny. The make-believe existence of a movie star would be perfect for her. Hollywood was where she belonged.

In her gut Cat Bracken had always known that she was a survivor.

Chapter Thirty-three

Jan woke up in a private clinic in Los Angeles.

Jaafar and Leancia had attended to the details. A white-coated doctor came into the room, wearing a comforting smile.

"I'm Dr. Klein. How are you feeling?"

Jan sat up and looked at him, feeling as if she were drunk.

"I don't know how I feel. Why am I here? Have I had an accident?"

Casting her mind back, she remembered. She was getting married—that was it. She'd been on board *Pleasure Palace* with Nick, the man she loved. She'd gone looking for him. She could remember everything so clearly up to that point. But then nothing.

As if from a great distance, she again heard the doctor's voice.

"No, you've had no accident. You've been sedated. But we'll talk everything out later. I don't want you to get upset. You're in very good hands. Right now you just need to rest, so I'll give you another shot to help you sleep."

Jan felt the sharp, stinging prick of a needle in her arm. Then everything became a blur, and the smiling face of the doctor swam in front of her. As she closed her eyes, she felt herself moving off to a quiet place far beyond the shadows.

"Nick," she murmured as darkness gathered around her; her eyes were wet with tears.

Chapter Thirty-four

With a great sense of relief, Cynthia Tyson turned the key in the front door of Tyson Hall.

It was morning. Not another sound disturbed the silence of the house as she walked to her room.

All her fury had ebbed. All the betrayals were ended. There would be no more adulterous relationships ever again. In her mind, everything was settled at last.

Walking to the window, she looked out beyond the gracious grounds. Images flashed unbidden into her brain. She had no sense of reality, only the hazy recollection that she had fired her gun.

Leaving the ship had been easy. Her limo had driven her to the airport. The flight was on time and uneventful. It had all been quite simple.

"Thank God," she whispered. "All I have to do now is wait until Nick comes home."

Cynthia sat down. She stirred restlessly as she felt the start of a headache. Reaching for her brandy bottle, she switched on the bedroom TV. As she listened to the morning news, nothing registered. It was as if the world had stopped for her after last night.

The wide smile of popular anchorwoman Dallas Dillon flashed on the screen. After a few moments of trivia, her expression turned serious, her tone somber, as she chronicled the tragic shooting that had occurred the night before during a gala fund-raiser aboard the incredible luxury ship *Pleasure Palace.*

The words of the newscast penetrated Cynthia Tyson's

consciousness. She moved her body in the chair and stared with horror in her eyes as Dallas Dillon showed a film clip of the ship's disco. Then a photograph of the victim, Nick Tyson, was flashed on the screen. Dillon gravely explained that he was a scion of the wealthy founding family of Tysons Landing and *Pleasure Palace* co-owner.

The voice continued relentlessly. Dallas Dillon described how Nick Tyson had been shot on the stage of the ship's disco while the glamorous charity party was in full swing. Cameos were shown of many of the notables who had attended the black-tie affair.

The newscaster injected a personal note as she continued.

"Due to the noise and confusion, none of us in the audience realized what had happened at the time."

Then Dillon's voice turned breathless as she picked up a piece of paper that had just been handed to her.

"Our newsroom has just learned that the police have found the murder weapon. They have allegedly traced it to a member of the Tyson family."

Dallas Dillon's familiar smile once more flashed across the screen.

"Stay tuned to this channel. We'll interrupt our regular programming to bring you bulletins concerning this tragic affair as soon as they are received."

Cynthia stared at the TV set, numb with shock.

It was a few seconds before the pain hit her. She whipped her head from side to side, and her entire body heaved spasmodically. She was choking, drowning. She gasped for air. Then, with a soft moan, she slid to one side of the chair in a dead faint.

* * *

Later that morning, Alpha moved around quietly, not wanting to make noise for fear of waking Mrs. Tyson. She baked hot scones in the oven, tuned into her favorite morning sermon on TV, and filled the kettle to make the morning coffee.

About a half-hour later, the front doorbell rang.

Alpha walked to the kitchen window and peered out down the driveway. An official-looking black sedan was parked outside next to Sheriff Fogarty's patrol car.

The bell rang again, then again, as she opened the door.

"Lord a'mercy, Sheriff! What are you doing here so early in the morning?"

The man standing next to Fogarty had no warmth in his expression.

"We want to speak to Mrs. Tyson. May we come in?" he asked.

Alpha looked at Fogarty.

"It's all right, Alpha. You just go wake her up. We'll wait here in the hall till she comes down."

Alpha hesitantly tapped on Cynthia's bedroom door. Hearing no answer, she waited a full minute before entering.

The room was empty. The bed had not been slept in.

She turned and walked to the stairs. Maybe Mrs. Tyson had spent the night in her late husband's room. Alpha knew how crazy Mrs. Tyson had been acting, drinking herself into a stupor time after time. She had even spent whole evenings alone in Charles Tyson's bedroom.

The gloomy, vaulted hall was eerie and full of shadows. Alpha entered the stair-elevator, feeling nervous for some reason. She wanted to get this over with as soon as possible and return to the comfort of the kitchen.

Reaching the landing, she saw that the door ahead of

her was open. She stood there for a few seconds, then called out, "Mrs. Tyson, are you in there? Sheriff Fogarty and some gentleman are waitin' to see you."

Hearing no response, Alpha slowly entered the dimly lit room. Reaching for the wall switch, she turned on the lights and turned toward the wheelchair.

She stood frozen to the spot, paralyzed with shock.

Without conscious thought, she started to scream. Her screams reverberated through the house.

Within seconds, Sheriff Fogarty and Detective Lewis Waring had raced up the stairs.

They rushed into Charles Tyson's room, and then the two startled men came to an abrupt halt. Fogarty gave his head a shake like a dog, spitting out his toothpick in an involuntary, nervous motion.

"Holy shit!" was all he could say.

Cynthia's inert body was slumped over in the wheelchair. She was dressed in evening clothes. A half-spilled bottle of brandy and an empty bottle of pills were on the floor.

"Holy shit!" he said again.

He moved closer and took her pulse.

"She's still alive," he said, "but barely."

Cynthia's mouth was open. Her lips were moving, as if she were trying to talk, to tell him something.

Alpha stood by, keening in a loud voice. Tears ran down her face, and her quivering lips mouthed a silent prayer.

Detective Waring barked at her, "Pull yourself together, woman! Go downstairs and call Emergency. Have them send an ambulance right away."

Alpha was grateful for the order that allowed her to run away from the terrible scene of poor Mrs. Tyson in the wheelchair.

* * *

The two men talked for a few minutes, then decided to
wait downstairs in the kitchen until the ambulance came.

Alpha brewed some coffee. Detective Waring wanted to
find out more about the Tysons. He was good at asking
questions. But Alpha was able to provide him with very
little information, except for the fact that she thought Mrs.
Tyson had changed since her husband's stroke, and that
over time she had become a mentally sick woman.

When the ambulance arrived, the attendants moved
Cynthia onto a stretcher and down the stairs. The paramedics paused at the kitchen door. Cynthia's breathing
was becoming erratic. They placed the stretcher on the
floor, and one of the paramedics started to work on her.
After a few seconds of artificial respiration, he turned to
his partner.

"I think we're losing her."

The TV set was still on; the screen was still lit. An attendant moved to turn it off just as the news was coming on.

"Leave it, Ethel," Fogarty ordered, "and turn up the
sound."

The news was still full of the tragedy on *Pleasure Palace*.

"Holy shit!" muttered one of the ambulance attendants.
Then he pointed a thumb in the direction of the stretcher.
"Tyson—that's her name, ain't it?"

Alpha started to weep. She turned to Fogarty.

"Lord, oh Lord, what are they saying about Mr. Nick
being shot? That can't be true, can it? It couldn't be his
own mama that did it!"

"You heard it, Alpha. The news don't lie. Detective
Waring here is with homicide. He has a warrant with him.
He's filled me in on the details."

There was a long silence. Then Sheriff Fogarty inserted a
toothpick into his mouth, rolling it around until it felt

comfortable to him. He turned his eyes back to the stony-faced detective.

"The hardest part is believin' that it was his own mama who shot him. That's the real pisser in this case. One thing I know for sure—we ain't got the whole story yet. That boy meant everything to Mrs. Tyson. After what happened to her husband, he became her whole life, and that's a fact."

As they wheeled Cynthia into the ambulance, a silent shriek came from deep inside her. It forced itself up from the bottom of her own private hell. She screamed inwardly, working her mouth with no sound coming out.

Please, please! the voice inside her screamed. *Somebody help me. No, no, I haven't murdered my own child. Not Nick, my beloved son.*

Her face was contorted, her eyes huge, as if the horrors of the damned were lurking inside them. The young attendant felt a chill as he looked at her.

Nick! Nick! she mouthed.

Then she stopped breathing.

"Here they come," said Detective Waring as he looked out the window at the approaching reporters and TV crews. His expression was impassive as he watched the ambulance attendant cover Cynthia's face. Then he turned and responded to Fogarty's last remark.

"There's a reason, Sheriff. There's always a reason, even though we may never find out what it was."

Minutes later, a weeping Alpha closed the front door.

She walked into the kitchen. The TV was still on. The program had changed to *The Word of God,* her favorite religious show. What better time to watch it than now?

The preacher talked of an old friend of his who would be

appearing on the program that morning. Seconds later, Jim Boyd appeared on screen, wearing a gentle, almost martyred expression on his face. His smiling visage was infused with love. Sitting next to him on a velvet sofa was redheaded Cory Jones, dressed all in white. Her glittering sequins, catching the light, gave her the look of a Christmas tree angel.

Boyd's cajoling voice was soft, friendly, and full of love for his fellow man.

"Dear, dear brothers and sisters. You know this ministry has been built on your blessed dollars. Without your devoted support, it would not be possible for these God-fearing people to do the Lord's great work. And it is His work they do."

His voice became firmer, more determined. It rang with conviction and purpose.

"That is why we are launching a crusade to build Him a mighty tabernacle, and why I have dedicated myself to lead this crusade for His everlasting glory."

Boyd's voice grew softer as he held his Bible close to his breast.

"As you know, my dear wife Cory and I once were sinners. We were entrapped by the evil web of Satan. We were two sinners on our way to purgatory. But we repented because the Lord God showed us the way."

Cory smiled shyly. Her eyes were moist with tears, and her white garb and modest demeanor seemed to represent a perfect mix of purity and humility.

Boyd's flat brown eyes faced front, as he held his Bible close.

"Before Cory sings 'Let Jesus In,' join us in prayer. Pray to the Savior for the soul of any sinner that you know. Any sinner who might, at this very minute, be standing at the gate of hell. Remember, He who died for us on the cross forgives us all."

Alpha called in old Willie, and the two of them prayed along with the Reverend Jim Boyd—the blessed Reverend Boyd, as Alpha called him.

Weeping and praying, they prayed for the soul of Cynthia Tyson.

Chapter Thirty-five

Jan had lost track of the time she spent in the hospital. Her days and nights all seemed homogenized.

The only thing keeping her from uncontrollable hysterics, from plunging over the brink into madness, was her refusal to accept what had happened to Nick. Her mind simply blotted out the fact of his death. She was convinced that he would soon come walking through the door and take her away with him.

The months drifted by. She took no notice of their passing. All emotion seemed to have left her. She existed from hour to hour in a vacuum that was like a bottomless well of loneliness.

Jan sat quietly looking out the window—looking, but not really seeing anything. It would soon be time for another visit from Dr. Klein, the chief staff psychiatrist.

She turned her head slowly as he walked into her room. Then she sank back into comfortable silence.

"How are you feeling?" he asked.

Jan laughed a sad, bitter little laugh.

"Feeling? What a funny word. I'm not feeling anything. How can I feel anything until Nick comes back to me?"

Looking down at her, the doctor made no reply. After a few seconds Jan spoke again, as if she had forgotten his presence, as if she were addressing herself.

"While I'm waiting, I guess this is as good a place to be as any. People tell me what to do and when to do it. They study me, discuss me, and give me wonderful pills to help me sleep, to help me dream about nothing."

Dr. Klein sat down on a chair facing her. When he spoke, his voice was gentle.

"Jan, you're going to be angry with me, but we have to face up to the pain again. There's no way to avoid the awful pain of losing someone you love. You can't keep pretending about Nick Tyson."

Closing her eyes, Jan wondered why the doctor was talking to her that way. Why didn't he just go away and leave her alone? She didn't want him to bring the pain back to her again.

As she continued looking out the window, she thought she would try to change the subject.

"Doctor, do you think anyone can die of a broken heart?"

He looked at her gravely.

"Yes, I suppose it's possible. We can die from almost anything."

Jan leaned her head back on the chair.

"You see, if I face up to Nick's death, then there would be nothing left for me. I can't let him go, no matter how I try. What if I can never let him go?"

She seemed unaware that her tears were starting to flow. She looked up at Dr. Klein as if hoping to find some answer, as if searching his face for some relief from the awful pain that clutched at her heart again.

His voice was as gentle as before when he spoke to her softly, ever so softly.

"You will face it, Jan. Sooner or later, you will let go. Because, my dear, you must. But it will happen only after you face all that pain. You've got to endure it, to let it rush through you. There's no way to avoid it. You can't keep pushing it away forever."

He paused, as if not wanting to be too hard on her, and yet he knew he had to continue. Perhaps today would be the breakthrough.

"I know how difficult it is to accept such a terrible loss. The death of a loved one is a traumatic experience for everyone. But there must be a time when you face up to it, and that is when the grief will begin to diminish, as I promise it will. That is the time you'll slowly start to come alive again."

She had turned her head slightly. She was now staring out the window again. Tears were still flowing, but he felt he was reaching her. However, he mustn't overdo it. Just another few words, that was all.

"Soon the time will come when you'll be able to talk about Nick, to accept the fact that he's dead without suffering the pain. You'll be able to remember his laugh and his voice, and you'll be grateful for the time you knew him, for the happiness that was given to you to share with him. I'm here to help you till that time comes."

Jan was still facing the window. She heard the doctor open her door, ready to leave. He paused for a moment; then she heard his voice from over her shoulder. It was slightly hesitant as he spoke.

"Of course, there are some few people who never let go. They're the ones who never get their lives back together again. But my money's on you. Somehow I don't see you as a quitter."

Then Dr. Klein gently closed the door behind him.

Three months later Jan left the sanitarium.

Jaafar and Leancia had come to her rescue. They insisted she stay at their beach house in Montauk, on the easternmost tip of Long Island. There would be servants to look after her, yet she could be as private as she pleased.

At times Jan's depression seemed to fill the beach house. The evenings were a never-ending series of nightmares, filled with dreams of Nick, in which she was continually running up and down corridors, turning corners, endlessly searching for him. He would be just within her reach, she'd be just about to hold him, and then he'd dissolve in a vapor, and she'd wake up drenched in sweat.

On the nights when she couldn't sleep at all, she would walk the beach desperately, tirelessly, oblivious to the cold, the wind, or the fog.

On her return to the beach house, she'd drug herself with Valium to ease her pain.

There were also nights when she would get drunk. But mostly she would just sob herself to sleep when tears finally came.

Slowly, almost imperceptibly, a sense of balance seemed to take over. It was very tentative, very fragile, but it was there.

One night she actually watched a TV program from beginning to end. She even laughed at a situation comedy.

Later, while walking in the village, Jan picked out some attractive postcards from the local store and sent them to friends.

She was surprised when she found she could finally read a romantic novel without weeping.

One morning, as streaks of early color edged the sky, Jan went for a walk along the beach. The air was still; the chill autumn frost lightly covered the wild grass atop the dunes.

After twenty minutes of meandering in solitude, she came to her favorite cove. Touched, as always, by the stillness and the beauty of the scene, she sat down near the water's edge on an old log that had been washed up by the tide.

It was a peaceful time for her, just sitting and letting her mind drift while gazing out to sea. She wrapped her heavy sweater closer to ward off the cool, damp air.

Tucking her hands deep into the sweater's oversize pockets, she pulled out a bottle of sleeping pills. They had been with her for months—old friends, always available.

With a sigh, she unscrewed the cap and slowly dropped them on the moist sand at her feet. She watched as the encroaching waves greedily sucked them up, taking them out with the tide.

A soft fog was rolling in.

Jan stood up and watched the swirling mist. Warm tears filled her eyes. She knew that Nick was lost to her. He was dead, never to return. She would never again be held in his arms. But he would always be alive in her heart. She would always see his beautiful face, hear his laugh, and hold his memories close to her.

"Good-bye, my love," she whispered. "You will be with me forever."

Turning, she walked back along the beach. Her stride was strong; her heart was finally free.

She saw the figure of a man walking toward her.

Jan hesitated just long enough to be sure her eyes weren't playing tricks on her.

They weren't. It was Mark Squire.

She started running toward him; her long hair flew in the wind.

Soon she was in his arms, laughing and crying as he swung her around.

"Mark! Mark! Where on earth did you come from?"

His eyes were filled with love as he felt Jan's heart beating against his. Nevertheless, his reply was flippant.

"Oh, I just happened to be in the neighborhood, so I thought I'd drop by."

He looked at her lovely face, so full of questions as they walked toward the beach house. His thoughts were racing. He sensed that Jan was coming out from behind her wall. He'd lost her twice before, but never would he lose her again.

He placed his arm protectively around her shoulder. They had a lifetime ahead of them. In time, Jan Julliard would become Mrs. Mark Squire.

He had enough love to make it happen.

Unity Hall
Secrets £2.99

Les Hirondelles – the mansion where three generations of the de
Courtenays gather under the Mediterranean sky and languish amidst
wealth and luxury. Three generations of secrets: the father's passion
for an Algerian masseuse; the eldest son and his illicit love of his
own half-sister; the daughter's insatiable sexuality schooled by her
father; the granddaughter a hireling of the sensuality of pain; and
Anne, the outsider looking for a man to free her from twisted lust . . .
Among them walks a stranger of powerful wealth – the man who
knows the biggest secret of all . . .

The White Paper Fan £2.99

Jade had just made love in the jacuzzi in Aspen, Colorado with the
big blond American when she got the phone call. The man who'd
always been her father, who'd adopted her and Poppy when they
were just tiny Chinese baby girls, had been killed in a hit-and-run
accident. He bequeathed them not only money, but many
unanswered questions. Who were those names in his address book?
What did the clippings from the Hong Kong newspapers mean? And
who were Poppy and Jade, anyway? The answers lay in Hong Kong,
in a labyrinth of drugs and death, sinister Triad connections and dark
secrets – hidden behind the white paper fan.

Sidney Sheldon
Master of the Game £3.99

Kate Blackwell is one of the richest and most powerful women in the world – an enigma, surrounded by a thousand unanswered questions. Her father was a diamond prospector who struck it rich beyond dreams; her mother, the daughter of a crooked Afrikaaner merchant; her conception was an act of hate-filled vengeance. At the celebrations of her ninetieth birthday, there are toasts from a Supreme Court judge and a telegram from the White House. But for Kate there are ghosts – of absent friends and absent enemies, from a life of blackmail, deceit and murder, ghosts from an empire spawned by naked ambition.

If Tomorrow Comes £3.99

Tracy Whitney was young and on top of the world, about to marry into wealth and glamour. Until suddenly, betrayed by her own innocence, she was in prison, framed by the Mafia, abandoned by the man she loved. Tracy emerged from her savage ordeal determined to revenge herself ... From New Orleans to London and on to Paris, Madrid and Amsterdam, with intelligence and beauty her only weapons, Tracy played for the highest stakes in a deadly game ...

'Sheldon's most bewitching heroine yet ... Another winner'
PUBLISHERS WEEKLY

All Pan books are available at your local bookshop or newsagent, or can be ordered direct from the publisher. Indicate the number of copies required and fill in the form below.

Send to: **CS Department, Pan Books Ltd., P.O. Box 40, Basingstoke, Hants. RG21 2YT.**

or phone: 0256 469551 (Ansaphone), quoting title, author and Credit Card number.

Please enclose a remittance* to the value of the cover price plus: 60p for the first book plus 30p per copy for each additional book ordered to a maximum charge of £2.40 to cover postage and packing.

*Payment may be made in sterling by UK personal cheque, postal order, sterling draft or international money order, made payable to Pan Books Ltd.

Alternatively by Barclaycard/Access:

Card No.

Signature:

Applicable only in the UK and Republic of Ireland.

While every effort is made to keep prices low, it is sometimes necessary to increase prices at short notice. Pan Books reserve the right to show on covers and charge new retail prices which may differ from those advertised in the text or elsewhere.

NAME AND ADDRESS IN BLOCK LETTERS PLEASE:

Name

Address

3/87